The Early Fiction of H. G. Wells

The Early Fiction of H. G. Wells

Fantasies of Science

Steven McLean

palgrave
macmillan

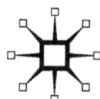

No portion of this publication may be reproduced, copied or transmitted save with written permission or in accordance with the provisions of the Copyright, Designs and Patents Act 1988, or under the terms of any licence permitting limited copying issued by the Copyright Licensing Agency, Saffron House, 6-10 Kirby Street, London EC1N 8TS.

Any person who does any unauthorized act in relation to this publication may be liable to criminal prosecution and civil claims for damages.

The author has asserted his right to be identified as the author of this work in accordance with the Copyright, Designs and Patents Act 1988.

First published 2009 by
PALGRAVE MACMILLAN

Palgrave Macmillan in the UK is an imprint of Macmillan Publishers Limited, registered in England, company number 785998, of Houndmills, Basingstoke, Hampshire RG21 6XS.

Palgrave Macmillan in the US is a division of St Martin's Press LLC, 175 Fifth Avenue, New York, NY 10010.

Palgrave Macmillan is the global academic imprint of the above companies and has companies and representatives throughout the world.

Palgrave® and Macmillan® are registered trademarks in the United States, the United Kingdom, Europe and other countries.

ISBN-13: 978–0–230–53562–6 hardback
ISBN-10: 0–230–53562–3 hardback

This book is printed on paper suitable for recycling and made from fully managed and sustained forest sources. Logging, pulping and manufacturing processes are expected to conform to the environmental regulations of the country of origin.

A catalogue record for this book is available from the British Library.

Library of Congress Cataloging-in-Publication Data

McLean, Steven, 1973–
    The early fiction of H.G. Wells : fantasies of science / Steven McLean.
       p. cm.
    Includes bibliographical references and index.
    ISBN 978–0–230–53562–6
       1. Wells, H. G. (Herbert George), 1866–1946 – Knowledge – Science. 2. Science fiction, English – History and criticism. 3. Literature and science – Great Britain – History – 19th century. 4. Fantasy in literature. I. Title.
PR5778.S35M35 2009
823'.912—dc22   2008050876

10 9 8 7 6 5 4 3 2 1
18 17 16 15 14 13 12 11 10 09

Transferred to Digital Printing in 2014

To Caiden
and
The Discovery of the Future

Contents

Acknowledgements

My principal intellectual debt in the gestation and completion of this book is to Professor Sally Shuttleworth (now of the University of Oxford) who, as my doctoral supervisor, first encouraged me to investigate the interconnections between Wells's scientific romances and the discourses of contemporary science. Indeed, many of Professor Shuttleworth's earlier observations have proven invaluable in transforming my PhD into the monograph which follows.

Professor Patrick Parrinder, of the University of Reading, examined an earlier version of this book as a PhD thesis and has continued to encourage and inspire my interest in Wells. Dr Richard Steadman-Jones, the second examiner of my PhD, earnestly encouraged me to develop my thesis into a monograph. I would also like to express my gratitude to Dr Simon J. James, of the University of Durham, for reading chapter drafts at various stages and giving me the benefit of his expertise. I wish to thank Professor David C. Smith, of the University of Maine, who read my manuscript for Palgrave Macmillan and recommended its publication.

Dr Richard Canning supported the early stages of my doctoral research, and I record my appreciation here. I express my gratitude to Professor Ann Heilmann, of the University of Hull, for her vigorous support and for her suggestions regarding the introduction to this book. I am indebted to Dr John Bolland, formerly of Manchester Metropolitan University, the very first person to encourage me to write on Wells. Similarly, Dr Nick Cox, now of Leeds Metropolitan University, not only supported my early academic studies but also was instrumental in encouraging me to undertake postgraduate work.

I wish to thank staff at the University of Sheffield Library, particularly those in the Document Supply Unit. I am similarly indebted to staff at Sheffield Central Library.

I would like to acknowledge the support I have received from the members of the H. G. Wells Society. While it is not possible to mention everyone here, some I must not omit. Dr John Hammond, the founder of the Society and author of several important studies on Wells, has been both an inspiration and an unceasing source of encouragement. Professor Bernard Loing, Dr Sylvia Hardy, Mark Egerton, Paul Allen and John Green (as well as Patrick Parrinder) have all supported my Wellsian endeavours, as did the late Giles Hart and Peter Lonsdale.

I would like to express my sincere gratitude to the editorial staff at Palgrave Macmillan. In particular, I thank Paula Kennedy for commissioning this book and Christabel Scaife and Steven Hall for their helpful efficiency.

Throughout the time it has taken to complete this project, I have been blessed with the friendship and support of the following individuals: Rodney Polydore (a steadfast friend), Dong-Uk (Martin) Kim (a scholar and a gentleman), Wendy Halsall, Judith Jones, David Dickin, Susan Shackford, Jane Allan-Brown and Anna Pluta.

Finally, I would like to acknowledge my deep gratitude to my parents, Margaret and John, and to my sisters, Grace, Shona and Sarah. I wish to thank my brother in law Jamie Macaskill and Sarah's partner, Luke Hardy. Of course, I should also like to mention my nephew Caiden, to whom this book is faithfully dedicated.

An extract from Chapter 3 was originally published in *The Undying Fire: Journal of the H. G. Wells Society, the Americas*; an earlier version of Chapter 4 appeared in *Cahiers Victoriens Et Edourdiens* and extracts of Chapter 7 appeared in *Papers on Language and Literature*. Thanks are due to these publications for permission to reprint.

There is a possibility that the cover illustration was by C. R. Ashbee, though this is by no means certain. I wish to thank the Ashbee family for their assistance in this respect. Every effort has been made to trace all copyright holders, but if any have been inadvertently overlooked, the publisher will be pleased to make the necessary arrangements at the first opportunity.

1
Introduction

> I am simply a story-teller who happens to be a student of science. If a man writes the best that is in him, he cannot help some of his serious speculations appearing.
>
> H. G. Wells, Interview with
> the *Weekly Sun Literary Supplement*, 1 December 1895[1]

In 1887, H. G. Wells left the Normal School of Science, though without taking a degree. After a stint as a schoolteacher – and having finally completed his degree in zoology in 1890 – he discovered journal editors to be highly receptive to the endeavours of a recent 'student of science' who was able to formulate 'some of his serious speculations' in a digestible form. It would, indeed, be difficult to understate the role of the periodical press in shaping the fortunes of the young Wells. His first published scientific essay, 'The Rediscovery of the Unique', appeared in the *Fortnightly Review* in July 1891. Following this initial success, he took advantage of a number of opportunities in the early 1890s to publish his scientific, literary and educational journalism in such prestigious journals as the *Saturday Review* and *Nature*.

As Wells merged his 'serious speculations' with the skills as 'a story-teller' he had been developing since 1884, the periodicals were again pivotal to his success. The first significant breakthrough in his literary career occurred when *The Time Machine*, the first of his quick succession of brilliant scientific novels, or 'scientific romances', was published in the pages of the *New Review* between January and May 1895.[2] Subsequently, he continued to serialise his scientific romances in the lucrative periodical market prior to their publication in book form. This market included, of course, popular magazines such as *Pearson's*, in which *The War of the Worlds* was serialised between April and December 1897.[3]

1

From the mid 1890s onwards Wells not only sustained a high level of journalistic output alongside his fictional endeavours, but also diverted his energies into other fields. This meant that by the time later scientific romances like *The First Men in the Moon* (1901) and *A Modern Utopia* (1905) appeared, he had published contributions to the nascent discipline of sociology and immersed himself in the contemporary debates of social reform.

Critics have often explored the interconnections between Wells's scientific romances and the non-fiction he was concurrently producing.[4] However, they have neglected to examine how his journalistic speculations begin to reveal the full extent to which his scientific romances are immersed in the discourses of contemporary science, and indeed in the social, psychological and moral disputes that were stimulated by scientific advances.

The assessment of Wells as something of a 'founding father' of science fiction has, perhaps, worked to obscure a full examination of the relevance of contemporary science in understanding his early fiction. This assessment encourages the popular conception that the significance of his scientific romances lies not so much in their engagement with scientific debates, but rather in the contribution of a number of literary tropes toward the creation of the modern genre of science fiction. Yet, his statements at the time he was actually producing scientific romances are highly instructive in revealing how Wells himself conceived of his work. In a very early interview with the *Weekly Sun Literary Supplement* at the end of 1895, he assessed the status of modern-day fiction in the following terms:

> 'It is singular enough,' went on Mr Wells, 'how fiction is widening its territory. It has become a mouthpiece for science, philosophy and art. That is the natural tendency of things. You cannot blame science for welcoming so popular an expression, and then speculation itself is so romantic. The dream of the philosopher has all the richness and variety of imagination necessary to a fascinating novel. The only difference is that the scientist builds his airy palace on solid ground. Thus his speculation becomes the recreation of other men'.[5]

At the moment he gave this interview, *The Time Machine* was Wells's only published scientific romance, although *The Island of Doctor Moreau* would appear just a few months later. This statement is especially relevant, therefore, because it suggests the influence that contemporary debates – scientific, philosophical and sociological – would have on the development of his conception of the scientific romance.

This book investigates the relationship between Wells's scientific romances and the discourses of science in the 1890s and early years of the twentieth century. More specifically, I examine how Wells was drawing upon the discourses of contemporary science – primarily evolutionary biology, but also physical science, astronomy, anthropology, linguistics and entomology – in the creation of the imaginative worlds of his scientific romances. I also investigate how – still more importantly – he used his own fiction as 'a mouthpiece for science', since his scientific romances participate directly in topical scientific debates. The contribution of his early romances to contemporary scientific disputes incorporates Wells's evolving response to the work of leading 'men of science', particularly T. H. Huxley, Herbert Spencer and Francis Galton. The discussion further investigates how his scientific romances were immersed in other present-day discourses, including those concerned with social reform, which might – following Wells himself – be loosely defined as the 'philosophy' of the contemporary moment.

A significant part of the methodology employed in this work consists of resituating Wells's scientific romances in their initial publishing context. It is rather surprising that critics have yet to examine his early fiction in the crucial publishing milieu of the contemporary periodical press. The significance of the periodicals for Wells in the 1890s and 1900s was not restricted simply to his publishing material within them. His relationship to the periodical press was, rather, a reciprocal one.

It would be remarkable indeed if Wells were not also reading the periodicals in which his journalism appeared.[6] There was a substantial amount of space dedicated to science within those journals which published his scientific writings. In order to maintain the basis of his fiction in contemporary science, Wells appears to have appropriated numerous scientific ideas from the pages of various journals. As I indicate in the chapters which follow, he sometimes makes explicit reference to these periodical sources within his scientific romances. More often, however, his appropriation of scientific ideas from journals is implicit. Wells's own scientific, educational and literary journalism, as well as his early correspondence, reveal precisely which scientific debates and sources – both from within the periodical context and otherwise – informed the construction of his scientific romances.

Some of the earliest examples of his scientific journalism reveal the eagerness of the young Wells to engage in debate with the leading scientific figures of his time. His emphasis on the importance of co-operation in the evolution of species in 'Ancient Experiments in Co-Operation' (1892), for example, aligns him with T. H. Huxley in his opposition to the economic individualism of Herbert Spencer. In this work, I examine how the imaginative endeavour of his scientific romances enabled Wells to participate in debates with Huxley, Spencer and Galton. Throughout his scientific romances, he was continually adjusting his position in relation to Huxley and Spencer (though he was more consistent in his attitude towards Galton). While he is widely considered to have thoroughly endorsed Huxley's conception of 'ethical' evolution,[7] this book demonstrates that the work of Spencer was increasingly important to the development of Wells's scientific romances.

Huxley and Spencer represent opposing interpretations of the implications of evolutionary theory for humanity. Huxley rejected the gladiatorial theory of existence as a guide for ethical conduct, and instead argued that humanity should initiate a programme of co-operative ethical evolution in order to ensure the survival of as many as possible. Spencer, conversely, was adamant that humanity could not escape the model of competition between individuals suggested by nature. Indeed, it was for Spencer imperative that humanity did not interfere with this model. To do so would only result in the propagation of the weak, which would in turn lead to the degradation of the species as a whole.

While Francis Galton was active in many fields of scientific research, his primary significance in the context of this book concerns his work towards establishing the nascent science of eugenics. In a number of works, Galton researched family genealogies and advanced the conception of 'positive' eugenics. This consisted of the public endowment of marriages between gifted individuals, in order to accelerate the evolution of humanity.

The impact of the disputes between such figures as Huxley, Spencer and Galton was not restricted to scientists alone. Science in the late Victorian and Edwardian period encompassed a wide range of social debates. The difference between a Huxleian and a Spencerian interpretation of the implications of evolutionary biology, for example, amounted to a clash of worldviews which could influence such issues as conceptions of social reform and the provision of social welfare. Alongside those scientific speculations published in the periodical press – including of course Wells's own – appeared articles dealing with the social, psychological and ethical implications of science. In this book, I investigate how in his scientific romances Wells endeavoured to engage in debate with those articles dealing with the social implications of science that were published at the same time, and often in the same journals, as his own scientific journalism.

Wells's educational journalism indicates a further context which is significant in developing our understanding of his early fiction. As Brian Stableford has pointed out in his stimulating history of the genre, the development of the scientific romance was facilitated by an unprecedented period of literary experimentation from the 1880s onwards.[8] This period found publishers attempting for the first time to cater for the demands of near universal literacy that had been achieved as a result of the 1870 Education Act.[9] Since the Education Acts implemented earlier in the century had provided Wells with access to higher education and so – in an indirect sense – created him as a writer, it seems somehow appropriate that his scientific romances contain a definite educational function. Wells was fully aware of the interest in scientific topics among the newly created popular readership. Consequently, his use of comical incidents in such novels as *The First Men in the Moon* – which was serialised in the popular *Strand Magazine* – indicates his intention to communicate scientific ideas to a non-specialist readership of the scientific romances.

The emergence of the Wellsian scientific romance as a literary mode that satisfied the public curiosity about science depended upon the adoption and transformation of other popular late-Victorian genres, such as the adventure narrative and the future war story. Simultaneously, Wells's scientific romances continue long-standing literary genres as he engages with satirical and utopian discourse, from Jonathan Swift to William Morris.[10] It is important to acknowledge that, in addition to participating in topical scientific discussions, these works continue intellectual debates from earlier in the Victorian era. This is particularly true of Wells's theorising of individuality.

While the focus of this work is on those of his romances which engage with contemporary science, Wells was concurrently publishing novels that might be defined as purely fantastic. Thus shortly after *The Time Machine* appeared in 1895, he also published *The Wonderful Visit*, the story of an angel that falls to earth. Similarly, one year after *The First Men in the Moon* appeared, *The Sea Lady* (1902) – a story featuring a mermaid – was published. The fact that they do not have a scientific basis, however, means that these fantastic novels fall outside the scope of the present study.

The development of Wells's scientific romance was, I will argue, characterised by three distinct – and yet related – stages. These three stages parallel the development of the author's thought as he adjusts his position in relation to specific contemporary debates and leading scientific figures. This book comprises a series of six case studies of individual texts, beginning with *The Time Machine* and ending with *A Modern Utopia*, and its three parts correspond to the successive stages in Wells's development as an author of scientific romances.

The first of these stages, which I have entitled 'Misadventures in a Post-Darwinian Universe', concerns the pessimistic vision of Wells's 'evolutionary fables'. The discussion of *The Time Machine* in Chapter 2 considers how Wells deliberately extrapolates the pessimistic implications of evolutionary theory regarding the creation of a disturbing vision of future humanity. In particular, I consider how the potential for retrogression in human evolution identified in the work of Huxley and – more especially – Ray Lankester informed his construction of the Eloi and the Morlocks, the two degenerate remnants of humanity the Time Traveller encounters in the future. In this initial case study, I examine how the disturbing future portrayed in Wells's first novel signifies something of a break from Huxley.

In my discussion of *The Island of Doctor Moreau* (1896) in Chapter 3, I indicate how in his second scientific romance Wells continues to draw upon the pessimistic implications of evolutionary theory for humanity. By examining the novel in relation to periodical debates that concerned the capacity of animals to attain reason through language, my analysis reveals a new context in which to understand *The Island of Doctor Moreau*. I also investigate how his fictional engagement with these debates provided Wells with an alternative means of exploring the degenerative potential of humanity, since the entire species *homo sapiens* represented in the novel is implicated in the linguistic retrogression of the Beastfolk.

The theme of misadventure is especially prominent in the evolutionary fables, as the protagonists are confronted with temporal and spatial displacement respectively. I examine how both the temporal explorer of *The Time Machine* and Prendick, the shipwrecked survivor of *The Island of Doctor Moreau*, are subjected to the harsh realities of existence in a post-Darwinian universe. In my discussion of each of these protagonists, I investigate how their degradation to bestiality in the space of less than a single generation relates to existing fears concerning 'acquired characteristics'.

I have labelled Wells's second stage of development as a writer of scientific romances 'Science and Society'. The title refers to the fact that in the two novels included in this category, *The Invisible Man* (1897) and *The War of the Worlds* (1898), Wells for the first time presents his reader with a recognisable social setting. This enables him to explore the implications of recent advances in scientific knowledge for society. The analysis of *The Invisible Man* in Chapter 4 centres on Wells's exploration of the complexities inherent in the relationship between scientist and society. I investigate how in the novel he warns against both the reticence of scientists to communicate their knowledge effectively and a continued failure on the part of society to facilitate a broader understanding of scientific knowledge. I also examine how *The Invisible Man* contributes to existing debates over the nature of scientific method itself.

In *The War of the Worlds*, Wells shifts the focus from the relationship between scientist and society onto disputes over the implications of Darwin's theory of natural selection for human ethical conduct. Chapter 5 investigates how he uses the social disintegration created by the Martian invasion in the novel as a means to participate in the debate between Huxley's ethical evolution and the economic individualism of Spencer. The analysis also explores the implications of the Martian invasion for the conduct of Western humanity towards supposedly 'inferior' races and species.

The final stage I have identified in the development of Wells's scientific romances is entitled 'Towards the Shaping of Humanity'. As the title implies, in the last phase of his development in this genre of writing Wells became much more interested in utilising the scientific romance to suggest possible future directions for humanity. This emerges in *The First Men in the Moon* and is more explicitly stated in *A Modern Utopia*. His interest in using his fiction to suggest the future shape of humanity is signalled by Wells's divergence after 1901 into the emerging field of sociology.

Chapter 6 examines *The First Men in the Moon* in the context of Wells's first full-length sociological work, *Anticipations* (1901). The opposition between earthly and lunar society in the novel is understood in the context of the analysis in *Anticipations* of the emergence of a unified 'world state' in the twentieth century. I investigate how the human society portrayed in the novel corresponds to Wells's assessment of those factors which obstruct the emergence of the world state in the contemporary world. The global unity of the Selenites is considered as a tentative articulation of this world state – though it is clear that the writer never univocally endorses the lunar global order since his satirical intentions are distinctly apparent.

A Modern Utopia was intended as a form of hybrid between the type of philosophical engagement Wells had himself earlier identified as significant for contemporary fiction and novelistic endeavour. In order to understand the element of philosophical discussion in the work, Chapter 7 traces how the social policies advanced in Utopia emerge from the process of intellectual development Wells underwent between the publication of *Anticipations* and the appearance of *A Modern Utopia*. However, I also consider how, as a consequence of the artistic limits he imposes upon himself in *A Modern Utopia*, Wells cannot endorse the Utopia his protagonists visit as a practical means of instigating social reform.

This study is not the first book to examine the scientific basis of Wells's work. As its title implies, Roslynn D. Haynes's *H. G. Wells: Discoverer of the Future, The Influence of Science on His Thought* (1980) examines the impact of science on the writer.[11] However, the broad focus of Haynes's study on Wells's entire output between 1895 and 1946 generates a series of overviews which results in the specific scientific engagement of the early romances being largely overlooked. William Greenslade's *Degeneration, Culture and the Novel, 1880–1940* (1994) examines some of Wells's early fiction as part of a wider response to degeneration theory, thereby pre-empting something of the discussion in Part One of this book.[12] Yet Greenslade's preoccupation with degeneration – and indeed his focus on a number of authors – means that he touches only slightly on the scientific engagement of Wells's early work. What distinguishes *The Early Fiction of H. G. Wells: Fantasies of Science* from previous studies is that it investigates the full extent to which Wells's romances are immersed in the discourses of science in the 1890s and 1900s.

Part I
Misadventures in a Post-Darwinian Universe

2
Heart of Darkness: *The Time Machine* and Retrogression

> Suppose the monkey drives the machine, the gullible, mischievous, riotous and irresponsible monkey?
>
> V. S. Pritchett, *The Living Novel* (1946)[1]

The Time Machine is a unique portrayal of the devolutionary potential of evolution. Other novelists had already examined theories of degeneration in a fictional form. The latent atavism of humankind had also been explored, and comparisons with Robert Louis Stevenson's *The Strange Case of Dr Jekyll and Mr Hyde* (1886) were made immediately after *The Time Machine* was published in May 1895.[2] Yet most late-Victorian stories which investigate the implications of degeneration do so within a contemporary setting. Wells's innovative use of the convention of time travel, on the other hand, enables him to depict the entire Victorian era as subject to a disturbing future retrogression.[3]

Contemporary reviews instantly recognised the iconoclasm of the novel. The *Daily Chronicle*, for example, regarded the concept of the Time Machine as a literary device allowing Wells to travel into the narrative space of the future as 'that rarity which Solomon declared to be not merely rare but non-existent – a "new thing under the sun"'.[4] The author of an unsigned notice in the *Review of Reviews* called the writer 'a man of genius' who possessed an imagination 'as gruesome as that of Poe'.[5] Such positive responses appear to have fully justified the aspirations Wells attached to the publication of *The Time Machine*.[6] His hopes for the novel were openly expressed in a letter he wrote to his friend, Elizabeth Healey, in December 1894:

> You may be interested to know that our ancient Chronic Argonauts of the Science Schools Journal has at last become a complete story

and will appear as a serial in the *New Review* for January. [...] It's my trump card and if it does not come off very much I shall know my place for the rest of my career.[7]

The high degree of emphasis Wells placed on the success of the novel is indicative of the fact that the final version of *The Time Machine* was the culmination of an idea which he had developed over a period of seven years. Following his introduction of the concept of time travel in 'The Chronic Argonauts' (1888), Wells worked on two further versions of the story, both of which were lost.[8] He next produced 'The Time Traveller's Story', a series of seven linked articles commissioned by W. E. Henley and published in the *National Observer* between March and June 1894.[9] The 'complete story' then appeared in the *New Review* between January and May 1895, before William Heinemann finally published *The Time Machine* in book form.[10]

In the development of successive versions of the novel, the vast earthly chronology uncovered by the scientific advances of the nineteenth century becomes increasingly evident.[11] Lyellian geology forced a reassessment of the timescale of human occupation of the earth. Rather than having been the immutable creation of God in 4004 BC, humanity was now to be regarded as the outcome of tens of millions of years of evolution. In consecutive drafts of *The Time Machine*, Wells increasingly foregrounds the vast timescale of human evolution, as post-Darwinian thinkers now understood it. Thus in the *National Observer* version of the text, the protagonist journeys forward to AD 12,203. In the final version of *The Time Machine*, however, this future date is extended to 802,701. In his book *Shadows of the Future* (1995), Patrick Parrinder offers a persuasive explanation for Wells's final choice of date. For him, there are two timescales at work in *The Time Machine*: 'The two scales, those of historical time measured by the rise and fall of cultures and civilisations, and of biological time measured by the evolution and devolution of the species, are superimposed upon one another.'[12] Parrinder hypothesises that Wells added 800 years of historical time to a story set in 1901, thus arriving at the number 2701. A further 800,000 years of evolutionary time was then superimposed, arriving at a figure that would have appealed to Wells: 'Supposing the number 802,701 to have been determined by a process such as this, its poetic appeal as a symbol of entropy would have ensured its adoption.'[13] While Parrinder's idea that there are two timescales at work in *The Time Machine* is generally accepted, his assumption that the story is set in 1901 is not supported by textual evidence.[14] The Time Traveller's reference to Simon Newcomb's address to the New York Mathematical Society ' "only a month or so ago" ' provides a valuable clue in determining the probable date of his dinner party.[15] Newcomb spoke on the possibility of constructing a four dimensional geometry in December 1893. Further, the Medical Man recollects ' "that ghost you showed us last Christmas" ' (14). These references indicate that the Traveller's guests visited his home during the festive period in December 1893, or perhaps early in January 1894.[16]

The appeal that the number 802,701 would have possessed for Wells as a countdown to the 'extinction of man' perfectly concurs with the pessimism of *The Time Machine*, which is particularly highlighted by the highly entropic ending to the novel. The narrator of *The Time Machine* makes an explicit reference to the Linnaean Society, at a meeting of which Charles Darwin and Alfred Russel Wallace jointly announced the theory of natural selection. With its emphasis on the mutability of all organic beings, the theory of natural selection implied that *homo sapiens* is subject to the same evolutionary forces as other animals. Wells in *The Time Machine* is endeavouring to explore the pessimistic implications of evolution for humanity. The disconcerting future he creates in his very first scientific romance should therefore be understood in the context of the post-Darwinian debates which influenced its construction.

The discussion which follows investigates how the portrayal of both the surface dwelling Eloi and their subterranean counterparts, the Morlocks, is directly influenced by Ray Lankester's notion of retrogressive metamorphosis. It further examines how the work of T. H. Huxley – especially his Romanes Lecture of 1893 – provides a crucial context in which to understand *The Time Machine*. Although Huxley taught Wells, it is important to establish at the outset that in *The Time Machine* the author appears determined to extrapolate the most pessimistic implications of his former Professor's work.

Previous critics have hinted at the fact that an additional site of retrogression in *The Time Machine* is located in the figure of the Traveller himself.[17] My analysis substantiates these inferences by examining how the protagonist increasingly reveals the same evolutionary plasticity as those future inhabitants he interacts with. This is particularly apparent in his savage struggle with the Morlocks. His battle for supremacy with the Morlocks is understood as the Time Traveller's attempt to reassert the volition he had initially lost in his fearful introduction to the future. Since the protagonist's loss of willpower emerges in part from Wells's endeavour to undercut an existing tradition of utopian literature, it is appropriate to begin by examining the relationship of *The Time Machine* to previous late-Victorian 'tales of the future'.

Recent studies of *The Time Machine* have examined its somewhat ironic relationship to near contemporary utopian novels, particularly Edward Bellamy's *Looking Backward* (1888) and William Morris's *News From Nowhere* (1890).[18] These studies have successfully demonstrated that the various utopian references Wells makes in the course of his first novel constitute a significant reassessment of the entire genre of utopian literature. Indeed, Stephen Derry has persuasively argued that the Time Traveller's reading of recent utopian literature shapes his interpretation of the future landscape. While the focus of recent research on formal characteristics has proven invaluable to revealing how *The Time Machine* constitutes a significant moment in the emergence of twentieth-century dystopian writing, this approach to the text overlooks the ways in which the characterisation of the Time Traveller relates to the protagonists of other late-Victorian utopian novels. Such an oversight is unfortunate, because in *The Time Machine* Wells subverts such texts as *Looking Backward* by making his protagonist's introduction to the future overwhelmingly fearful. More pertinently, the Traveller's fear-driven behaviour means his reactions to its inhabitants shape his reading of the future just as much as his understanding of recent utopian novels.

A statement in which Julian West, the protagonist, supposedly explains the extraordinary circumstances in which he had awoken from a 103-year sleep to find his native Boston radically transformed prefaces *Looking Backward*. This not only allows the protagonist to ingratiate himself with the potentially disbelieving twenty-first century citizen, but also enables Bellamy to encourage his contemporary readership to suspend its disbelief. In *The Time Machine*, contrastingly, the protagonist recounts the narrative of his futuristic adventures to a disbelieving audience: ' "I cannot expect you to believe it" ' (112), he says. This invites the reader of *The Time Machine* to become actively engaged in the interpretation of the future.

Julian West's introduction to the future is much more reassuring than that experienced by the Time Traveller. Bellamy's protagonist awakes from his almost hypnotic sleep to discover that: 'A fine-looking man of perhaps sixty was bending over me, [with] an expression of much benevolence mingled with great curiosity upon his features.'[19] It is not only this man's compassion that contributes to removing any potential fear from West's awakening in the future, but also the fact that his host is able to explain his circumstances there. While West laments that he awakes in what had been his own house to discover 'an utter stranger' standing over him, the Time Traveller (who had witnessed the apparent destruction of his own home while journeying through time) encounters no such conveniently placed guide to the future. Indeed, the Time Traveller himself emphasises that: ' "I had no convenient cicerone in the pattern of the Utopian books" ' (65).

The fact that he does not encounter a guide upon his arrival undoubt-edly accounts in part for the Time Traveller's fear in confronting the world of the future.[20] Faced with the ' "sightless eyes" ' of the ' "colossal figure" ' which exerts such a profound domination over the landscape of the future, the Traveller is immediately hypnotised by the Sphinx: ' "I stood looking at it for a little space – half a minute, perhaps, or half an hour" ' (27). The instant fascination which the future holds for the Wellsian observer is at once accompanied by the fear it stimulates:

'I looked again up at the crouching white shape, and the full temer-ity of my voyage came suddenly upon me. What might appear when that hazy curtain was altogether withdrawn? What might not have happened to men? [...] What if in this interval the race had lost its manliness, and had developed into something inhuman, unsympa-thetic, and overwhelmingly powerful? I might seem some old-world savage animal, only the more dreadful and disgusting for our com-mon likeness – a foul creature to be incontinently slain. [...] I felt naked in a strange world. I felt as perhaps a bird may feel in the clear air, knowing the hawk wins above and will swoop. My fear grew to frenzy. I took a breathing space, set my teeth, and again grappled fiercely, wrist and knee, with the machine. It gave under my desper-ate onset and turned over. It struck my chin violently. One hand on the saddle, the other on the lever, I stood panting heavily in attitude to mount again'. (27–8)

The most similar near contemporary utopian novel in terms of con-textualising the Time Traveller's fearful introduction to the future is Edward Bulwer Lytton's *The Coming Race* (1871). Following the death of his travelling companion as they descend into the underworld of the Vril-ya, the narrator's actions anticipate the frenzied behaviour of the Time Traveller:

While I was bending over his corpse in grief and horror, I heard close at hand a strange sound between a snort and a hiss; and turning instinctively to the quarter from which it came, I saw emerging from a dark fissure in the rock a vast and terrible head, with open jaws and dull, ghastly, hungry eyes – the head of a monstrous reptile resem-bling that of the crocodile or alligator, but infinitely larger than the largest creature of that kind I have ever beheld in my travels. I started to my feet and fled down the valley at my utmost speed. I stopped at last, ashamed of my panic and my flight, and returned to the spot on which I had left the body of my friend. It was gone; doubtless the monster had already drawn it into its den and devoured it. The rope and the grappling hooks still lay where they had fallen, but they afforded me no chance of return: it was impossible to re-attach them to the rock above, and the sides of the rock were too sheer and smooth for human steps to clamber. I was alone in this strange world, amidst the bowels of the earth.[21]

There are definite parallels between the frightened actions of these two protagonists. Each possesses an intense desire to escape from his new environment, which is frustrated by impracticality for the narrator of *The Coming Race* and by panic on the part of the Time Traveller. There are exact equivalents in the language used, with each protagonist expressing a fear that he will be trapped in a 'strange world'. However, whereas the protagonist of *The Coming Race* flees a menacing monster, the Time Traveller's fear emerges from his imagined speculation that *homo sapiens* might have evolved into an inhuman, unsympathetic and overwhelmingly powerful being.[22]

The Vril-ya conform more neatly to the Time Traveller's speculations of a powerful and inhuman race than the ' "indescribably frail" ' (29) creatures he actually meets. This perhaps explains why the first encounter with an alien inhabitant has the opposite effect on each of these fearful protagonists. The narrator of *The Coming Race* is completely unnerved by his first encounter with the Vril-ya:

But the face! it was that which inspired my awe and my terror. [...] I felt that this manlike image was endowed with forces inimical to man. As it drew near, a cold shudder came over me. I fell on my knees and covered my face with my hands.[23]

Coming face to face with the first of the Eloi, however, restores the Time Traveller's courage following his initial frenzy: ' "At the sight of him I suddenly regained confidence. I took my hands from the machine" ' (29). This moment not only provides an early indication of how his attitude to the future is shaped by his response to its inhabitants, it also foreshadows the Time's Traveller's alignment with the Eloi as he uses his struggle with the Morlocks as a means to reassert his volition.

Following his introduction to its passive inhabitants, the protagonist speculates on the emergence of the pastoral world of 802,701, the date as revealed by the dial on his Machine. He assumes that the utopian setting of the future – with its unmistakable connotations of Eden, ' "the whole earth had become a garden" ' (39) – is the logical consequence of the scientific and technological processes begun in his own age. Hence science, still at its ' "rudimentary stage" ' (39) in the Traveller's contemporary moment, has, by the time he arrives 'In The Golden Age',[24] uncovered the secrets of nature, and scientific knowledge has at last united humanity in the subjugation of nature: ' "The whole world will be intelligent, educated, and co-operating; things will move faster and faster towards the subjugation of Nature. In the end, wisely and carefully we shall readjust the balance of animal and vegetable life to suit our human needs" ' (40). The Traveller also reflects upon the ' "social paradise" ' he encounters, and speculates that the playful lives of the Eloi, who perhaps owe something to William Morris's Nowherians, are the necessary outcome of the amelioration of social life. The protagonist hypothesises that the condition of passivity in which he finds the Eloi renders strength – the outcome of hardship – redundant: ' "Under the new conditions of perfect comfort and security, that restless energy, that with us is strength, would become weakness" ' (42). Again, the beginnings of the diminishing need for struggle is something the protagonist finds in his contemporary era: ' "Physical courage and the love of battle, for instance, are no great help – may even be hindrances – to a civilised man" ' (42). Thus the ' "physical slightness of the people, [and] their lack of intelligence" ' (41–2) – which accounts for 'The Sunset of Mankind' – affirms the Traveller's belief in ' "a perfect conquest of Nature" ' (42). Just as bodily strength 'become[s] weakness' (42) in a society that has removed physical danger, so intelligence or inventiveness would no longer be required in an automatic society. The protagonist indeed conceives the arranging of flowers by the Eloi as the last artistic impetus of humanity.

Musing over ' "this too perfect triumph of man" ' (43), the Traveller's complacency is chilled suddenly by a ' "queer doubt" ' (44), as he realises he is unable to locate the Time Machine on the lawn where he had left it. Soon he is ' "in a passion of fear" ' as he races down the slope to reach the lawn, where his ' "worst fears were realised" ' (45). The protagonist is forced to acknowledge that this world may not be so simple as he had first imagined: ' "That is what dismayed me: the sense of some hitherto unsuspected power, through whose intervention my invention had vanished"' (45). The fearful response of the protagonist to the loss of his invention is of course consistent with what might be expected of a man who risks being severed from his own world, for as he puts it himself: ' "At once, like a lash across the face, came the possibility of losing my own age, of being left helpless in this strange new world"' (44). Yet, the Traveller's immediate response to the 'intervention' of this 'unsuspected power' in removing the Machine from his grasp might also be considered as a loss of volition.

The emphasis on the importance of self-control was a constant feature of nineteenth-century thought. John Barlow, writing at the inception of the Victorian period, identifies the power of will as the crucial factor in distinguishing between sanity and insanity.[25] Later, post-Darwinian, conceptions of volition also retain, to a greater or lesser extent, a degree of emphasis on the role of will in preventing mental disorders. Henry Maudsley, who does not place such a high emphasis as Barlow on the role of individual agency in the attainment of self-control, sees the 'dethronement of will, [as] the loss of power of co-ordinating the ideas and feelings'.[26] The Traveller's actions in the overnight period in which he discovers the disappearance of the Machine conform precisely to Maudsley's curt definition of the loss of volition. The Traveller's heightened state of emotional arousal amounts to the diminished power of co-ordinating thoughts and feelings that accompanies the dethronement of will. His immediate reaction to the loss of his invention is both intensely irrational and unproductive: ' "I ran round it [the lawn] furiously, as if the thing might be hidden in a corner, and then stopped abruptly, with my hands clutching my hair"' (45). The futility of the protagonist's actions as he loses his capacity to co-ordinate his ideas is recalled when we consider his somewhat abrupt threatening of the Eloi, a people whom he himself acknowledges show no sign of possessing the adequacy to remove the Machine. Wells in the scientific romances tends to conceive human destiny in animal terms.[27] Hence, it is unsurprising that the Traveller articulates being stranded in an alien world in the following terms: ' "I felt hopelessly cut off from my own kind – a strange animal in an unknown world"' (46). It is perhaps this acute sense of isolation which generates the Time Traveller's most violent emotional outburst, where, appearing to have lost all self-control, he begins searching for the Machine ' "in this impossible place and that"', before finally throwing himself ' "on the ground near the sphinx and weeping with absolute wretchedness"' (47).[28]

The profound effect that the disappearance of the Time Machine has on the protagonist can be explained by recourse to Maudsley's notion that mental degeneration occurs most frequently in individuals who remain skilled solely in 'the special work of their lives', at the expense of 'a deliberate culture and sustained activity of the mind as an aim in itself'.[29] The centrality of the Time Machine to the Traveller's life can be understood within the same paradigm as Maudsley's single-minded businessman, who by virtue of his 'long concentration of desire and energy' upon the single aim of success is particularly vulnerable to mental degeneration.[30] Indeed, Maudsley's observation that any sudden loss to such a person 'destroys the pride of his previous accomplishments, [and] lays low the fabric which he has been building with all the eagerness of an intense egoism', is a wholly adequate description of the Traveller's unexpected loss of the invention which had consumed all his energy.[31] Wells in *The Time Machine* explicitly indicates his awareness of contemporary discourses concerning the necessity of conserving nervous energy.[32] This is revealed by the narrator's remark that: 'The Medical Man looked into his face and, with a certain hesitation, told him he was suffering from overwork, at which he laughed hugely' (114). If the diagnosis of the medical man is to be accepted – and the 'usually pale face' (3) of the protagonist apparently reveals its symptoms – then the debilitating effects of overwork as a drain on nervous energy could have increased the Traveller's susceptibility to 'A Sudden Shock' such as that he receives when he discovers the disappearance of the Time Machine.

Subsequent to its mysterious removal, the recovery of the Time Machine becomes the identifiable 'quest' of the protagonist's narrative. Indeed, locating his invention in space is bound inextricably in the Traveller's mind with solving 'the riddle of the sphinx', and thus revealing the true basis of this future world: ' "I determined to put the thought of my Time Machine and the mystery of the bronze doors under the sphinx as much as possible in a corner of memory, until my growing knowledge would lead me back to them in a natural way" ' (51).[33]

As indicated, Wells in *The Time Machine* makes significant departures from an established tradition of utopian writing. Unlike Morris and Bellamy, he does not introduce to his protagonist 'some obliging scandal-monger [who] appears at an early stage, and begins to lecture on constitutional history and social economy'.[34] Indeed, in a passage which openly satirises Morris's use of a cicerone in *News From Nowhere*, Wells has the Traveller explicitly emphasise his status as a 'real' explorer: ' "But while such details are easy enough to obtain when the whole world is contained in one's imagination, they are altogether inaccessible to a real traveller amid such realities as I found here" ' (52). It is perhaps his being 'a real traveller' that accounts for the determined rationalism of the protagonist in uncovering the knowledge of this society that he is sure will allow him to regain his Machine.[35]

Nowhere is the, at times, ruthless rational individualism of the Traveller more apparent than in his absurd relationship with Weena, the Eloi woman whom he prevents from drowning. Though Weena serves an important function in affiliating his sympathies to the Eloi, she also serves to illustrate that no emotional interest will distract the Traveller from his desire to recover the Time Machine. Commenting on the reassessment of the utopian genre that occurs in the emergence of the scientific romance, Fernando Porta points out that: 'A female companionship would almost always be present in any utopian romance, thus creating a strong emotional involvement for the lonely explorer who finally finds love in a world or in an epoch where he is a stranger.'[36] He emphasises that in breaking away from this convention Wells creates a more serious purpose for his protagonist, which 'is to see and report back to the present the incredible things of the future'.[37] This purpose means that the almost callous attitude of the Traveller towards Weena underlines 'the male individualism and the rational commitment of a scientist'.[38]

Weena disrupts the flow of the Traveller's narrative ('"But my story slips away from me as I speak of her"' (57))[39] and obstructs his capacity for action in critical moments ('"It was time for a match. But to get one I must put her down"'(93)). Yet while the protagonist feels '"the intensest wretchedness for the horrible death of little Weena"', she still cannot be allowed to interfere with discovering the far more important fate of the Time Machine, '"I tied some grass about my feet and limped on across smoking ashes and among black stems, that still pulsated internally with fire, towards the hiding-place of the Time Machine"' (99).

In his determination to uncover the knowledge that he is certain will restore the Machine to him, the Traveller is careful to emphasise at the outset the importance of action, as opposed to merely sitting '"among all those things before a puzzle like that"' and yielding to the tendency to preoccupation he associates with '"monomania"' (50). The movement of the text's narrative constitutes the constant modification of the Traveller's initially confident hypothesis regarding the world of 802, 701, as he gradually uncovers the true foundation of the future. Dissatisfied with his '"first theories of an automatic civilisation"' (53), the protagonist soon discovers the Morlocks:

'A pair of eyes, luminous by reflection against the daylight without, was watching me out of the darkness. The old instinctive dread of wild beasts came upon me. I clenched my hands and steadfastly looked into the glaring eyeballs. I was afraid to turn. Then the thought of the absolute security in which humanity appeared to be living came to my mind. And then I remembered that strange terror of the dark. Overcoming my fear to some extent, I advanced a step and spoke. I will admit that my voice was harsh and ill-controlled. I put out my hand and touched something soft. At once the eyes darted sideways, and something white ran past me'. (59)

The primary significance of this passage is that, in illustrating how the Traveller uses his superior aggression to meet the challenge of this first subterranean inhabitant, it prefigures the outcome of the protagonist's eventual struggle for supremacy with the Morlocks.[40] This scene is also noteworthy because the wanderings stirred up in the Traveller's mind in this encounter – 'the absolute security in which humanity appeared to be living', 'then I remembered that strange terror of the dark' – emphasise the importance of the Morlocks to solving the Sphinx's riddle.

Indeed, before too long the protagonist is mustering the courage to descend into the underworld that the Morlocks inhabit, which opposes the paradisal surface world of the Eloi. *The Time Machine* can be considered as a manifestation of the literature of descent. The protagonist of the classical descent text, such as Orpheus, visits Hell in order to rescue the woman. However, the Time Traveller's descent is motivated by his desire to recover the Machine. Thus in the scientific romance, the technological creation replaces the woman as the object of emotional gratification. This is revealed explicitly in the moment when the Traveller finally regains his Machine, where he finds ' "a pleasure in the mere touch of the contrivance" ' (102). The narrator of the novel captures the almost irresistible fascination which machines hold for men:

I stared for a minute at the Time Machine and put out my hand and touched the lever. At that the squat substantial-looking mass swayed like a bough shaken by the wind. Its instability startled me extremely, and I had a queer reminiscence of the childish days when I used to be forbidden to meddle. (115)

The Morlocks, and the underworld they inhabit, relate to the proliferation of late-Victorian discourses on the poor. This is recognised in the modified hypothesis put forward by the Traveller, in which he explains his discovery that humanity has split into two species by recourse to the concepts employed in writings on the poor.[41] In posing a rhetorical question the protagonist appears to draw directly upon the research into East London conducted by such figures as Charles Booth: ' "Even now, does not an East-end worker live in such artificial conditions as practically to be cut off from the natural surface of the earth?" ' (63). The darkness of the Morlocks' dwellings is the first definite sign that something has gone awry in the future. It suggests that the problems of Outcast London, identified by Andrew Mearns among others, do not just remain unresolved, but have been accentuated. The anxiety of Mearns and others that the living conditions of the poor were becoming unacceptable is taken to its extreme in *The Time Machine*.[42] A particular concern of Mearns was that the houses of the poor were not receiving adequate air or indeed light:

> Should you have ascended to the attic, where at least some approach to fresh air might be expected to enter from open or broken window[s], you [...] discover that the sickly air which finds its way into the room has to pass over the putrefying carcases of dead birds or cats, or viler abominations still.[43]

This type of environment is endured by the Morlocks on a permanent basis, the Traveller noting that the ' "place, by the bye, was very stuffy and oppressive, and the faint halitus of freshly shed blood was in the air" ' (70). The darkness endured by the poor is recalled in the ' "black shadows, in which [the] dim spectral Morlocks sheltered from the glare" ' (70). The continuous darkness of the Morlocks' cavern is also recalled in the protagonist's statement that ' "the unbroken darkness had had a distressing effect upon my eyes" ' (69).

It is subsequent to his descent into the Morlocks' caverns that the Traveller begins to realise the true foundation underlying the apparent harmony of this future world. Though the Heart of Darkness explored in 1899 by his friend and correspondent Joseph Conrad would implicate contemporary London in the atavism of the supposedly more primitive peoples, Wells's own particular dark heart warns that – unless radical social reform is immediately implemented – the future will become the site of a disturbing retrogression.[44]

Wells's use of *The Time Machine* to emphasise the urgent necessity of social reform was undoubtedly influenced by the work of Huxley. In 'The Struggle for Existence in Human Society' (1888), Huxley writes approvingly of recent attempts to improve the conditions of the industrial classes: 'There is, perhaps, no more hopeful sign of progress among us, in the last half-century, than the steadily increasing devotion which has been and is directed to measures for promoting physical and moral welfare among the poorer classes.'[45] In direct opposition to Herbert Spencer, he is emphatic that this benevolence must be eventually upheld by the sponsorship of the State: 'the endeavour to improve the condition under which our industrial population live, to amend the drainage of densely peopled streets, to provide baths, washhouses, and gymnasia [...] is not only desirable from a philanthropic point of view, but an essential condition of safe industrial development'.[46]

Taking his cue from Huxley, Wells in *The Time Machine* endeavours to demonstrate the probable future outcome of a failure to introduce systemised reform in the contemporary moment.[47] This is apparent as the Traveller finally realises that the divergence between social classes he had earlier identified as the key to understanding this world has become an evolutionary distinction.

It would be difficult to overestimate the profound influence of Huxley on Wells. The author himself repeatedly acknowledged the indebtedness he felt towards his former Professor at the Normal School of Science. In his *Experiment in Autobiography* (1934), for example, Wells wrote: 'That year I spent in Huxley's class was, beyond all question, the most educational year of my life.'[48] With this comment in mind, it is unsurprising that Huxley's work is crucial to understanding *The Time Machine*. However, it is important to emphasise again here that – in his first novel at least – Wells undercuts the optimism of Huxley's position. The degradation of humanity the Time Traveller discovers in the world of 802, 701 reveals how Wells extrapolates the most pessimistic implications of Huxley's famous Romanes Lecture (1893).

In that lecture, Huxley had challenged the appropriation of Darwin's theory of natural selection by proponents of individualism. For Huxley, it is necessary to pit humanity's ethical system against the 'cosmic process' that has functioned so well in the natural world:

> Social progress means a checking of the cosmic process at every step and the substitution for it of another, which may be called the ethical process; the end of which is not the survival of those who may happen to be the fittest [...] but of those who are ethically the best.[49]

However, Huxley is keen to emphasise that this does not mean that we can simply disregard the importance of the cosmic process: 'Let us understand, once for all, that the ethical progress of society depends, not on imitating the cosmic process, still less in running away from it, but in combating it.'[50] Though he acknowledges that humanity remains in perpetual combat 'with a tenacious and powerful enemy', he is equally certain concerning the means of subjugating it. This should entail the application on the part of humanity of sound and collective will.

Wells's endeavour to extrapolate the pessimistic implications of Huxley's theory is emphasised as the Traveller realises that, rather than having successfully attained a conquest over nature, humanity ' "had differentiated into two distinct animals" ' (60). The protagonist's use of the term 'animal' is wholly appropriate in this instance, since *homo sapiens* is now subject to the exact same 'cosmic process' of evolution as the animal and plant kingdoms. That this is the case inverts the scientific rationalism of the Traveller's earlier statement, ' "we shall readjust the balance of animal and vegetable life to suit our human needs" ', which is confident in its assurance of humanity's capacity to control the entire course of earthly evolution.

Significantly, the Time Traveller learns that ' "like the Carlovingian kings" ', the once aristocratic Eloi ' "had decayed to a mere beautiful futility" ' (74). Hence, the playful lives of the upperworlders – which the protagonist had misinterpreted within a utopian frame – are not at all humanity's reward for the application of a sustained and collective will in guiding its own course along the evolutionary path. Instead, the entire existence of the Eloi is indicative of a species that is subject to the far more powerful and tenacious process of cosmic evolution. Moreover, the traveller's comparison of the automatic organic habits of the Morlocks with the behaviour of horses – ' "They did it as a standing horse paws with his foot" ' (74) – is acutely suggestive of a species that is subject to the identical evolutionary influences as animals and plants.

For the model of degradation which characterises the Eloi, Wells again reveals his indebtedness to the work of Huxley. In 'The Struggle For Existence In Human Society', Huxley stresses that 'it is an error to imagine that evolution signifies a constant tendency to increased perfection':

> That process undoubtedly involves a constant re-modelling of the organism in adaptation to new conditions; but it depends on the nature of those conditions whether the direction of the modifications effected shall be upward or downward. Retrogressive is as practicable as progressive metamorphosis.[51]

In a letter which accompanied a presentation copy of *The Time Machine* that he sent to Huxley in May 1895, Wells wrote: 'I am sending you a little book that I fancy may be of interest to you. The central idea – of degeneration following security – was the outcome of a certain amount of biological study.'[52] Wells might well have intended this statement to direct Huxley's attention to the endeavour of this 'little book' to illustrate that retrogression 'is as practicable as progressive metamorphosis'. After all, the diminished size, intellect and strength of the Eloi in response to the amelioration of social life demonstrate perfectly Huxley's point that the course of evolution 'involves a constant re-modelling of the organism in adaptation to new conditions'. However, by identifying the degeneration that must inevitably follow security as the 'central idea' of *The Time Machine*, Wells not only points to the didactic purpose of his first novel to warn against the assumption that evolution implies constant progression but also to an imperative that is crucial to understanding his subsequent work: that an element of risk and competition is essential to the continuing evolution of *homo sapiens*. While Huxley's reference to the plasticity of *homo sapiens* was undoubtedly pivotal to the formation of the novel's didactic intention, the degradation that the Time Traveller uncovers in the future reveals the influence of a more extensive account of the significance of retrogression in evolution.

The primary source for Wells's concept of degeneration in *The Time Machine* is Ray Lankester's *Degeneration: A Chapter in Darwinism* (1880).[53] Wells and Lankester became firm friends and allies, and the characterisation of both the Eloi and the Morlocks is informed by Lankester's account of the antithetical potential of degeneration in the evolutionary process.[54] Speaking from a strictly zoological basis, Lankester identifies three possible outcomes that can emerge from the influence of natural selection on an organism: Balance, Elaboration and Degeneration.[55] While in Balance the complexity of an organism's structure remains constant, and in Elaboration its complexity increases, Lankester is most interested in examining the third of these possible outcomes, Degeneration, in which the complexity of an organism decreases. 'Degeneration may be defined as a gradual change of the structure in which the organism becomes adapted to *less* varied and *less* complex conditions of life [emphasis in original]', he writes.[56] For Lankester, degeneration is most likely in circumstances where there is a 'new set of conditions occurring to an animal which render its food and safety very easily attained'.[57] Lankester identifies the parasite as a long recognised instance of degeneration, which is subject to what he terms retrogressive metamorphosis: 'Let the parasitic life once be secured, and away go legs, jaws, eyes, and ears; the active, highly-gifted crab, insect, or annelid may become a mere sac, absorbing nourishment and laying eggs.'[58]

The influence of Lankester, and in particular his notion that degeneration constitutes a suppression of form in the organism, is revealed as the Traveller adjusts his assessment of the Eloi: ' "The too-perfect security of the Upperworlders had led them to a slow movement of degeneration, to a general dwindling in size, strength, and intelligence" ' (65). The noncerebral lives of the passive Eloi eloquently articulate Lankester's foreboding that 'With regard to ourselves, the white races of Europe', it is possible 'we are all drifting, tending to the condition of intellectual Barnacles or Ascidians'.[59] The parasitic nature of the Eloi's existence is most explicitly stated as the protagonist learns the eventual fate of humanity, ' "Man as I knew him, had been swept out of existence" ' (79):

> 'It is a law of nature we overlook, that intellectual versatility is the compensation for change, danger, and trouble. An animal perfectly in harmony with its environment is a perfect mechanism. Nature never appeals to intelligence until habit and instinct are useless. There is no intelligence where there is no change and no need of change. Only those animals partake of intelligence that have to meet a huge variety of needs and dangers'. (100–1)

The above statement from the Traveller appears to draw directly upon Lankester's notion of retrogressive metamorphosis, which he associates directly with parasitism. Thus the Eloi, whose needs are attended to by the Morlocks – who ' "made their garments, I inferred, and maintained them in their habitual needs" ' (74) – become rather like 'the [once] active, highly gifted crab', thereby losing the necessity to adapt that more varied circumstances would bring.

The Morlocks' parasitism is recalled in what the protagonist conceives as a cannibalistic feeding on the Eloi. Like the Eloi, these other descendants of humanity are also an instance of retrogressive metamorphism. The Morlocks' eyes, which, through an enhanced sensitivity to the dark demonstrate how one particular organ can undergo elaboration in spite of the degeneration of the organism as a whole, also reveal the influence of Lankester: ' "Then, those large eyes, with that capacity for reflecting light, [which] are common features of nocturnal things – witness the owl and the cat" ' (62).[60] Yet despite being unquestionably degenerate, the Morlocks have adapted to their environment far more successfully than the Eloi. This is because, due to a shortage of food, they have not been introduced to the same biological security that inevitably tends to retrogression, and hence intelligence, induced by what the protagonist terms '"Mother Necessity"' (101), has returned. Thus the Traveller concedes that the Morlocks, due to the thought necessitated by the continued use of machinery, '"had probably retained perforce rather more initiative, if less of every other human character, than the upper [worlders]"' (101).

The degeneracy of the Morlocks, and their cannibalistic relationship to the Eloi, can also be examined in the light of the work of Francis Galton, whose Sociological Society would later include H. G. Wells among its members. In his *Inquiries into Human Faculty and its Development* (1883), Galton expressed fears regarding national fitness. For Galton, the rural section of the population was the 'fittest' (in the sense of healthiest) section of English society. The urban section of society is, by contrast, deteriorating with alarmingly rapidity.[61] Galton found that members of the rural population were far more fertile than their urban counterparts, whose town existence proved harmful to their biological constitution. However, Galton noted with concern in his *Inquiries* that the rural population too was beginning to show signs of deterioration, 'owing to the continual draining of the more stalwart of them to the towns'.[62]

The opposition between country and city implicit in the relationship between the Morlocks and the Eloi articulates the type of anxieties apropos national fitness expressed by Galton, among others. Galton's conception that the healthier rural population are to be considered the fittest to reproduce is cruelly inverted in the Morlocks' subversion of the Eloi's pastoral existence.[63] For the grossly unfit, urban Morlocks not only feed on the now sparsely numbered rural population that has become the Eloi, they '"probably [even] saw to the breeding of"' (81) them. The work of Galton is also instructive in illuminating another aspect of the successful downward adaptation of the Morlocks. Galton writes that it is 'by no means [always] the most shapely or the biggest personages who endure hardship the best' and that 'Sickly-looking and puny residents in towns may have a more suitable constitution for the special conditions of their lives'.[64] The Morlocks, regardless of their '"pallid bodies"' (66), which bear witness to their unfit physical constitution, have, like 'the puny residents in towns' from which they descend, retained precisely the appropriate hardiness for their underground existence.

The sardonic reference to positive eugenics revealed in the protagonist's statement that the Morlocks '"saw to the breeding of"' the Eloi indicates that *The Time Machine* strongly resists the teleology of the early eugenics movement (though we should note that just a few years afterwards Wells himself would be outlining the scope of future human-ity, in such texts as *A Modern Utopia*).[65] Although similar concepts were widely articulated, it is appropriate to remain with the *Inquiries Into Human Faculty and its Development* since Wells would later continue his critical engagement with Galton.

In his *Inquiries Into Human Faculty*, Galton argues that a list of emi-nent families should be drawn up as part of an endeavour to improve humanity. The genealogies of these families should reveal the heredi-tary transmission of certain desirable traits. While he insists 'on the certainty that our present imperfect knowledge of the limitations and conditions of hereditary transmission will be steadily added to', Galton regrets 'the serious want of adequate materials for study in the form of life-histories'.[66] However, he is strongly impressed with the necessity of endowing the favoured classes immediately these materials become available: 'local endowments, and perhaps adoptions, might be made in favour of those of both sexes who showed evidences of high race and of belonging to prolific and thriving families'.[67]

Although he acknowledges additional research will be necessary to establish a list of families whose members should be thus endowed, Galton is already certain what he considers to constitute the most desir-able qualities. The most transmissible of all traits is energy, which he defines as 'the capacity for labour'.[68] Galton also indicates that these desirable qualities are most likely to be found in the most privileged sections of society. While he is obviously concerned that the bulk of the population is deteriorating, Galton notes 'there are many signs that the better housed and better fed portion of it improves'.[69] This improve-ment is characterised by greater athletic feats and indeed by an increase of height, chiefly among the middle classes. Galton recounts the con-trast between the present and his own days at Cambridge, and notes that the undergraduates are now generally taller.

The ideas concerning eugenics in *Inquiries Into Human Faculty* are rele-vant in considering the characterisation of the Eloi, since they consti-tute precisely the descendants of those privileged groups Galton would choose to endow. Rather than possessing an increased amount of the energy which Galton considers to be the most highly transmissible trait, however, the Traveller points to the Eloi's incapacity for labour: ' "I never met people more indolent or more easily fatigued" ' (35).

The protagonist's description of the first of the Eloi he meets – ' "He was a slight creature – perhaps four feet high" ' (29) – reveals how Wells in *The Time Machine* also undercuts Galton's notion that increased stature necessarily accompanies improved conditions. Indeed, in the

National Observer version of *The Time Machine* the Traveller refers explicitly to the type of idea expressed by Galton as he considers the reduced
stature of the upperworld inhabitants:

> 'You believe the average height, average weight, average longevity
> will all be increased, that in the future humanity will all be increased,
> that in the future humanity will breed and sanitate itself into human
> Megatheria. I thought the same until this trip of mine. But, come to
> think, what I saw is just what one might have expected. Man, like
> other animals, has been moulded, and will be, by the necessities of
> his environment. What keeps men so large and strong as they are?
> The fact that if any drop below a certain power and capacity for com-
> petition, they die'.[70]

In this passage, Wells opposes the teleology of the early eugenics movement to Huxley's imperative that the future metamorphosis of the
human animal is contingent upon its environment. The extract reveals
that regardless of all those contemporary schemes which aim to breed
for certain traits – increased height and weight, for example – until such
time as 'humanity will breed and sanitate itself into human Megatheria',
the Eloi's diminished stature is a consequence of the fact that man will
ultimately be moulded 'by the necessities of his environment'. Thus
all elaborate schemes to improve the constitution of humanity will be
rendered irrelevant if *homo sapiens* does not continue to encounter the
risk that induces the capacity to adapt. Precisely what has occurred in
the case of the Eloi – both in the *National Observer* version of the text
and in the edition of *The Time Machine* eventually published in May
1895 – is that the amelioration of social life has long since erased any
danger or risk, resulting in the reduction of stature and intelligence
which accompanies any animal, including *homo sapiens*, 'drop[ping]
below a certain power and capacity for competition'. This again indicates how the understanding of the plasticity of *homo sapiens* he derives
from Huxley's foreboding concerning the potential for retrogressive
metamorphosis is more persuasive for Wells in *The Time Machine* than
the teleology of the early eugenics movement. However, it is important
to recognise that in his emphasis on the necessity of competition to the
evolutionary progress of humanity, Wells introduces an element that is
largely absent from Huxley's thought.

There is a degree of incompatibility in *The Time Machine* between the
emphasis on biological competition on the one hand, and the recognition of the need for co-operation in order to implement social reform on

the other.[71] The 'dilemma' faced by Wells in this respect is eloquently summarised by Kathryn Hume:

> not improving conditions leads to nightmare, but improving them in the direction of equality gets us back to Utopia and its degeneration. If one accepts the biological message – physical competition – one must ignore the social message; if one accepts the social – improved conditions – one must ignore the biological. Wells offers us no way to accept both.[72]

These two seemingly irreconcilable elements of the novel correspond to the terms of the individualism-collectivism debate that began earlier in the nineteenth century.[73] The individualist position, taken by proponents and opponents alike to be synonymous with the name of Herbert Spencer,[74] advocated the independent actions of individuals as opposed to state interference. Individualists argued that competition was imperative for the evolutionary progression of the human race, and that excessive state intervention would encourage the propagation of the weak, thus resulting in the degradation of humanity as a whole. The collectivist position maintained that state intervention was an integral aspect of social life, and a necessary part of social reform. Collectivists argued that the removal of material obstacles would facilitate the development of humanity, and drew support from 'the long-standing anxiety about the effect of extreme poverty upon the religious and moral habits of the working class'.[75] While he offers no means of reconciling these positions in *The Time Machine*, Wells would later attempt to resolve the individualist-collectivist debate in *A Modern Utopia*.

In *A Modern Utopia* the author would also synthesise the industrial world with the fabric of his utopian vision. In *The Time Machine*, however, the manner in which the Morlocks emerge from the industrialised underworld of their caverns to prey on the weakened Eloi satirises the pastoral setting associated with an existing lineage of utopian writing, particularly Morris's *News From Nowhere*.

As they emerge to subvert the seemingly Edenic world of the Eloi, the Traveller becomes increasingly preoccupied with the Morlocks, and what he describes as the ' "inhuman and malign" ' (73) quality of their being. Indeed, the protagonist's near obsession with the Morlocks – ' "I fancied I could even feel the hollowness of the ground beneath my feet: could, indeed, almost see through it the Morlocks in their ant-hill going hither and thither and waiting for the dark" ' (77) – almost threatens to emerge as an instance of the monomania he had earlier been so careful to avoid. Almost, that is, were it not for the considerable significance the Traveller attaches to the importance of action: ' "I could work at a problem for years, but to wait inactive for twenty-four hours – that is another matter" ' (50). The Time Traveller, who is conscious not only of the need for action but also of the tears which accompanied his loss of volition (' "They were the only tears, except my own, I ever saw in that Golden Age" ' (65)), has to find a source against which he can reassert his will power.[76]

In *The Logic of Fantasy* (1982), John Huntington notes how both the Eloi and the Morlocks make an identical gesture of touch towards the Traveller, who reacts warmly towards the Eloi but violently towards the Morlocks.[77] The protagonist's opposing reactions to the Eloi and the Morlocks can be explained by recourse to his need to regain his volition. Thus there is a hint that the source of the protagonist's comfort with the Eloi is his own physical superiority: ' "they looked so frail that I could fancy myself flinging the whole dozen of them about like nine-pins" ' (30). The instant animosity which characterises his feelings towards the Morlocks, conversely, can be attributed to the fact that, in these descendents of the unfit town dwellers, the Traveller finds an outlet for his desire to act, and – since the Morlocks constitute an opponent that is physically and intellectually superior to the Eloi, but ultimately inferior to himself – the perfect source against which to reassert his will power.[78]

It is his realisation of their cannibalistic feeding on the Eloi that generates the Traveller's most intensive violence towards the Morlocks. Deeply offended by ' "these inhuman sons of men" ' (80), the protagonist is moved to abandon the rationalism associated with the man of science and to align his sympathies fully with the Eloi. The Traveller claims that, despite the greater initiative retained by the Morlocks, his allegiance to the Eloi is the consequence of the fact that they have ' "kept too much of the human form not to claim my sympathy" ' (81). However, there is perhaps an underlying reason for the Traveller's unswerving support of the Eloi.

The Time Traveller's relationship with the Morlocks has always been understood in terms of class antagonism. Bernard Bergonzi, in his article '*The Time Machine*: An Ironic Myth', identifies the Morlocks as standing 'on one level for the late nineteenth century proletariat, [and hence] the Traveller's attitude towards them clearly symbolises a contemporary bourgeois fear of the working class'.[79] More recent discussions of class in *The Time Machine* have, however, focused on the ambiguities of the text which emerge from the sudden class mobility of Wells himself in the early 1890s. In his article 'The Time Machine and Wells's Social Trajectory', John Huntington examines the possible parallels between the ambiguous class position occupied by the Time Traveller and the difficulties faced by Wells in his meteoric rise to fame.[80] Huntington argues that, as a man who has achieved sudden social mobility, the protagonist – perhaps like Wells himself – is not entirely at ease with his new found status, and that this is revealed in the opening scenes of *The Time Machine*: 'The Time Traveller's upbringing has conditioned him so that as he rises in class he has difficulty behaving the way people born to the higher position do.'[81] According to Huntington, the evolutionary split that has emerged between the Morlocks and the Eloi in *The Time Machine* enables Wells to vent his class anger at the conditions endured by his mother at Uppark House, since the rich are preyed upon by the poor. However, the fact that the Time Traveller eventually understands the relationship between the Morlocks and the Eloi as that between members of different species concurrently masks class differences, thus accounting for the ambiguous class perspective of *The Time Machine*: 'In this shift away from class back to species we see exactly Wells's own double consciousness as he aspires to become a successful writer. He is filled with anger at the inequalities that his mother accepted, but his ambitions are not revolutionary or anarchistic.'[82]

Huntington's reading offers a valuable tool for uncovering some of the complex layers of meaning in the text. In particular, supposing Huntington's surmise that his first protagonist shares Wells's own humble class origins to be correct, then this provides a chilling resonance to the Traveller's statement that it is: ' "Very inhuman, you may think, to want to go killing one's own descendants!" ' (86–7). However, the Time Traveller's extreme violence towards the Morlocks is also significant in uncovering exactly how intense the contemporary bourgeois fear of the proletariat was.

The opening scenes of *The Time Machine* reveal the protagonist to be a liberal-minded man whose thought is well ahead of his era. He begins his account of time travel by challenging the principles his guests had learned at school and is indeed described by the narrator as ' "one of those men who are too clever to be believed" ' (15). That the Time Traveller possesses a social conscience is indicated by the sympathy for the plight of the East End worker he had revealed in his earlier identification of the opposition between capitalist and labourer as the key to understanding the future. Yet for all his liberalism, the protagonist is immediately offended upon encountering the Morlocks: ' "Instinctively I loathed them" ' (74). The Time Traveller's almost 'instinctual' loathing of the Morlocks emphasises just how deeply ingrained prejudices towards the proletariat were, even among the most liberal sections of the bourgeois community.

Resolving to stand firm against the perpetual nocturnal menace posed by the Morlocks, the Traveller affirms that: ' "I came out of this age of ours, this ripe prime of the human race, when Fear does not paralyse and mystery has lost its terrors. I at least would defend myself" ' (75). This affirmation from the protagonist illustrates another aspect of *The Time Machine*'s status as an evolutionary fable which warns against the complacent assumption that humanity's upward progression in the evolutionary scale is assured, or what Wells terms elsewhere 'Excelsior biology'.[83] For within the narrative framework of the novel, the ripe prime of the human race is located, not in the future which the protagonist visits only to be disappointed by the discovery that humanity has devolved into two distinct species of animal, but in the contemporary moment from which he had himself emerged. Further, we might specify that the apex of human evolution is located in the figure of the Traveller himself. He alone is able to fully understand, and indeed master, both the worlds represented in the novel. The protagonist not only has the knowledge of Time Travel which places him in an exclusive position among his contemporaries (whose objections he is able to meet with astounding ease), but also retains the privileged position in the future age of being able to adapt to the diametrically opposed environments in which the Eloi and Morlocks exist.

As he struggles to come to terms with the enormity of the truth that humankind has been ' "swept out of existence" ', the Time Traveller finds looking at the stars an unexpected source of reassurance: ' "Looking at these stars suddenly dwarfed my own troubles and all the gravities of terrestrial life. I thought of their unfathomable distance, and the slow inevitable drift of their movements out of the unknown past into the unknown future" ' (79). In his classic study of *H. G. Wells* (1970), Patrick Parrinder comments on the 'appeal to the stars' in the author's fiction.[84] For Parrinder, the above passage reveals how: 'The deterministic and pessimistic cast of *The Time Machine* corresponds to the sense of human belittlement implicit in the scientific humanism of the period.'[85] More specifically, it is possible to supplement Parrinder's account by stating that this passage implicates the whole of humanity in the same cosmic process as the stars the protagonist derives comfort from, since the pessimism of *The Time Machine* suggests that the evolution of *homo sapiens* also constitutes a 'slow inevitable drift' from an 'unknown past' into an 'unknown future'.

The Time Traveller's circumstances at this moment in the text correspond to Wells's speculations in 'On Extinction', an article published in *Chambers Journal* in September 1893.[86] In that article, Wells reviews the extraordinary number of species that once existed but have left no evidence of their time on earth: 'The long roll of palaeontology is half filled with the records of extermination; whole orders, families, groups and classes have passed away and left no mark and no tradition upon the living fauna of the world.'[87] He then speculates on whether the members of endangered species are conscious of their impending extinction, before turning his attention to man. Wells acknowledges that 'These days are the days of man's triumph' and the consequent anthropocentrism means that the 'future is full of men to our preconceptions, whatever it may be in scientific truth'.[88] However, he also introduces the possibility of human extinction: 'the most terrible thing that man can conceive as happening to man: the earth desert through a pestilence, and two men, and then one man, looking extinction in the face'.[89]

The challenge of *The Time Machine* to the anthropomorphic preconceptions Wells mentions in 'On Extinction' is indicated in the instance where the protagonist reveals the constitution of those creatures that have replaced man: ' "Instead were these frail creatures who had forgotten their high ancestry, and the white Things of which I went in terror" ' (79). In the world of 802,701, then, the Traveller is in many senses 'the last man'.[90] Indeed in 'The Further Vision' which functions as a highly entropic ending to the novel, the Traveller actually is 'looking extinction in the face' since the last remnants of humanity have already reverted to the slime from which it emerged and large crab like creatures are the last remaining living things.

Returning to the world of 802,701, the Eloi can be also understood in the context of the analogy between the development of the individual and the evolution of the species that was commonplace in nineteenth-century anthropology. The characterisation of the upperworld inhabitants of *The Time Machine* undercuts what Ernst Haeckel outlines as '*the fundamental law of organic evolution* [emphasis in original]':

The fundamental law [...] is briefly expressed in the proposition: that the History of the Germ is an epitome of the of the History of the Descent; or, in other words: that Ontogeny is a recapitulation of Phylogeny; or, somewhat more explicitly: that the series of forms through which the Individual Organism passes during its progress from the egg cell to its fully developed state, is a brief, compressed reproduction of the long series of forms through which the animal ancestors of that organism (or the ancestral forms of its species) have passed from the earliest periods of so-called organic creation down to the present time.[91]

Haeckel's theory of development is an optimistic one, since it implies a continually progressive evolution of the organism. Perhaps the popularisation of this *'fundamental law of organic evolution'* is what Wells had in mind in 'Zoological Retrogression' (1891), where he wrote that 'the educated public': 'has decided that in the past the great scroll of nature has been steadily unfolding to reveal a constantly richer harmony of forms and successively higher grades of being, and it assumes that this "evolution" will continue with increasing velocity under the supervision of its extreme expression – man'.[92] Wells is, however, at pains to point out that – like that of a man moving about in a busy city – the course of evolution can take many different paths: 'Sometimes it goes underground, sometimes it doubles and twists in tortuous streets, now it rises far ahead along some viaduct, and, again, the river is taken advantage of in these varied journeyings to and fro.'[93]

In *The Time Machine*, Wells challenges any complacency on the part of his readers by illustrating how human evolution could take a downward course. In his characterisation of the Eloi, Wells inverts what Haeckel calls *'the first principle of Biogeny'*. Whereas Haeckel claimed that the development of the individual recapitulates the earlier phases of evolution of the entire species, Wells in his construction of the Eloi portrays the future development of *homo sapiens* as a retrogressive movement back towards the primitive stages of human development. This concurs with the overall implication that human evolution is moving backwards in *The Time Machine*, which is, of course, also suggested by the use of the number 802,701 almost as a countdown to extinction.

The depiction of the Eloi is indeed explicitly child-like. Their lack of abstract reflection, and indeed lack of concentration, is revealed as the Traveller feels ' "like a schoolmaster amidst children" ' (35) in his strenuous efforts to learn the language. The simplicity of the upperworlders' language not only relates to the general discussion of primitive language in anthropological circles but also more specifically to Lankester's discussion of language in *Degeneration: A Chapter in Darwinism*. Lankester insists that 'True' degeneration of language is 'only found as part and parcel of a more general degeneration of mental activity'.[94] The absence of abstract terms and concepts in their language is symptomatic of the fact that the Eloi have undergone 'a more general degeneration of mental activity'.[95]

Towards the end of his sojourn in the future, the protagonist considers his hasty conclusions as he returns to the spot from which he had first viewed the future: '"About eight or nine in the morning I came to the same seat of yellow metal from which I had viewed the world upon the evening of my arrival"' (99). This implies that the Traveller not only journeys into the future, but also that his unravelling of the eventual fate of humanity in 802,701 takes the form of a journey which returns him to his original point of departure. The protagonist does not function as an unchanging observer who merely reports on events in the future. Rather, in the course of the journey in which he discovers the eventual fate of humanity, the Time Traveller is himself subjected to retrogression. This is immediately apparent as, having discovered the disappearance of his Machine, the Time Traveller himself regresses to the same child-like characteristics as his hosts: '"'Where is my Time Machine?' I began, bawling like an angry child"' (46). The regression of the protagonist to the same childhood state as the Eloi is further emphasised as he acquires their fear of the dark and loathing of the Morlocks.

His violent conduct towards the Morlocks emphasises the latent savagery underlying the Time Traveller's own apparently civilised being.[96] Throughout his narrative, the protagonist creates a careful distinction between the civilised man and the savage. Thus while explaining the principles of time travel to his dinner guests he emphasises how the '"civilised man is better off than the savage"' (8) in his capacity to defy gravity by travelling in balloons. In the context of the future world which the Traveller initially identifies as the apex of evolution, contemporary men are nonetheless '"savage survivals, [and] discords in a refined and pleasant life"' (41). Wells's source for the protagonist's speculations in this respect is again Huxley's Romanes Lecture. In that lecture, Huxley points out that man's evolutionary position has been purchased by the same struggles that characterise the animal and plant kingdoms:

> For his successful progress, throughout the savage state, man has been largely indebted to those qualities which he shares with the ape and the tiger; his exceptional physical organization; his cunning, his sociability, his curiosity, and his imitativeness; his ruthless and ferocious destructiveness when his anger is roused by opposition.[97]

However, Huxley is at pains to point out that such characteristics are unnecessary with the advancement of social organisation, and that modern man would be pleased to see the 'ape and tiger' within him die. Indeed, Huxley argues that manifestations of the ape and tiger are considered as 'sins': 'he punishes many of the acts which flow from them as crimes; and, in extreme cases, he does his best to put an end to the survival of the fittest of former days by axe and rope'.[98] Huxley's emphasis on the diminished need for savage struggle enables him to strengthen his case against proponents of individualism by underlining the necessity for 'ethical' evolution.

Wells again indicates his intention in *The Time Machine* to extrapolate the most pessimistic implications of Huxley's theory by making the Traveller draw on precisely this primitive energy in his savage struggle with the Morlocks. Indeed, immediately his Machine disappears the protagonist states his plan to '"recover it by force or cunning"' (47), thereby unleashing the 'ape' and 'tiger' within him.

Feeling '"like a beast in a trap"' (74) with the approach of longer periods of nightfall during which he must inevitably encounter the Morlocks, the protagonist himself begins to reveal the 'ruthless and ferocious destructiveness' of a man whose 'anger is aroused by opposition'. Lamenting his reluctance to take into the future any technological aids from his own epoch – arms or medicine – the Traveller is left to fight the Morlocks '"with only the weapons and the powers that Nature had endowed me with – hands, feet, and teeth"' (71). Therefore, the protagonist's battle for supremacy with the Morlocks constitutes the kind of struggle Huxley had identified with an earlier phase of humanity's development, rather than with any process of ethical evolution.

Huntington has suggested that both the fire otherwise absent from the world of 802,701 and the protagonist's iron bar act as symbols linking him to the technological advancement of his own age. He considers that the use of both as weapons sublimates the Traveller's aggression, since it is his self-control that 'marks his difference from both Morlock and Eloi'.[99] Yet at the most crucial moment in the narrative – where he struggles to retain the levers that set his machine in motion in the face of an onslaught from the Morlocks – the Traveller is in possession of neither of these aids, having already discarded the iron bar and being unable to light the matches in his possession. Rather, in order to recover the lever that the Morlocks almost prise from his grasp, the Traveller is forced to use sheer physical aggression: '"As it slipped from my hand, I had to butt in the dark with my head – I could hear the Morlock's skull ring – to recover it"' (103). That it is his superior physical strength in this moment that enables him to recover his Machine and escape overturns the Time Traveller's previous idea that physical courage may provide a hindrance for the civilised man.

Furthermore, rather than asserting his technological superiority, the protagonist's forest-fire leads to a substantial massacre of the subterranean inhabitants of the future as well as apparently killing Weena, the only friend he has made in this new world. This moment in *The Time Machine* anticipates a scene in *Heart of Darkness*, in which a blindfolded missionary holds up a torch. In these scenes from each of their respective novels, first Wells and then Conrad critique the 'civilising' light of imperial expansion by foregrounding the ignorance of the colonial agent.

As his violence towards them intensifies, so the Traveller's simian affiliation with the 'ape-like' Morlocks is increasingly emphasised. Wells was certainly aware of the controversy in the pages of the *Fortnightly* over August Weissman's theory of germ plasm. In 'The Biological Problem of To-day', published in the *Saturday Review* in December 1894, Wells expresses his support of Spencer's view of the importance of acquired characteristics in the hereditary process as opposed to Weissman's germ-plasm theory: 'the public have been devouring the fruit of the tree of Weismannism, [in]spite of the warnings of Herbert Spencer and Romanes that it is bitter'.[100]

As the Time Traveller gradually acquires those characteristics associated with the Morlocks, he first becomes ' "accustomed to the darkness" ' (92) of their nocturnal environment before he finally matches their pattern of rest: ' "I awoke a little before sunsetting. I now felt safe against being caught napping by the Morlocks" ' (101). The protagonist's acquiring of such characteristics is seemingly complete when – having returned to his contemporary moment – he explicitly reproduces (or rather, anticipates) the traits of the Morlocks. He is 'dazzled by the light' (17) of his dining room in much the same manner as the Morlocks are dazzled by the light of his matches. He also reproduces the carnivorous habits of those future degenerates: ' "I'm starving for a bit of meat" ' (18); ' "What a treat it is to stick a fork into meat again!" ' (20). That the Traveller so easily acquires the traits of the Morlocks relates to contemporary fears that characteristics acquired within a single lifetime could be transmitted to future generations. Indeed, his affiliation with the simian Morlocks is emphasised right up until the moment the Traveller again disappears. The Traveller had initially mistaken the subterranean inhabitants of the future for ghosts. This prefigures the narrator's description of the protagonist as he departs on the final voyage from which he does not return: ' "I seemed to see a ghostly, indistinct figure sitting in a whirling mass of black and brass for a moment – a figure so transparent that the bench behind with its sheets of drawings was absolutely distinct; but this phantasm vanished as I rubbed my eyes" ' (116).

The pessimism of the Traveller's narrative is to some extent countered by the epilogue. The sentimentalism lacking in the Traveller's relationship with Weena is restored by the narrator's possession of 'two strange white flowers – shrivelled now, and brown and flat and brittle – to witness that even when mind and strength had gone, gratitude and a mutual tenderness still lived on in the heart of man' (118). The darkness which characterises the Traveller's vision of the futuristic retrogression – and indeed ultimate regression of humankind back to the slime from which it emerged – recalls an important passage from 'The Rediscovery of the Unique', in which Wells stresses the potential of scientific knowledge to reveal the comparative insignificance of contemporary humanity in the cosmic process:

> Science is a match that man has just got alight. He thought he was in a room – in moments of devotion, a temple – and that his light would be reflected from and display walls inscribed with wonderful secrets and pillars carved with philosophical systems wrought into harmony. It is a curious sensation, now that the preliminary splutter is over and the flame burns up clear, to see his hands lit and just a glimpse of himself and the patch he stands on visible, and around him, in place of all that human comfort and beauty he anticipated – darkness still.[101]

Avoiding such pessimism, the narrator of *The Time Machine* characterises the future as 'still black and blank – [it] is a vast ignorance, lit at a few casual places by the memory of his story' (117). The appropriate response to the apparent inevitability of the Traveller's vision, is, for the narrator of the novel, 'for us to live as though it were not so' (117). Instead, he anticipates the coming time when the riddles of his own era, which he cannot conceive as 'man's culminating time!' have been solved by those descendents of humanity whose efforts constitute 'the manhood of the race' (117). The narrator's hopes for 'the manhood of the race' offer a contrast to the childhood imagery which the protagonist uses to describe the Eloi.

The overall impact of *The Time Machine* on its reader, however, remains one of extreme pessimism. It is the Time Traveller's vision of a retrogressive child-like humanity, rather than the narrator's aspirations for 'the manhood of the race', which endures. In his first scientific romance, Wells synthesises his understanding of contemporary science with his literary skills in order to create a chilling vision of the future. In drawing effectively on the work of Huxley and Lankester, he is able to create the Eloi and the Morlocks, his memorable future inhabitants. That the protagonist is forced to actively interpret the future before he realises the extent of the retrogressive metamorphosis of humanity emerges from Wells's endeavour in *The Time Machine* to critique such utopian novels as Bellamy's *Looking Backward*. This critique also relates to the retrogression of the Time Traveller himself, since his loss of volition in his fearful introduction to the future generates his desire to reassert his willpower. While the subterranean inhabitants of 802,701 provide the perfect source against which he can reassert his volition, the Time Traveller's struggle with the Morlocks increasingly unlocks the 'ape' and 'tiger' which underlie his apparently civilised being. While Wells himself always celebrated the towering influence of his Professor at the Normal School of Science, *The Time Machine* can be considered as anti-Huxley. Since the protagonist's 'primitive' energy helps defeat the Morlocks, this would appear to suggest that Wells sees something of the 'ape' and 'tiger' as necessary to human progress. Relatedly, Wells reveals in *The Time Machine* that he considers competition to be crucial to the continuing development of humanity. This emphasis on competition is largely absent from Huxley's writings. *The Time Machine* most explicitly undercuts the optimism of Huxley's principle of ethical evolution as the Time Traveller announces his final assessment of the Eloi and the Morlocks. Rather than having initiated a process of ethical evolution in order to guide its own evolutionary course, humanity has in fact devolved into two species, each of which is subject to the tenacity of the 'cosmic process'. The removal of any rigid distinction between human and animal that is implicit in *The Time Machine*, and indeed the protagonist's simian affiliation with the 'ape-like' Morlocks, prefigures Wells's second scientific romance, *The Island of Doctor Moreau*.

3
'An Infernally Rum Place':
The Island of Doctor Moreau
and Degeneration

> He who fights with monsters should look to it that he himself
> does not become a monster. And when you gaze long into an
> abyss the abyss also gazes into you.
>
> Friedrich Nietzsche, *Beyond Good and Evil* (1886)[1]

The Island of Doctor Moreau was first written in 1895; through subsequent revisions Wells transformed a relatively conventional adventure narrative into a disconcerting evolutionary fable which offended critical sensibilities following its publication in April 1896. Basil Williams, in a review in *Athenaeum*, found that: 'The sufferings inflicted in the course of the story have absolutely no adequate artistic reason, for it is impossible to feel the slightest interest in any one of the characters, who are used as nothing but groundwork on which to paint the horrors.'[2] Similarly, the author of an unsigned notice in the *Review of Reviews* warned that 'the frontispiece alone of his [Wells's] new story is enough to keep it out of circulation'.[3] The conservative tone of such reviews is perhaps symptomatic of the fact that Wells's second scientific romance was published in the climate of moral suppression which followed the Wilde trials of April and May 1895. Writing in 1924, Wells acknowledged the trials as a partial inspiration for the novel:

> There was a scandalous trial about that time, the graceless and pitiful downfall of a man of genius, and this story was the response of an imaginative mind to the reminder that humanity is but animal rough-hewn to a reasonable shape and in perpetual internal conflict between instinct and injunction.[4]

The text's Wildean inspiration is reflected in its characterisation and plot structure. Moreau flees England following the sensational exposure of his researches. Montgomery is similarly forced to flee due to a possible homosexual lapse.[5] Prendick is himself – albeit temporarily – a prisoner on the island. Moreau's expulsion is the consequence of breaking a social law. Laws restricting vivisection had been passed in 1876 and hence Moreau was doing something that had been declared unlawful.[6] The unnatural connotations which might be associated with vivisection are revealed in the mock human status that Moreau confers on the Beast People. Wilde's removal from society was similarly a consequence of transgressing the societal conceptions which cluster around the natural/ unnatural opposition.

In addition to responding to the Wilde trials, *The Island of Doctor Moreau* sustains Wells's fictional engagement with the discussions surrounding the implications of evolutionary theory. Like *The Time Machine*, the novel should be read in the context of the various discourses involved in disseminating Darwin's theory of natural selection, and in assessing its model of humanity, to adopt Wells's phrase, as an 'animal rough-hewn to a reasonable shape'. Such texts of course include Wells's own scientific writings, particularly 'Zoological Retrogression'. In that article, which traces his indebtedness to Ray Lankester's *Degeneration: A Chapter in Darwinism*, Wells challenges the optimistic (or ' "excelsior" ') contemporary interpretations of evolutionary theory. 'Scientific observers', writes Wells, 'certainly fail to discover that inevitable tendency to higher and better things with which the word "evolution" is popularly associated'.[7] He emphasises instead that recent times have seen an increasing awareness of 'the enormous importance of degeneration as a plastic process in nature', and the examination of its 'entire parity with evolution'.[8] Such an acknowledgement has for Wells been facilitated by the recognition of oversights in the classification of micro-organisms which have led to the mistaken identification of a universal progression in the evolutionary scale. Wells is careful to stress the 'antithetical' potential of degeneration: 'rapid progress has often been followed by rapid extinction or degeneration'.[9]

Wells's scientific journalism also provides a challenge to the hegemony of humanity's place in the universe. There is a passage in 'Zoological Retrogression' that does much to undermine the contemporary faith that humanity's progression along the evolutionary path was assured. Wells writes that nature may be 'in unsuspected obscurity, equipping some now humble creature with wider possibilities of appetite, endurance, or destruction, to rise in the fulness of time and sweep *homo* away into the darkness from which his universe arose'.[10] The challenge to anthropocentrism contained in this passage is revealed in *The Island of Doctor Moreau* by Prendick's remark that: 'The creatures I had seen were not men, had never been men. They were animals – humanised animals – triumphs of vivisection' (88).

Previous critics have established that the examination of social and natural laws unites the text's Wildean inspiration and its post-Darwinian considerations.[11] Yet there is another, more explicit, link between the Wilde trials and the 'plastic process in nature' that is degeneration. The concept of degeneration provided the late Victorians with a very powerful model of explanation for numerous forms of deviant behaviour, including homosexuality.[12] Indeed, as will be examined, Wilde's association with degeneracy extended beyond his infamous sexuality, particularly through his name being linked to the supposedly degenerate aesthetic movement in the arts.[13]

The Island of Doctor Moreau is the most intensely gruesome of all Wells's scientific romances, its early chapters setting a pessimistic tone. They also establish the relative nature of many social laws. Set adrift and near starvation, Prendick and his companions almost engage in a retrogressive cannibal act.[14] Aboard the *Ipecacuanha*, Captain Davis's somewhat arbitrary system of justice – ' "I'm the law here, I tell you" ' (16) – prefigures the Faustian pursuits of Moreau in the enclosed space that is the island. From its very outset, then, *Moreau* is preoccupied with the inscription and transgressing of boundaries. Prendick himself has the experience of crossing the ultimate demarcation, that which marks off this world from the next: 'I had a persuasion that I was dead' (6).

Contemporary reviews of the novel seem to affirm its gruesome nature. To the anonymous reviewer in the *Review of Reviews*, the portrayal of the metamorphosis of man into animal proves more offensive than the hint of bestiality in the novel. 'The law against sex[ual] intercourse with animals may be, and is, unduly severe, but it is an offence against humanity to represent the result of the intermingling of man and beast', he writes.[15] The text activates fears of atavism not only in its 'intermingling of man and beast', but also in its exploration of the latent bestiality which modern man attempts to conceal.

Prendick's insertion into Moreau's island space marks the beginning of a transformation in the Wellsian observer that will eventually lead to his living as one among the creations of Doctor Moreau. In the section of the text entitled 'The Thing in the Forest', Prendick is unable to define the exact status of a threatening antagonist. He variously accords to this mysterious entity the status of 'man' and 'the unmistakable mark of the Beast' (51), before confronting his confusion over the issue: 'What on earth was he – man or animal?' (52). Finally he settles for the term 'man-animal'. That Prendick is hunted like a fearful animal concurs with the ultimate failure of the text as a whole to make any enduring distinction between man and beast:

> It was some time before I could summon resolution to go down through the trees and bushes upon the flank of the headland to the beach. At last I did it at a run, and as I emerged from the thicket upon the sand I heard some other body come crashing after me. (56)

Prendick's fearful actions in his encounter with the Leopard Man relate to the wider discussion of fear in the late-Victorian periodical context. In his 'The Human Animal in Battle', published in the *Fortnightly Review* in August 1896, H. W. Wilson speculates on the implications of fear for the conduct of soldiers in future military confrontation.[16] Of immediate significance is the article's title, with its emphasis on the human animal. In 'Human Evolution, An Artificial Process', published in the *Fortnightly Review* just two months later, Wells similarly makes use of the term 'the human animal' to underline humanity's status as an animal species.[17] Mankind's status as only one among a number of species is emphasised in the equality implied by Prendick's recollection of 'some other body' which came 'crashing after me'.

In terms of contextualising Prendick's behaviour when confronted with the Leopard Man, the most crucial aspect of Wilson's discussion is its emphasis on the necessity to control fear, which for him remains 'the most powerful emotion in the human animal'.[18] Uncontrolled fear can have devastating consequences for the soldier, making both him and his comrades vulnerable to an adversary: 'If flight takes place it is the flight of panic, a reflex and involuntary act. [...] [Which] is rarely the best road out of danger'.[19] In order to counter the contagious effects of panic, Wilson advocates the instillation of self-control: 'Only strength of will can overcome this tendency to run.'[20] Combatants who are able to control their fear gain an immediate advantage over an assailant: 'To go forward and die is certainly better than to go backward and die [...] [since] the enemy, who is experiencing precisely the same emotions, will lose courage and shoot less steadily'.[21]

In his initial confrontation with the Leopard Man, Prendick seems to anticipate the conceptual framework Wilson invokes. First of all, he manages to control 'an impulse to headlong flight with the utmost difficulty' (51). Moving still closer to his then unknown assailant, Prendick notes that 'Flight would be madness' (52). His actions then prefigure Wilson's view that there is an advantage to be gained in controlling one's fear and confronting an adversary: 'My heart was in my mouth, but I felt my only chance was to face the danger, and walked steadily towards him. He turned again and vanished into the dusk' (52). Thus Prendick's 'strength of will' has, on this occasion, caused the Leopard Man to 'lose courage'.

Such courageous behaviour is subsequently abandoned as Prendick – perfectly in accordance with the post-Darwinian concerns of the novel – becomes the hunted. Significantly, he is now subject to Wilson's dictum that 'Fear is greatest where the imagination is strongest.'[22] Hastily retreating in a 'perplexed' state of mind, Prendick considers the possibility that his pursuer 'was a mere creation of my disordered imagination' (54). The adverse effects of Prendick's imagination are now such that: 'Every dark form in the dimness had its ominous quality, its peculiar suggestion of alert watchfulness' (55). The sheer power of Prendick's imagination is undoubtedly a major contributing factor to his complete unnerving: 'I completely lost my head with fear, and began running along the sand' (56).

The narrator of *The Island of Doctor Moreau* is further subjected to what Wilson considered one of the greatest enemies to courage in 'the human animal': hunger. An important biological theme in the novel is that of food; through lack of it Prendick is forced to recognise himself as part of an animal species: 'Hunger and a shortage of blood-corspuscles take all the manhood from a man' (26).[23] Rescued at the point of starvation, Prendick becomes the object of Montgomery's medical scrutiny, thus prefiguring the objectification of the Beastfolk at the hands of Moreau. Montgomery's explanation of Prendick's recovery further highlights the specifically physical aspect of being a man (or for Wells, a member of the species *homo sapiens*): ' "I've put some stuff into you now" ' (8). The conception of man as a biological rather than an intellectual species is extended when Prendick is again pursued (tellingly, in 'The Hunting of the Man'), this time by Moreau, Montgomery and various of the Beastfolk. Most notably here, Prendick is again reminded of his physicality: 'with my heart beating loudly in my ears' (66).

Prendick's experiences in the text take the form of a journey: 'The rafters, I observed, were made out of the timbers of a ship' (60). The protagonist's occupation of the role of the hunted in the early part of this journey forces him – and by extension, the reader – to begin to reconsider his own anthropocentric views. Particularly, the textual treatment of humanity's apparently superior evolutionary adaptation is worthy of note. The imagination was believed to be a product of language (which was considered by many at this time to separate humanity from the animals). Yet, it is precisely this supposedly enhanced evolutionary attribute that intensifies Prendick's animalisation at particular points in the text.

While the animalisation of humanity represented in the novel invited a barrage of moral censor, Wells vigorously defended the scientific basis of *The Island of Doctor Moreau*, which was, after all, subtitled 'A Possibility'. Wells responded furiously to the claim, made by P. Chalmers Mitchell in a review of *The Island of Doctor Moreau*, that the grafting of tissue between different animals conducted by the novel's eponymous character was not possible. In a letter to the Editor of the *Saturday Review* published on 7 November 1896, he wrote that:

> I was aware at the time that Mr Chalmers Mitchell was mistaken in relying upon Oscar Hertwig as his final authority in this business, that he was making the rash assertion and not I, but for a while I was unable to replace the stigma of ignorance he had given me, for the simple reason that I knew of no published results of the kind I needed.[24]

Wells then pointed to a report in the *British Medical Journal* of 31 October 1896 of a successful graft of connective tissue between man and rabbit.[25]

Moreau himself conceives of his life work as ' "the study of the plasticity of living forms" ' (89). He informs Prendick that: ' "it is a possible thing to transplant tissue from one part of an animal to another or from one animal to another, to alter its chemical reactions and methods of growth, to modify the articulation of its limbs, and indeed to change it in its most intimate structure" ' (90). Wells had outlined the substance of Moreau's explanation in 'The Limits of Individual Plasticity', an article published in the *Saturday Review* in January 1895.[26] In that article, Wells speculates: 'a living being may also be regarded as raw material, as something plastic [...] [so that it] might be taken in hand and so moulded and modified that at best it would retain scarcely anything of its inherent form and disposition'.[27]

For Prendick, the most incredulous attribute of Moreau's 'monsters manufactured' is their linguistic capacity: ' "These things – these animals *talk!* [emphasis in original]" ' (90). *The Island of Doctor Moreau* is responding to new theories of the relation between humans, animals and language which were threatening to overturn the existing dominant idea, popularised by Max Müller and C. Lloyd Morgan, that animals could not possess language.[28] The American naturalist Richard Garner provided one of the most serious challenges to this view, and his initial experiments with monkeys appeared to reveal a simian language much like a simplified version of our own speech.[29]

Garner accepted the inextricability of language and reason: what he did not accept was that language belonged to humans only. Garner began conducting experiments with monkeys in his native America in 1884 and concluded he had found a number of Capuchin monkey words including those for food and drink. For Garner, the importance of studying simian language was that it provided clues to the origins of speech. In 'The Simian Tongue [I]', the first of a series of three articles published in the *New Review* between June 1891 and February 1892, Garner wrote that he was 'willing to incur the ridicule of the wise' and 'assert that "articulate speech" prevails among the lower primates'.[30] Furthermore, Garner thought his research significant because it revealed a close correlation between the uniformly progressive nature of evolution and the level of reason attained through language: 'To reason, they [simians] *must think*, and if it be true that *man cannot think without words*, it must be true of monkeys [emphasis in original]'.[31] In order to validate his theories, Garner next announced his plans 'to arrange for a trip to interior Africa to visit the *troglodytes* in their native wilds'.[32] This, he hoped, would enable him to confirm his theories concerning the progressive scale of language and reason, allowing him to examine at close quarters what he considered to constitute the intermediate region of this scale. British readers first learned from a report in *Harper's Weekly* in December 1891 of Garner's plan to use a seven-foot square cage as the basis from which to conduct his research.[33]

Wells's awareness of the debates concerning animals and language is revealed in his 'The Mind in Animals', a review of Morgan's *An Introduction to Comparative Psychology* (1894).[34] In this review, Wells is critical of Morgan's 'perceptions of relations' which 'does not seem to give proper weight to the difference in mental operations that must exist' between, to use the example cited by Wells, the olfactory functions of man and dog. Morgan had of course argued that there was a distinction between men and animals based on language. However, Wells explores the possibility that the dog's enhanced powers of olfactory discrimination could provide the basis for something akin to rationality: '[the dog] may have on that basis a something not strictly "rational" perhaps, but higher than mere association and analogous to and parallel with the rational'.[35] Emphasising this point in a passage that does much to prepare the reader for the anthropomorphism of animals in *The Island of Doctor Moreau*, Wells intimates that his opinion of animal intelligence is higher than Morgan's. 'It may even be that Professor Lloyd Morgan's dog, experimenting on Professor Lloyd Morgan with a dead rat or a bone to develop some point bearing upon olfactory relationships, would arrive at a very low estimate indeed of the powers of the human mind', he writes.[36] I can find no evidence that Wells encountered the work of Garner. It is, however, a distinct possibility that, in the period of his apprenticeship as a journalist, the young Wells read 'The Simian Tongue' in the pages of the *New Review*, the same periodical that would later serialise *The Time Machine*.

The narrator of *The Island of Doctor Moreau* appears to follow Morgan in identifying language as the distinguishing feature of humanity. In his early encounter with the Ape Man, Prendick identifies his interlocutor as a man, 'for he could talk' (67). Yet, Moreau's imposition of a 'humanising process' on the Beastfolk seems to confirm Garner's conception of an unbroken chain of expression. Gradually, Prendick comes to accept that animals might reason: 'never before did I see an animal trying to think' (86). Rather like Garner in his African experiments, Prendick is forced into an anthropological relationship with the Beastfolk following his initial inability to understand them from an observational distance: 'The speaker's words came thick and sloppy, and though I could hear them distinctly I could not distinguish what he said' (50).

Once among them, Prendick gains an understanding of the abilities and limitations of the Beastfolk in relation to their capacity to reason. Thus although the Ape Man had seemed perfectly human due to his use of speech, there remains a gulf between his speech and the higher levels of reasoning associated with humanity. His responses to questions are for Prendick highly unsatisfactory, being but 'chattering prompt responses [which] were, as often as not, at cross purposes with my question' (68–9). Later in the novel, the Ape Man himself creates a distinction which summarises much of the limitations of the Beastfolk's capacity for reasoning: 'He had an idea, I believe, that to gabble about names that meant nothing was the proper use of speech. He called it "big thinks," to distinguish it from "little thinks" – the sane everyday interests of life' (159–60). The Ape man's 'big thinks' are nothing but signifiers that have become dislodged from their concepts or that have been conjured up from nothing. It would seem, then, that the Beastfolk conform to Garner's notion of an evolutionary chain – their communication only of relatively simple ideas reflects their comparatively lowly placing in a great chain of articulation.

Despite endowing the Beast People with the linguistic faculty that enables them to transcend what Morgan had considered to constitute an immutable barrier, *The Island of Doctor Moreau* is distinctly cautious concerning the possibility of these hybrid animals further developing that faculty to attain truly abstract reasoning. This cautiousness is foregrounded in the chapter 'The Sayers Of The Law' in which a somewhat perplexed Prendick is forced to participate in the recital of Moreau's Law:

'Not to go on all-fours; *that* is the Law. Are we not Men?'
'Not to suck up Drink; *that* is the Law. Are we not Men?'
'Not to eat Flesh nor Fish; *that* is the Law. Are we not Men?'
'Not to claw Bark of Trees; *that* is the Law. Are we not Men?'
'Not to chase other Men; *that* is the Law. Are we not Men?' (72–3)

The prohibitory nature of Moreau's law effectively binds his creations' imaginations, limiting them to little more than idiocy. This cruelly eliminates the potential for abstract reasoning that is created in the increased scope of the Beastfolk's intelligence. In their recital of the Law the Beastfolk do not employ anything which resembles abstract reasoning. Instead, they are subject to a 'kind of rhythmic fervour [which] fell on all of us; [as] we gabbled and swayed faster and faster' (73). Rather than substantiate Garner's theory that simian language 'contains rudiments from which the tongues of mankind could easily develop', the heavily ritualised nature of the Beastfolk's 'rhythmic fervour' tends to support Morgan's view that, although animals often display intelligent behaviour, abstract reasoning remains exclusively the property of the human species.[37] However, we should not overlook the parallels of the Beast People's recital of the Law with human religious practices.[38]

The Island of Doctor Moreau's engagement with the debates concerning animals and language concurs with its overall suppression of the biological limen between man and beast. In this hybrid world of 'humanised animals' and 'animalised humans', the Beastfolk's recital of the Law functions as a comment on the status of those philosophical and religious activities considered to constitute the most advanced forms of human reasoning. To the anonymous author of an unsigned review in *The Guardian*, there is a definite hint of blasphemy in the novel: 'his [Wells's] object seems to be to parody the work of the Creator of the human race, and cast contempt upon the dealings of God with His creatures'.[39] Moreau's Law is undoubtedly the most blasphemous element of the novel.[40] Its recital by the Beastfolk recalls the prayers of a Christian Church: ' "*His* is the House of Pain. *His* is the Hand that makes. *His* is the Hand that wounds. *His* is the Hand that heals [emphasis original]" ' (73). The droning insistence that accompanies the Beast People's fearful worship of a mock deity reduces the metaphysical system of belief that is the Christian religion to a series of monotonous 'gabbles', which is entirely bereft of any conceptual dimension. The Ape Man's 'Big Thinks' similarly parodies what Frank McConnell has identified as 'the self-serving, metaphysical pretensions of the philosophical community'.[41] In the figure of the Ape Man, these ideas perform an acute degradation, being represented in the last instance by a 'gabble about names which meant nothing'.

The Ape Man is undoubtedly the most deliberately allegorical figure to appear in the text, and as such, his presence does much to emphasise the continuity between humanity and the animal species. At the time of his first encounter with this creature, the narrator is still, significantly, subject to the mistaken assumption that his interlocutor is another man, thus stressing a common heritage shared by all members of the species *homo sapiens*. Yet the Ape Man's use of speech is nothing like the 'true articulate speech' which Wells elsewhere identifies as the foundation of human society.[42] The 'artificial' education of the Ape Man falls distinctly short of the process of 'artificial' evolution or education which Wells would later advocate in 'Human Evolution, An Artificial Process', written only six months after the *The Island of Doctor Moreau*. Rather than providing the basis of 'true' articulate speech, his 'parrot-like' (69) answers to questions function only for Prendick to identify him as a 'creature [who] was little better than an idiot' (68).

The support that *The Island of Doctor Moreau* provides to the view that there exists an evolutionary continuum between the use of language in humans and animals is further underlined by the imagination that is created by the Beastfolk's newly-found linguistic status. The endowment of the Beastfolk with a linguistic faculty also brings with it the fear which had earlier overwhelmed Prendick to such a great extent. This is particularly recalled in the case of the sheep, which despite having 'no more than the wits of a sheep', was 'terrified beyond imagination' (95) following its most basic humanisation by Moreau.

The one factor that does separate humanity from these hybrid animals is the capacity for untruths. In order to contain the Beastfolk following Moreau's demise, Prendick insists that Moreau has merely transformed the manner of his existence, and that the Law still applies. In Prendick's statement that 'An animal may be ferocious and cunning enough, but it takes a real man to tell a lie' (157), Wells offers a sardonic commentary on those powers of abstract reasoning that Morgan and others considered the exclusive property of the human species. The uniqueness which Prendick represents as the sole human survivor on the island is therefore accompanied by another textual representation of the negative aspects of humanity's supposedly enhanced evolutionary status. As John R. Reed points out, Wells seems to use the protagonist of his 1932 novel *The Bulpington of Bulp* to identify lies as a universal fact of humanity's status as 'the culminating ape'. He states that the one gift that man, 'the poor ape' had to aid his development was that he could lie: 'Man is the one animal that can make a fire and keep off the beasts of the night. He is the one animal that can make a falsehood and keep off the beasts of despair.'[43] Prendick's status as the sole remaining representative of humanity on the island therefore highlights the double function of mankind's ability to imagine what does not exist. Falsehood is construed as a negative aspect of humanity's supposedly enhanced evolutionary status but it is precisely the same capacity for mental inventiveness which enables the future development of the species as a whole.

In order to gain a sense of the Beast People, Prendick implores the reader to 'Imagine yourself surrounded by all the most horrible cripples and maniacs it is possible to conceive' (74). The figures of the Beastfolk are projections and intensifications of those groups considered to have constituted the most degenerate sections of Victorian society. Such groups included criminals and the mentally ill, and also radically alien groups. Particularly, the characteristics of the Beastfolk as described by Prendick are markedly similar to Herbert Spencer's taxonomy of the physical constitution of the primitive as outlined in *The Principles of Sociology* (1876).[44] To begin with, Spencer notes that 'Men of inferior types appear to be generally characterized by relatively-defective development of the lower limbs'.[45] This is recalled in the description of the first of the Beast People encountered by the protagonist, who reflects on the apparent stature of the island's inhabitants: 'I found afterwards that really none were taller than myself, but their bodies were abnormally long and the thigh part of the leg short and curiously twisted' (29–30). Spencer further 'discovers' the following traits in the primitive man:

> Among other structural traits of the primitive man which we have to note, the most marked is the larger size of jaws and teeth. This is shown not simply in that prognathous form characterizing various inferior races [...] but it is shown also in the races otherwise characterized: even ancient British skulls have relatively massive jaws.[46]

It is with the above description of primitive man that the physical tropes of the Beastfolk most strikingly concur. On Davis's ship, Prendick meets 'The Strange Face', which 'startled me profoundly' (11). The protagonist proceeds to describe what he finds most disturbing about this 'singularly deformed' face: 'The facial part projected, forming something dimly suggestive of a muzzle, and the huge half-open mouth showed as big white teeth as I had ever seen in a human mouth' (11). Relieved – though not morally appeased – to find that Moreau is in fact vivisecting animals, the narrator organises his recollections 'Concerning the Beast Folk'. Following his reiteration of the disproportionate nature of these creatures' bodies, Prendick further details the 'obvious deformity' of the Beastfolk's faces. As he does so, his language draws directly on that of Spencer and other contemporary evolutionary theorists: the faces of the Beastfolk 'were prognathous, malformed about the ears, with large and protuberant noses, very furry or very bristly hair, and often strangely coloured or strangely placed eyes' (104).

The Beastfolk similarly conform to Spencer's ideas on the intellectual characteristics of the primitive type. Spencer identifies in the savage a parallel with 'the young of our own race', which amounts to an 'inability to concentrate the attention on anything complex or abstract'.[47] The limited mental capacity in these creatures is revealed in Prendick's relationship with the Ape Man, who assumes he is the equal of the protagonist merely because of the number of digits on his hand.

In the preface to Prendick's narrative, supposedly written by his nephew Charles Edward, the island is termed 'Noble's Isle', which may be an ironic reference to Rousseau's notion of the 'Noble Savage'.[48] Prendick notes how the inhabitants of the island look at him 'in a peculiar furtive manner, quite unlike the frank stare of your unsophisticated savage' (38). The 'peculiar furtive manner' of the Beastfolk's stare is a consequence of the conditioning imposed upon them by Moreau. Throughout the novel, the Beastfolk are unable to make substantial eye contact with the protagonist. However, when they do, the experience is for Prendick a disturbing one. Meeting M'ling's gaze under the darkness of the starlight, he is 'struck down through all my adult thoughts and feelings, and for a moment the forgotten horrors of childhood came back to my mind' (21–2). Prendick's eye contact with the Beast People forms part of what William Greenslade defines as a wider late-Victorian 'poetics of recognition' where 'the moment of glimpse, glance or gaze' means 'that commonly accepted co-ordinates of knowledge have gone awry'.[49] Through eye contact, Prendick is forced to acknowledge the 'utter strangeness and yet [...] strangest familiarity' (50). His observations of the island are predicated on the recognition of a haunting familiarity, which makes him, for example, sure that he had met the Fox-Bear woman 'in some city byway' (107). He also compares another of the Beast Folk to a 'yokel trudging home from his mechanical labours' (107). Looking at the Beastfolk makes Prendick aware of the latent bestiality that resides in his own humanity. It also emphasises that the text creates a line of continuity between the civilised and the primitive as well as between humans and animals.

That Prendick should use a prostitute and a proletarian as central points of reference is not only in accordance with the novel's preoccupation with degenerate sections of the community but also relates more specifically to late nineteenth-century discourses on the bestial working class. Though more implicitly than *The Time Machine*, the text is engaged with contemporary concerns regarding the living conditions endured by the poorest sections of the community. Particularly, there was a fear that the conditions in which the poor were housed were creating animals out of them. One of a number of identically entitled articles produced in the latter decades of the 1800s, Mary Jeune's 'The Homes of the Poor' outlines the hardships of the poor in London.[50] Focusing on specific areas such as Bethnal Green, Jeune reports on the lack of daylight and circulating air: 'every other inch being covered by miserable houses, except where huge warehouses rear their heads, shutting out only too effectively both air and light'.[51] Prendick similarly reports on the singularly harsh nature of the Beastfolk's living conditions. The dens in which the Beast People live – which are organised in a manner akin to a 'shanty-town' – are characterised by a lack of both light and circulating air. (Thus Prendick remarks the 'stench' of the 'hovels' in which he finds Moreau's creations).

I have already indicated that the Law recited by the Beastfolk in these darkened hovels constitutes the most blasphemous element of the text. That the novel horrified many of its first reviewers is indicative of the fact that Moreau's 'island paradise' might be read as a parody of Genesis, complete with Serpent: ' "a limbless thing with a horrible face that writhed along the ground" ' (97). Moreau is like a God to the inhabitants of this island paradise; Montgomery – with a hint of beastiality in his relationship with M'ling – is a Christ-like figure who dies for the Beast People's sins. Prendick himself is at points identified with Christ (with references to ' "he that walks weeping into the sea" ' (109)). Moreau's recollections of his early experiments in vivisection sound like a grotesque juxtapositioning of the story of Creation and a ruthlessly post-Darwinian logic:

'I began with a sheep, and killed it after a day and a half by a slip of the scalpel; I took another sheep and made a thing of pain and fear, and left it bound up to heal. It looked quite human to me when I had finished it, but when I went to it I was discontented with it; it remembered me and was terrified beyond imagination, and it had no more than the wits of a sheep. The more I looked at it the clumsier it seemed, until at last I put the monster out of its misery'. (94–5)

As many modern critics have noted, the text is strikingly Darwinian in its emphasis on the waste or chance that is inherent in the evolutionary process.[52] Prendick is taken to an island that is not his intended destination and this is illustrated by particular chapter headings used in the text: he is 'The Man who was going Nowhere'; and then 'The Man who had Nowhere to go'. Similarly, Montgomery is at pains to point out the role of chance in human life: ' "It's chance, I tell you [...] as everything is in a man's life" ' (20).

Like *The Time Machine*, *The Island of Doctor Moreau* can be read in the context of those social theories which emerged in response to Darwin's theory of natural selection. Moreau's activities on the island are most revealingly explored in the light of T. H. Huxley's famous Romanes Lecture (1893). As indicated in the discussion of *The Time Machine*, Huxley argued that it is imperative for humanity to pit its ethical system against the 'cosmic process' of evolution which functions in the natural world. Huxley is adamant that this is the only way that *homo sapiens* can overcome the threat posed by degeneration, since cosmic evolution is relentless in its operation.

Moreau's experiments should not be understood merely as the undertaking of a willful individual whose act of hubris is defined as an attempt immediately to overcome the cosmic process. Rather, his project constitutes an attempt to deflect the wider mechanics of evolution away from the island. In other words, Moreau is attempting to procure for himself a secluded space in the universe in which a cessation of the cosmic process occurs. In its place, he optimistically aims to impose on his creations his own vision of evolutionary control and then perfection. ' "I have been doing better; but somehow the things drift back again, the stubborn beast flesh grows, day by day, back again [...] I mean to do better things still" ' (96).

Moreau is indifferent to the impact of ethics on the conduct of his research. Yet, when he does comment on it, he delivers the chilling statement: ' "The study of Nature makes a man at last as remorseless as Nature" ' (94). Thus Moreau's project differs from Huxley's both in its disregard of ethics and in its emphasis on the imposition of an individual rather than the collective will. Nevertheless, we must attribute a certain degree of success to this modern Faust. The sheep and the Gorilla may be seen as early experiments (or as evolutionary mistakes), while Montgomery's attendant M'ling represents the most exemplary of Moreau's creations.

Finally, however, Moreau's undertakings on the island collapse into the chaos that is represented by the pursuit of the Leopard Man. Just as he cannot prevent the Beastfolk's reversion to their instinctively carnivorous habits, so Moreau is powerless to prevent the effects of another process, the cosmic one, emerging on the island space. One of Prendick's final comments before the demise of Moreau is that all on the island are subject to:

> a vast pitiless mechanism, [which] seemed to cut and shape the fabric of existence, and I, Moreau by his passion for research, Montgomery by his passion for drink, the Beast People, with their instincts and mental restrictions, were torn and crushed, ruthlessly, inevitably, amid the infinite complexity of its incessant wheels. (123)

Prendick's first observation on the island is of: 'a thin white thread of vapour [which] rose slantingly to an immense height, and then frayed out like a down feather' (30). This ominous sign is symptomatic of the fact that the island itself has something of an organic unity; we are reminded of its 'faint quivering', its 'gusts of steam' and its volcanic activity.[53] It is as though the island in its function as a living organism provides a trope for the cruel reality of the 'cosmic process', the remorseless assertion of which renders Moreau's ideas of grandeur comparatively insignificant.

As I have already indicated, the characterisation and action of *The Island of Doctor Moreau* were apparently influenced by the Wilde trials. Moreau, of course, had been a high achieving scientist before his exile. Yet he is, in another sense – like Wilde – an artist; though in a somewhat crude manner, Moreau is a sculptor.[54] He finds in ' "the human form" ' something ' "that appeals to the artistic turn of mind" ' (91). There is a moment shortly after Doctor Moreau 'explains' which brings together his dual role as an artist and biological scientist:

> Now they [the Beast people] stumbled in the shackles of humanity, lived in a fear that never died, fretted by a law they could not understand; their mock-human existence began in an agony, was one long internal struggle, one long dread of Moreau – and for what? It was the wantonness that stirred me. (122–3)

On the one hand, the 'wantonness' of Moreau's activities refers to the waste inherent in the evolutionary process as a whole. The Beastfolk's suffering is all the more intense because they are the perverse products of an attempt to circumvent the cosmic process. On the other, the above quotation recalls the fact that the text is working in an established literary tradition of the scientist as creator. In this respect, two of the most important intertexts for *The Island of Doctor Moreau* are *Frankenstein* (1818) and *The Strange Case of Dr Jekyll and Mr Hyde*, which shares a fascination with bestiality and male sexual deviance.[55] The Beast People are but the creations of a scientist remorselessly indulging in his 'passion for research'.[56] The result of this is science for its inherent sake or indeed art for art's sake.[57]

In his *Degeneration* (1892), Max Nordau examines what he considers to be the degenerate nature of the modern artist. In his preface to that text, dedicated to Lombroso, Nordau warns that *'some among these degenerates in literature, music, and painting have in recent years come into extraordinary prominence* [emphasis in original]'.[58] For Nordau, 'everyone capable of logical thought will recognise that he commits a serious error if, in the aesthetic schools which have sprung up in the last few years, he sees the heralds of a new era'.[59] Those targeted by Nordau include Oscar Wilde, as an English representative of the aesthetes. In many senses we might regard Moreau as a degenerate artist in the same sense as Nordau targets Wilde. For Moreau's 'art' is similarly the result of the self-indulgent practices against which Nordau warns. Certainly, the removal from English society of both Moreau and Wilde is a consequence of their respective attempts to elevate their individual will over the consensus of the wider community.[60] Yet, a difference between Moreau and Wilde is that Moreau has a choice; his exile is in part a consequence of his refusal to conform to social laws. Having chosen to ignore social laws, he then attempts – and fails – to circumvent natural ones.

It is in the 'Reversion of the Beastfolk' that *The Island of Doctor Moreau* makes its most explicit contribution to discourses of degeneration, thus making a strong challenge to the ' "excelsior" ' biology of the time. As the lone human survivor on the island following the deaths of Moreau and Montgomery, Prendick witnesses the final degradation of Moreau's 'shackles of humanity':

Of course these creatures did not decline into such beasts as the reader has seen in zoological gardens – into ordinary bears, wolves, tigers, oxen, swine and apes. There was still something strange about each; in each Moreau had blended this animal with that; one perhaps was ursine chiefly, another feline chiefly, another bovine chiefly – but each was tainted with other creatures – a kind of generalised animalism appeared through the specific dispositions. (162)

Returning to the anonymous writer in the *Review of Reviews*, he considers the 'hybrid monsters' of the story 'loathsome' on the grounds that: 'the result in the picture is exactly that which would follow as the result of the engendering of human and animal'.[61] As well as generating such fears of atavism, the reversion of the Beastfolk might also be understood in the context of discourses considering the degenerate artist. In his 'The New Naturalism' of 1885, W. S. Lilly objects to the degenerate artist. For Lilly, the New Naturalism represents precisely the opposite of potential human ascendency in the evolutionary scale. The passage which follows seems neatly to summarise Prendick's description of Moreau's 'art' as well as Lilly's objection to the New Naturalism: 'It eliminates from man all but ape and tiger. It leaves of him nothing but the *bête humaine*, more subtle than any beast in the field, but cursed above all beasts of the field.'[62]

Following the demise of Moreau, Montgomery seems to regress excessively rapidly. As he regresses, his liking for the Beast People becomes increasingly intense; until he at last shows his final preference for them in the chapter of the novel ironically entitled 'Montgomery's Bank Holiday'.[63] Although he does not engage in degenerate activities like Moreau, or degenerate behaviour like Montgomery, Prendick's actions do little to enhance humanity's capacity to overcome the cosmic process. This is established long before he reaches the Wellsian abyss. When cut adrift by Davis, Prendick's passitivity does little to inspire confidence in the prospect of combating the evolutionary process: 'Abruptly the cruelty of this desertion became clear to me. I had no means of reaching the land unless I should *chance* to drift there [emphasis added]' (27). On the island, the protagonist again shows his inability to adapt to sudden environmental changes. He twice contemplates suicide rather than attempting to assert an influence over his environment. The second of these occurs as Prendick broods over his inability to build an effective raft: 'But at the time my misery at my failure was so acute, that for some days I simply moped on the beach and stared at the water and thought of death' (164).

Significantly, the narrator is unable to secure for himself a staple source of food. Prendick frankly admits that 'I knew no way of getting anything to eat' (65). Moving into the 'shanty-town' of the Beastfolk, he is forced somewhat apologetically to ask the Ape Man for food. This means that Prendick's behaviour recalls Lankester's conception of parasitism. As indicated in the discussion of *The Time Machine*, Lankester observes that an organism loses its capacity to adapt in circumstances where its food is easily attainable. Prendick's reliance upon the Beastfolk for food as the last human survivor on the island similarly reduces his capacity to adapt.

Prendick's admission that he is not a practical man provides a stark contrast to the narrator of a significant precursor of *Moreau*, *Robinson Crusoe* (1719).[64] An important difference, however, exists in that Moreau's island seems to actively frustrate Prendick's attempts to act: 'The only insurmountable obstacle was that I had no vessel to contain the water I should need if I floated forth upon untravelled seas. I would have even tried pottery, but the island contained no clay' (166). Prendick – who had taken to natural history 'as a relief from the dulness of my comfortable independence' (9) – is destined to discover its harsher realities.

With no means of escape from the island, Prendick is forced to lower his anthropocentric conceptions and adapt, sharing both the Beastfolk's food and living space. Prendick's comments on the initial suitability of this arrangement read like an absurd parody of Garner's use of a cage in Africa: 'We were in just the state of equilibrium that would remain in one of those "Happy Family" cages that animal-tamers exhibit, if the tamer were to leave it for ever', he says (162). However, as the reversion of the Beastfolk accelerates and his own increasingly fear-driven and violent behaviour comes to mimic that of Moreau's creations, the 'cage' which encloses Prendick renders him distinctly animalistic.

Revealingly, the acceleration of this reversion is accompanied by a chronic degradation of the Beastfolk's use of language. 'My Ape Man's jabber', reports Prendick 'multiplied in volume, but grew less and less comprehensible, [and] more and more simian' (160). Others of the Beast People seem to be 'slipping their hold upon speech', so that language that was 'once clearcut and exact' becomes 'mere lumps of sound again' (160).

The Beast People's final reversion to a distinctly meaningless simian tongue reveals that the status of their linguistic faculty is contingent upon Moreau's Law and the perpetual engineering that occurs in the 'House of Pain'. To this end, there is the Ape Man's comments regarding the punishment he received as the consequence of a lapse in his linguistic capabilities: ' "I did a little thing, a wrong thing, once. I jabbered, jabbered, stopped talking. None could understand. I am burned, branded in the hand" ' (75). The Ape Man's 'humanisation' was always bound to fail, since Moreau can never entirely 'burn out' the Ape within him, and this creature's mock human status was only ever achieved by the continual application of violent means.[65] The 'artificial' education of the Ape Man could never be met with success, since there is no 'man' present in him for Moreau to teach the power of *logos* to.

As well as commenting on the Beastfolk, Prendick reports on the considerable transformation which he undergoes himself: 'My clothes hung about me as yellow rags, through whose rents glowed the tanned skin. My hair grew long, and became matted together. I am told that even now my eyes have a strange brightness, a swift alertness of movement' (162–3). That bourgeois Prendick undergoes such a hugely discernible transformation further relates to discourses concerning the bestial working class. Forced to inhabit the same living space, the protagonist's behaviour comes to resemble that of Moreau's creations. Thus this bourgeois character has degenerated into bestiality in the space of less than one generation.[66]

Eventually, however, the same boat that had helped deliver him to the island facilitates Prendick's return to England. In a highly Gulliverian touch, a distinctly misanthropic Prendick – now 'The Man Alone' – isolates himself from the rest of humanity, tending to:

> spend my days surrounded by wise books, bright windows in this life of ours lit by the shining souls of men [...] There is, though I do not know how there is or why there is, a sense of infinite peace and protection in the glittering hosts of heaven. There it must be, I think, in the vast and eternal laws of matter, and not in the daily cares and sins and troubles of men, that whatever is more than animal within us must find its solace and its hope. (172)

It is through the comfort he finds in 'the vast and eternal laws of matter', and by invoking some typically Huxleian terminology – 'the glittering hosts of heaven', the 'souls of men' and 'books' – that Prendick identifies the potential for overcoming the 'ape' and 'tiger' that resides within us all.[67] In 'Human Evolution, An Artificial Process', Wells is similarly influenced by Huxley as he articulates his method for escaping the biological pessimism of natural selection. 'Natural Selection', he writes, 'is selection by Death.'[68] Beginning with the fact that natural selection works comparatively slowly on humanity due to the great length between generations, Wells stresses the importance of the 'acquired factor', which constitutes the morals, culture and traditions of human society. It is through the accumulation of this 'acquired factor' that humanity may be able to steer 'itself against the currents and winds of the universe in which it finds itself'.[69]

At the time of writing *The Island of Doctor Moreau*, however, Wells had yet to make that crucial distinction between biological man ('the culminating ape') and the traditions and customs which might ultimately save humanity from retrogression.[70] This explains the overwhelmingly pessimistic ending of the novel. Fearing 'that presently the degradation of the Islanders will be played over again on a larger scale' (171), a deeply traumatised Prendick now observes that the whole of England is ripe for degeneration:

> I would go out into the streets to fight with my delusion, and prowling women would mew after me, furtive craving men glanced jealously at me, weary pale workers go coughing by me with tired eyes and eager paces like wounded deer dripping blood, old people, bent and dull pass murmuring to themselves, and all unheeding a ragged tail of gibing children. Then I would turn aside into some chapel, and even there, such was my disturbance, it seemed that the preacher gibbered Big Thinks even as the Ape Man had done; or into some library, and there the intent faces over the books seemed but patient creatures waiting for prey. (171–2)

It is precisely those elements that he had first encountered on Moreau's island space which an overwhelmingly fearful Prendick now identifies in his fellow human beings. Significantly, those who share the degenerate traits of those 'others' of Moreau's island come to occupy central place in contemporary England.[71] Most poignantly, the entire species *homo sapiens* is subjected to the same retrogressive use of language as the Beast People, with even those of the religious order – 'the preacher gibbered Big Thinks even as the Ape Man had done' – unable to escape this form of linguistic damnation. The final juxtapositioning of the bestial traits of *homo sapiens* – 'like wounded deer dripping blood' – with the reduction of its most advanced conceptual activities into a distinctly animalistic trait – 'there the intent faces over the books seemed but patient creatures waiting for prey' – not only underlines the allegorical intentions of the novel as a whole but also reinstates its overall suppression of any enduring distinction between man and beast.

It is possible to conclude by stating that Wells creates a distinction between humans and animals, but then undercuts it by showing humanity to be subject to reversion, or even more radically, its higher conceptual reaches turn into the same forms of gabble as that of the Beastfolk. This is especially apparent as humankind is ultimately subjected to the same retrogressive use of language as the Beast People at the end of the novel.[72] Thus, the extreme pessimism of its ending can be attributed to the fact that *The Island of Doctor Moreau* represents the superiority of human evolution as a futile achievement. The final effect of the novel clearly reinstates Prendick's observation that the island of Doctor Moreau is a microcosm which implicates the entire human cosmos: 'I had here before me the whole balance of human life in miniature, the whole interplay of instinct, reason, and fate in its simplest form' (122).

Part II
Science and Society

4
Science behind the Blinds: Scientist and Society in *The Invisible Man*

> I discovered that I was one of those superior Cagots called a genius – a man born out of my time – a man thinking the thoughts of a wiser age, doing things and believing things that men now *cannot* understand, and that in the years ordained to me there was nothing but silence and suffering for my soul – unbroken solitude, man's bitterest pain.
>
> H. G. Wells, 'The Chronic Argonauts' (1888)[1]

The Invisible Man has often been commended for the scientific verisimilitude granted to the (in)credible discovery of invisibility. As an anonymous reviewer in *Literature* wrote, 'one is really almost persuaded that one's own ignorance of the true meaning of scientific formulae alone prevents a full apprehension of the process by which Griffin is able [...] at last to fade away himself out of human sight'.[2] Though keenly impressed by 'Mr Wells's peculiar gift' of achieving for his story 'a scientific glamour', which – 'with a reference to the Rontgen Rays [sic] and other still more mysterious vibrations' – allows him to 'reduce the impossible into terms of the probable' and thus uphold the fictional illusion of a man who has attained corporeal invisibility, the author of the review adds a cautionary note:

> A doubt might suggest itself to the curious whether by further manipulation of the refractive index Griffin ought not to have been able at once to bring himself back [to a visible state] again without having to retire to a remote village in Sussex with bottles and dynamos to find out how to do so.[3]

Wells himself was acutely aware of the scientific paradoxes which accompany the invisible status he bestows upon Griffin. In a letter written to fellow novelist and friend Arnold Bennett shortly after the publication of the novel he identified an implausibility in the concept of an invisible man which he believed to be 'insurmountable': 'Any alteration in the refractive index of the eye lens would make vision impossible. Without such alteration the eyes would be visible as glassy globules.'[4]

Yet the significance of Wells's third scientific romance lies not so much in the engagement with actual scientific possibilities, but instead in its exploration of the potential complexities inherent in the relationship between scientist and society. Clement Shorter's observation, in an early review of *The Invisible Man*, that 'Scientific research is indeed vanity if we are to accept Mr Wells as a guide' is borne out as the most gifted of Wells's early scientists are reticent to utilise their scientific gifts towards the benefit of society.[5] In *The Time Machine*, the Time Traveller returns only to tell of his adventures before he disappears on a final temporal voyage. In *The Island of Doctor Moreau*, Moreau chooses to exile himself to a lonely Pacific island to continue his research on vivisection. Since *The Invisible Man* is the first of his scientific romances in which 'we are shown a recognisable society', it is through the grotesque figure of Griffin that Wells most thoroughly investigates the factors which can lead potentially to the scientist's alienation from the community, and thus to the loss of outstanding scientific capacity which could be of far greater benefit to society as a whole.[6]

Kirpal Singh concludes that 'Wells's uncanny insight into the mind of the disgruntled but talented scientist sounds a warning to both the scientist and his fellowmen'.[7] Like other accounts of *The Invisible Man*, however, Singh's brief analysis fails to consider how the novel participates in wider debates which determine the relationship between scientist and society. In the first half of the novel, Wells dramatises the need to disseminate a broader understanding of scientific method through the education system. At the same time, however, the Iping section reveals the limits of induction and *The Invisible Man* points to the importance of the imagination to scientific enquiry – thus making a distinctive contribution to the wider dispute over the nature of scientific method itself. As Robert Sirabian puts it in his article 'The Conception of Science in Wells's *The Invisible Man*', 'The achievement of *The Invisible Man* is Wells's treatment of science beyond its oversimplified conceptions, either as a purely imaginative, speculative pursuit or as an analytical activity concerned only with facts.'[8] In addition to highlighting how the public must inevitably come to terms with forms of scientific thinking, Wells concurrently indicates how scientists must endeavour to popularise their research in order to facilitate the public understanding of science.

The Invisible Man has often been classified alongside Robert Louis Stevenson's *The Strange Case of Dr Jekyll and Mr Hyde* as a novel which reveals the bestiality unleashed in the irresponsible pursuit of knowledge. However, there is a significant difference between the two novels in this respect. Hyde's inherent bestiality and disposition towards violence are immediately apparent at the outset of Stevenson's novel. Yet as Bernard Bergonzi points out, we first see Griffin, 'not directly as weird or terrifying, but through the matter-of-fact eyes of the Iping villagers'.[9] The absurdity of his bandaged appearance immediately marks the visitor out as a figure to be mocked, disdained and feared by the local Sussex people. Consequently, the identity of the stranger – who remains nameless for the entire first half of the narrative – becomes the subject of intense speculation amongst the villagers. By making Griffin's identity mysterious to the people of Iping – rather than immediately foregrounding his bestiality – Wells is able to render his concerns regarding the teaching of scientific method in a fictional form.

Wells's discontent with the current state of science teaching in schools is revealed in his correspondence and educational journalism of the early 1890s. In a letter written to the Editor of the *Educational Times*, dated August 1891, he criticises the Royal College of Preceptors for its encouragement of 'unintelligent list cramming' in a current zoology examination paper.[10] Wells suggests that the College might instead consider the 'type' method of teaching favoured by T. H. Huxley, which encourages a more inquisitive frame of mind: 'a few types are dissected, the dissections drawn, and comparisons drawn and homologies traced between them'.[11] Wells's own indebtedness to the type method of teaching can be traced in his *Textbook of Biology* (1893), which, by focusing on a few specific instances of dissection, emphasises the importance of an understanding of scientific processes rather than the mere presentation of scientific fact.

In 'Science, in School and After School', an article published in *Nature* in September 1894, Wells turns his attention to teaching practice in schools.[12] He identifies two distinct methods of teaching science to school pupils. The first, and most prevalent, is that which merely imparts a series of scientific facts. The second, which 'occurs at present most abundantly in theoretical pedagogics' is the truly educational science teaching which has its basis in practical experimentation as a means to develop scientific reasoning: 'that takes the pupil still undeveloped and trains hand, eye, and mind together, enlarges the scope of the observation, and stimulates the development of the reasoning power'.[13] Wells is without doubt that this is the proper method of science teaching, particularly in the light of the modern consensus of the school as a training place where 'the vessel is moulded rather than filled'.[14] This metaphor relates to his identification of two significant obstructions to 'moulding the vessel' that is the child's mind. The first is the misconception that the school pupil's education should be treated as analogous to that of the adult. This situation, Wells notes, has not been helped by the College of Preceptors, which 'has done nothing to promote practical work in schools'.[15] The second is the tendency of 'many middle class schools' to generate financial remuneration by cramming students' heads with factual knowledge.[16]

In 'Science Teaching – An Ideal and Some Realities', an article appearing in the *Educational Times* in January 1895, Wells makes explicit his own conception of the teaching of scientific method.[17] Ideally, training in scientific method should be at the core of the school curriculum; the interrelatedness of subjects should be stressed in an overall 'Sequence of Studies'.[18] In each specific area of study, 'generalisations' are to be arrived at 'inductively' by means of 'object lessons and physical measurements'.[19] This will enable 'the children to see certain visible facts as connected with certain other visible facts'.[20] Rather than continue to present facts in isolation from one another without regard for the development of an investigative use of the senses, 'an ample background of inductive study' would encourage the pupil's skill of 'exact thinking'.[21] Wells attaches considerable importance to the role of practical work in the school curriculum, since this encourages pupils 'to imagine and describe the laws they had already become familiar with under new conditions'.[22]

Wells's advocacy of a predominantly scientific education reveals the unmistakeable influence of Huxley's 'Science and Culture' (1880).[23] In that essay, which forms part of a broader debate between advocates of scientific education and those seeking to preserve the influence of the classics, Huxley dismisses the notion that 'the study of physical science is incompetent to confer culture; that it touches none of the higher problems of life'.[24] Indeed, Huxley is adamant that 'for the purpose of attaining real culture, an exclusively scientific education is as least as effectual as an exclusively literary one'.[25] The diffusion of a 'thoroughly scientific education', moreover, is imperative to the prosperity of a nation, since it is 'an absolutely essential condition of industrial progress'.[26]

His proposal in 'Science Teaching' that chemistry and physics should be placed at the centre of the school curriculum indicates that Wells concurs with Huxley's insistence on the importance of scientific education. Indeed, Wells develops Huxley's position, arguing that 'science study affords a discipline in the use of language such as direct language-teaching fails to give'.[27] During object lessons, children should be encouraged to 'express [their] thought[s]' about what they have observed.[28] Improved clarity of expression among pupils would thus be a useful by-product of teaching scientific method. 'Almost unconsciously he will acquire the power of writing and expressing his thought clearly', writes Wells.[29] For Wells, then, the study of science can subsume those functions typically associated with the exclusively literary education earlier opposed by Huxley.

Wells's purpose in selecting the secluded village of Iping as the setting for the first half of *The Invisible Man* is to depict a society that has not been trained in scientific modes of reasoning. Prior to the novel's publication, he expressed admiration for the detective stories of Arthur Conan Doyle, writing that 'the public delights in the ingenious unravelling of evidence'.[30] The influence of the detective genre is apparent as the characters make a series of increasingly sophisticated guesses as to the identity concealed by the stranger's bandaged condition. The multifocal narrative viewpoint thus generated anticipates the wider societal perspective of *The War of the Worlds*.

First Mrs Hall, taking her guest at his word that he is an experimental investigator, supposes that ' "The poor soul's had an accident or an operation or something" '.[31] Next, Teddy Henfrey, ' "taken aback" ' by the stranger's grotesque appearance, supposes him to be a criminal: ' "If the police was wanting you you couldn't be more wropped and bandaged" ' (15). Mr Gould, the probationary assistant at the National School, theorises 'that the stranger was an Anarchist in disguise, preparing explosives, and he resolved to undertake such detective operations as his time permitted' (27). Mr Fearenside, certain he has discovered that the stranger's legs are ' "black" ' in contrast to his ' "pink" ' nose, decides he is a piebald: ' "He's a kind of half-breed, and the colour's come off patchy instead of mixing" ' (24).

Such a myriad of speculations concerning the identity of this newcomer to Iping relates to the preoccupation of *The Invisible Man* with what Anne B. Simpson has called 'the ways in which Otherness affects the condition of the world, and the modes in which Otherness is discovered in the world'.[32] While unsuccessful in revealing the stranger's identity, the more sophisticated guesses contain an element of truth concerning the 'discovery' of his Otherness. Thus the piebald explanation is not far from the truth of an albino who had sought invisibility to escape a life of marginality, while Gould's explosives theory ironic-ally anticipates Griffin's fate as a murderous anarchic menace.

The more elaborate speculations concerning the strange man's iden-tity seem contrived to reveal the limits of a purely imaginative approach to scientific enquiry. The anarchist theory, for example, is 'Elaborated [solely] in the *imagination* of Mr. Gould [emphasis added]' (27) and thus, crucially, does not emerge from the observational data that is available to the villagers (Gould's attempts to gather information amount to lit-tle more than 'asking people who had never seen the stranger, leading questions about him' (27)). Such wildly imaginative conjecture, in cir-cumstances where sensory data could have been obtained, affirms the significance of nurturing an understanding of scientific method in the educational process.

The invisibility of the scientist is essential to Wells's purpose in the first half of the novel. Thus through their incapacity to connect certain invisible facts together in the fertile exchange of gossip concerning the stranger Wells demonstrates the absence of inductive reasoning amongst the villagers. *The Invisible Man* is a novel in which the senses – especially vision – feature prominently. As if to point to the necessity of the devel-opment of the senses in the context of practical experimentation as a means to enlarge scientific understanding, all of the potential clues as to the strange man's condition as it is later revealed are of a sensory nature. Thus the evidence available to Mrs Hall is visual. Catching her guest unawares in the parlour, 'it seemed to her that the man she looked at had an enormous mouth wide open, – a vast and incredible mouth that swallowed the whole of the lower portion of his face' (12). Later, 'she saw he had removed his glasses; they were beside him on the table, and it seemed to her that his eye sockets were extraordinarily hollow' (22). Though disturbed enough by the grotesque appearance of her vis-itor to dream 'of huge white heads like turnips, that came trailing after her at the end of interminable necks' (17), her lack of scientific educa-tion prevents her from utilising the clues before her. The next sensory evidence is presented to the villagers when 'Mr Cuss Interviews The Stranger'. Recounting his experience to Bunting, the local vicar, Cuss tells of how from an apparently empty sleeve: ' "Something – exactly like a finger and a thumb it felt – nipped my nose" ' (32). In his article, Sirabian argues that villagers 'decide to try an "inductive approach" by attempting to gather information in order to determine the stran-ger's identity and situation'.[33] However, it is clear that the villagers do not reason inductively. Mrs Hall does not share her impressions of her visitor with anybody. Similarly, Cuss – for all his scientific training as a general practitioner – only shares his experience with Bunting and makes no apparent attempt to link this to the other facts regarding Griffin. Despite the intense conjecture concerning their visitor, none of the villagers, in fact, makes a genuine attempt to gather all the available information. Wells's appropriation of the detective genre, then, merely underlines the unscientific manner in which the villagers approach the question of the stranger's identity – thereby emphasising the urgent need to facilitate the instruction of scientific method.

The inability of the villagers to articulate what they observe reiterates Wells's insistence in 'Science Teaching' that increased powers of expression would be an advantageous by-product of scientific study. This is particularly apparent as – following the attack on the stranger by Fearenside's dog – the sympathetic Mr Hall attempts to offer some comfort to his wife's guest. Hall encounters 'A waving of indecipherable shapes', but is unable to describe what he has seen since 'his vocabulary was altogether too limited to express his impressions' (20). This leaves him 'wondering what it might be that he had seen' (20).

Setting out as it does Griffin's invisibility as a puzzle before the villagers, *The Invisible Man* works to suggest that scientific training is applicable to wider social problems. The implication of the novel in this respect aligns Wells with other writers who argued for a broader dissemination of instruction in scientific method. One such writer was Karl Pearson. In his book, *The Grammar of Science* (1892), Pearson argues that the acquisition of the 'scientific frame of mind' is essential to good citizenship.[34] For Pearson, 'The classification of facts [and their relative significance] and the formation of absolute judgements upon the basis of this classification – judgements independent of the idiosyncrasies of the individual mind – is peculiarly *the scope and method of modern science* [emphasis in original].'[35] The capacity to form judgements that hold true for each individual mind, and are thus free of personal feeling, 'is characteristic of what we shall term the scientific frame of mind'.[36] Pearson is careful to stress that 'the scientific method of examining facts' is 'applicable to social as well as to physical problems'.[37] He further emphasises that the scientific frame of mind should not be regarded as 'a peculiarity of the professional scientist'.[38] Indeed, Pearson is adamant that the means of acquiring the scientific frame of mind should be placed within the reach of all, since it would enable citizens to make unbiased judgements about political issues such as Home Rule.

Confronted with the question of the strange man's identity, the inhabitants of Iping make no attempt to form an unbiased judgement based on the classification of facts (indeed, as I have already noted, they make no attempt to gather all the available facts). Rather, they splinter into various schools of thought – with 'waverers and compromisers' (28) between the main groups – according to personal bias. The tendency of the villagers to impose the idiosyncrasies of the individual mind is particularly evident in those who 'either accepted the piebald view or *some modification of it*; as, for instance, Silas Durgan, who was heard to assert that "if he cho[o]ses to show enself at fairs he'd make his fortune in no time [emphasis added]" ' (27–8).

It might be possible to conclude that Wells's sole purpose in the first section of the novel is to reaffirm the need to implement his educational ideals – and, by extension, to promote the type of diffusion of a scientific frame of mind advocated by Pearson. This, however, would be to neglect the way in which *The Invisible Man* participates in the ongoing nineteenth-century dispute over scientific method itself. At the beginning of the century, induction was firmly established – and, in some cases, revered – as the principal method of scientific investigation. In the latter decades of the nineteenth century, however, the status of induction was increasingly questioned by those arguing for the importance of the imagination to scientific enquiry.[39]

Even had the villagers been trained in scientific method, it would not be reasonable to expect them to solve the enigma of the stranger's circumstances. This is because an invisible man is outside of experience and (by definition) observation – hence exposing the limits of induction. The complexity of the narrative is such that even some of the instances in which the villagers are presented with sensory clues as to Griffin's distinctiveness contrive to indicate how induction is 'hampered when data cannot be obtained or is inconclusive'.[40] Hence, although training in inductive reasoning might have made her more likely to connect certain facts together, Mrs Hall is confronted with her visitor's apparently odd characteristics in dim light which renders conclusive observation impossible.[41] Similarly, while instruction in scientific method could have equipped Mr Hall to describe better what he does witness, 'he had *no time* to observe [emphasis added]' (20) the unusual graphic array in the stranger's room. As well as warning of the hazards of a purely imaginative approach to science, then, the first part of the novel simultaneously 'reveals the limits of a scientific methodology based solely on inductive reasoning'.[42] Sirabian establishes the novel's recognition of the necessity of the imagination in scientific investigation. He does not, however, identify the importance of the scientific imagination as a means which might have helped the villagers solve the mystery surrounding their visitor.

The reference to encouraging the development of the imagination in 'Science Teaching – An Ideal and Some Realities' is indicative of this important context in which to understand *The Invisible Man*. John Tyndall's 'Scientific Use of the Imagination' (1870) forms part of the whole debate that undermines many naive critical assumptions regarding nineteenth-century positivism.[43] Tyndall sets out his purpose in the following terms: 'I wished, if possible, to take you beyond the boundary of mere observation, into a region where things are intellectually discerned'.[44] Tyndall's argument is that science has to proceed by hypothesis, imagining what cannot be seen and making a new world of enquiry available to our coarser senses: 'we can lighten the darkness which surrounds the world of the senses'.[45] Tyndall is not denying that the senses have a role to play in scientific enquiry. Rather, he is suggesting that this role should be supplemented by the scientific use of the imagination: 'We can also magnify, diminish, qualify and combine experiences, so as to render them fit for purposes entirely new.'[46] Tyndall uses the example of sound to demonstrate how the imagination is exercised in understanding even those phenomena 'a very little way from downright sensible experience'. 'The bodily eye, for example, cannot see the condensations and rarefactions of the waves of sound', he says.[47] A degree of scientific imagination, moreover, is necessitated by the increasingly invisible nature of the units of scientific inquiry. Concerning Darwin's theory of pangenesis, Tyndall writes that: 'According to this theory, a germ already microscopic is a world of minor germs. Not only is the organism as a whole wrapped up in the germ, but every organ of the organism has there its special seed.'[48] Tyndall distinguishes between 'two men, one educated in the school of the senses, having mainly occupied himself with observation; the other educated in the school of imagination as well, and exercised in the conceptions of atoms and molecules to which we have so frequently referred'.[49] To the man trained solely in observation, a minute particle will seem small. To the man trained and equipped with both powers of observation and scientific imagination, conversely, it will appear large.

In the context of Tyndall's discussion, it is highly appropriate that Wells should utilise Griffin's status as a 'hollow man' to emphasise the increasingly invisible nature of scientific research. Indeed, the unpreparedness of the village community for the invisible identity of the stranger supports Tyndall's point that the general public, as well as the more conservative members of the scientific community, must inevitably come to terms with the significance of the scientific imagination:

> 'You don't understand,' he said, 'who I am or what I am. I'll show you. By Heaven! I'll show you.' Then he put his open palm over his face and withdrew it. The centre of his face became a black cavity. 'Here,' he said. He stepped forward and handed Mrs. Hall something which she, staring at his metamorphosed face, accepted automatically. Then, when she saw what it was, she screamed loudly, dropped it, and staggered back. The nose – it was the stranger's nose! pink and shining – rolled on the floor.
>
> Then he removed his spectacles, and every one in the bar gasped. He took off his hat, and with a violent gesture tore at his whiskers and bandages. For a moment they resisted him. A flash of horrible anticipation passed through the bar. 'Oh, my Gard!' said some one. Then off they came.
>
> It was worse than anything. Mrs. Hall, standing open-mouthed and horror-struck, shrieked at what she saw, and made for the door of the house. Every one began to move. They were prepared for scars, disfigurements, tangible horrors, but *nothing*! The bandages and false hair flew across the passage into the bar, making a hobbledehoy jump to avoid them. Every one tumbled on every one else down the steps. For the man who stood there shouting some incoherent explanation, was a solid gesticulating figure up to the coat-collar of him, and then – nothingness, no visible thing at all! (47–8)

The villagers' shock at the walking nothingness by which they are confronted is understandable since it does not conform to the possibilities generated by their narrow range of experience (thus Mrs Hall supposes that her visitor has suffered an accident because her nephew had one).[50] The implication of the first part of the novel, however, is that the scientific use of the imagination could have lightened the darkness around the world of the villagers' experiences (to adopt Tyndall's phrase). In order to solve the enigma of the strange man's situation, the inhabitants of Iping would need to combine the type of observational skills advocated in Wells's educational journalism with the scientific use of the imagination. Linked together by the scientific imagination, the sensory clues which provide the basis for the wrongheaded guesses concerning his identity – the bandage, the pink nose, the apparently black legs – could have successfully anticipated the disguise later discarded by the stranger. Having revealed the limitations of an approach to science based exclusively on either imagination or observation, then, the Iping section of *The Invisible Man* points to the necessity of an integrated conception of science – thereby making a distinctive literary contribution to the contemporary debate over scientific method.[51]

Revealed as a disturbing non-entity, the gifted scientist is destined to remain invisible because society does not understand even the most elementary modes of scientific thinking that would allow him to assume a social identity. In a community where most people think unscientifically, the inhabitants would have only been able to attribute a social role to the stranger had his identity conformed to their own narrow preconceptions – 'They were prepared for scars, disfigurements, tangible horrors'. This would still have resulted only in his remaining grotesquely visible, and consequently one of the most gifted of Wells's early scientists is – in the context of the village of Iping at least – forced into isolation in order to retain his status as a researcher.[52]

In order to protect this status, and conceal the identity for which the community is unprepared, Griffin must go abroad by twilight, 'muffled up enormously', walk 'the loneliest paths' (26) and even ensure he is free from prying eyes before he can enjoy a meal: 'He took a mouthful, glanced suspiciously at the window, took another mouthful, then rose and, taking the serviette in his hand, walked across the room and pulled the blind down to the top of the white muslin that obscured the lower panes' (7). Bergonzi notes the similarities between Griffin's circumstances and those of Nebogipfel, the protagonist of 'The Chronic Argonauts'.[53] Although 'The Chronic Argonauts' is generally acknowledged as the precursor of *The Time Machine*, 'Wells seems to have been consciously using this material [in writing *The Invisible Man*] and there are one or two verbal parallels'.[54] One aspect that Wells certainly developed from the earlier story is the scientist's use of a barrier to isolate himself from the community: '[he was] engaged in the curious operation of nailing sheet-tin across the void window sockets of his new domicile – "blinding his house", as Mrs Morgan ap Lloyd Jones not inaptly termed it'.[55] Unlike Nebogipfel's use of an identical means of creating a barrier between scientist and society in 'The Chronic Argonauts', Griffin's concealment behind the blinds is not a matter of choice but of necessity.

It is important to emphasise that, for all their lack of scientific knowledge, Wells does not blame the villagers for Griffin's isolation – he is simply pointing to the need to disseminate a broader public understanding of scientific modes of thinking as a partial means of reconciling scientist and society. Nor does Wells endorse Griffin's behaviour towards them. On the contrary, his position is also that scientists should endeavour to communicate the nature of their research to the rest of society. The characterisation of *The Invisible Man*'s scientist protagonist relates to the concerns expressed by Wells in 'Popularising Science', a short article which appeared in *Nature* in July 1894. In that article, Wells warns the scientific community that 'in an age when the endowment of research is rapidly passing out of the hands of private or quasi-private organisations into those of the State, the maintenance of an exterior intelligent interest in current investigation becomes of almost vital importance to continual progress'.[56] Wells notes that the scientist was once able to disregard the scorn of such an influential man as Swift and still progress with research funded through private means. Intelligent exchange with the outside world is, however, imperative for the modern scientist since, 'now that our growing edifice of knowledge spreads more and more over a substructure of grants and votes, and the appliances needed for instruction and further research increase steadily in cost, even the affectation of a contempt for popular opinion becomes unwise'.[57] Contempt for public opinion is unwise not only because it invites 'the danger of supplies being cut off', but also 'of their being misapplied by a public whose scientific education is neglected'.[58]

Wells identifies scientific writing as a means of facilitating productive exchange between the scientist and the exterior world, as 'even the youngest and most promising of specialists [should be reconciled] to the serious consideration of popular science'.[59] Lamenting the decline of scientific writing addressed to 'the general reader' since Darwin's generation, Wells, 'as a mere general reader', says 'a little concerning the defects of very much of what is proffered to the public as scientific literature'.[60] The most common error he detects on the part of scientific writers is their failure to write in the language of the reader. Some he finds 'write boldly in the dialect of their science, and there is certainly a considerable pleasure in a skilful and compact handling of technicalities; but such writers do not appreciate the fact that this is an acquired taste, and that the public has not acquired it'.[61] Others avoid technicalities altogether with the result that this writing too 'often rests contented with vague, ambiguous, or misleading phrases'.[62] Worst of all, for Wells, emerges when the scientific writer attempts to communicate his point by using jokes. 'Now this kind of thing is not popularising science at all', he writes, 'it is merely making fun of it'.[63] Scientific writers should ideally endeavour to satisfy the public thirst 'for problems to exercise their minds upon [...] [since] there is a keen pleasure in seeing a previously unexpected generalisation skilfully developed'.[64]

Griffin's characterisation can be read as a warning to scientists of the dangers that accompany the refusal to popularise their subject matter. Griffin's actions work against Wells's suggestions in 'Popularising Science', and he thus contributes to his own status as a reviled social outcast. Already on the verge of alienating the entire population of the village of Iping by his grotesque appearance and brash manner, Griffin's position as an outsider is further accentuated by his outright refusal to make the language of his science accessible to them. Thus Hall, already suspicious of his wife's paying guest, 'went aggressively into the parlour and looked very hard at his wife's furniture, just to show that the stranger wasn't master there, and scrutinised closely and *a little contemptuously* a sheet of mathematical computation the stranger had left [emphasis added]' (17). The episode of 'The Thousand and One Bottles', in which his experimental apparatus is delivered to him, illustrates Griffin's unwillingness to record his scientific investigations in a manner that might lead to the popularisation of his ideas: 'in addition there were a box of books, – big, fat books, of which some were just in incomprehensible handwriting' (18). Griffin's unwillingness to use accessible English is emphasised when Cuss and Bunting, two readers who hope to discern clues to the stranger's identity from his diary, discover that it is written in 'cypher': ' "Some of it's mathematical and some of it's Russian or some such language (to judge by the letters), and some of it's Greek" ' (69).[65] In the epilogue of course – which Wells added to the New York edition of the novel and incorporated in subsequent reprints of the text – Mr Marvel scrutinises the dead man's books, but is unable to translate the formula of invisibility into comprehensible language: ' "Hex, little two up in the air, cross and a fiddle-de-dee" ' (205).

Griffin's violent response to those curious to discover the nature of his research blunts the public curiosity regarding science, which Wells had identified in 'Popularising Science' as a potential market for scientific writers. This is apparent in the episode in which Griffin ejects his sympathetic host from his room. That the arrival of the stranger had aroused Hall's interest in science is revealed in his 'tugging with a casual curiosity at the straw' (18) of the boxes containing the newcomer's experimental apparatus. Hence, instead of slamming the door in his face, Griffin might have facilitated Hall's scientific interest by explaining the nature of the 'indecipherable shapes' in language that was accessible to him.

Refusing to enter the system of scientific publication, which he holds in open contempt, Griffin is therefore unable to gain the recognition that would enable him to seek funding from one of the growing number of state funded mechanisms in order to continue his exciting and extra-ordinary research.[66] This refusal on the part of Griffin points to the dangers faced by scientists who alienate themselves from the potential benefits offered by state funding. Lacking the resources to fund the completion of his research, Griffin resorts to the theft of money, which results in his father's suicide. As though to emphasise the hardships faced by researchers who show contempt for their potential benefactors, this substantial sum is not enough to cover the costs of both Griffin's experimental apparatus and a reasonable standard of living, and he is forced to rent a room in a slum in London as a base from which to conduct his research. There Griffin encounters another hazard faced by scientists who hold public opinion in contempt. Having achieved only partial success in making a cat invisible, he must face its owner, the old woman from one of the rooms below, who suspects him of vivisection.[67] Griffin politely denies any knowledge of the cat, though it is audible in the background. Her suspicions heightened, the old lady informs the landlord of the property. Confronted by the landlord, who reminds him of the severe laws punishing vivisection, Griffin's habitual bad temper gives way as he again ejects from his room an individual whose curiosity is aroused by his appliances. In this instance the refusal of the scientist to explain the nature of his research and the purpose of his appliances results in his becoming homeless, since the landlord whom he regards with severe contempt – ' "an old Polish Jew in a long grey coat and greasy slippers" ' (132) – serves him with a notice of eviction.

Returning to his period of residence in Iping, Griffin reveals his tendency to use his invisible persona to 'make fun of science'. A source which certainly informed Wells in this respect is Christopher Marlowe's *Dr Faustus* (1604). Faustus acquires absolute power from the devil and wastes it, in part, by playing silly tricks when invisible. This is particularly evident as he is magically transported to Rome, where Faustus makes himself 'a frolic guest' of the Pope.[68] One of Faustus's tricks is to snatch food and drink from the Pope, thus making it appear as though dishes and cups are moving of their own accord. Another is to amuse himself by inflicting mild physical abuse on others when they arouse his anger: 'How now? Must every bit be spiced with a cross? / Nay then, take that. / Faustus *hits him a box of the ear*' (*Doctor Faustus* III, 2, 86–7).

That Griffin amuses himself by playfully pinching Cuss on the nose with an apparently empty sleeve recalls the moment in which Faustus strikes the Pope.[69] Like Faustus, Griffin uses his invisible persona to amaze others with the seemingly inexplicable movement of physical objects. He pursues the prying Mrs Hall with a chair in the instance of

'The Furniture That Went Mad'. Wells was undoubtedly aware that the comedy of such moments would have appealed strongly to a popular readership. Following the barrage of criticism he received upon the publication of *The Island of Doctor Moreau*, Wells might well have been motivated to use comedy as a means of making his third scientific romance less intense than his evolutionary fables.[70] However, these moments of comedy cannot disguise the more serious implications of Griffin's tendency to 'make fun of science'. Such actions as that towards Mrs Hall bring science into disrepute since it means the local villagers, whose scientific education has been neglected, revert to a supernatural explanation of these unexplained phenomena. Of course, his mocking of Mrs Hall leads to his final alienation and then rejection by the community of Iping. His exclusion is emphasised on the occasion of Whit-Monday: 'And inside, in the artificial darkness of the parlour, into which only one thin jet of sunlight penetrated, the stranger, hungry we must suppose, and fearful, hidden in his uncomfortable hot wrappings, pored through his dark glasses upon his paper or chinked his dirty little bottles' (45).

Following his comical escape from the village authorities, Griffin attempts to force his will on his fellow outcast, Mr Marvel, a superstitious tramp. When this fails, he stumbles accidentally upon the house of his university contemporary Kemp, to whom he recounts the narrative of his adventures. Immediately apparent from his monologue is the moral regression which characterises his preoccupation with achieving corporeal invisibility. While *Frankenstein* almost certainly provided Wells with the literary model for his monomania, the bestiality that Griffin uncovers within himself due to his misapplication of science unmistakeably recalls *Dr Jekyll and Mr Hyde*.

Griffin undercuts the ideology of the scientist as hero advanced by Wells in 'Morals and Civilisation', an article which appeared in the *Fortnightly Review* seven months prior to the publication of *The Invisible Man*:

> And yet one may dream of an informal, unselfish, unauthorised [undemocratic] body of workers, a real and conscious apparatus of education and moral suggestion, held together by a common faith and common sentiment, and shaping the minds and acts and destinies of men.[71]

Uninterested in the unselfish application of his scientific expertise towards the goal of improving humanity, Griffin instead keeps his discovery to himself, ' "because I meant to flash my work upon the world with crushing effect, – to become famous at a blow" ' (123). As he

becomes increasingly immersed in the research he hopes will bring him
fame and fortune, Griffin gradually severs himself from the human species he would ideally help shape the future of in accordance with Wells's
ideal. Instead of being part of an organised body, Griffin has alienated
himself from the scientific community: ' "In all my great moments I
have been alone" ' (124). One of the moments which define his severance from mankind follows Griffin's return to his research after attend-
ing his father's funeral. Attributing his own loss of sympathy to 'the
general inanity of things', Griffin's alienation from the social world now
appears complete: ' "Re-entering my room seemed like the recovery of
reality. There were the things I knew and loved. There stood the apparatus, the experiments arranged and waiting" ' (127).[72] Griffin's desire to
achieve an advantage over his fellow humanity is acutely emphasised
when, having attained his dream of corporeal invisibility, his head is
'teeming with plans of all the wild and wonderful things I had now
impunity to do' (138).[73]

Griffin's moment of initial elation is soon broken as he discovers the
reality of the transformation he has effected:

'But hardly had I emerged upon Great Portland Street, however (my
lodging was close to the big draper's shop there), when I heard a
crashing concussion and was hit violently behind, and turning saw a
man carrying a basket of soda-water syphons, and looking in amaze-
ment at his burden. Although the blow had really hurt me, I found
something so irresistible in his astonishment that I laughed out
aloud. "The devil's in the basket," I said, and suddenly twisted it out
of his hand. He let go incontinently, and I swung the whole weight
into the air'. (139)

While he derives an irresistible Faustian pleasure in astonishing this
man, what Griffin himself later calls the 'absurdity' of an invisible man
is immediately apparent. Examined within an evolutionary frame, his
corporeal invisibility constitutes a downward adaptation. Griffin himself soon realises that being an invisible man increases his susceptibility
to the material elements, and that he must proceed quickly to avoid
either rain or snow from settling and thus exposing him as ' "a greasy
glimmer of humanity" ' (154). However, as the inhabitants of central
London threaten to infer his presence, the most appropriate metaphor
to describe Griffin's situation is that of a hunted animal. In his short
analysis of 'The Origin of the Senses', which appeared in the *Saturday
Review* of May 1896, Wells stresses the line of continuity between man

and animal. 'Men share the higher senses with a larger number of the lower creatures', he writes.[74] Perhaps with this in mind Wells retains a degree of 'visibility' for Griffin in his dealings with dogs: ' "I had never realised it before, but the nose is to the mind of a dog what the eye is to the mind of a seeing man. Dogs perceive the scent of a man moving as men perceive his vision" ' (141). Other incidents recounted by Griffin seem contrived to emphasise how his attainment of invisibility leaves him out of harmony with his environment. Indeed, those factors that make him grotesquely visible compound Griffin's status as the hunted.

Griffin's status as the hunted is again foregrounded in the chapter 'In The Emporium'. In this instance his presence is inferred, not by the nose of a dog or the innocent curiosity of a child, but by the noises of his movements. In 'The Origin of the Senses', Wells writes of the origin of the ear as 'an organ for translating vibrations into touches'.[75] The sound of his sudden movements caused by the arrival of two shop assistants following his overnight stay in the emporium alerts them to his existence. Griffin's comparison of himself to a ' "rabbit hunted out of a wood-pile" ' (152) does much to reinforce the conception of him as an animal unfitted to meet the challenges of its environment.

From its moment of conception, then, corporeal invisibility is fated as a downward evolutionary course, since it makes social interaction impossible. Through his misapplication of the scientific gift, which could be better directed, Griffin learns that although ' "invisibility made it possible to get" ' things, ' "it made it impossible to enjoy them when they are got" ' (165). As Griffin somewhat embarrassedly admits, the unassimilated matter of the digestive process would grotesquely reveal him to others, and thus he cannot even eat in the company of his fellow human beings. Hence, as a now passive observer on visible reality, he must watch others enjoy this pleasure: ' "On the table was his belated breakfast, and it was a confoundedly exasperating thing for me, Kemp, to have to sniff his coffee and stand watching while he came in and resumed his meal" ' (157). Nor can Griffin retain any hope of propagating his species: ' "What is the good of the love of woman when her name must needs be Delilah?" ' (165). Griffin himself confesses his lack of judgment in a statement which seems to confirm his severance from humanity:

'I made a mistake, Kemp, a huge mistake, in carrying this thing through alone. I have wasted strength, time, opportunities. Alone – it is wonderful how little a man can do alone! To rob a little, to hurt a little, and there is the end'. (168–9)

In order to enter into any social interaction whatsoever, Griffin must now seek to conceal his invisibility beneath a disguise, which may make him appear as a caricature of a man, but at least has the benefit of making him 'feel [like] a human being again' (149).

Even as Griffin seems to have completed his severance from the species *homo sapiens*, there remains the potential for some reconciliatory gesture to restore him to humanity and, in one sense of the word, visibility. His scientific colleague Kemp urges him to ' "take the nation at least – into your confidence. Think what you might do with a million helpers" ' (170). In this attempt to reconcile Griffin's discovery of invisibility with the social community – ' "Publish your results" ' (170), he implores – Kemp comes much closer to adhering to Wells's ideal of the scientist as hero, and is the perfect antithesis to Griffin's egotistical ambitions. The chapter 'The Man Who Was Running' serves to illustrate the contrasting fortunes of these two former university peers. Instead of repressing his scientific enquiries, Kemp contemplates the prospect of becoming a fellow of the Royal Society in a room which signifies an open relationship with the rest of society: 'It was a pleasant little room, with three windows, north, west, and south, and bookshelves crowded with books and scientific publications, and a broad writing-table, and, under the north window, a microscope, glass slips, minute instruments, some cultures, and scattered bottles of reagents' (92).

The Invisible Man, however, resists the absolute distinction between good and evil that is a feature of the traditional romance genre, so that 'the Other is presented as at once isolate and rabble; the terms of the discourse shift so that the "us" of some sections [...] are the "them" of others, as foregrounded by the narrator's changes in distance from the characters and events he narrates'.[76] In a monologue reminiscent of *Frankenstein*, the reader is presented with Kemp's shortcomings as well. While Griffin's story evokes sympathy from the reader, Kemp is more preoccupied with awaiting the arrival of the authorities to whom he has already reported the presence of his visitor. Concerning Kemp's hypocrisy, Singh writes that: 'Dr. Kemp's betrayal, even if understandable in the light of social obligation, invites our censure on grounds of guilt. At the end of the novel we read of Dr. Kemp's trying to get the secret of invisibility himself!'[77]

It is important to emphasise that Griffin does not entirely misplace his trust in Kemp. After all, the intellectual affinity between the two men is recalled when Kemp, like Griffin, uses the stars as a source of scientific inspiration: 'his mind had travelled into a remote speculation of social conditions of the future, and lost itself at last over the time dimension' (101). Perhaps the opposition between the two men can be attributed to their distinct conceptions of science. For Sirabian, Griffin – like Victor Frankenstein before him – conceives the imagination as an integral part of his scientific method. Kemp, conversely, retains a strictly conventional (i.e., empirical) conception of scientific method. This is why he 'can only see the unconventionality of his [Griffin's] science'.[78] Griffin's explanation of the method he uses to discover the secret of invisibility 'demonstrates the power and delight of his imaginative vision', thus revealing that: 'Science's contribution to progress lies in its ability to make new discoveries and to envision new possibilities that can become workable methods and solutions, a view held by those who argued for the necessity of hypothesizing as part of scientific method in the nineteenth century.'[79] Although he does not draw the connection, Sirabrian's comment indicates how the scientific method employed by Griffin reveals an additional parallel between *The Invisible Man* and Tyndall's 'Scientific Use of the Imagination'. In his explanation to Kemp of those 'Certain First Principles' he used to guide his research, Griffin concurs with Tyndall's emphasis on the importance of formulating hypotheses as an aid to scientific investigation: ' "But this was not a method, it was an idea that might lead to a method by which it [invisibility] would be possible" ' (120).[80] Griffin states emphatically that: ' "Fools, common men, even common mathematicians, do not know anything of what some general expression may mean to the student of molecular physics" ' (120). His reference to 'molecular physics' suggests that – like Tyndall's ideal man of science – Griffin is able to supplement sensory investigation with the scientific use of the imagination. Like the type of investigator endorsed by Tyndall, Griffin undoubtedly possesses the necessary scientific imagination to regard even the minutest of particles as significant. Indeed, even Kemp realises that many objects of scientific enquiry lie outside the normal range of the senses:

'Is there such a thing as an invisible animal? In the sea, yes. Thousands! millions! All the larvae, all the little nauplii and tornarias, all the microscopic things, the jelly-fish. In the sea there are more things invisible than visible! I never thought of that before. And in the ponds too! All those little pond-life things, – specks of colourless translucent jelly!' (113–4)

This passage is significant because it reveals that Griffin's attainment of invisibility forces Kemp to reassess his own prejudices regarding the practice of science. His consideration of 'all the microscopic things' forces him to acknowledge the limitations of his own empirically based science ('I never thought of that before').[81] Kemp's statement unwittingly reveals the importance of imagination in scientific investigation, since only hypothesis can reveal the working of those 'invisible animal[s]' in the sea.

Aside from their opposing conceptions of science, Kemp's apparent belief in a universal morality leads him to reveal Griffin's whereabouts in a letter to Colonel Adye. Despite his obvious hypocrisy, Kemp echoes Wells's insistence in 'Morals and Civilisation' that it is necessary to construct 'a rational code of morality to meet the complex requirements of modern life'.[82] For his part Griffin is scornful of universal morality and modern critics have identified a possible Nietzschean influence in his contempt for the ' "common conventions of humanity" ' (160).[83]

During his flight from Kemp's house, there is an explicitly Stevensonian moment which illustrates Griffin's kinship with the alter ego of the protagonist in *Dr Jekyll and Mr Hyde*. This occurs as the narrator reports that, 'A little child playing near Kemp's gateway was violently caught up and thrown aside, so that its ankle was broken' (176). This brief episode recalls the opening scene of Stevenson's novel, in which a child is needlessly trodden by a malevolent man: ' "Well, sir, the two ran into one other naturally enough at the corner; and then came the horrible part of the thing; for the man trampled calmly over the child's body and left her screaming on the ground." '[84] The chapter 'The Wicksteed Murder' more tellingly reveals Wells's indebtedness to Stevenson for the model of Griffin's wanton bestiality. In Stevenson's novel, the chapter 'The Carew Murder Case' begins with an account of a maid servant who witnesses Hyde's brutal killing 'of an aged and beautiful gentleman with white hair', whose face seemed to her to 'breathe such an innocent and old-world kindness of disposition'.[85] She beholds Hyde, who 'had in his hand a heavy cane, with which he was trifling' suddenly break 'out in a great flame of anger' and beat the gentleman with it 'like a madman'.[86] In *The Invisible Man*, Wells changes the peripheral details but retains the essence of an unjustifiably wanton act. Thus Mr Wickstead, a middle aged man 'of inoffensive habits and appearance, [was] the very last person in the world to provoke such a terrible antagonist' (179). An iron rod, rather than a cane, is the invisible man's weapon, and the deceased was in this instance last seen alive by a little girl. Like Hyde's killing of the old gentleman, Griffin's murder of Wickstead is an unprovoked act of rage.

Following his betrayal by Kemp, Griffin is forced into an openly anarchic relationship with society. This section of the novel draws on the stereotypical conceptions of the anarchist that would have been fixed in the mind of the British reading public by such novels as Stevenson's *The Dynamiters* (1885) and may have influenced Conrad's characterisation of Karl Yundt in *The Secret Agent* (1906), which was dedicated to H. G. Wells.[87] Griffin's stated intention to unleash a 'Reign of Terror' indicates the parallels between *The Invisible Man* and 'The Country of the Blind', a short story Wells published in 1904. Griffin announces that 'the Epoch of the Invisible Man' will begin with ' "one execution for the sake of example, – [of] a man named Kemp" ' (182). Griffin's plan to control the population through fear resembles Nunez's endeavours to bring the inhabitants of the blind valley to their senses by affirming his superiority by violent means: 'He thought of seizing a spade and suddenly smiting one or two of them to earth, and so in fair combat showing the advantage of eyes.'[88] In each of these stories, the protagonists soon find themselves overwhelmed by the social unit they had hoped to coerce.

Despite Griffin's proclamation, the remainder of the novel is preoccupied with the combined efforts of the social community to track down this 'tangible antagonist' (177). That the theme of collectivity is reasserted so strongly towards the end of the text recalls one of the earliest pieces of scientific journalism that Wells ever produced. Wells wrote 'Ancient Experiments in Co-Operation' as a reaction to the use of evolutionary theory, by Herbert Spencer and others, as a justification for economic individualism. Revealing the influence of Huxley's 'ethical' evolution, Wells begins by stressing that 'an even cursory examination of the biologist's province will show that this element of individual competition is over-accentuated in current thought'.[89] He is at pains to point out not only that various cases of mutual aid exist among social animals, particularly in the community of the termite, for the greater benefit of the species, but also that the very existence of the species *homo sapiens* is a testimony to the prevalence of union. 'The first attempts at mitigating competition by union are of hugely remoter date than the first of human cities', he writes, 'and their success or failure is written, not on the dead and decaying papyrus and stone, but vividly and with an animation, variety, and colour that a Carlyle or Froude must envy, in the whole volume of living things.'[90]

In severing himself from his own species, Griffin must face the might of its co-operated efforts to hunt him, for as Kemp rightly states: ' "He has *cut himself* off from his kind. His blood be upon his own head [emphasis added]" ' (175). Hence, the young scientist who might have helped facilitate the union of mankind is now a monstrous Other to be hunted by any necessary means, including dogs, powdered glass and the extraordinary opponent that is a species uniting in co-operation:

> Every passenger train along the lines on a great parallelogram between Southampton, Manchester, Brighton, and Horsham, travelled with locked doors, and the goods traffic was almost entirely suspended. And in a great circle of twenty miles around Port Burdock, men armed with guns and bludgeons were presently setting out in groups of three and four, with dogs, to beat the roads and fields. (177)

The victory scored by the species over this potential threat to its harmony is, however, an ironic one. For there is an atavistic quality in the crowd which beats him to death that is a least equal to the more wanton of Griffin's actions. The manner in which Griffin is killed can be related to the work of the French social psychologist Gustave Le Bon, whose book *The Crowd: A Study of the Popular Mind* was published in 1896.[91] Le Bon theorised that once part of a psychological crowd, 'the intellectual aptitudes of the individuals, and in consequence their individuality, are weakened'.[92] Once part of a crowd, individuals acquire, according to Le Bon, a sentiment of invincibility and are subject to contagion, in much the same manner as individuals under hypnosis are suggestible. Individuals in crowds descend 'several rungs in the ladder of civilisation' and possess 'the spontaneity, the violence, the ferocity, and also the enthusiasm and heroism of primitive beings'.[93] The crowd that kills Griffin possesses the exact characteristics identified by Le Bon:

> In another second there was a simultaneous rush upon the struggle, and a stranger coming into the road suddenly might have thought an exceptionally savage game of Rugby football was in progress. And there was no shouting after Kemp's cry, – only a sound of blows and a heavy breathing. [...] Down went the heap of struggling men again and rolled over. There was, I am afraid, some savage kicking. Then suddenly a wild scream of 'Mercy! Mercy!' that died down swiftly to a sound like choking. (199–200)

The savagery with which Griffin is pounded to death by the mob concurs with Le Bon's contention that crowds revert to a primitive phase of evolution. The moralising intrusion of the narrator in this instance ('There was, I am afraid, some savage kicking') further underlines the uncivilised actions of the crowd. Evidence of the hypnotic suggestibility of individuals in crowds is apparent in the simultaneous rush upon the struggle involving Griffin. The cries of mercy that dispel this hypnotic influence correspond to the moment at which the civilised identities previously weakened by the crowd reassert themselves.

Griffin's restoration to a visible state after his brutal murder by the mob suggests that the only time the gifted scientist can become visible in the novel is through death. This conclusion to Griffin's endeavours perfectly concurs with Wells's purpose in *The Invisible Man* to reveal the necessity for an urgent reassessment of the relationship between scientist and society. Wells therefore utilises the remote setting provided by the remote Sussex village of Iping to dramatise the need for a broader dissemination of scientific method. The inability of the local inhabitants to reason inductively constitutes an elaboration of the critique of contemporary scientific education – particularly in schools – that Wells had initiated in his early scientific journalism. At the same time, however, the Iping section indicates the limits of induction. The implication that the inhabitants might have supplemented the sensory data they gather with the use of the scientific imagination, in particular, reveals that *The Invisible Man* supports Tyndall's point that scientific method must increasingly involve the formulation of hypotheses. Yet some of the more elaborate theories as to Griffin's identity mean that the first half of the novel also exposes the dangers of a purely imaginative approach to scientific enquiry. Since solving the mystery of Griffin's identity would require the villagers to combine the type of sensory skills advocated in Wells's educational journalism with the scientific imagination, the first half of *The Invisible Man* points to the need for an integrated conception of science. As well as emphasising the need to disseminate a broader understanding of scientific reasoning, in this initial segment of the text Wells concurrently critiques Griffin's attitude and his behaviour towards the local community. The didactic purpose of Griffin's bizarre behaviour should be understood in the context of Wells's insistence that scientists must endeavour to facilitate effective communication with the rest of society, or else risk alienating the ever proliferating public sources of funding for scientific research.

As Griffin recounts his narrative to Kemp, the importance of *The Invisible Man* as a contribution to the debate over the role of imagination in science resurfaces. The whole opposition between Griffin and Kemp can be attributed, in part, to the opposing conceptions of scientific method they uphold. Whereas Kemp relies heavily upon empirical research, Griffin is able to draw upon both sensory data and imaginative method. However, Kemp is forced – albeit temporarily – to acknowledge the importance of imagination to scientific practice. This occurs as he considers the invisible creatures in the sea. Following Griffin's failure to gain any recognition for his endeavours he is forced into a battle against his species. The might of the united humanity that defeats Griffin recalls the emphasis Wells places on co-operation in his scientific writings. However, the victory of the united species over this lone transgressor remains an ironic one, since Wells concurrently reveals the atavistic quality in the crowd that beats Griffin to death. Overall, *The Invisible Man* constitutes an investigation of the issues to be resolved between scientist and society before science itself can take on the pivotal role Wells would ideally ascribe to it.

5
The Descent of Mars: Evolution and Ethics in *The War of the Worlds*

> Man, we are assured, is descended from ape-like ancestors, moulded by circumstances into men, and these apes again were derived from ancestral forms of a lower order, and so up from the primordial protoplasmic jelly. Clearly then, man, unless the order of the universe has come to an end, will undergo further modification in the future, and at last cease to be man, giving rise to some other type of animated being. At once the fascinating question arises, What will this being be? Let us consider for a little the plastic influences at work upon our species.
>
> H. G. Wells, 'The Man of the Year Million' (1893)[1]

The publication of *The War of the Worlds* elaborates the range of the scientific involvement of Wells's fiction. The novel substantiates the curiosity with astronomical speculation that is, to varying degrees, implicit in his first three scientific romances.[2] The novel's engagement with discourses of evolutionary theory marks a further development in Wells's fiction. Whereas the early fables (broadly speaking) accentuate the degenerative potential of 'the plastic influences at work upon our species', *The War of the Worlds* explores the ethical implications of humanity's capacity for evolutionary progression. Through the apocalyptic plot device of the Martian invasion, the novel raises concerns about the ethics of evolution, or perhaps, the evolution of ethics. It should be noted here that, in *The War of the Worlds*, the Darwinian precepts introduced in the evolutionary fables – such as the critique of anthropocentrism and the establishment of a line of continuity between humans and animals – are, to large extent, inextricable from the novel's preoccupation with evolution and ethics.

At the outset of the novel, the narrator is comfortably 'busy upon a series of papers discussing the probable developments of moral ideas as civilisation progressed'.[3] He also concludes that, 'The intellectual side of man already admits that life is an incessant struggle for existence' (215). This early reference to the 'struggle for existence' invokes the language of the dispute between T. H. Huxley and Herbert Spencer over the ethical questions associated with the process of determining the 'further modification in the future' of the species *homo sapiens. The War of the Worlds* should therefore be read in the context of the opposition between Huxley's 'ethical' evolution and the economic individualism of Spencer. The complex characterisation of the Martians, moreover, invites questions regarding human ethical conduct.

The preoccupation of *The War of the Worlds* with ethics encapsulates the novel's castigation of the expansionist tendencies of the New Imperialism. The narrator explains the decision of the Martians to colonise the earth by reminding the reader of the 'ruthless and utter destruction [of] our own species' (215), citing in particular the atrocities of the European immigrants who swept the Tasmanians 'out of existence in a war of extermination' (216). Critics have commented on how the novel dramatises the 'fear of invasion that was an intermittent preoccupation of English society in the final decades' of the nineteenth century.[4] The novel has been classified alongside such invasion fictions as George Chesney's *The Battle of Dorking* (1871) and William Le Queux's *The Great War in England in 1897* (1893).[5] These comparisons hint at how *The War of the Worlds* participates in debates over British military efficiency conducted in the periodical press at the time of the novel's serialisation in *Pearson's Magazine* between April and December 1897.

Following the publication of *The War of the Worlds* in book form in January 1898, an anonymous reviewer in the *Saturday Review* commented that, 'No astronomer, no physicist, can take it upon himself to declare that it is absolutely certain that this planet will never be invaded from a foreign world.'[6] The novel's central idea of an invasion of the earth by highly evolved beings from Mars is a brilliant extrapolation from contemporary speculation concerning life on other worlds. Mars, and the possibility of its being inhabited, was a subject of particularly intense interest in the late-Victorian era.[7] Works such as Percival Lowell's *Mars* (1895) applied Darwinian principles to celestial bodies. Wells later acknowledged the indebtedness of his work to Lowell in an article on 'The Things that Live on Mars' published in 1908.[8]

Lowell emphasises that our neighbouring planet is already bearing the stresses associated with its comparatively advanced stage of evolution: 'He [Mars] is older in age, if not in years; for whether his birth as a separate world antedated ours or not, his smaller size, by causing him to cool more quickly, would necessarily age him faster.'[9] Like Lowell, the narrator of *The War of the Worlds* observes a close correlation between the size of Mars and its phase of evolution: 'Nor was it generally understood that since Mars is older than our earth, with scarcely a quarter of the superficial area and remoter from the sun, it necessarily follows that it is not only more distant from life's beginning but nearer its end' (214). Lowell stresses the correlation between planetary and organic evolution in his discussion of the red planet. 'Mars being thus old himself, we know that evolution on his surface must be similarly advanced', he says.[10] Crucial to the construction of a scientific justification for the Martian invasion of the earth is that Wells, following Lowell, extends the conception of the advanced evolution of Mars to cover organic existence: 'long before this earth ceased to be molten, life upon its surface must have begun its course' (214). In his consideration of the highly advanced creatures that might inhabit Mars, Lowell speculates that 'Quite possibly, such Martian folk are possessed of inventions of which we have not dreamed'.[11] This passage is recalled explicitly as Wells portrays his Martians capably 'looking across space with instruments and intelligences such as we have scarcely dreamed of' towards 'a morning star of hope, [which is] our own warmer planet' (215).

One source that has been overlooked by critics but which undoubtedly influenced Wells in his creation of a means for the Martians to reach that 'morning star of hope' is Robert S. Ball's 'Mars', an article that appeared in the *Fortnightly Review* in September 1892.[12] Wells's awareness of Ball's work is revealed in two sources prior to the publication of *The War of the Worlds*. The first is the article 'Another Basis For Life', in which Wells criticises Ball for limiting the possibilities of extraterrestrial existence to those elements associated with life on earth before considering the prospect of silicon-aluminium based life forms as an 'at least fascinatingly plausible [one]'.[13] The second is a letter to the *Academy* in which Wells responds to the Editor's proposal for the formation of an English Academy. Wells laments that the Editor's list of possible candidates for inclusion contains no such ' "scientific" ' literary men as 'Norman Lockyer, [Robert] Ball, and Ray Lankester'.[14]

In endowing the Martians with a level of technological advancement which enables them to realise their ambition of travelling to earth, Wells's indebtedness to Ball is strikingly apparent. Ball speculates that both oxygen and water are likely to be found on Mars since the molecules of these elements could not achieve the velocity required to escape the Martian atmosphere. In order to demonstrate this point, Ball cites the example of the relative velocity at which an artillery shell would be able to escape the gravitation of a particular celestial body. Having established that even the most powerful piece of artillery constructed could not launch a projectile capable of escaping the terrestrial atmosphere, Ball notes that 'on a globe much smaller than the earth, not larger for instance than are some of the minor planets, it is certain that a projectile shot from a great Armstrong gun would go up and up and would never return'.[15] In his use of a piece of artillery as a means for transporting the Martians to the earth, Wells borrows directly from Ball's example: 'I am inclined to think that this blaze may have been the casting of the huge gun, in the vast pit sunk into their planet, from which their shots were fired at us' (216). The timing of the Martian descent also bears the hallmarks of Ball's article. The Martians' choice of August as the month in which to launch their offensive concurs exactly with Ball's observation that this presents the most favourable moment at which the opposition of Mars to our own world occurs.[16]

Further derivations from Ball's item are discernible in later passages of *The War of the Worlds*. Concerning the redness of the planet Mars, Ball notes that,

> It has been sometimes thought that the ruddy colour of the planet may be due to vegetation of some peculiar hue, and there is certainly no impossibility in the conception that vast forests of some such trees as copper-beeches might impart to continental masses hues not unlike those which come from Mars.[17]

This observation is cleverly incorporated into the fabric of Wells's novel, as the Martian invasion is inevitably accompanied by the appearance on earth of the red weed and other vegetation from their planet. One additional, more explicit appropriation of Ball's work occurs towards the end of the novel. As well as examining the likely constitution of Mars, Ball considers Venus to be much more of a companion to the earth, in terms of both its size and conditions. 'Everything, therefore, so far as we can judge, points to the conclusion that Venus is a world resembling our own in important features of physical constitution, so that quite possibly it is adapted to be a residence for organised beings', he concludes.[18] Such speculation concerning Venus undeniably influenced Wells's decision to make it the final destination of the Martians in the flight from entropy:

> Venus and Mars were in alignment with the sun; that is to say, Mars was in opposition from the point of view of an observer on Venus.

Subsequently a peculiar luminous and sinuous marking appeared on the unillumined half of the inner planet, and almost simultaneously a faint dark mark of a similar sinuous character was detected upon a photograph of the Martian disc. (449)

That the Martians flee a dying world exposes the irony of the narrator's analogy between the invasion of earth and European colonists' annihilation of the Tasmanians. The invasion of earth has, at least, the moral justification of being essential to the survival of the Martian species. The extermination of the Tasmanians, conversely, was in no way necessary to the survival of the European immigrants. Furthermore, the Martians (who do not intend to eradicate the human species) are not recognisably related to *homo sapiens*.[19] European imperialism, on the other hand, was supported by discourses of racial 'science' which accentuated the supposed evolutionary hierarchy within the human race. The rights of 'civilised' European settlers over 'primitive' indigenous populations were enough to justify the obliteration of the Tasmanians 'in spite of their *human likeness* [emphasis added]' (215–6).

The assured supremacy of the imperial subject partly explains why the humanity portrayed at the beginning of *The War of the Worlds* is oblivious to the possibility of being observed by more advanced beings, as is revealed in the story's famous opening paragraph:

No one would have believed in the last years of the nineteenth century that this world was being watched keenly and closely by intelligences greater than man's and yet as mortal as his own; that as men busied themselves about their various concerns they were scrutinised and studied, perhaps almost as narrowly as a man with a microscope might scrutinise the transient creatures that swarm and multiply in a drop of water. With infinite complacency men went to and fro over this globe about their little affairs, serene in their assurance of their empire over matter. It is possible that the infusoria under the microscope do the same. No one gave a thought to the older worlds of space as sources of human danger, or thought of them only to dismiss the idea of life upon them as impossible or improbable. It is curious to recall some of the mental habits of those departed days. At most, terrestrial men fancied there might be other men upon Mars, perhaps inferior to themselves and ready to welcome a missionary enterprise. Yet across the gulf of space, minds that are to our minds as ours are to those of the beasts that perish, intellects vast and cool and unsympathetic, regarded this earth with envious eyes, and slowly and surely drew their plans against us. (213)

Aside from the imperial conceit that there might be 'inferior' humans on Mars, the deliberate repression of informed contemporary astronomical speculation from the somewhat melodramatic first passage of the novel is immediately evident. The proliferation of late-Victorian speculations concerning the possibility of life on other worlds reveals the claim that contemporary thinkers dismissed 'the idea of life upon them as impossible or improbable' to be demonstrably untrue. This is apparent not only in Wells's use of astronomical writings as a source of scientific verisimilitude but also in his own contributions to the debate on extraterrestrial life, notably 'Intelligence on Mars' (1894).[20] The suppression of informed astronomical speculation can be attributed to the fact that *The War of the Worlds* constitutes perhaps the author's most sustained critique of anthropocentrism. This is immediately indicated by the quotation from Kepler which prefaces the novel: ' "*But who shall dwell in these Worlds if they be inhabited? [...] Are we or they Lords of the World? [...] And how are all things made for man?*" ' Wells appears to have developed the novel's opening from an earlier piece of journalism, 'Through A Microscope' (1894).[21] In a passage which undoubtedly inspired the comparison between the scrutiny of men and that of 'the transient creatures that swarm and multiply in a drop of water' in *The War of the Worlds*, the narrator of 'Through A Microscope' imagines that the micro-organisms visible in the slide of a microscope conduct their lives in a manner equally oblivious to the eye of the detached observer: 'And all the time these creatures are living their vigorous, fussy little lives in this drop of water they are being watched by a creature of whose presence they do not dream'.[22] There is also a moment in 'Through A Microscope' that anticipates the novel's direct comparison of human species arrogance with that of 'the infusoria under the microscope': 'Even so, it may be, the dabbler himself is being curiously observed.... The dabbler is good enough to say that the suggestion is inconceivable. I can imagine a decent Amoeba saying the same thing.'[23]

The early chapters of the novel carefully establish the complacency of humanity at the time of the Martian invasion. On 'The Eve of the War', the narrator is unable even to imagine the import of what he had observed erupting from Mars during his vigil with Ogilvy and comments on the reassuring serenity of the evening: 'My wife pointed out to me the brightness of the red, green, and yellow signal lights hanging in a framework against the sky. It seemed so safe and tranquil' (221).

The emergence of the Martians from their cylinders and the devastating initial use of the Heat-Ray is not enough to unsettle human confidence, since 'the daily routine of working, eating, drinking, sleeping, went on as it had done for countless years – as though no planet Mars existed in the sky' (254).

Wells's deliberately selective use of those sources which inform the scientific verisimilitude he grants to the Martian invasion underlines his endeavour in the first half of the novel to critique anthropocentrism. Ball begins his article on 'Mars' by stressing the continued journalistic interest in the planet in the year of its opposition: 'The newspapers, crowded as they are with their staple political matters, can still make room for paragraphs, columns, and even for long articles on the phenomena of our neighbouring globe.'[24] In *The War of the Worlds*, however, the reluctance of the newspaper industry to inform the public of the object astronomers have observed approaching the earth from Mars comprises a significant aspect of humanity's species arrogance: 'Yet the next day there was nothing of this in the papers except a little note in the *Daily Telegraph*, and the world went in ignorance of one of the gravest dangers that ever threatened the human race' (217).

Examining the evidence which suggests the Martians had meticulously prepared their invasion, the narrator reports that during the 1894 opposition of Mars 'a great light was seen on the illuminated part of the disc, first at the Lick Observatory, then by Perrotin of Nice, and then by other observers' (216). English readers did indeed hear 'of it first in the issue of *Nature* dated August 2nd' (216), as Wells is referring here to an actual notice in that periodical of 'A Strange Light on Mars'.[25] In this instance, Wells has modified the report in *Nature* of a 'luminous projection [which] is not a light outside the disc of Mars, but in the region of the planet not lighted up by the sun at the time of observation' for his purpose of establishing a scientifically accurate basis for the plot of his novel.[26] He is, however, meticulously selective in his use of this source. The *Nature* article relates the fact that this 'strange light' appears to be located on the surface of the planet itself to the revival of 'the old idea that the Martians are signalling to us'.[27] Wells is forced to omit this particular aspect of 'A Strange Light on Mars' because its inclusion would have conflicted with the insistence of the novel that humanity's own 'blindness' had prevented any consideration of the possibility of life on other worlds.

The way in which the first part of *The War of the Worlds* fuses indigenous complacency with the sudden materialisation of a challenge to human supremacy corresponds to a suggestive passage of 'The

Extinction of Man' (1894), in which Wells warns:

> No; man's complacent assumption of the future is too confident. We
> think, because things have been easy for mankind as a whole for a
> generation or so, we are going on to perfect comfort and security in
> the future. We think that we shall always go to work at ten and leave
> off at four and have dinner at seven for ever and ever. But these four
> suggestions out of a host of others must surely do a little against this
> complacency. Even now, for all we can tell, the coming terror may be
> crouching for its spring and the fall of humanity be at hand. In the case
> of every other predominant animal the world has ever seen, I repeat,
> the hour of its complete ascendency [sic] has been the eve of its entire
> overthrow. But if some poor story-writing man ventures to figure this
> sober probability in a tale, not a reviewer in London but will tell him
> his theme is the utterly impossible. And when the thing happens, one
> may doubt if even then one will get the recognition one deserves.[28]

Wells's caution in the above passage against assuming we will 'have
dinner at seven for ever and ever' is explicitly recalled as the narrator
consumes 'the last civilised dinner I was to eat for very many strange
and terrible days' (252). As the Martians take increasingly violent measures to establish themselves on earth, the narrator is forced to confront
the precariousness of his previously comfortable existence: 'And this
was the little world in which I had been living securely for years, this
fiery chaos!' (276).

As he realises the magnitude of the threat to the security of this 'little
world', the narrator moves quickly to secure the conveyance of the unsus-
pecting proprietor of the Spotted Dog, admitting that: 'At the time it did
not seem nearly so urgent that the landlord should leave his [home]' (263).
The narrator's actions in this instance prefigure the human self-interest
apparent in later chapters of the novel.[29] Whereas in *The Invisible Man* a
united humanity co-operates in order to hunt down an anarchic fugitive,
The War of the Worlds emphasises how the species *homo sapiens* becomes
increasingly atomised in the course of the Martian conquest. Wells's construction of the chapters dealing with the flight from London undercut
the insistence of Herbert Spencer that his economic theories should be
used to direct the 'further modification in the future' of humankind. In
1894, Wells wrote to his friend Arthur Morley Davies:

> I am very glad of the change in your views regarding our excellent
> Herbert Spencer – a noble & wondrous thinker but lacking humour,

the trick of looking at things with two eyes, the stereoscopic quality that makes a view real. The way you put it 'individualism in ethics, socialism in economy' expresses I think my own position as well as yours.[30]

His friend and correspondent Grant Allen, who was a devotee of Spencer, might also have informed Wells's understanding of Spencer.[31]

Spencer had delineated his views on economic individualism in a series of four articles published in the *Contemporary Review* in 1884.[32] The final instalment of this series, 'The Sins of Legislators', makes explicit the reasoning behind his insistence that human interaction should be governed by the mechanism of natural selection which operates in the natural world.[33] Spencer argues that the continuance of higher species depends on the conformity 'of two radically-opposed principles'.[34] These principles are the extra nurturing required by the young of the higher species in reaching maturity and the struggle for survival faced by the individual in adulthood: 'Placed in competition with members of its own species and in antagonism with members of other species, it dwindles and gets killed off, or thrives and propagates, according as it is ill-endowed or well-endowed.'[35] If by some mechanism, the 'multiplication of the inferior was furthered and multiplication of the superior hindered, progressive degradation would result' with the probable consequence that the species 'would fail to hold its ground in [the] presence of antagonistic species and competing species'.[36] In human society, according to Spencer, the fitness of an individual to propagate is determined by their economic status. The sin of legislators who seek to redress the disproportion of wealth that exists between rich and poor is that they actively encourage the propagation of the weak members of the human species: 'Society in its corporate capacity, cannot without immediate or remote disaster interfere with the play of those opposed principles under which every species has reached such fitness for its mode of life as it possesses, and under which it maintains that fitness.'[37] For Spencer, social activities produced through the combined efforts of individuals 'have done much more towards social development than those which have worked through governmental agencies'.[38] Spencer advocates a greatly diminished role for the State, reserved primarily to ensuring justice as the various members of society pursue gratification through economic individualism, thus ensuring the 'survival of the fittest'.

In the response of the indigenous population to the increasing dominance of the invaders in *The War of the Worlds*, Wells vigorously opposes

Spencer's insistence that the competition apparent in the natural world translates into an appropriate framework for human ethical conduct. As the Martian fighting machines advance upon London, Wells sardonically recreates the diminished influence of government which Spencer had identified as crucial to the competition between individuals: 'He [the narrator's brother] heard that about half the members of the government had gathered at Birmingham' (351). The absence of government and the wider breakdown of social agency in the chapter 'The Exodus From London' indeed result in competition between numerous individuals in their desperation to escape the Martians. Yet the struggle for existence invoked implies the brutalisation of humanity rather than the necessary stage in its evolutionary ascendancy envisaged by Spencer. The first indication that the survival of the fittest merely reveals the latent bestiality underlying the civilised individual occurs as 'People were fighting savagely for standing-room in the carriages even at two o'clock. By three, people were being trampled and crushed [...] revolvers were fired, [and] people stabbed' (331).

The characterisation of the 'multitudes' which engage in a savage struggle to escape the oncoming Martians reveals how the functioning of the cosmic process in human society results only in turning humans into animals. This is apparent, for instance, in the description of trains 'swarming' (347) with fugitives. The competition within *homo sapiens*, moreover, resembles the type of automatic response associated with the lower animals: 'Yet a kind of eddy of people drove into its mouth [the road]; weaklings elbowed out of the stream, who for the most part rested but a moment before plunging into it again' (342). Far from endorsing Spencer's view that an individual's economic status determines their fitness and hence suitability for propagation, those best adapted to survive the brutal struggle for existence invoked by Wells are the labouring poor: 'There were sturdy workmen *thrusting* their way along, wretched, unkempt men, clothed like clerks or shop-men, struggling spasmodically [emphasis added]' (341).

Wells satirises the economic basis of Spencer's individualism by highlighting the futility of the obsessive pursuit of wealth in the context of the immediate threat to human supremacy posed by the Martians. One particular caricature constructed to this end is that of the man encountered by the narrator's brother, who attempts to retain his financial status in the face of the Martian invasion. As his bag of money is split open in the rush to escape the invaders, this man 'flung himself, with both hands open, upon the heap of coins, and began thrusting handfuls in his pocket' (344). The unrelenting greed of this individual leads him to cause his own disablement as his back is broken by the rim of a cart just as he attempts to recover these coins amid the flood of retreating individuals. As the narrator's brother and his two companions attempt to escape England by sea, their fate rests in the hands of the steamer captain; an individual prepared to place in jeopardy not only his own life but also those of others in his pursuit of financial gain. Having charged an extortionate amount of money for passage on his vessel, and 'picking up passengers until the seated decks were even danger- ously crowded' (354), only the sound of gunfire is sufficient to prompt him to disregard his desire for profit and begin the voyage to safety. The actions of some crewmen on boats carrying passengers to safety con- firm Wells's view that connecting an individual's right to survive and propagate with their capacity to accumulate wealth would merely result in unleashing the savagery within *homo sapiens*. Those unable to pay 'the enormous sums of money offered by fugitives' are simply 'thrust off with boat-hooks and drowned' (350).

The absurdity of such preoccupation with financial gain is empha- sised since the potential hegemony of the Martians on earth renders obsolete the system of commodity exchange by which humankind determines the relative status of its individual members. Thus emerging upon 'Dead London', the narrator notes that plunderers had broken into a jeweller's leaving 'a number of gold chains and a watch [which] were scattered on the pavement' (430). He does 'not trouble to touch them' (430) because these commodities are now devoid of the exchange values once associated with them and their use value serves no purpose for the narrator in his will to survive.

In emphasising how the imitation of the cosmic process in the strug- gle to escape the Martians leads merely to the breakdown of social bonds just as they are most needed, Wells points to the importance of co-operation in human evolution.[39] Wells thus reveals his adher- ence in *The War of the Worlds* to Huxley's ethical evolution which, of course, has its basis in co-operation. Huxley emphasises the importance of co-operation to the ethical process by which humanity is able to interfere with the cosmic process and thus ensure its own survival in a cosmos largely indifferent to human concerns. 'In place of ruthless self-assertion it demands self-restraint; in place of thrusting aside, or treading down, all competitors, it requires that the individual shall not merely respect, but shall help his fellows', he writes.[40] The serialised ver- sion of *The War of the Worlds* contains a passage in which the narrator explicitly recalls Huxley's reasoning: 'But, as for right, I do not believe that there is any right in the world, save the sense of justice between man and man. All the rest, I hold, is physical law'.[41] In the final version of the text, the narrator remarks approvingly of a solitary instance of co-operation which stands out amid all the brutality witnessed by his brother: 'A little way down the lane, with two friends bending over him, lay a man with a bare leg, wrapped about with bloody rags. He was a lucky man to have friends' (342).

The conduct of the narrator's brother himself perfectly adheres to the principles of ethical evolution. While those involved in the physical tussles around him revert to the characteristics associated with the 'ape' and 'tiger', the narrator's brother maintains his self-restraint. He resorts to violence only when it is inevitable and necessary to help others, as is apparent in his rescue of the two women, who later become his companions, from three men attempting to ruthlessly steal their carriage: 'One of the men desisted and turned towards him, and my brother, realising from his *antagonist's face that a fight was unavoidable*, and being an expert boxer, went into him forthwith and sent him down against the wheel of the chaise [emphasis added]' (334). The reciprocal bonds which form the basis of ethical evolution are distinctly apparent as one of the women he has just saved in turn rescues the narrator's brother from the two remaining antagonists:

> He would have had little chance against them had not the slender lady very pluckily pulled up and returned to his help. It seems she had a revolver all this time [...] She fired at six yards' distance, narrowly missing my brother. The less courageous of the robbers made off, and his companion followed him, cursing his cowardice. (335)

In resolutely escorting the two women to safety, the narrator's brother further underlines his commitment to the co-operative principles of ethical evolution.

Notwithstanding such instances of co-operation, Roslynn Haynes writes that 'there is no effective counter-impression [in the novel] to that of confused, self-centred men feeling in confusion before the advance of an efficient, amoral, technological power'.[42] The savage struggle to escape London is, however, juxtaposed to a cosmic perspective which exposes the fragility of earthly existence. As he observes Mars with Ogilvy, the narrator comments that: 'Few people realise the immensity of vacancy in which the dust of the material universe swims' (218). This observation reiterates Huxley's conception of the human race as 'Fragile reed' in an inhospitable universe.[43] The celestial perspective of the passage just cited also recalls the novel's opening, in which 'the globe is reduced to the size of a water-drop, humanity becomes an ant-like swarm and its affairs look contemptibly petty'.[44] Viewed from a cosmic standpoint which reveals the fragility of terrestrial life, the need for humanity to abandon its anthropocentric preconceptions and co-operate as a means to combat its precarious position in the natural order becomes imperative.

Moving from the human response to the invasion to the aliens themselves, the narrator of *The War of the Worlds* comments that, 'To me it is quite credible that the Martians may be descended from beings not unlike ourselves' (381). The Martians are indeed posited in the narrative as a potential evolutionary future for humanity. As he and the Curate observe the Martians through the peep-hole in the ruined house, the narrator refers to a prophecy which 'appeared in November or December, 1893, in a long defunct publication, the *Pall Mall Budget*, and I recall a caricature of it in a pre-Martian periodical called *Punch*' (380). The article being referred to here is Wells's own 'The Man of the Year Million', which in fact appeared in the *Pall Mall Gazette* in November 1893.[45]

In that article, Wells ironically explores the potential of the intellect in human evolution. He begins his speculation by stressing that ' "man is the creature of the brain; he will live by intelligence, and not by physical strength, if he live at all" '.[46] This will lead inevitably to the hypertrophy of his intellect and to the suppression of ' "much that is purely 'animal' about him" '.[47] The beginning of this suppression is revealed by the diminishment of man's primitive instincts, the residual effects of which are a burden in contemporary life: ' "Cabs, trains, trams, render speed unnecessary, the pursuit of food becomes easier; his wife is no longer hunted, but rather, in view of the crowded matrimonial market, seeks him out." '[48] The existing capacity of medicine artificially to supersede bodily functions suggests 'parallel modifications will also affect the body and limbs' so that the ' "many hours" ' spent each day digesting food ultimately 'may and can be avoided'.[49] Parallel with the diminishment of humanity's bestial inheritance, 'The coming man, then, will clearly have a larger brain, and a slighter body than the present.'[50] This is with the exception of the hands, as ' "the teacher and interpreter of the brain" '.[51] Bringing together these developments, Wells presents a comical vision of future humanity:

'They are descendents of man – at dinner. Watch them as they hop on their hands – a method of progression advocated already by Bjornsen – about the pure white marble floor. Great hands they have, enormous brains, soft, liquid, soulful eyes. Their whole muscular system, their legs, their abdomens, are shrivelled to nothing, a dangling, degraded pendant to their minds'.[52]

Wells's characterisation of the Martians builds upon those speculations on future humanity first introduced in the above piece of journalism. In the first instance, the Martians display that hypertrophy of the intellect which Wells had sardonically characterised as the essential feature of humanity's evolutionary progression. 'They were huge round bodies – or, rather, heads – about four feet in diameter, each body having in front of it a face' (376), the narrator states. Wells's earlier speculative vision of future humanity as 'hopping heads' is recalled in the narrator's observations of the invaders: 'Even as I saw these Martians for the first time they seemed to be endeavouring to raise themselves on these hands, but of course, with the increased weight of terrestrial conditions, this was impossible' (377). The Martians are also characterised by the 'soft liquid soulful eyes' of Wells's anticipated future humanity, each having 'a pair of very large, dark-coloured eyes' (377). As 'the teacher and interpreter of the brain', the Martians are endowed with disproportionately large tentacles, which 'have since been named rather aptly, by that distinguished anatomist, Professor Howes, the *hands*' (377). The evolutionary advancement of the Martians is underlined by the fact that they do not even possess the 'degraded pendant' of a body which Wells had anticipated in future humanity: 'Entrails they had none' (377–8).

The narrator, who periodically displays a preoccupation with what he perceives as the superiority of the Martians reminiscent of Gulliver's relationship to the Houyhnhnms in *Gulliver's Travels* (1726), points to the comparative advantages enjoyed by the Martians' lack of a digestive system: 'Men go happy or miserable as they have healthy or unhealthy livers, or sound gastric glands. But the Martians were lifted above all these organic fluctuations of mood and emotion' (378). He then comments on the suppression in the Martians of 'the animal side of the organism by the intelligence' thus indicating Wells's didactic purpose in *The War of the Worlds*: 'Without the body the brain would, of course, become a mere selfish intelligence, without any of the emotional substratum of the human being' (381).

In his insistence on the continued importance of the body in human evolution, Wells is overturning Jonathan Swift's position in book four of *Gulliver's Travels*. In 'A Voyage to the Houyhnhnms', Swift appears determined to highlight the status of humankind as an animal among animals. Swift's Yahoos continually indulge in excesses which emphasise the bestiality of *homo sapiens*. The first of these excesses occurs as the Yahoos attack Gulliver shortly after his arrival: 'Several of this cursed brood getting hold of the branches behind leaped up into the tree, from whence they began to discharge their excrements on my head.'[53] His apparent disdain for bodily functions suggests Swift would be attracted to the vision of a diminished body and hypertrophied brain Wells presents in 'The Man of the Year Million'. For Wells himself, however, the animal side of the human organism is crucial to the evolution of the species. This didactic purpose of *The War of the Worlds* is thus to point to the crucial significance of the body in human evolution. This is because the animal side of the human organism possesses the emotions that ensure the capacity for sympathy and co-operation among humankind.[54]

Despite this insistence on the importance of the body in preserving sympathy, the novel invites questions as to whether the human possession of a digestive system necessarily results in conduct that is more ethical than that of the 'selfish' Martians. As Warren Wagar puts it, 'were contemporary human beings, under the influence of their gastro-intestinal tracts, better judges of ethical behaviour than the "selfish" Martians? If so, why would Englishmen, fully equipped with stomachs and intestines, do away with the Tasmanians?'[55]

Recent criticism has also demonstrated that the conduct of the Martians does not support the narrator's claim that the invaders are mere 'selfish intelligence[s]' devoid of the emotional capacities of human beings. In his article, 'How Far Can We Trust the Narrator of *The War of the Worlds*?', Patrick Parrinder points out that the narrator bases his claim that the Martians' intellects are 'unsympathetic' solely on their behaviour towards humans, which is 'not relevant, unless we agree to judge human beings by their general behaviour towards the animals and plants necessary for their food supply'.[56] In considering whether or not the Martians possess emotions 'we should look at their behaviour towards one another, and not towards human beings'.[57] Judged by their conduct towards one other, the Martians reveal precisely those attributes associated with the 'emotional substratum' of human beings. Parrinder emphasises how the Martians' mutual sympathy is demonstrated in their recovery of a fallen comrade from the field of battle and in their mourning of each other's deaths.

The Martians' sympathy for one another, moreover, is bound inextricably with their capacity for co-operation. In a suggestive passage of 'Ancient Experiments in Co-Operation', Wells speculates on the development of the co-operative principle in future and concludes:

> The village commune of the future will be an organism; it will rejoice and sorrow like a man. Men will be limbs – even nowadays in our

public organisations men are but members. One ambition will sway the commune, a perfect fusion of interest there will be, and a perfect sympathy of feeling.[58]

The increased level of co-operation discernable in their conduct towards one another symbolises a positive aspect of the Martians' status as a potential evolutionary future for humanity. Under fire from the earthly artillery, the Martians collaborate in the face of adversity: 'After this it would seem that the three took counsel together and halted, and the scouts who were watching them report that they remained absolutely stationary for the next half-hour' (321). The co-operation of the Martians in this instance enables them to facilitate a solution to the difficulty arising from the gunner's destruction of one of their tripod legs, as one of the Martians emerges from its mount to repair the damage. In contrast to the way in which contemporary humanity fragments immediately it is subjected to external pressure, the level of co-operation which characterises the evolutionary advancement of the Martian enables them to overcome such difficulties and proceed with that 'One ambition [that] [...] sway[s] the commune'. That the Martians are like the 'limbs' of a larger 'organism' is revealed by the narrator's assertion that: 'I have seen four, five and (once) six of them sluggishly perform the most elaborately complicated operations together without either sound or gesture' (382). Indeed, the degree of collaboration between the Martians is such that it would appear to substantiate Wagar's hint that their conduct towards each other can be reconciled with Wells's belief in the Huxleian principle of ethical evolution grounded in co-operation and mutual aid.[59]

While their disregard for human beings does not obscure the Martians' ethical conduct towards one other, it does suggest the need for a reconsideration of how humans in turn treat animals. Indeed, the narrator's initial observations of the Martian fighting machines cause him to question 'for the first time in my life how an iron-clad or a steam-engine would seem to an intelligent lower animal' (276). Similarly, although repulsed as he witnesses the Martians feeding on the blood of human beings, the narrator acknowledges 'how repulsive our carnivorous habits would seem to an intelligent rabbit' (378). In such passages, Wells uses anthropomorphism to encourage empathy with animals thus discouraging their cruel treatment or exploitation by humans. The narrator's empathy towards animals is, of course, developed as 'He becomes literally rabbit-like when he scrabbles for young onions and immature carrots after escaping from the [ruined] house'.[60]

The narrator's account of life under the Martians not only high-lights the plight of animals, it articulates the predicament of those supposedly inferior races subjugated by British imperialism. Indeed, Herbert Sussman remarks of the novel, 'This anti-imperialist fable is even told from the viewpoint of the oppressed'.[61] The inverted imperialism of *The War of the Worlds* signifies its affinity to the emerging genre of the invasion novel. As Bernard Bergonzi notes of the novel, 'The word "war" in its title would have had a significance then which is now lost.'[62] The novel undoubtedly related in the contemporary mind to numerous other books and pamphlets expressing anxieties concerning 'the invasion of England followed by – in some cases – national defeat and humiliation at the hands of a foreign enemy – usually either the French or Germans'.[63] Bergonzi hints that *The War of the Worlds* might be related to those publications of authors who 'wished to expose national unpreparedness and to warn of the fate that might befall the country if its defences were not put in order'.[64] This hint can be substantiated by examining the novel in the context of the debates concerning the alleged shortcomings of the British armed forces which permeated the late-Victorian periodical press.

The particular intensity of debate in 1897 concerning Britain's apparent incapacity to field an efficient, adequately numbered army provides an appropriate context in which to examine the militaristic subtext of *The War of the Worlds*, which of course began serialisation in April of that year. One representative contributor to these debates was H. M. Havelock-Allan, whose two articles 'A General Voluntary Training To Arms *Versus* Conscription' and 'England's Military Position', appeared in the *Fortnightly Review* in January and July 1897 respectively.[65] In the first of these articles, Havelock-Allan suggests that a system of voluntary training to arms can 'supply for England, under her now vastly increased liabilities, what Conscription supplies for the nations of the Continent'.[66] He begins by emphasising that 'The primary and paramount duty of every Englishman, [is] to take up arms in defence of his country in case of invasion'.[67] For Havelock-Allan, Britain's military strength can be increased greatly by encouraging the latent patriotism of the population to 'enable the Volunteer movement to include within its numbers practically all the able-bodied men of the nation'.[68] The training of volunteers will, Havelock-Allan is confident, fulfil the necessity for a strengthened British land force, since despite its naval supremacy, Britain has learned 'that a fleet alone cannot act on dry land, or as Lord Salisbury aptly put it, "That our ironclads cannot travel over the mountains of the Taurus"'.[69] Havelock-Allan begins 'England's Military

Position' with the exaggerated warning that Britain's inadequately sized field force 'puts us in about the same military position as Belgium or Roumania'.[70] He cautions that the prioritisation of overseas regiments is leaving our home battalions in 'such weakness and inefficiency as can scarcely be exaggerated'.[71] Havelock-Allan not only notes the deterioration of the infantry due to the demands placed upon it from the system whereby home battalions have to supply men to those overseas, but also the graver impact of this system on the Horse and Field artillery. The home batteries had previously been left intact as 'the Horse and Field Artillery in India were kept at their full strength by drafts taken from two large depots which existed at Woolwich'.[72] Despite such demands, Havelock-Allan expresses his admiration of the determined efficiency of these batteries: 'It only shows of what magnificent material our Royal Artillery is composed, that under such discouraging circumstances they can continue to be effective at all.'[73]

The militaristic subtext of *The War of the Worlds* engages with the exact concerns apropos the efficiency of the British military articulated by Havelock-Allan. In the first instance, the increasing challenge to Britain's imperial hegemony is revealed as an important context for the novel: 'Many people had heard of the cylinder, of course, and talked about it in their leisure, but it certainly did not make the sensation that an ultimatum to Germany would have done' (253). The narrator's account of the military resistance to the Martian invasion of England is comparable to the type of war correspondence popularised in the late nineteenth century by such writers as Archibald Forbes. Like numerous war correspondents, the narrator not only endeavours to interview army personnel, he also displays a considerable interest in military tactics: 'I sat at tea with my wife in the summer-house talking vigorously about the battle that was lowering upon us' (261).

By locating the site of the Martian landing close to the British army headquarters in Aldershot, and including artillery resources drawn from such towns as Woolwich, Wells uses his war correspondent narrator to comment on the preparedness of the military forces in Britain for an invasion by a malign alien adversary. The success of the hidden batteries at Weybridge in destroying one of the vastly superior invaders would appear to allay the fears of Havelock-Allan and others that the demands placed on the resources of the home artillery are excessive: 'The shell burst clean in the face of the Thing. The hood bulged, flashed, was whirled off in a dozen tattered fragments of red flesh and glittering metal' (292). As the Martians retreat to their triangle around Woking, the authorities employ all their energy in preventing the invasion of London: 'Guns were in rapid transit from Windsor, Portsmouth, Aldershot, Woolwich – even from the north; among others, long wire-guns of ninety-five tons from Woolwich' (312). The conduct of the gunners defending the capital undercuts Havelock-Allan's idea that the volunteer system should be extended to include all able bodied men. For the actions of the Ripley Gunners, 'unseasoned artillery volunteers who ought never to have been placed in such a position, [and who] fired one wild, premature, ineffectual volley, and bolted on horse and foot through the deserted village' (320), not only underlines their own ineffectiveness but also enables the Martian to come 'unexpectedly upon the guns in Painshill Park, which he destroyed' (321). The actions of the St George's Hill men, conversely, are perhaps more worthy of the praise Havelock-Allan heaped on the overstretched artillery. A consequence of being either 'better led or of a better mettle', they retain their composure to such a high degree that they are able to lay 'their guns as deliberately as if they had been on parade' (321).

The valiant artillery eventually succumbs to the black smoke employed by the Martians. In his preface to the Atlantic Edition of *The War of the Worlds*, Wells wrote that: 'Once or twice in reading this book, written a quarter of a century ago, the reader will be reminded of phases and incidents in the Great War: the use of poison-gas, for instance, or the flight before the Martians' (ix).[74] While Wells correctly identifies the prophetic aspect of its representation of war, the novel can be related to contemporary speculation concerning the future of warfare. One such speculation is Archibald Forbes's 'The Warfare of the Future', which appeared in the *Nineteenth Century* in 1891.[75] Two particular elements of Forbes's analysis find resonance in the pages of *The War of the Worlds*. The first of these is that 'Magazine and machine guns would seem to sound the knell of possible employment of cavalry in battle'.[76] Regardless of the cavalry's determination, Forbes is certain that 'the quick-firing arms of the future must apparently stall off the most enterprising horsemen'.[77] Although the Martian Heat-Ray is far more futuristic than machine-gun fire, Forbes's principle can be applied to the ineffective nature of the cavalry used to combat it. So although the narrator reports on the flying hussars who gallop boldly towards the invaders, the artillery-man who takes refuge in his home relates the eventual fate of such men, as he 'found himself lying under a heap of charred dead men and dead horses' (278). The second element of Forbes's article of relevance to the novel is his idea that 'The fortress of the future will probably be in the nature of an entrenched camp'.[78] On encountering the artillery-man on a second occasion, the narrator learns of the entrenched base the Martians have constructed in London: ' "I guess they've got a bigger camp there. Of a night, all over there, Hampstead way, the sky is alive with their lights. It's like a great city, and in the glare you can just see them moving" ' (413).

That the navy should provide the last significant military opposition to the establishment of a Martian base is highly appropriate. The anonymous critic in the *Saturday Review* points to the ambiguity surrounding the success of the *Thunderchild* in heroically rescuing the threatened shipping at Clacton: 'Are we to believe that he had not heard of the three which H.M.S. "Thunder Child" blew up at Clacton, or were these three soused and scalded, but not killed?'[79] The apparent achievement of a single ironclad in destroying at least two of the invaders – thereby proving doubly as efficient as the combined efforts of the army – reiterates Havelock-Allan's notion of a disparity between Britain's undisputed naval supremacy and the comparative weakness of its land based forces. Notwithstanding the partial success of the *Thunderchild*, what Havelock-Allan had called Britain's lesson 'that a fleet alone cannot act on dry land' is recalled by the description of the remainder of the Channel Fleet in the novel: 'which hovered in an extended line, steam up and ready for action, across the Thames estuary during the course of the Martian conquest, vigilant and yet powerless to prevent it' (353).

The failure of the British military to defeat the invaders perfectly concurs with the novel's castigation of imperial pride. Yet the fact the invaders are defeated by the one factor they had failed to include in their supposedly meticulous preparations reveals how the Martians are characterised by the same blindness as the imperial subject. They are, 'slain by the putrefactive and disease bacteria against which their systems were unprepared; [...] slain, after all man's devices had failed, by the humblest things that God, in his wisdom, has put upon this earth' (436). This plot device not only provides Wells with an ingenious means of ending the novel, it also reveals his support for Huxley's contention that it is the survival of the most fitted – rather than the survival of the fittest – that determines the evolutionary success of a species. Arguing against a Spencerian assessment of the implications of evolutionary theory for humanity, Huxley emphasises that 'what is "fittest" depends upon the conditions':

> I ventured to point out that if our hemisphere were to cool again, the survival of the fittest might bring about [...] a population of more and more stunted and humbler and humbler organisms, until

the 'fittest' that survived might be nothing but lichens, diatoms, and such microscopic organisms as those which give red snow its colour.[80]

The maladaptation of the Martians on the earth entirely concurs with Huxley's point that, under altered conditions, the 'strongest' might not necessarily be the 'fittest'. Still more poignantly, Wells's use of the 'humblest' creatures upon the earth finally to end the Martian conflict explicitly recalls Huxley's insistence that a different environment could bring creatures now considered to be 'humble' to prominence.

While the eventual overthrow of the Martians on earth is widely celebrated, there is one figure who embraces the invasion as a perfect opportunity to reinvigorate the human species. On the second occasion the narrator encounters him, the artilleryman stresses the need for chosen members of the human race to adapt to the circumstances indicated by the emerging Martian hegemony and to degenerate in a manner akin to a species of giant, savage rat. His selectivity regarding those fitted to ensure the continuance of the human race – ' "Mind you, it isn't all of us that are made for wild beasts; and that's what it's got to be" ' (418) – recalls the class inversion implied by the fact that it is the poor who had retained the capacity for adaptation in the struggle to escape London. The artilleryman is certain that the ideal fate of ' "all those damned little clerks" ' is to be captured by the Martians as they mould humanity into a source of nourishment: ' "Well, the Martians will just be a godsend to these. Nice roomy cages, fattening food, careful breeding, no worry" ' (418).[81]

According to John Huntington, the artilleryman's schemes for humanity are 'undercut by the [narrator's] discovery that it is all bluster, that the man is a lazy hypocrite who has no intention of living up to his arduous declaration'.[82] This, however, should not imply that the narrator's rejection of the artilleryman is also a refutation of his proposed programme for the regeneration of the human species. Rather, it is a consequence of the artilleryman's failure to fulfil the narrator's desire for action, which had been revealed in his earlier statement that: 'My imagination became belligerent, and defeated the invaders in a dozen striking ways; something of my school-boy dreams of battle and heroism came back' (260–1).[83] While the scheme outlined by the artilleryman had at first appealed to the narrator's sense of the urgent need for humanity to respond proactively to the Martian invasion, the protagonist becomes disillusioned with his interlocutor's lack of application: 'when I saw the work he had spent a week upon – it was a burrow scarcely ten yards long, which he designed to reach to the main drain on Putney Hill – I had my inkling of the gulf between his dreams and his powers' (423).

The significance of the artilleryman's ideas is that they are nascent articulations of those ideas which Wells himself would later delineate in his first major sociological work, *Anticipations* (1901).[84] Particularly, the artilleryman's proposed use of eugenics to determine the fittest members of the human species anticipates Wells's discussion of eugenics in the sociological text. To the artilleryman, the reinvigoration of humanity requires ruthless selectivity:

'Those who stop obey orders. Able-bodied, clean minded women we want also – mothers and teachers. No lackadaisical ladies – no blasted rolling eyes. We can't have any weak or silly. Life is real again, and the useless and cumbersome and mischievous have to die. They ought to die. They ought to be willing to die. It's a sort of disloyalty, after all, to live and taint the race. And they can't be happy. Moreover, dying's none so dreadful; it's the funking makes it bad'. (421)

The artilleryman's emphasis on the opposing fates of the 'Able-bodied' and the 'weak or silly' is echoed in Wells's expectation in *Anticipations* that the ethical system of the future will on the one hand favour 'beautiful and strong bodies', while on the other checking 'the procreation of base and servile types, of fear-driven and cowardly souls, of all that is mean and ugly and bestial in the souls, bodies, or habits of men'.[85] The preparedness of the artilleryman – revealed in such statements as ' "It's a sort of disloyalty, after all, to live and taint the race" ' – to envisage lethal methods of eliminating the weak members of the human species prefigures the ethical perspective of the men of the New Republic who 'will hold life to be a privilege and a responsibility, not a sort of night refuge for base spirits out of the void'.[86] Consequently, Wells relates that in specific circumstances 'I do not foresee any reason to suppose that they will hesitate to kill when that sufferance is abused'.[87] The artilleryman is especially scornful of the religious piety he expects will be displayed by those human beings captured by the Martians: ' "Now whenever things are so that a lot of people feel they ought to be doing something, the weak, and those who go weak with a lot of complicated thinking, always make for a sort of do-nothing religion, very pious and superior, and submit to persecution and the will of the Lord" ' (419). In this respect, he presages the pragmatic outlook of Wells's New Republicans, to whom 'the idea of airing their egotisms in God's presence through prayer, or any such quasi-personal intimacy, [is] absurd'.[88]

The ruthless selectivity of the artilleryman's proposal to use the Martian invasion as an excuse to purge humanity of its weak members might appear as a mere variation of Social Darwinism. Yet Wells himself had, of course, questioned the relevance of natural selection to *homo sapiens* in his 'Human Evolution, An Artificial Process'. As indicated in the discussion of *Moreau*, he uses this article to point out that in contrast to such animals as the rabbit, the long intervals between each generation of man means that the role of natural selection in human evolution is negligible. 'In view of which facts, *it appears to me impossible to believe that man has undergone anything but an infinitesimal alteration in his intrinsic nature since the age of unpolished stone* [emphasis in original].'[89] In order to explain the evolution that has occurred in man since the Stone Age, Wells underlines the role of 'an acquired factor', 'the artificial man, the highly plastic creature of tradition, suggestion, and reasoned thought'.[90] The artificial factor in man can be extended through the accumulation of knowledge, hence: 'If this new view is acceptable it provides a novel definition of Education, which obviously should be the careful and systematic manufacture of the artificial factor in man.'[91] The most significant element of the scheme of regeneration proposed by the artilleryman is the first fictional articulation of Wells's acquired factor: ' "But saving the race is nothing in itself. As I say, that's only being rats. *It's saving our knowledge and adding to it is the thing* [emphasis added]" ' (421). The artilleryman also stresses the role of education in ensuring the continuation of the human species: ' "We must make great safe places down deep, and get all the books we can; not novels and poetry swipes, but ideas, science books" ' (421).

This emphasis on accumulating scientific ideas is recalled by the fact that one of the benefits of the Martian invasion is that it enables humanity to extend radically its understanding of science. This enlarged understanding of science is not limited to the experimental laboratories that reveal specific aspects of the Martians' technology. It also facilitates the popular conception of science. Such statements as 'Few of the common people in England had anything but the vaguest astronomical ideas in those days' (228) imply that popular understanding of scientific ideas has increased since the Martian invasion. To the narrator, the Martians suggest an optimistic future direction for humanity: 'Dim and wonderful is the vision I have conjured up in my mind of life spreading slowly from this little seed-bed of the solar system throughout the inanimate vastness of sidereal space' (450).[92]

However, the optimism of the narrator's 'remote dream' for humanity is undercut by those aspects of *The War of the Worlds* which – rather like

The Island of Doctor Moreau – appear to emphasise the futility of evolution. Notwithstanding their supposedly advanced evolutionary status, various characteristics of the Martians in fact suggest retrogression. That the invader which repairs its tripod is 'oddly suggestive from that distance of a speck of blight' (321), together with the 'oily brown skin' (234) of the extraterrestrials, emphasise how the descriptions of the Martians recall the micro-organisms of the novel's opening. The similarity between the Martians and those creatures occupying the lowest point in the earthly evolutionary scale can be further explored with reference to 'Through A Microscope'. In that article, Wells notes how 'the simple protozoon has none of that fitful fever of falling in love, that distressingly tender state that so bothers your mortal man'.[93] In the novel, the narrator's assessment of the absence of sex among the Martians underlines their identification with creatures apparently existing at the opposite end of the evolutionary scale: 'the Martians were absolutely without sex, and therefore without any of the tumultuous emotions that arise from that difference among men' (379). One of the most striking elements of the Martians' characterisation that suggests retrogression is that they are parasites: 'Let it suffice to say, blood obtained from a still living animal, in most cases from a human being, was run directly by means of a little pipette into a recipient canal' (378). The feeding method of the Martians would suggest they are subject to the diminished capacity for adaptation that Lankester had identified with the parasitical animal. Humanity is also subject to retrogression in the novel. The artilleryman's conception of humanity reverting to primitivism is prefigured in the narrator's admission that 'Something very like the war-fever that occasionally runs through a civilised community had got into my blood' (265) at the start of the Martian invasion.

While *The War of the Worlds* contains elements which recall the evolutionary fables, the novel constitutes a development from these earlier works in that it focuses primarily on the ethical implications of humanity's capacity for evolutionary development. Wells utilises his fourth scientific romance as a means to participate in the debate between Huxley and Spencer over the application of evolutionary theory to human society. Wells undercuts Spencer's individualism by indicating how humanity fragments just as social bonds are most needed. By highlighting the necessity for co-operation in the novel, Wells reveals his adherence to the ethical evolution of Huxley for the first time as an author of scientific romances. Indeed, the Martian invasion facilitates the co-operation of humanity, as is revealed in the narrator's comment that 'it has done much to promote the conception of the commonweal of mankind' (449). Moreover, the Martian invasion shatters the anthropocentrism which had prevented humanity from recognising its comparative insignificance in the cosmic order: 'We have learned now that we cannot regard this planet as being fenced in and a secure abiding place for man. [...] it has robbed us of that serene confidence in the future which is the most fruitful source of decadence' (449). Yet for all this Huxleian emphasis, Spencer's work will become increasingly important to Wells as he begins to outline the future direction of humanity.

Although the narrator rejects his schemes, the artilleryman nonetheless constitutes an early attempt on the part of Wells to define the future shape of humanity. Indeed the artilleryman's plans for humanity prefigure the ideas expressed by Wells himself in *Anticipations*. More especially, the artilleryman's emphasis on the 'acquired factor' – and indeed on the necessity for humanity to retain its capacity for adaptation – prefigure two of Wells's key concerns as he becomes increasingly preoccupied with his role as a writer who imagines 'the shape of things to come'.

Part III
Towards the Shaping of Humanity

6

'Science is a Match that Man Has Just Got Alight':[1] Science and Social Organisation in *The First Men in the Moon*

My examination of the evolutionary fables suggested that Wells began his literary career by extrapolating the pessimistic implications of evolutionary theory for humanity. However, in the scientific romances he published in the twentieth century, beginning with *The First Men in the Moon*, Wells started to dream of an end for – rather than the end of – humanity. Yet, as the following discussion of *The First Men in the Moon* reveals, Wells could not immediately create a blueprint for the future of humanity in simple or univocal terms.

Immediately discernible from the novel's plot is a significant reduction in the moments of narrative crisis which had characterised Wells's earlier scientific romances. Wells, in *The First Men in the Moon*, begins to adapt his narrative technique for the increasingly didactic purpose of his fiction in the twentieth century. This observation is not intended to detract from the literary quality of the novel. Indeed, Wells himself regarded the novel highly, terming it probably his 'best "scientific romance" '.[2] He also emphasised the status of *The First Men in the Moon* as a scientific work: 'Except for Cavorite, that substance opaque to gravitation, the writer has allowed himself no liberties with known facts; there is no impossibility in the tale' (ix).[3] The literary quality Wells himself identifies in the novel depends to a high degree on the appropriation of raw scientific data in the creation of moments of dramatic intensity and comedy.

The most significant example of Wells's skill in embedding scientific concepts within the fabric of the novel is the invention of the gravity-defying substance Cavorite. Despite his later claim that it has no basis in scientific theory, Wells's inspiration for this crucial plot device was in fact provided by contemporary research into the effects of gravitation. Richard Gregory, a friend of Wells's from his days as a student at the Normal School of Science who was working for the science periodical *Nature*, provided the author with an advance copy of an article by Professor Poynting on 'Recent Studies In Gravitation' during the period of the novel's construction in 1899.[4]

Appearing in *Nature* in August 1900, Poynting's article considers whether gravitation is subject to the same external influences as other known forces: 'we are at once led to inquire whether the lines of gravitative force are always straight lines radiating from or to the mass round which they centre, or whether, like electric and magnetic lines of force, they have a preference for some media and a distaste for others'.[5] Poynting reviews recent research which seeks to determine whether the force of gravity may be 'screened' like that of magnetism: 'If we enclose a magnet in a hollow box of soft iron placed in a magnetic field, the lines of force are gathered into the iron and largely cleared away from the inside cavity, so that the magnet is screened from external action.'[6] He cites the work of the American scientists Austin and Thwing, whose recreation of the force of gravity in miniature focused exactly upon detecting the possible influence of external forces: 'With screens of lead, zinc, mercury, water, alcohol or glycerine, the change in attraction was at most 1 in 500 [...] That is, they found no evidence of a change of pull with a change of medium.'[7] Considering such evidence, Poynting concludes that it is not possible to screen the force of gravity: 'Yet the work I have been describing is not a failure. We at least know something in knowing what qualities gravitation does not possess.'[8]

Wells's appropriation of Poynting's article underlines his serious intention to popularise science for the more general readership of *Strand Magazine*, in which *The First Men in the Moon* was serialised between December 1900 and August 1901. Bedford's explanation of the nature of Cavor's investigations functions as a fictional device that allows Wells to convey the object of contemporary gravitational research to a non-specialist audience. The narrator's statement that he intends to avoid the 'highly scientific language [...] that would bring upon me the mockery of every up-to-date student of mathematical physics in the country' (17) undoubtedly constitutes a necessary evasion of empirical reality in terms of upholding the fictional illusion of a substance that can defy gravity. Yet it can also be read as Wells's attempt to render the material forwarded by Gregory into a form of expression suitable for the target readership of the novel.

Wells achieves this by utilising Bedford's status as a non-scientist as a method of legitimising his own translation of Poynting's ideas into more accessible language. Having 'forgotten' the exact phrase Cavor applied to the property he hopes to isolate in a revolutionary new substance, Bedford makes use of the more comprehensible word 'opaque' to explain the capacity of a medium to screen the influence of a particular force: 'The object of Mr. Cavor's search was a substance that should be "opaque" – he used some other word I have forgotten, but "opaque" conveys the idea – to "all forms of radiant energy" ' (17). Wells's employment of the term 'radiant energy' enables him to relate to his general readership the essential idea of lines of force. His use of contemporary scientific ideas that have acquired a popular usage facilitates this process:

'Radiant energy,' he made me understand, was anything like light or heat or those Röntgen rays there was so much talk about a year or so ago, or the electrical waves of Marconi, or gravitation. All these things, he said, *radiate* from centres and act on bodies at a distance, whence comes the term 'radiant energy'. Now almost all substances are opaque to some form or other of radiant energy. Glass, for example, is transparent to light, but much less so to heat, so that it is useful as a fire-screen; and alum is transparent to light, but blocks heat completely. (17)

Having established the principle associated with lines of force, Wells can then popularise the nature and conclusions of contemporary experiments in gravitation:

You can use screens of various sorts to cut off the light or heat or electrical influence of the sun, or the warmth of the earth from anything; you can screen things by sheets of metal from Marconi's rays, but nothing will cut off the gravitational attraction of the sun or the gravitational attraction of the earth. (18)

Wells's emphasis on communicating the principles of experiments in gravitation to a wider readership here reveals a continuation from his earlier work, especially the article 'Popularising Science'. However, *The First Men in the Moon* indicates a significant development in Wells's conception of the scientific romance, since it constitutes his first fictional world state.[9] This takes the form of the subterranean lunar society of the Selenites.[10] While John Huntington has examined the implications of this global community, he does not proceed to link it to the fact that in 1901 Wells embarked on an entirely new form of endeavour.[11] Beginning serialisation in the *Fortnightly Review* in the April of that year, *Anticipations* constitutes Wells's first attempt to provide 'a rough sketch of the coming time, a prospectus, as it were, of the joint undertaking of mankind in facing these impending years'.[12] Significantly, the serialised version of *Anticipations* was accompanied by the subtitle 'An Experiment in Prophecy'. This means that its vision of the world of the year 2000 assumes the same provisional status as the fragmentary, incomplete messages which Cavor radios back to the earth from within the interior of the moon. The publication of *Anticipations* in book form in November 1901 meant that Edwardian readers could have understood the lunar society of the Selenites created by Wells in *The First Men in the Moon* as a version of the world state he envisaged in his sociological work.

Indeed, in a letter to Winston Churchill dated November 1901, Wells himself establishes a link between *The First Men in the Moon* and *Anticipations*. Responding to a short analysis of *Anticipations* sent to him by Churchill, Wells wrote that:

> My predominating people to come are to be 'educated not trained' and in your litany where it came to 'from the drum of all specialists' I too will most heartily join in the 'god [illegible word, perhaps finally] delivers us' with you. Indeed, in another book, The First Men in the Moon [...] I have been giving the specializer sort to the best of my ability.[13]

This passage reveals that Wells intended the Selenites – 'giving the specializer sort to the best of my ability' – to satirise specialisation. However, the lunar experts of *The First Men in the Moon* are unmistakeably endowed with certain traits that characterise the class of experts Wells foresees arising to prominence in *Anticipations*. Further, it is possible to consider that Cavor – the scientist-protagonist of the novel – represents the expert class portrayed in *Anticipations* as it exists in its nascent form in contemporary society.

In his characterisation of Cavor, Wells draws extensively on preexisting stereotypes concerning the 'man of science':

> He was a short, round-bodied, thin-legged little man, with a jerky quality in his motions; he had seen fit to clothe his extraordinary mind in a cricket cap, an overcoat, and cycling knickerbockers and stockings. Why he did so I do not know, for he never cycled and he never played cricket. It was a fortuitous concurrence of garments arising I know not how. He gesticulated with his hands and arms and jerked his head about and buzzed. He buzzed like something electric.

You never heard such buzzing. And ever and again he cleared his throat with a most extraordinary noise. (7)

Cavor's characterisation constitutes a significant development in Wells's portrayal of the scientist following the anarchic figure of Griffin in *The Invisible Man*. Critics have identified how his ruthless absent mindedness creates an affinity between Cavor and earlier figures such as Moreau and Griffin. Huntington, for example, notes that: 'Though his personality remains uncorrupted by the egomaniacal hatreds of Moreau and Griffin, he shares with them a blindness to the needs of society and to the consequences of his experiments'.[14] It is possible to supplement Huntington's account by stating that Cavor displays the exact disdain towards the system of exchange for scientific ideas as Griffin: ' "So much pettiness," he explained, "so much intrigue! And really when one has an idea – a novel, fertilising idea – I don't wish to be uncharitable, but –" ' (14).

It should be noted, however, that there is an element of comedy in Cavor's innocent ruthlessness that is entirely absent from the more intentional gruesome activities of Moreau and Griffin. This is particularly evident in the moment in which Cavor almost entirely depopulates the terrestrial globe with the first making of Cavorite: ' "Good heavens! Why, it would have squirted all the atmosphere of the earth away! It would have robbed the world of air!" ' (30).[15] Cavor's eccentricity emerges from the Swiftian stereotype of the scientist. Wells probably derived the otherworldliness of his protagonist from the voyage to Laputa in *Gulliver's Travels*. Interestingly Cavor's characterisation in this respect prefigures that of the experts in lunar society, which is also informed by Swift's voyage to Laputa. The fact that Cavor 'buzzed like something electric' further anticipates the Selenites in their status as machine-tenders.

With the similarity between Cavor and the lunar experts in mind, this Chapter examines the opposition between earthly and lunar society in the context of the concept of global unity established in *Anticipations*. Particularly, the analysis will focus upon the contrasting role of science in these two societies. Human society, it is argued, is characterised by a lack of application of science to the greater social fabric which reiterates Wells's statement in 'The Rediscovery of the Unique' that: 'Science is a match that man has just got alight'. The eccentric scientist Cavor is considered as a figure in whose hands science is only just beginning to reveal its potential as the force that Wells believes will emerge to shape the future destiny of humanity. His role as a theoretical man of science emphasises his shortcomings in comparison to that body of men Wells foresees as facilitating science and the scientific method throughout the world in *Anticipations*. The global co-operation of the Selenites is examined as a possible articulation of the world state of *Anticipations*, which has already undergone the process of segregation which must inevitably result from the application of science to every facet of human society. Although the Selenites are endowed with specific attributes that Wells foresees as characterising the twentieth century of *Anticipations*, it is important to emphasise here that he is not endorsing lunar society as a possible future for humanity. Indeed, the unsettling impact of Selenite society on the reader emerges from Wells's engagement with the satirical tradition of Jonathan Swift. The lunar society depicted in the novel is further considered as an arena in which Wells tests his emerging sociological ideas, since the organisation of the Selenites also foregrounds the complexities of the author's thought at the moment he wrote *The First Men in the Moon*.

In order to understand the didactic purpose fulfilled by Cavor's characterisation, it is necessary to review Wells's analysis of the emergence of the twentieth century in *Anticipations*. Wells begins *Anticipations* by examining how the improvements in transportation already apparent in the contemporary moment will inevitably lead to 'The Probable Diffusion Of Great Cities', as the distance commutable within a reasonable space of time increases. The primary focus of Wells's analysis in *Anticipations*, however, centres on the new social classes that have emerged as a consequence of the development of mechanism in the mid-eighteenth century:

> Correlated with the sudden development of mechanical forces that first began to be socially perceptible in the middle eighteenth century, has been the appearance of great masses of population having quite novel functions and relations in the social body, and together with this appearance such a suppression, curtailment, and modification of the older classes as to point to an entire disintegration of that system. The *facies* of the social fabric has changed, and – as I hope to make clear – is still changing in a direction from which, without a total destruction and rebirth of that fabric, there can never be any return.[16]

Wells identifies four 'Developing Social Elements' or classes whose beginnings are discernable in the social constitution of his day. The most striking of these is the shareholder. Unlike their predecessors the owners of 'real estate', shareholders are liberated from social responsibility due to the fact that 'share property is property that can be owned at any distance and that yields its revenue without thought or care on the part of its proprietor'.[17] However, the shareholder can never become the predominant social class, since it derives all of its members from pre-existing social groups: 'It is a class with scarcely any specific character-istics beyond its defining one of the possession of property and all the potentialities property entails, with a total lack of function with regard to that property.'[18] The second class to emerge since the mid-eighteenth century, which 'consists of people who have failed to "catch on" to the altered necessities the development of mechanism has brought about' is also deemed incapable of becoming the dominant social group.[19] A third class identified by Wells consists of a 'great number of non-productive persons living in and by the social confusion'.[20]

Wells then turns his attention to 'the really living portion of the social organism'.[21] Although engineers, men of science and medical professionals constitute an unorganised social myriad, Wells foresees the development in the coming years of the only emerging social elem-ent to possess 'a certain common minimum of education and intel-ligence, and probably a common-class consciousness – a new body, a new force, in the world's history'.[22] His statement to Churchill that 'My predominating people to come are to be "educated not trained"' refers to Wells's emphasis in *Anticipations* that 'this new, great, and expand-ing body of mechanics and engineers will tend to become an educated and adaptable class in a sense that the craftsmen of former times were not educated and adaptable'.[23] The adaptability of this class is a con-sequence of its possession of 'a common fund of intellectual training' which enables its members to 'get a grasp of that permanent something that lies behind the changing immediate practice'.[24] As the adaptabil-ity of this 'new force' begins to establish itself it will have a discern-ible influence on the more established sections of the community. This influence consists of a 'process of attraction' which constitutes the application of science to a diversity of social practices.[25]

Wells considers that the current intermingling of these nascent social classes accounts for the 'greyness' of contemporary life: 'The grey expanse of life to-day is grey, not in its essence, but because of the minute confused mingling and mutual cancelling of many-coloured lives.'[26] He is most interested in the expert since it is that class alone that will retain a functional role in the increasingly technological soci-ety of the future. Wells therefore encourages the conscious assumption of predominance by this 'really living portion of the social organism':

The practical people, the engineering and medical and scien-tific people, will become more and more homogenous in their fundamental culture, more and more distinctly aware of a common 'general reason' in things, and of a common difference from the less functional masses and from any sort of people in the past.[27]

His use of the phrase 'the social organism' indicates that, in *Anticipations*, Wells is modifying the work of Herbert Spencer. Although his ideas will be discussed later, it is worth noting here that in his essay, 'The Social Organism' (1860), Spencer outlines his development hypothesis which states that all evolution is characterised by a movement from homogeneity to heterogeneity, or from the simple to the complex.[28] In emphasising how the development of society beyond its existing confusion depends upon the increasing homogeneity of one particular social group, Wells is modifying Spencer's development hypothesis. Whereas Spencer insists that increasing heterogeneity is the unifying principle underlying all evolution, Wells is emphatic that increasing homogeneity of the expert class in his contemporary moment will lead to greater differentiation in the social organism of the future.

Despite his potential for future development, the expert is notoriously absent from the political sphere in the modern democratic state. When he is consulted by existing powers, 'The man of special equipment is treated always as if he were some sort of curious performing animal.'[29] Wells draws attention to the manner in which the expert is never fully active in the application of his particular skill: 'The gunnery specialist, for example, may move and let off guns, but he may not say where they are to be let off – some one a little ignorant of range and trajectory does that'.[30] Modern democracy, however, is for Wells only a transitional form of government. It constitutes the political equivalent of the 'greyness' which defines the current intermingling of emergent social classes. Its appearance was also the consequence of the social and mechanical changes of the eighteenth century. Modern democracy owes its existence solely to the fact that at its moment of conception, 'It was impossible then – it is, I believe, only beginning to be possible now – to estimate the proportions, possibilities, and inter-relations of the new social orders out of which a social organisation has still to be built in the coming years.'[31]

As a transitional form of government, democracy carries it own antithesis. In order to retain power, political parties must stimulate the patriotism of the voting public. 'The party conflicts of the future', writes Wells, 'will turn very largely on the discovery of the true patriot'.[32] However, the threat of warfare that inevitably accompanies the base nationalism unleashed by patriotism will prove crucial to the emergence of the expert class: 'But as a supersaturated solution will crystallise out with the mere shaking of its beaker, so must the new order of men come into visibly organised existence through the concussions of war.'[33] It is at the moment of warfare or other social crises that these men will decide to assume control of a society that relies increasingly upon their technological knowledge. They will choose to ignore the ruling powers of the democratic states, the ineffectual multitudes of society and formulate a new global order: 'as the embryonic confusion of the cocoon creature passes, into the higher stage, into the higher organism, the world-state of the coming years'.[34]

As indicated, Cavor's eccentric personality and unusual clothing draw upon pre-existing stereotypes concerning 'the man of science' as impractical and otherworldly. Yet the didactic purpose fulfilled by Cavor's characterisation in *The First Men in the Moon* is to point to the necessity for experts to apply their knowledge to the wider social fabric. Cavor's role as a theoretical man of science is emphasised at the outset of the novel in particular, and can be contrasted to the expert class Wells foresees arising to prominence in *Anticipations*, which has as one of its defining characteristics the practical application of science to other spheres of life. An astonished Bedford neatly summarises the lack of application which accompanies Cavor's scientific genius, having himself instantly recognised the vast potential of Cavorite:

> This astonishing little man had been working on *purely theoretical* grounds the whole time! When he said it was 'the most important' research the world had ever seen he simply meant it squared up so many theories, settled so much that was in doubt; he had troubled no more about the application of the stuff he was going to turn out than if he had been a machine that makes guns [emphasis added]. (20–1)

This analogy is highly significant, since it relates to Wells's point in *Anticipations* that while the expert's knowledge is often utilised in contemporary society, he has no control over its application.

The relationship between Bedford and Cavor implicit at the moment he states that 'He was to make the stuff and I was to make the boom' (22) parallels that between the expert and the democratically elected politician in *Anticipations*. Indeed, Wells's comment in *Anticipations* that 'The man of special equipment is treated always as if he were some sort of curious performing animal' is recalled in Bedford's initial preoccupation with Cavor: 'But he was very much in my mind, and it had occurred to me that as a sentimental comic character he might serve a useful purpose in the development of my plot' (11).

The fact that Cavorite has the potential to become ' "more universally applicable even than a patent medicine!" ' (22) underlines Cavor's shortcoming in comparison to the expert class of *Anticipations*. Bedford describes Cavor as 'childish', his only desire being that 'If he made it, it would go down to posterity as Cavorite or Cavorine and he would be made an F. R. S. and his portrait as a scientific worthy given away with *Nature*' (21). While Bedford's assessment undoubtedly emerges from his naked self-interestedness, it is clear that Wells – albeit for different reasons – agrees with his assessment of Cavor as 'childish'. In the light of Wells's insistence in *Anticipations* that the universal application of science is imperative to the development of human society in the twentieth century, Cavor is indeed responsible for manufacturing his revolutionary new substance.

Although tainted with the characteristic desire of a capitalist, Bedford appears also to speak for Wells addressing such members of the scientific community as Cavor when he implores: 'I tried to make him understand his duties and responsibilities in the matter – *our* duties and responsibilities in the matter' (21). The lack of cohesion in that community is recalled in Cavor's isolation from other men of science. Wells summarises his feelings concerning the state of present-day science in a statement which stems directly from that in the epigraph: 'He would have dropped this bombshell into the world as though he had discovered a new species of gnat, if it had not happened that I had come along. And there it would have lain and fizzled, like one or two other little things these scientific people have lit and dropped about' (21). Of course, in view of *Anticipations* the tendency of 'these scientific people' to merely light and drop 'one or two other things' has implications for society, since its progression beyond the 'greyness' which characterises the contemporary world depends entirely upon the increasing consciousness of experts as they form a coherent class.

Although he plays a pivotal role in the practical realisation of Cavorite, Bedford also represents the evolutionary competition which characterises the human species in the novel. The motives that underlie Bedford's enthusiasm for the entire Cavorite project relate to Wells's critique of those contemporaries who argue that the psychology of the capitalist constitutes an unalterable identity that has its origins in the primitive stages of human evolution. One such contemporary is Robert Wallace, whose article 'The Psychology of Capitalist and Labourer' appeared in the *Fortnightly Review* in 1893.[35]

Wallace begins by stating that capitalist and labourer respectively are to be considered fixed and separate types of being. He argues that, since these separate types of being were forged early in the evolution of the human species, social theorists – socialists included – must accept the fact that the capitalist constitutes a necessary identity that must inevitably find expression. Wallace identifies salient traits that distinguish the psychology of the successful capitalist from that of the labourer. For him, 'the capitalist is a being of vaster cupidity than the labourer. [...] He wants to possess all he sees, and his desires are really bounded only by the resources of the planet.'[36] Wallace is careful to distinguish the true capitalist from the 'shopkeeper' or 'miser'. Not to be confused with pure greed, the motive of the 'Titanic' capitalist 'is [a] delight in the large, in the magnificent, in the adaptation of gigantic means to corresponding ends'.[37] In the psychological type of the pure capitalist 'Size redeems from the petty and the mean'.[38]

Wells satirises the entire argument that the successful capitalist possesses an exclusive psychological constitution by endowing a failed businessman like Bedford with the type of imaginative traits outlined by Wallace. His 'delight in the large, in the magnificent, [and] in the adaptation of gigantic means to corresponding ends' is comically revealed the moment Bedford enthusiastically grasps the potential of Cavorite as a substance that might be marketed as a universally applicable substance: 'My first natural impulse was to apply this principle to guns and ironclads and all the material and methods of war and from that to shipping, locomotion, building, every conceivable form of human industry' (19–20). Bedford appears to underline his status as a 'true' capitalist since the 'Size [of his ambitions] redeems [him] from the petty and the mean'. The scope of his vision would appear to affirm Wallace's conception that the desires of the capitalist 'are really bounded only by the resources of the planet' since it not only includes 'a parent company and daughter companies, [with] applications to the right of us, [and] applications to the left' but culminates in 'one vast stupendous Cavorite Company [that] ran and ruled the world' (20).[39] Indeed, as Cavor's proposal to journey to the moon inspires his imagination, Bedford dreams of becoming a capitalist of 'Titanic' proportions unequalled in history. As his attention turns to the cosmic potential of Cavorite, Bedford's desires need no longer be 'bounded only by the resources of the planet', as he conjures up a vision through which Wells makes his most sardonic response to the type of personality classification offered by Wallace: 'Suddenly I saw as in a vision the whole solar system threaded with Cavorite liners and spheres *de luxe* [...] It wasn't as if it was just this planet or that – *it was all of them* [second emphasis added]' (38).

Bedford's aspirations for Cavorite in many senses prefigure the activities of Edward Ponderevo in *Tono-Bungay* (1909). Indeed his desire to make Cavorite ' "more universally applicable even than a patent medicine" ' directly anticipates that substance successfully marketed as a wonder drug in the later novel. While Ponderevo's schemes reach fruition, however, Bedford's aspirations amount to little. Wells thus undercuts the argument made by Wallace and others by separating Bedford's aspirations from his practical achievements. Thus while he possesses the psychological traits Wallace identifies as the exclusive property of the successful capitalist, Bedford acknowledges himself in the opening page of the novel that he was never destined to become a businessman: 'It may be there are directions in which I have some capacity; the conduct of business operations is not among these' (3).

As Huntington points out in his book *The Logic of Fantasy*, Bedford's return from the moon presents him with a potentially life changing perspective.[40] Rather than learn from this experience, however, 'when he returns to earth he sets about turning his information to profit, and the old Bedford, the con man who knows no other way of being, resumes'.[41] Bedford is in many ways a morally reprehensible character. This is emphasised by his lack of remorse concerning the boy who blasts off in the sphere: 'I must confess that hitherto I have not acknowledged my share in the disappearance of Master Tommy Simmons, which was that little boy's name' (209).[42] Bedford's lack of remorse in this instance fulfils a significant function in the novel. For his lack of morality underlines the fact that disregard for ethical principles can be uncovered in any strata of society, and is not exclusive to scientists like Cavor.

Bedford's competitiveness and lack of moral values invite the reader to question his reliability as a narrator. Bedford's claims are often only partially substantiated – if at all – within the frame of the novel. For example, he claims that: 'I think he [Cavor] underrates the part my energy and practical capacity played in bringing about the realisation of his theoretical sphere' (216). Yet Bedford's statement fails to account for the fact that he is also primarily responsible for the loss of Cavorite. In this particular instance, however, there is some truth in the narrator's claim. The presence of Bedford is to a large degree responsible for the practical realisation of Cavorite in the form of the sphere that lifts them into space.

T. S. Eliot later admired the novel's poetic quality and considered 'the description of sunrise on the moon' to be 'quite unforgettable'.[43] Commenting on the moment in which Bedford and Cavor observe awakening plant life in *The First Men in the Moon*, Patrick Parrinder observes that: 'The source of the sense of revelation which fills this passage is surely Wells's experience as a biology student.'[44] The connection Parrinder makes here between Wells's literary endeavour and his scientific training is instructive, for it testifies to the extensive care taken by Wells to construct a scientific frame for Bedford and Cavor's lunar adventures.

In a letter which accompanies the advance copy of Poynting's article, Gregory informs Wells that the surface gravity of the moon is approximately one sixth of that on the earth, and that consequently: 'A man who can step two feet here could with the same exertion step 12 feet on the moon, but I don't see how he could do it unless he had very long legs.'[45] In drawing imaginatively upon the information supplied to him by Gregory, Wells again underlines his serious intentions to popularise science for the periodical readership of *The First Men in the Moon*. The sense of wonder, adventure and comedy that characterises the descent of his dual protagonists onto the lunar surface also provides an effective vehicle enabling Wells to convey the probable effects of human beings walking on the moon.

Thus as Bedford takes his first overzealous step upon the lunar surface and is soon 'flying through the air', he reminds himself – and concurrently informs the popular readership – of the factors which account for the lesser gravitational force of the moon: 'I had forgotten that on the moon, with only an eighth part of the earth's mass and a quarter of its diameter, my weight was barely a sixth what it was on earth' (76). The popularisation of science in the novel was also facilitated by the illustrations which accompanied the serialisation of *The First Men in the Moon* in the *Strand Magazine*. One such illustration was used to support Wells's adaptation of Gregory's point that 'A man who could step two feet here could with the same exertion step 12 feet on the moon.' It depicts the moment where, having established that a stride that 'would have carried me a yard on earth; on the moon [...] carried me six' (78), Bedford 'realised my leap had been altogether too violent. I flew clean over Cavor's head, and beheld a spiky confusion in a gully spreading to meet my fall' (79) (see Illustration 6.1). The illustration contributes to the comedy of this amusing scenario, since it captures the instant where Bedford is already 'over Cavor's head' and advancing helplessly toward the 'spiky confusion': 'I hit a fungoid bulk that burst all about me, scattering a mass of orange spores in every direction, and covering me with orange powder' (79).

In the excitement of discovering their increased strength on the moon, Bedford and Cavor become 'Lost Men in the Moon', at which

Illustration 6.1   "I realized my leap had been too violent."
Source: Appeared in the January 1901 edition of the *Strand Magazine*.

point they encounter the Selenites. Intoxicated by eating the moon fungus, Cavor proclaims that he is not ' "going to crawl about on my stomach – on my vertebrated stomach!" ' for mere insects (101). Yet while Cavor's moment of aggression towards the Selenites is founded purely on zoological classifications, Bedford's plan to 'annex' the moon reveals a more politicised dimension to the discovery of a method of transportation to the moon:

> In some way that I have now forgotten my mind was led back to projects of colonisation. 'We must annex this moon,' I said. 'There must be no shilly-shally. This is part of the White Man's Burden. Cavor–we are–*hic*–Satap–mean Satraps! Nempire Caesar never dreamt. B'in all the newspapers. Cavorecia. Bedfordecia. Bedfordecia. Hic–Limited. Mean–unlimited! Practically.'
>
> Certainly I was intoxicated. I embarked upon an argument to show the infinite benefits our arrival would confer upon the moon. I involved myself in a rather difficult proof that the arrival of Columbus was, after all, beneficial to America. I found I had forgotten the line of argument I had intended to pursue, and continued to repeat 'sim'lar to C'lumbus' to fill up time. (100–1)

While Bedford and Cavor's lunar intoxication is undoubtedly one of the most hilarious moments in all of Wells's scientific romances, it also fulfils a function within the novel. This moment does not concur with Bedford's intoxicated proclamation of 'the infinite benefits our arrival would confer upon the moon'. Rather, it reveals the underpinnings of the competition and lack of organisation that are inherent in earthly society, which Bedford and Cavor threaten to introduce to the moon.

Bedford's comment that the moon might become a home for '"Our poor surplus population"' (99) establishes a link between imperialism, unemployment and overpopulation that was commonly made in the periodical press of the 1890s. In his article on 'The Unemployed', Arnold White proposes emigration as a solution to the problem of the unemployed.[46] Building on long-standing earlier debates, he points to the dangers of stifling 'in these small islands a population underfed and wrongly educated, [which] is to court an explosion'.[47] He suggests that the British government might partially alleviate the unemployment and overpopulation problem by policing tracts of land in Africa that could then receive the capable unemployed as emigrants. White informs his reader of the potential benefits of such an endeavour to Britain: 'Each female child emigrant from Great Britain is an envelope in which is the potentiality of five consumers of British clothes, ploughs, and other goods manufactured here.'[48] Thus Bedford's proposal to transform the moon into a home for '"our poor surplus population"' has political ramifications. His 'curiously benevolent satisfaction that there was such good food in the moon' (99) might be attributed to a vision of the alleviation of the suffering of his fellow countrymen. Perhaps his initial vision of a fleet of Cavorite liners could be supplemented with an idea of trade, with the moon providing future consumers of British goods.

Wells himself would not have agreed with Bedford's plans to 'annex' the moon, or indeed with his idea that the moon would provide an ideal home for the 'surplus' population of the British Empire. In accordance with his views in *Anticipations*, any 'scramble for the moon' would simply intensify the feeling of base nationalism that obstructed the emergence of the world state. In *Anticipations*, Wells is adamant that rather than competing with other nations for territorial expansion, the British Empire – together with the larger English-speaking Atlantic community of which it forms a part – provides the perfect foundation for the establishment of the world state.[49]

Despite his initial moment of aggression, Cavor remains deeply fascinated by the Selenites and begins to speculate on establishing communication with them. The Selenites do not possess the overwhelming malignancy of the Martians in *The War of the Worlds*, and this enables Wells to examine the whole question of communication with aliens in *The First Men in the Moon*. In order to attempt communication with the Selenites, Cavor recalls the principles of 'a paper by the late Professor Galton on the possibility of communication between the planets' (114).[50] This is a reference to an article written by Francis Galton entitled 'Intelligible Signals Between Neighbouring Stars', which was published in the *Fortnightly Review* in 1896.[51] In that article, Galton endeavoured to demonstrate that it was possible to devise signals 'that are *intrinsically* intelligible, so that the messages may be deciphered by any intelligent man, or other creature, who has made nearly as much advance in pure and applied science as ourselves [emphasis original]'.[52]

To demonstrate his point Galton provided a fictional account which 'suppose[s] that Mars began to signal, to the wonderment of our astronomers, who sent descriptive letters to the newspapers from day to day'.[53] The method that Galton envisaged being employed by the Mars creatures, in their attempt to establish intelligent communication with the earth, began with their identification of universal mathematical and geometrical truths, effected by means of a series of dots and dashes. Having established a mutual understanding of these universal truths, the Mars folk could then exchange sociological data with the earth, using the geometrical figures as a basis for picture drawing: 'The power of the method is easily seen by drawing any outline with dots at equal distances apart, and counting those dots'.[54]

In *The First Men in the Moon*, Cavor explicitly recalls Galton's proposed method of communication between planets: '"His idea was to begin with those broad truths that must underlie all conceivable mental existences and establish a basis on those"' (114). Remembering Galton's idea that by demonstrating '"for example, that the angles at the base of an isosceles triangle are equal, and that if the equal sides be produced the angles on the other side of the base are equal also [...] we should demonstrate our possession of a reasonable intelligence"' (114), Cavor determines a method of communicating with the Selenites: '"I might draw the geometrical figure with a wet finger or even trace it in the air"' (114).

In his method of enabling communication between Cavor and the Selenites, Wells again appears to have drawn on Galton's article. Phi-oo and Tsi-puff, the two Selenites appointed to attend Cavor for the duration of his stay in the moon, are able to make substantial progress with terrestrial speech by repeating certain words, indeed they 'mastered over one hundred English nouns at their first session' (233). The crucial factor in accelerating their comprehension of the English language is the employment of a lunar artist: 'Subsequently it seems they brought an artist with them to assist the work of explanation with sketches and diagrams – Cavor's drawings being rather crude' (233). Wells thus reveals his indebtedness to the sketch method employed in Galton's article.

In their tireless 24-hour activity, the Selenites extend the fascination with ants that Wells had implicitly revealed in the characterisation of the Martians in *The War of the Worlds*. Bedford makes explicit the analogy between the lunar community described by Cavor and a colony of ants:

> He does not mention the ant, but throughout his allusions the ant is continually brought before my mind, in its sleepless activity, its intelligence, its social organisation and, more particularly, the fact that it displays, in addition to the two forms, the male and the female, produced by all other animals, a great variety of sexless creatures – workers, soldiers, and the like, differing from one another in structure, character, power and use and yet all members of the same species. (226)

This statement could be related to a number of nineteenth-century studies of insect communities. Indeed, in a recent study, Charlotte Sleigh has examined Wells's work in the context of the contemporary fascination with insect communities.[55] However, she omits to investigate how John Lubbock's book on *Ants, Bees, and Wasps* (1885) appears to have specifically informed the characterisation of the Selenites and the construction of the lunar world they inhabit.[56] Wells's awareness of Lubbock's work is revealed in 'The Duration of Life', published in the *Saturday Review* in February 1895.[57] In that article, Wells noted how 'Sir John Lubbock kept a queen-ant alive for thirteen years' thus making an explicit reference to a passage in *Ants, Bees, and Wasps* which considered the duration of life among the insects studied.[58]

Like other nineteenth-century studies of the same subject, Lubbock's study of insects reveals the same fascination with non-human rationality displayed in contemporary discussions concerning the reasoning power of animals. Indeed, Lubbock claims that while the anthropoid apes remain closest to man in terms of bodily constitution: 'when we consider the habits of Ants, their social organisation, their large communities, and elaborate habitations; their roadways, their possession of domestic animals [...] it must be admitted that they have a fair claim to rank next to man in the scale of intelligence'.[59] Wells would no doubt have been attracted to Lubbock's claim that ants possess an alternative rationality to man: 'their [ants] mental powers differ from those of men, not so much in kind as in degree'.[60] He would perhaps have also appreciated the tantalising comment in the preface to Lubbock's book that, under more favourable conditions, ants 'may well be expected not only to manifest a more vivid life, but to develop higher powers'.[61] Wells utilises the more favourable conditions provided by the lesser gravitational pull of the moon, which has drastically reduced the restrictions on the development of the lunar brain, as a basis to make the Selenites – in Cavor's eyes at least – superior to man: 'And these Selenites are not merely colossally superior to ants, but, according to Cavor, colossally, in intelligence, morality and social wisdom, higher than man' (227).[62]

One of the most obvious relations of Selenite society to a colony of ants is its subterranean nature. In locating an entire civilisation within the interior of the moon, Wells overturns the dominant consensus in contemporary astronomical speculation concerning the condition of our satellite. This consensus is epitomised by the work of Lowell, who comments of the moon: 'For that body, from which we might hope to learn much, appears upon inspection to be, cosmically speaking, dead.'[63] It is by representing the moon as hollow that Wells effectively upholds his challenge to the dominant conception that it is 'cosmically speaking, dead': 'And if the moon is hollow, then apparent absence of air and water is, of course, quite easily explained' (224). Indeed, Wells's own conception that the structure of the moon is simply an inversion of that of the earth – 'The sea lies within at the bottom of the caverns, and the air travels through the great sponge of galleries, in accordance with simple physical laws' (224) – indicates that the novel provides a critique of anthropocentrism. There is an implication that the absence of speculation on the part of earthly astronomers regarding the possibility of the moon possessing an interior is a consequence of mankind's species arrogance: 'There was no necessity, said Sir Jabez Flap, F. R. S. [...] that we should ever have gone to the moon to find out such easy inferences' (224). Thus by entitling the novel *The First Men in the Moon*, Wells immediately emphasises the need to move beyond conceptions of the universe which focus exclusively upon the conditions of life for the species *homo sapiens*.[64]

There are more explicit analogies between the society of the Selenites and the ant community and its social habits as recorded in Lubbock's study. Lubbock notes how it 'has long been known that ants derive a very important part of their sustenance from the sweet juice excreted by aphides' and that it has been observed that they are the 'cows' of ants.[65] Lubbock is keen to emphasise the services which ants render aphids. This includes building the equivalent of 'cowsheds' for aphids in order to protect them. In *The First Men in the Moon*, the Selenites similarly derive sustenance from the mooncalves. Lubbock's emphasis on the protection ants provide for aphids finds resonance in the 'cowsheds' the Selenites build to shelter mooncalves from the lunar night: 'There is an enormous system of caverns in which the mooncalves shelter during the night' (222).

Considering the range of vision possessed by insects, Lubbock cautions that while it is commonly assumed that they see the world as human beings do, a 'little consideration, however, is sufficient to show that this is very far from being certain, or even probable'.[66] As he and Bedford face the potential hazard of crossing 'The Giddy Bridge', Cavor similarly comments on the different visual range possessed by the moon dwellers: ' "I don't believe they see as we do. I've been watching them. I wonder if they know this is simply blackness for us" ' (131).[67] Lubbock records details of a number of experiments he conducted in order to determine the sensory range of insects. In one such experiment he establishes that 'blue is the favourite colour of bees'.[68] The ' "everlasting blue" ' (223) which disturbs Cavor for the entire duration of his stay among the Selenites reveals the probable influence of Lubbock on Wells's choice of colour for the moon's interior.

Wells draws most explicitly upon Lubbock's work in his characterisation of the Selenites. Particularly, Wells utilises Lubbock's descriptions in *Ants, Bees, and Wasps* in order to substantiate the critique of anthropocentrism in the novel. Lubbock notes that ants possess one of two kinds of eyes: 'Large compound eyes, one on each side of the head; and ocelli, or so-called simple eyes.'[69] By endowing the Selenites with compound eyes, Wells frustrates the anthropocentric conceptions of his narrator. This is highlighted in the chapter 'The Selenite's Face', in which Bedford's confusion concerning the compound eyes of the first lunar inhabitant he scrutinises closely contributes to the horror of his recognition that 'the human features I had attributed to him were not there at all!' (106): 'There was no nose, and the thing had bulging eyes at the side – in the silhouette I had supposed they were ears' (107).

Bedford is not only shocked by the absence of human characteristics among the inhabitants of the moon, he is also unable to regard the Selenites as anything other than a threat to the domination of humanity. While Bedford represents the extreme evolutionary competition that characterises humanity, the Selenites represent evolutionary harmony. Wells again appears to have been informed by Lubbock here. In *Ants, Bees, and Wasps*, Lubbock observes the absence of conflict in the termite community, remarking that: 'This differentiation of certain individuals so as to adapt them to special functions seems to me very remarkable; for it must be remembered that the difference is not one of age or sex.'[70] Similarly, in *The First Men in the Moon*, Bedford comments specifically – in the passage cited above – on the even greater gradations among the Selenites, who differ 'from one another in structure, character, power and use and yet all [remain] members of the same species'.[71]

Concerning the specialisation of function among the Selenites, Bedford remarks that: 'The moon is indeed a kind of super-ant-hill' (227). The global co-operation of the Selenites can be related to the world state foreseen in *Anticipations*. While Wells was undoubtedly committed to the formation of the world state at the moment he wrote *The First Men in the Moon*, it would be a mistake to consider that he proposes the community of the Selenites as a possible future for humanity. Rather, Wells endows lunar society with certain characteristics emerging from his analysis of the probable direction of humanity in the twentieth century in *Anticipations* at the same time as he draws on the pre-existing tradition of satire. In his preface to the collected edition of the scientific romances, Wells recalls that: 'My early, profound and lifelong admiration for Swift, appears again and again in this collection'.[72] Nowhere is his indebtedness to Swift more apparent than in Wells's construction of the lunar community in *The First Men in the Moon*. Contemporary reviewers immediately identified the satirical dimension to the novel's plot. The anonymous reviewer in *Nature*, for example, noted how 'Mr. Wells sometimes allows himself a sly hint at terrestrial matters in describing lunar affairs'.[73] Perhaps the most accurate way of conceiving the lunar setting of *The First Men in the Moon* is as an arena in which Wells tests his embryonic sociological ideas, since Selenite society also reveals the ambiguities of the author's thought at the moment he wrote the novel.

Selenite society has perfected the social segregation that Wells identifies in *Anticipations* as an inevitable consequence of the progression of the twentieth century. This perfected segregation relates to an especially suggestive passage in chapter 4 of *Anticipations*, in which Wells describes how those developing social elements currently intermingled in contemporary life segregate to form the distinct classes of the coming century.

Wells begins the relevant passage by pointing to the increasing dissolution of universal moral values which will initiate the inevitable process of segregation, since 'it will only be with persons who have come to identical or similar conclusions in the matter of moral conduct and who are living in similar *ménages* [...] that really frequent and intimate intercourse can go on'.[74] Such a process of 'moral segregation' will, according to Wells, 'mean very frequently an actual local segregation'.[75] Wells thus foresees the co-existence of 'districts that will be clearly recognised and marked as "nice"' with 'fast regions, areas of ram-shackle Bohemianism, [and] regions of earnest and active work'.[76] He also considers that 'these segregations, based primarily on a difference in moral ideas and pursuits and ideals, will probably round off and complete themselves at last as distinct and separate cultures'.[77] Wells also speculates that the segregation of social groups might assume a physiological aspect: 'segregating groups will develop fashions of costume, types of manners and bearing, and even, perhaps, be characterised by a certain type of facial expression'.[78]

As inferred in my discussion of *Anticipations*, Wells uses colour as a metaphor to describe the social segregation of the twentieth century: 'Presently these tints and shades will gather together here as a mass of one colour, and there as a mass of another.'[79] The prevalence of the expert class to Wells's vision of the future is revealed by the fact that he identifies this emerging social element as the 'one colour [that] must needs have a heightening value amidst this iridescent display'.[80] For Wells, the culture of the expert will be defined in part by developing its own literature. Individual experts will be 'linked in professions through the agency of great and sober papers – in England the *Lancet*, the *British*

Medical Journal, and the already great periodicals of the engineering trades, foreshadow something, but only very little, of what these papers may be'.[81]

Wells's prediction that the segregations of the twentieth century 'will probably round off and complete themselves at last as distinct and separate cultures' finds ample resonance in the already segregated lunar society of *The First Men in the Moon.* The distinct culture of those Selenites appointed as mooncalf minders, for example, is characterised not only by such customs as the mooncalf lore but is more especially emphasised by the local 'dialect [which is] an accomplished mooncalf technique' (237). The physical characteristics of the mooncalf minders confirms Wells's speculation in *Anticipations* that the segregations of the twentieth century might ultimately assume a physiological dimension: 'He is trained to become wiry and active, his eye is indurated to the tight wrappings, the angular contours that constitute a "smart mooncalfishness"' (237).

The segregation of lunar society surpasses Wells's expectation in *Anticipations* 'that really frequent and intimate intercourse can go on' only between those individuals 'living in similar *ménages*'. The segregation of the lunar community portrayed in *The First Men in the Moon* into separate cultures has been perfected to such a degree of extremity that individual Selenites display considerable hostility to those members of society living outside their own particular social group. Thus the mooncalf minder 'takes at last no interest in the deeper part of the moon; he regards all Selenites not equally versed in mooncalves with indifference, derision, or hostility' (237). Similarly, the artist introduced to Cavor displays intense derision towards most other Selenites '"Hate most people. Hate all who not think all world for to draw. Angry. M'm. All things mean nothing to him–only draw"' (234).[82] The experts within Selenite society also finds 'his sole society [in] the other specialists in his own line', thereby recalling the point in *Anticipations* that experts will be 'linked in professions through the agency of great and sober papers'.

The segregation of lunar society is initially revealed in an early segment of Cavor's transmission, in which Bedford reflects upon the constitution of those Selenites living on the exterior of the moon: 'It would seem the exterior Selenites I saw were, indeed, mostly of one colour and occupation – mooncalf herds, butchers, fleshers and the like' (226–7). Immediately discernible in this statement is the fact that the colour used by Wells as a metaphor to describe the process of social segregation in *Anticipations* has become an actual physical characteristic which defines the distinct classes of moon-dwellers in *The First Men in the*

Moon.[83] The *ménage* characterised by those Selenites who are 'mostly of one colour and occupation' and who live on the exterior of the moon forms 'an actual local segregation' in a region which – as its population of 'mooncalf herds, butchers, fleshers and the like' indicates – is devoted to 'earnest and active work'.

The use of colour as a means of social segregation in the novel has unmistakeable racial connotations. In *Anticipations*, Wells foresees that a form of racial hierarchy will prove to be a crucial moment in the formation of the world state. There are parallels between the particularly harsh statements Wells makes concerning race in *Anticipations* and Bedford's competitive attitude towards the Selenites in *The First Men in the Moon*. One of the severest passages in *Anticipations* concerns Wells's examination of the problem posed to the emergence of the New Republic by the ever multiplying number of rejected among the white and yellow races, to which 'have been added a vast proportion of the black and brown races'.[84] Wells considers that 'collectively those masses will propound the general question, "What will you do with us, we hundreds of millions who cannot keep pace with you?"'[85] Similarly, it was their number and capacity for rapid reproduction which made insects such a threat to human domination. Sleigh notes that: 'The most frightening thing about insects was probably their sheer number.'[86] Given that the overwhelming numbers among an alien society which is construed as a potential obstruction to human progress is a factor in each case, it is unsurprising to uncover parallels in the manner in which Wells and Bedford conceive non-whites and the Selenites respectively. Hence in *Anticipations*, Wells stresses that answering the question posed by rapid multiplication among the 'vast proportion of the black and brown races' will constitute a crucial moment in the formation of the world state: 'If the New Republic emerges at all it will emerge by grappling with this riddle; it must come into existence by the passes this Sphinx will guard.'[87] The fear of outnumbering implicit in Wells's euro-centric views on race in *Anticipations* is echoed in the equally dramatic attitude Bedford displays towards the Selenites in *The First Men in the Moon*. Undoubtedly motivated by what Sleigh has identified as the horror conjured up by 'the image of mass insect invasion',[88] Bedford envisages a battle for domination between humanity and the Selenites, 'a strange race with whom we must inevitably struggle for mastery' (245).

The entire notion of racial hierarchy extends Wells's conception of the efficient state in *Anticipations*. In order to achieve the level of efficiency necessary to compete in the twentieth century, a nation 'must foster and accelerate that natural segregation' of social groups envisaged by Wells.[89] This will enable the successful nation to produce a substantial number of intellectually active people of all sorts. That lunar society has successfully accelerated 'that natural segregation' into distinct social groups reveals that it constitutes a model of the efficient state concurrently advocated by Wells in his sociological work.

At the head of his efficient world state in *Anticipations* are Wells's New Republicans. Wells's lunar experts, like his New Republicans, trace their indebtedness to Plato, and more especially the Greek philosopher's idea of the non-democratic elite that is the Guardian class: ' "These beings with big heads to whom the intellectual labours fall, form a sort of aristocracy in this strange society, and at the head of them, quintessential of the moon, is that marvellous gigantic ganglion the Grand Lunar" ' (237).

Whereas the future prevalence of his class is discernable only in its nascent form in contemporary human society, the expert has successfully attained a 'heightening value' amidst the colours that, quite literally, characterise the different social groups of lunar society. Unlike their earthly counterpart Cavor, the lunar experts apply their scientific knowledge to the wider social fabric. The lunar mathematician, for example, finds that 'his one delight lies in the exercise and display of his faculty, [and] his one interest in its *application* [emphasis added]' (236).

While notoriously absent from the political sphere of contemporary human society, the expert participates directly in the administration of Selenite society. Of the three classes of lunar experts – the administrators, the experts and the erudite – it is the administrators who assume responsibility for social organisation. Wells had in *Anticipations* criticised those 'obsolete' areas of administration that continue to be applied to the territorial boundaries of every country in the world without 'the slightest reference to the practical revolution in topography that the new means of transit involve'.[90] The persistence of such boundaries disregards the increasingly global nature of trade as well as transportation:

> The nations and boundaries of to-day do no more than mark claims to exemptions, privileges, and corners in the market – claims valid enough to those whose minds and souls are turned towards the past, but absurdities to those who look towards the future as the end and justification of our present stresses.[91]

However, as an already established world state, the community of the Selenites has successfully adjusted its administrative areas to account for 'the practical revolution in topography' that must inevitably have an impact on the organisation of human society.[92] Indeed, the administrators in Selenite society who are 'responsible each for a certain cubic content of the moon's bulk' (238), closely conform to Wells's ideal type of administrator as expressed in *Anticipations*:

> The man who has concerned himself with the public health [...] or with the vital matters of transport and communication, if he enter the official councils of the kingdom at all, must enter ostensibly as the guardian of the free and independent electors of a specific district that has long ceased to have any sort of specific interests at all.[93]

It should be noted, however, that the conception of the efficient state Wells advances in *Anticipations* is not entirely without irony. Wells was subject to a barrage of hostile criticism in response to the publication of *Anticipations*. *The Daily Telegraph*, for instance, concluded that he 'advocates such extreme doctrines as the lethal chamber for the criminal and the lunatic' and 'praises the suicide of the melancholic, diseased or helpless persons'.[94] In a response to such criticism, Wells protested to the Editor of *Clarion* that his publication's review of *Anticipations* 'quotes passages that are couched in a vein of savage irony as though they were my heart's desire'.[95] His protestations of irony would be unlikely to convince those modern commentators who rate Wells too limitedly and read select passages of *Anticipations* as though they were Wells's only remarks on eugenics. However, the passages of *Anticipations* in question work in the tradition of Jonathan Swift's 'A Modest Proposal' (1729).[96] 'A Modest Proposal' constitutes Swift's sardonic response to the problem of poverty in Ireland. It concerns the author's proposal for a scheme to prevent the children of the poor – and indeed their parents – from being a burden to society. Swift proposes that, since babies provide a plentiful source of nutrition, the children of the poor should be sold as food to the wealthier classes: 'A child will make two dishes at an entertainment for friends, and when the family dines alone, the fore or hind quarter will make a reasonable dish, and seasoned with a little pepper or salt will be very good boiled on the fourth day'.[97] Swift ironically suggests that his 'modest proposal' would not only allow those landlords purchasing babies as food to gain the esteem of their tenants but that it would also prevent the child's mother from being a burden to others: 'Thus the Squire will learn to be a good landlord and grow popular among his tenants, the mother will have eight shillings net profit, and be fit for work until she produces another child.'[98]

Somewhat like Swift's 'modest proposal', Wells's solution to the difficulty raised by the 'People of the Abyss' constitutes a sardonic response to the fears of his contemporary moment. Regarding the obstruction to progress apparently posed by the proliferation of the 'unfit', Wells defines the efficient state of the future as one which 'resolutely picks over, educates, sterilises, exports, or poisons its People of the Abyss'.[99] In a highly Swiftian moment, Wells satirically suggests eradicating large portions of humanity as a means of foregrounding the inadequacy of the entire concept of the 'unfit', which obscures the material inequalities in society. Swift's notion that the mothers of those children sold as food can return to work – thereby reducing the burden on the remainder of society – finds ample resonance in Wells's statement that the nation which 'turns the greatest proportion of its irresponsible adiposity into social muscle [...] will certainly be the ascendant or dominant nation before the year 2000'.[100]

The entire constitution of lunar society is inextricably bound with Wells's satirical purpose. The characterisation of the lunar expert, for example, fulfils a double function in the novel. In addition to revealing the prevalence of the expert in Selenite society, the more cerebral of the lunar experts are obviously indicative of Wells's intentions to chastise the arrogance of earthly intellectuals: ' "In front and behind came his bearers, and curious, almost trumpet-faced, news disseminators shrieked his fame" ' (239).

Part of Swift's satirical intention in the voyage to Laputa in *Gulliver's Travels* was to emphasise how their preoccupation with science prevented the educated population of this flying island from participating fully in social life: 'it seems, the minds of these people are so taken up with intense speculations, that they can neither speak, nor attend to the discourses of others, without being roused by some external taction upon the organs of speech and hearing'.[101] Wells's lunar experts are similarly immersed in their own private speculations to the detriment of genuine social interaction: ' "The experts for the most part ignore me completely, even as they ignore each other, or notice me only to begin a clamorous exhibition of their distinctive skill" ' (238). That the attention of the inhabitants of Laputa must be aroused by some external taction finds resonance in the description of the erudite class of lunar expert: ' "The erudite with very few exceptions are rapt in an impervious and apoplectic complacency from which only a denial of their erudition can rouse them" ' (238–9).

In order to engage in conversation each eminent individual in Laputa employs a flapper, a person who uses a bladder to gently gain the attention of the intended interlocutor. This flapper must frequently accompany his master on walks 'because he is always so wrapped up in cogitation, that he is in manifest danger of falling down every precipice, and bouncing his head against every post'.[102] The danger posed by physical obstructions to the preoccupied individual in lunar society is revealed by a highly Swiftian moment in which Cavor encounters the expert who assists in establishing communication: ' "He entered in a preoccupied manner, stumbling against a stool, and the difficulties that arose had to be presented to him with a certain amount of clamour and hitting and pricking before they reached his apprehension" ' (233–4).

Inspired by Gulliver's audience with the King of Brobdingnag in *Gulliver's Travels*, Wells utilises Cavor's interview with the Grand Lunar as a means of reinstating the type of critique of contemporary society outlined in *Anticipations*. Thus the Grand Lunar reveals his disdain for the democratic method sketched by Cavor by his action of ordering ' "cooling sprays upon his brow" ' (258). Cavor's attitude towards the Grand Lunar indicates the limitations of his narrative. Whereas Bedford's account is prejudiced by his naked self-interestedness, Cavor's willingness to submit to the rationality of the Selenites invites the reader to question the objectivity of his narrative. Notably, Cavor's eagerness to ingratiate himself with the Grand Lunar indicates his readiness to distort information. This is revealed as he responds to the astonishment of the Grand Lunar that – despite not having different shapes to fit them to their distinctive functions – men must vary from one another a great deal: ' "In order to bring myself into *a closer harmony with his preconceptions*, I said that his surmise was right [emphasis added]" ' (259).

Yet as well as providing insights which empower the reader to determine the unreliability of the protagonist's narrative, the section of the novel dealing with this interview enables Wells to effect an additional critique of Cavor's lack of consciousness as a member of the expert class. Hence, Cavor's statement that ' "our science was growing by the united labours of innumerable little men" ' (260) assumes a marked irony in the light of his own conduct. Cavor's unwillingness to associate with his fellow researchers and his reticence to apply science mean that he is not contributing to the increasing class consciousness that will enable those 'innumerable little men' to emerge as the dominant social constituent of tomorrow. The fact that the Grand Lunar ' "was greatly impressed by the folly of men in clinging to the inconvenience of diverse tongues" ' (261) also relates to Wells's reinstatement of his critique of Cavor in this section of the novel. Having established in *Anticipations* the inevitability of the world state, Wells then considers those factors that determine which nations are most likely to emerge dominant in its formation. By far the most significant factor in this determination centres on 'The Conflict of Languages'. While many languages compete in the world, it is for Wells that which produces the greatest proportion of scientific literature that will emerge to dominate the world state since 'the decisive factor in this matter is the amount of science and thought the acquisition of a language will afford the man who learns it'.[103]

While Wells himself would campaign for the English-speaking countries to lead the formation of this world state, he nonetheless laments the lack of serious scientific literature produced in English: '[It is] a fact of very great significance that the actual number of books published in English is less than French or German, and that the proportion of serious books is conspicuously less.'[104] However, Wells does envisage a concerted effort to publish scientific work in English with the result 'that the whole functional body of human society would read, and perhaps even write and speak, our language'.[105] Examined in the light of these considerations in *Anticipations*, Cavor's refusal to enter the existing system of scientific publication threatens Wells's campaign to establish English as the dominant global language. In order for the English language to form the linguistic foundation of the world state that he apparently promises in his statement to the Grand Lunar that ' "Our States and Empires are still the rawest sketches of what order will some day be" ' (261), it is imperative that scientists such as Cavor publish substantially.

As indicated, Wells's emphasis on the need for increasing homogeneity amongst experts such as Cavor modifies Spencer's development hypothesis. The characterisation of the Selenites can be examined as a more direct response on the part of Wells to Spencer's notion of a single principle governing all evolution. In 'The Social Organism', Spencer notes the essential simplicity of the lowest living forms, Protozoa in the animal kingdom and Protophyta in the vegetal kingdom. Although these cells often congregate together, Spencer insists that they do not form societies in the strictest sense since: 'there is no subordination of parts among them – no organization. Each of the component units lives by and for itself'.[106] The lack of mutual dependence in the lowest form of evolved life is paralleled in the impermanence of group associations in the primitive stage of human evolution. The absence of specialised function in these initial groups of cells is reciprocated in the lack of organisation in early humanity: 'We see nothing beyond an undifferentiated group of individuals, forming the germ of a society; just as in the homogeneous groups of cells above described, we see only the initial stage of animal and vegetal organization.'[107]

Spencer next points to how in the *Physalia*, 'instead of that tree-like group of similar individuals forming the original type of the class, we have a complex mass of unlike parts fulfilling unlike duties'.[108] Similarly, this differentiation upon differentiation is precisely what occurs in the evolution of society: 'the several sections, at first alike in structures and modes of activity, gradually become unlike in both – gradually become mutually dependent parts, diverse in their natures and functions'.[109] For Spencer the phrase 'physiological division of labour' can not only be used to describe the increased specialisation of function of parts in the highly evolved organism but also to denote the analogous economic division of labour in the civilised society.

Spencer insists that increased specialisation of function constitutes an integral part of evolution: 'Not only is all progress from the homogenous to the heterogeneous; but at the same time it is from the indefinite to the definite.'[110] The increased specialisation of parts which accompanies evolution means that, as is the case with the interdependent parts of the living body, the constituent elements of the social organism are mutually dependent.

His use of the term 'physiological division of labour' indicates the economic dimension of Spencer's development hypothesis. He stresses that 'while citizens are locomotive in their private capacities, they are fixed in their public capacities'.[111] This means that although he may make the occasional journey, a farmer will continue to produce in that specific function. Spencer's development hypothesis upholds the argument against state interference elsewhere in his writings, since the inequality that results from specialisation of function is crucial to the growth of society.

Wells's construction of lunar society might well have been informed by Spencer's development hypothesis. The specialisation, or heterogeneity, of the Selenites is a consequence of the moulding of each individual until his or her personal identity becomes inextricable from the social role he or she is to fulfil. Like the interdependent parts of a living body in Spencer's thesis, the various elements of the lunar 'social organism' are also mutually dependent. This is emphasised by the way in which the meat produced by those Selenites who specialise in working with the mooncalves – fleshers and herders – is transferred in balloons to the interior of the moon, thus providing sustenance for those fulfilling a different specialist function.

The 'physiological division of labour' has become an actual attribute of the Selenites. Hence, Cavor remarks of certain members of the operative class: ' " 'Machine hands,' indeed some of these are in actual fact – it is no figure of speech"' (240). Such passages in the novel can be read as a sardonic response from Wells to Spencer's idea that men remain fixed in their public capacities. For the fact that the entire physiology and psychology of each Selenite is inextricable from his or her public capacity means that, as is implied by Spencer's model (to Wells at least), there is no scope for social mobility in the moon.

In 'The So-Called Science of Sociology', an article published in the *Independent Review* in May 1905, Wells severely criticises Spencer's development hypothesis.[112] He writes of Spencer that: 'he believed that individuality (heterogeneity) was and is an evolutionary product from an original homogeneity; and the thought that it might be inextricably in the nature of things probably never entered his head'.[113]

The characterisation of the Selenites appears to have been deliberately contrived to emphasise the limitations of the development hypothesis as a model for the evolution of humanity. This is emphasised by the ridiculous degree of specialisation among the Selenites. The construction of those Selenites who exist solely to replace the abortive physical powers of the lunar intellectuals in particular recalls Wells's criticism that Spencer continues to stress increasing heterogeneity 'until at last the brain reeled at the aggregation': 'Apart from their controlling intelligence, these subordinates are as *inert and helpless as umbrellas in a stand* [emphasis added]' (239).

There is a moment in the novel which opposes the evolutionary harmony of the Selenites to the competitive ethic of humanity. This occurs in the chapter 'The Fight in the Cave of the Moonbutchers' in which Bedford relentlessly attacks the Selenites. While this moment undoubtedly highlights his xenophobia towards the aliens, Bedford's actions also emphasise the superiority of a non-specialised evolutionary adaptability. Thus while the Selenite soldiers are able to perform only within the limits of a single specialised function, Bedford is able to improvise and use his jacket as a shield against the arrows of his opponents, thereby revealing his adaptability. This moment is important since it reinstates the didactic purpose of *The Time Machine*: that an element of risk and competition is essential to the continuing development of the human species.[114]

Lunar society seems deliberately contrived to highlight the failings of the Selenites. Like the King of Brobdignag in his interview with Gulliver, the Grand Lunar not only provides an organ for criticising the behaviour of *homo sapiens* but also concurrently highlights the shortcomings of his own species. Particularly his comment that '"from the solidity of the earth there had always been a disposition [among the

Selenites] to regard it as uninhabitable"' (255) reveals that the inhabitants of the moon are constrained by a species centred conception of the universe that performs an identical function to the anthropocentrism which characterises humanity in the novel.

It is through Cavor's reflections upon lunar education that Wells most explicitly draws attention to the shortcomings of the social organisation of the Selenites. The educators of the young in lunar society constitute a partial realisation of the ideal teachers envisaged in *Anticipations*. Wells insists in his first primarily sociological work that 'The shabby-genteel middle-class schoolmaster of the England of today [...] with his smattering of Greek, his Latin that leads nowhere, his fatuous mathematics, [and] his gross ignorance of pedagogics' will be superseded in the coming century by teachers who 'will be skilled and educated men'.[115]

Although the instructors of the young in the moon possess the educational expertise foreseen in *Anticipations*, Cavor emphasises the manner in which Selenite education restricts individual freedom of choice. While he attempts to justify the educational practices of the Selenites by appealing to scientific objectivity, Cavor admits that these methods '"have affected me disagreeably"' and that: '"That wretched-looking hand sticking out of its jar seemed to appeal for lost possibilities"' (241).

The lost potential by which Cavor is so deeply disturbed reveals that Wells encounters a difficulty faced by all educational reformers attempting to stimulate the development of individual talent. That is, the question of the extent to which it is legitimate to encourage the development of an individual's particular aptitude at the expense of their remaining faculties. There is, however, a further aspect of lunar education which reveals the difficulties Wells creates for himself. Cavor reports on how the Selenites have apparently supplanted natural selection with a process of artificial education which has indeed taken an organic form: 'All knowledge is stored in distended brains much as the honey-ants of Texas store honey in their distended abdomens. The lunar Somerset House and the lunar British Museum Library are collections of living brains' (238). The horrific image of the lunar brain-library concurs with the unsettling effect that lunar society has on the reader of the novel. Yet it also constitutes a perverse articulation of the 'acquired factor' of mankind that Wells had extensively argued for.[116] That this is the case indicates that at the time of writing *The First Men in the Moon*, Wells is yet to forge his conception of artificial education into a coherent social policy.[117]

The compression of individuality that occurs in Selenite society indicates another difficulty faced by Wells at the moment of writing. Cavor remarks on the uniqueness of each lunar inhabitant: 'Indeed, there seemed not two alike in all that jostling multitude. They differed in shape, they differed in size!' (229). The unique nature of each Selenite can be construed as an expression of a principle Wells first outlined in his earliest piece of published journalism, which was of course 'The Rediscovery of the Unique'. As its title suggests, the article is devoted to the assertion of a single principle: 'In a sentence it is, *All being is unique*, or, nothing is strictly like anything else.'[118] For Wells, no two items – he cites marbles, coins, and bricks as examples – are identical. While he acknowledges this principle might appear obvious, Wells insists it has far reaching implications for understanding how humans construct an apprehension of the world. Although the classification of objects and even abstract concepts into categories is necessitated by the limited capacity of the human mind to make sense of the objective world, it distorts an infinity of small differences: 'It implies, therefore, that we only arrive at the idea of similar beings by an unconscious or deliberate disregard of an infinity of small differences.'[119] This means that, strictly speaking, logic and other forms of classification are inaccurate. Number, for example, involves the inaccurate replication of a succession of unique objects.

While the characterisation of the Selenites explicitly foregrounds their uniqueness, that same uniqueness is compressed to the extent that is necessary to maintain the efficiency of lunar society, so that each being becomes as Cavor puts it: ' "a perfect unit in a world machine" ' (237). Hence, in *The First Men in the Moon* Wells encounters the difficulty of reconciling the scope for individual development demanded by his own insistence on the unique, with efficiency of social organisation.

The entire paradox in this instance is prefigured in 'A Slip Under the Microscope', a short story first published in the *Yellow Book* in 1895. Significantly, this piece was later collected in the same volume of the *Atlantic Edition* of his works as *The First Men in the Moon*, under the subtitle *Some More Human Stories*, which means the two were linked in Wells's mind. As the subtitle suggests, 'A Slip Under the Microscope' provides a more recognisable terrestrial setting in which to explore the theme of how the compression of individuality often results from efficient organisation.

'A Slip Under the Microscope' concerns the fortunes of William Hill, who – rather like Wells in his own student days – is an aspiring young man of humble social origins who has won a place at the Normal School of Science thanks to the proliferation of government-funded scholarships: 'Hill was the son of a Landport cobbler, and had been hooked by a chance blue paper the authorities had thrown out to the Landport Technical College.'[120] There is little doubt that, in the context of the predominantly bourgeois cohort of students to which he belongs, Hill is unique. Yet Hill's uniqueness is compressed at the precise moment his individuality is set to flourish. Accidentally undertaking a prohibited action, Hill confesses to his Professor that he has moved the microscope slide during an examination. Although privately sympathetic to his case, Hill's tutor informs him that: 'Professors in this College are machines [...] I am a machine, and you have worked me' (417). The professor's reference to himself as 'a machine' which Hill has 'worked' prefigures Cavor's description of each Selenite as 'a perfect unit in a world machine'. As is the case in the later novel, the efficient organisation of the college in 'A Slip Under the Microscope' results in the compression of individuality. For Hill's confession 'works' the regulations that result in his expulsion from the college, thereby stunting his imaginative liberty.

Returning to *The First Men in the Moon*, Wells appears to have been aware of this contradiction. Crucially, there can be no mistake that it is a dispute over roles that causes the accident which leads to the first making of Cavorite:

> But it chanced that, unknown to Cavor, dissension had arisen among the men about the furnace-tending. Gibbs, who had previously seen to this, had suddenly attempted to shift it to the man who had been a gardener, on the score the coal was soil, being dug, and therefore could not possibly fall within the province of a joiner; the man who had been a jobbing gardener alleged, however, that coal was a metallic or ore-like substance, let alone he was cook. But Spargus insisted on Gibbs doing the coaling, seeing that he was a joiner and that coal is notoriously fossil wood. (24)

A dispute over roles is possible only when social function and individual identity remain separate. For all its inefficiency in comparison to the highly specialised society of the Selenites, it is the maintenance of imaginative liberty that is ultimately responsible for generating the most ingenious application of science in either of the opposing worlds represented in *The First Men in the Moon*, Cavorite. That the application of Cavorite is a direct consequence of the above dispute over roles reveals that Wells has yet to reconcile the need for the efficient management of society with individual liberty. He would of course later attempt to resolve this contradiction in *A Modern Utopia*.

To conclude, the opposing societies created in *The First Men in the Moon* relate to Wells's earliest articulation of the world state in *Anticipations*. The human society represented in the novel considers those factors that obstruct the formation of the world state as well as foregrounding the competition inherent in the human species. It is also a society characterised by a lack of application of science to the wider social fabric. The subterranean lunar society of the Selenites, conversely, constitutes a tentative articulation of the world state. However, its satirical undertones indicate that Wells does not endorse lunar society. Rather, the community of the Selenites functions as an arena in which he tests his sociological ideas, since lunar society foregrounds the ambiguities and complexities of Wells's thought at the moment he wrote the novel. Such complexities include the fact that Wells has yet to reconcile individual freedom with efficient social organisation. This is an issue that he would return to in *A Modern Utopia*. While Wells does not endorse Bedford's capitalism or his extreme xenophobia, it is equally apparent that neither does he fully endorse the social harmony of the Selenites. Bedford's adaptability is indicative of the author's belief that risk and competition are essential to the continued evolution of the human species, and prefigures the 'kinetic' world order of *A Modern Utopia*.

7
The Limits of a Sociological Holiday: Social Progress in *A Modern Utopia*

While *A Modern Utopia* continues the ancient tradition of utopian writing, Wells is keen at the outset to stress its distinctly modern aspect:

> The Utopia of a modern dreamer must needs differ in one fundamental aspect from the Nowheres and Utopias men planned before Darwin quickened the thought of the world. Those were all perfect and static States, a balance of happiness won for ever against the forces of unrest and disorder that inhere in things. One beheld a healthy and simple generation enjoying the fruits of the earth in an atmosphere of virtue and happiness, to be followed by other virtuous, happy, and entirely similar generations until the Gods grew weary. Change and development were dammed back by invincible dams for ever. But the Modern Utopia must be not static but kinetic, must shape not as a permanent state but as a hopeful stage leading to a long ascent of stages. Nowadays we do not resist and overcome the great stream of things, but rather float upon it. We build now not citadels, but ships of state.[1]

For Wells, social progress post-Darwin demands that *homo sapiens* must continually adapt to its environment. Hence, the modern Utopia is necessarily 'kinetic' – and therefore 'must shape not as a permanent state but as a hopeful stage leading to a long ascent of stages' – precisely because it recognises the futility of attempting to overcome 'the forces of unrest and disorder that inhere in things'. Since these forces also exert an influence over the development of humanity, which can no longer be eternally 'dammed back by invincible dams', selection – both biological and artificial – is essential to social progress in *A Modern Utopia*.

Wells intends his conception of a 'kinetic' Utopia as a definite contribution to the emerging discipline of sociology. In 'The So-Called Science of Sociology', Wells argues vigorously against the positivist conceptions of the discipline advanced by Comte and Spencer. He reasons instead that the proper object of sociology is the creation of ideal societies against which the existing social organisation can be measured. In short, he argues for utopianism: 'I think, in fact, that the creation of Utopias – and their exhaustive criticism – is the proper and distinctive method of sociology.'[2] Wells's didactic intention to critique existing societies in *A Modern Utopia* is reflected in a change in the narrative strategy from his earlier scientific romances.

In *A Modern Utopia*, Wells adapts his narrative strategy to allow for the heavily didactic purpose of the work. The moments of crisis that are still to some extent present in *The First Men in the Moon* are entirely absent from *A Modern Utopia*. Whereas the transfer to another time or place in the early scientific romances is best described as fearful or overwhelming for the protagonist involved, the narrator of this fiction remains deeply fascinated by Utopia. Such a transformation is in fact necessary since a protagonist engaged in moments of crisis cannot be adequately used to delineate the authorial intention that in many senses emerges from Wells's engagement with sociological debates.

To conceive the narrator as a mere mouthpiece, however, would be to radically understate Wells's achievement in creating a complex narrative structure for *A Modern Utopia*. In 'A Note To The Reader' which accompanied the first edition, Wells wrote that: 'I am aiming throughout at a sort of shot-silk texture between philosophical discussion on the one hand and imaginative narrative on the other.'[3] Therefore, he intended *A Modern Utopia* to be read as something of a speculative fiction. A notable characteristic of many recent accounts of the work is the unwillingness on the part of critics to consider Wells's attempt at 'philosophical discussion' in the light of his concurrent novelistic endeavour.[4] This is unfortunate, because much of the comedy and irony of *A Modern Utopia* emerges from the opposition between the narrator's speculations concerning Utopia and the reality of the world he now finds himself in. In his book on *Utopianism* (1991), Krishan Kumar emphasises how the utopian writer is often burdened with a kind of 'double vision'. He not only 'looks down from utopian heights with a sometimes exasperated or pitying mien but more often with comic relish for the follies and vanities of his own world', he also 'looks up from his own world with a tragic sense of the unattainability of the ideal'.[5] Such a double perspective means invariably that 'there is no overriding sense that the one world must, or could, be made to conform to the other'.[6] For Kumar, the finest utopian writing is characterised by a 'high tension between the ideal and the real' and which 'is still to be found powerfully present in Wells's *A Modern Utopia*' among other examples of the genre.[7] The conformity of *A Modern Utopia* to the key features of the finest utopian writing identified by Kumar is a consequence of the artistic framework Wells imposes upon himself in the work. In this *Sociological Holiday*, to appropriate the subtitle given to the version of the work serialised in the *Fortnightly Review* between October 1904 and April 1905, Wells permits himself a 'free hand' with the institutions, culture and literature of humanity. While he acknowledges that radical alterations in human culture are characteristic of all utopian writings, Wells restricts himself to the capacities of those individuals alive in 1905. This means that although the alternative earth out beyond Sirius to which his protagonists are transferred by an instantaneous act of the imagination possesses a different history to earth, it is identical in terms of its physical constitution and the individuals who inhabit it. Each person alive on earth thus possesses a utopian 'double'. This device not only enables Wells to establish a narrative perimeter within which his protagonists can search for their utopian doubles – or in the case of the botanist, his 'lost love' – it also allows him to implicate his contemporary readers in a game of utopian hide and seek: 'and you, Sir or Madam, are in duplicate also, and all the men and women that you and I know' (24).

That Utopia is therefore inextricably bound with earthly intolerance and prejudice accounts for Wells's adherence to Kumar's notion of the utopian writer looking 'with comic relish' upon 'the follies and vanities of his own world', which in turn renders his narrator – for all the rationality of his utopian imaginings – viewing nowhere 'with a tragic sense of the unattainability of the ideal'. This is not to say that the ideals expressed in *A Modern Utopia* are entirely divorced from those in Wells's sociological thinking. There is a definite line of continuity, following the publication of *Anticipations*, in the development of Wells's thought up until the work's appearance in 1905, and *Mankind in the Making* in particular is essential to understanding the social policies advanced in *A Modern Utopia*. Wells is at pains to emphasise at the outset the distinction he creates between the narrator – or 'The Owner of the Voice' – and the author of the work: '*Now this Voice, and this is the peculiarity of the matter, is not to be taken as the Voice of the Ostensible author who fathers these pages. You have to clear your mind of any pre-conceptions in that respect* [emphasis in original]' (3). This creates deliberate ambiguity in the work, so that – while the narrator's ideas parallel those of the author in his sociological work – his aspirations cannot be easily identified with those of Wells himself. Sometimes the implied author of the work upholds the utopian ideals of the narrator. More frequently, however, his and the botanist's experience undercuts the narrator's conceptions of Utopia. The manner in which the fictional dimension of *A Modern Utopia* consistently overturns the narrator's hopes and ideals can indeed be considered as a blatant piece of self-irony on the part of Wells. It is almost as though he is aware from the beginning that his ideals are not attainable with the limited capacity of humanity in 1905.

In order to understand the significance of the ways in which the fictional aspect of the work undercuts the aspirations of the narrator, it is necessary to trace the parallels between the sociological debates Wells was immersed in and the social policies he advanced in *A Modern Utopia*. This Chapter begins by examining how his conception of Utopia is shaped by Wells's early rejection of the 'positive' eugenics advanced by Francis Galton. His opposition to Galton is in part understood as a consequence of Wells's insistence on the right of the individual to choose. Since this aligns Wells with the liberal tradition of John Stuart Mill, I examine the parallels between the two men. I investigate how Wells also objects to Galton's work because it fails to consider the significance of environmental factors in the development of human potential. Further, the insistence on minimum standards in *A Modern Utopia* is explored in the context of contemporary discourses of social reform.

My examination of the ambiguities of *A Modern Utopia* has implications for understanding Wells's position as he brings his work in the genre of the scientific romance towards a close.[8] I examine how – following on from *The First Men in the Moon* – Wells is again confronted with complexities as he attempts to reconcile individual freedom with social efficiency. Furthermore, I investigate the ways in which – for all his attempts to critique these principal scientific figures – Wells in *A Modern Utopia* in fact appropriates concepts from the work of both Spencer and Galton.

Crucial to initiating the process which led to the development of the social policies advanced in *A Modern Utopia* is Wells's response to Galton, founder of both the Sociological Society and the first professorship of eugenics at London University.[9] As indicated in the discussion of *The Time Machine*, Galton had already begun to delineate the nascent science of eugenics in his *Inquiries into Human Faculty and its Development*. However, his 'The Possible Improvement of the Human Breed Under The Existing Conditions of Law and Sentiment', published in *Nature* in October 1901, is a more elaborate account of the principles he hoped would soon be applied throughout contemporary society.[10] While he had earlier been hesitant concerning the availability of family genealogies, Galton endeavours to use the platform provided by this second Huxley Lecture of the Anthropological Institute as an opportunity to 'show that our knowledge is already sufficient to justify the pursuit of this perhaps the grandest of all objects'.[11]

Using statistical analysis of a representative section of the population, Galton concludes that parents derived from those sections of the community where the concentration of talent is highest are likely to produce gifted offspring. More particularly, the quality of offspring improves considerably in cases where both parents are of a high class: 'When both parents are of the V class the quality of parentages is greatly superior to those in which only one parent is a V.'[12] Having identified such an unmistakable correlation between the quality of parentage and the degree of talent in the offspring, Galton proceeds to state that: 'The possibility of improving the race of a nation depends on the power of increasing the productivity of the best stock.'[13] For Galton, this is a far more important endeavour 'than [that] of repressing the productivity of the worst'.[14] One exception to this rule, however, is the case of the criminal: 'Many who are familiar with the habits of these people do not hesitate to say that it would be an economy and a great benefit to the country if all habitual criminals were resolutely segregated under merciful surveillance and peremptorily denied opportunities for producing offspring.'[15]

As in his *Inquiries*, Galton proposes the public endowment of gifted couples. He accepts that, as a superficial objection to his directive that high calibre persons should intermarry, it 'is sure to be urged that the fancies of young people are so incalculable and so irresistible that they cannot be guided'.[16] However, he is assured that public opinion can emerge as a powerful coercive agent in ensuring the pairing of highly able individuals that he sees as imperative to producing the most gifted offspring.

Perhaps fearing that he had aligned himself with Galton's ideas in *Anticipations*, Wells uses 'The Problem of the Birth Supply' (1902) to distance himself from the notion of 'positive' eugenics.[17] In this second instalment of the serialised version of *Mankind in the Making* – which was subsequently published in book form in 1903 – Wells questions the existence of characteristics that are measurably transmissible to the next generation of humanity. He uses the example of beauty to demonstrate the complexities involved in such an apparently simple characteristic: 'If beauty were a simple thing it would be possible to arrange human beings in a simple scale according to whether they had more or less of this simple quality'.[18] However, the case becomes complicated immediately the different varieties and types of beauty are considered as part of the equation. For Wells, there are a number of incommensurable points in human appearance that may combine in a variety of ways to constitute beauty. Similarly, even an apparently unequivocal characteristic such as that of 'perfect health' cannot be regarded as suitable for universal application: 'we are scarcely more certain that the condition of "perfect health" in one human being is the same as the similarly named condition in another, than we are that the beauty of one type is made up of the same essential elements as the beauty of another'.[19]

Regardless of the complexities inherent in the constitution of such characteristics as beauty or health, Wells stresses that a distinct lack of knowledge among the contemporary scientific community remains the primary obstacle to utilising the laws of heredity to improve the standard of the human race. 'The fact is that in this matter of beauty and breeding for beauty we are groping in a corner where science has not yet been established', he writes.[20] For Wells, precisely the problem is that researchers remain unaware of the exact nature of those elements which contribute to the formation of beautiful appearance. Still more importantly, researchers are woefully ignorant of the principles governing the combination of these elements in the heredity process. Since this is the case, 'It is quite conceivable that you might select and wed together all the most beautiful people in the world and find that in nine cases out of ten you had simply produced mediocre offspring or offspring below mediocrity.'[21] Not only does Wells consider the laws of inheritance to be incalculable and too unreliable to be subject to statistical analysis, he also challenges Galton's claim that the offspring of two high calibre parents are more likely to possess a higher degree of a specified quality. Continuing with his example of beauty, Wells points out that children are often beautiful, not because both parents are beautiful, but rather simply by 'taking after' one parent or the other, 'through the predominance, the *prepotency,* of one parent over the other, a thing that might have happened equally well if the other parent was plain [emphasis original]'.[22] This being the case, Wells concludes that 'personal value and reproductive value may be two entirely different things'.[23]

Wells again engages with Galton's work at a meeting of the Sociological Society on 16 May 1904. Galton presented a paper entitled 'Eugenics: Its Definition, Scope and Aims', which was significantly accompanied by a list of genealogies of eminent families within the United Kingdom. Wells participated in the roundtable discussion which followed the delivery of this paper, and many of his criticisms of Galton's position reiterate those of 'The Problem of the Birth Supply'. Whereas in 'The Problem of the Birth Supply' he had stressed the value of research in order to learn about the laws of heredity, at this meeting of the Sociological Society Wells is adamant that no conscious selection of the best for reproduction is possible: 'I believe that now and always the conscious selection of the best for reproduction will be impossible, that to propose it is to display a fundamental misunderstanding of what individuality implies.'[24]

In *A Modern Utopia* Wells continues his critique of Galton's position, warning his reader against 'all nonsense of the sort one hears in certain quarters about the human stud farm' (163). To understand the specific nature of his critique of Galton in *A Modern Utopia*, it is necessary to examine what Wells himself understands individuality to imply. This is outlined in 'Scepticism of the Instrument', a paper first presented to the Oxford Philosophical Society in 1903 and included as an appendix to the publication of *A Modern Utopia* in book form.[25]

As he acknowledges, 'Scepticism of the Instrument' continues the line of speculation Wells had already begun in 'The Rediscovery of the Unique'. Wells begins by emphasising that essentially a doubt of the objective reality of classification forms 'the first and primary proposition of my philosophy'.[26] To him, 'classification is a necessary condition of the working of the mental implement but [...] a departure from the objective truth of things'.[27] Wells stresses that the human mind possesses a limited capacity to make sense of reality, and that consequently this obscures the objective truth that every individuality, both material and organic, possesses its own unique character.

In order to illustrate his point, Wells uses the example of the term chair. While the mention of this term brings an average chair to mind, this is to obscure not only the fact that there are different types of chair – arm chairs, reading chairs and so forth – but also the fact that each chair is unique by virtue of some small difference from all other chairs, even from others of the same set of machine made chairs. It is precisely 'because our brain has only a limited number of pigeon-holes for our correspondence with an unlimited universe of objective uniques, that we have to delude ourselves into the belief that there is a chairishness in this species common to and distinctive of all chairs'.[28] It is, for Wells, precisely the tendency of the human mind to delude itself into categorising groups of unique things together that renders those forms of thought derived from the Greeks – number, logic and class – equally illusory. Similarly, anyone involved in the study of anatomy will have been impressed with the suggestion of the vagueness and instability of biological species. 'A biological species', writes Wells, 'is quite obviously a great number of unique individuals which is separable from other biological species only by the fact that an enormous number of other linking individuals are inaccessible in time'.[29] Wells also points out that 'each new individual in that species does, in the distinction of its own individuality, break away in however infinitesimal degree from the previous average qualities of the species'.[30] Each of the above statements of course reveals the influence of Charles Darwin's *On the Origin of Species* (1859).[31] Darwin's entire argument is based on the breakdown of species barriers, since precise divisions are not possible because there are slight incremental changes all the time. Darwin thus emphasises the potential of continual individual variations in forming new species: 'Hence I look at individual differences, though of small interest to the systematist, as of high importance for us, as being the first step towards such slight varieties as are barely thought worth recording in works on natural history. And I look at varieties which are in any degree more distinct and permanent, as steps leading to more strongly marked and permanent varieties; and at these latter; as leading to subspecies, and to species.'[32]

Hence it is possible to understand precisely what Wells means in his statement in *A Modern Utopia* that 'State breeding of the population was a reasonable proposal for Plato to make, in view of the biological knowledge of his time and the purely tentative nature of his metaphysics; but from anyone in the days after Darwin, it is preposterous' (163–4). In proposing state breeding 'as the most brilliant of modern discoveries', Galton and his followers within the Sociological Society 'seem totally unable to grasp the modification of meaning "species" and "individual" have undergone in the last fifty years' (164). That is, Galton's ideal of understanding ourselves by looking at our forebears undercuts the idea of individuality as it is understood by post-Darwinian social thinkers. This is perhaps what Wells meant in *A Modern Utopia* when he wrote that: 'To them individuals are still defective copies of a Platonic ideal of the species, and the purpose of breeding no more than an approximation to that perfection' (164). While individuality may remain 'a negligible difference to them, an impertinence', successive generations of humanity do not reproduce the exact characteristics of their predecessors (164). Rather, in accordance with the perspective that Wells, following Darwin, advances, each new individual introduces its own individual distinctions which vary in some infinitesimal degree from the existing average of the species.

A Modern Utopia introduces an additional criticism of 'positive' eugenics that is entirely absent from Wells's two previous engagements with

Galton's work. This is explicitly entwined with the emphasis on individual liberty that Wells sees as an essential ingredient of social progress in *A Modern Utopia*. At the time of writing *Anticipations* Wells had specifically disavowed liberalism, stating that: 'Liberalism is a thing of the past, it is no longer a doctrine but a faction.'[33] However, a comment from Edmund Gosse appears to have been instrumental in changing Wells's mind concerning the value of individual freedom. Responding to a copy of 'The Discovery of the Future' (1902) sent to him by Wells, Gosse replied that: ' "I am sure the weak spot in all Utopias is the insufficient consideration of Man's intense instinctive determination to be happy. You prophets of the future are so occupied with the useful that you forget that it is only in individualism that we can be happy." '[34] It is perhaps not too fanciful to suppose that after reading Gosse's remarks Wells, ever sensitive to criticism, took steps to ensure that his Utopia would not neglect individualism as an essential ingredient of happiness.

In its emphasis on personal freedom, *A Modern Utopia* continues in a tradition of thought that had been forged into a coherent philosophy by the publication of Mill's *On Liberty* (1859).[35] Mill states that the purpose of his essay 'is to assert one very simple principle' which should be used to govern the dealings of society with the individual in the manner of compulsion and control: 'That principle is that the sole end for which mankind are warranted, individually or collectively, in interfering with the liberty of action of any of their number is self-protection. [...] His own good, either physical or moral, is not a sufficient warrant.'[36] Only in preventing harm to others does the civilised community have the right to exercise power over the individual. Otherwise, while it may be reasonable to entreat or remonstrate with an individual to behave in a certain way, or even to refrain from behaving in a certain way, an individual cannot rightfully be compelled to conform to opinions or standards of conduct imposed by others. In short, where the individual's conduct 'merely concerns himself, his independence is, of right, absolute. Over himself, over his own body and mind, the individual is sovereign.'[37] It is important to clarify that Mill's emphasis on the assertion of individuality does not diminish his sense of the individual's responsibility towards society. On the contrary, Mill points out that the continuation of society depends on 'each person's bearing his share (to be fixed on some equitable principle) of the labours and sacrifices incurred for defending the society or its members from injury and molestation'.[38] Further, it is worth noting that the assertion of individuality is, for Mill, limited in part by the freedom of others: 'The only freedom which deserves the name is that of pursuing our own good in our own way, so long as we do not attempt to deprive others of theirs or impede their efforts to obtain it.'[39] Mill is quick to emphasise that his doctrine applies only to those in the maturity of their faculties: 'We are not speaking of children or of young persons below the age which the law may fix as that of manhood or womanhood. Those who are still in a state to require being taken care of by others must be protected against their own actions as well as against external injury.'[40]

An important consideration for Mill in striving for the free development of individuality is the fact that human beings do not share a uniform character. Indeed, there is a strong implication in *On Liberty* that the nature of each individual character is unique: 'A man cannot get a coat or a pair of boots to fit him unless they are either made to his measure or he has a whole warehouseful to choose from; and is it easier to fit him with a life than with a coat, or are human beings more like one another in their whole physical and spiritual conformation than in the shape of their feet?'[41] It is precisely because human beings are more diverse in their sources of pleasure and pain than they are in the shape of their feet that Mill sees tolerance towards alternative modes of living as an essential ingredient leading to human happiness. A person's experience of the world might teach him or her that his or her circumstances or character are of an uncustomary nature and to deny him or her the right to conduct a 'different experiment of living' accordingly is to deprive him or her of that use of faculties which is crucial to the development of individuality in human beings.[42]

The innovation that results from the cultivation of originality is, for Mill, a valuable element in human affairs, since it is through the introduction of new truths, practices and modes of conduct that life is prevented from becoming a stagnant pool. Given the importance of originality of key individuals to continued progress, Mill insists 'emphatically on the importance of genius and the necessity of allowing it to unfold itself freely both in thought and in practice'.[43] For Mill, it is also important to make every reasonable effort to preserve the freedom of genius, since: 'Persons of genius are, *ex vi termini*, more individual than any other people – less capable, consequently, of fitting themselves, without hurtful compression, into any of the small number of moulds which society provides in order to save its members the trouble of forming their own character.'[44]

Wells's awareness of Mill's work is revealed in two slight references in *Mankind in the Making*, which was serialised in the *Fortnightly Review* between September 1902 and September 1903. The first of these references cites Mill's *Autobiography* alongside the writings of such figures as Henry George and John Ruskin.[45] The second refers to 'Mill's plural voting for educated men'.[46] While there is no direct reference to *On Liberty* in Wells's writings, it is possible that – following the type of criticism he received from Gosse – Wells was prompted to consider this account of individual freedom by one of a number of articles on Mill in the periodical press of the 1890s and 1900s, which included Frederic Harrison's item on 'John Stuart Mill', published in the *Nineteenth Century* in 1896.[47]

Mill's emphasis on the cultivation of individual difference would have been attractive to Wells in his endeavour to ensure that, unlike its ancient (and indeed some of its immediate) predecessors, his modern Utopia ensures scope for individual development. Thus, *A Modern Utopia* necessarily conforms to the 'the modern view', which:

> with its deepening insistence upon individuality and upon the significance of uniqueness, steadily intensifies the value of freedom, until at last we begin to see liberty as the very substance of life, that indeed it is life, and that only the dead things, the choiceless things, live in absolute obedience to law. To have free play for one's individuality is, in the modern view, the subjective triumph of existence. (31)

The parallels between Wells's emphasis on individual liberty and that formulated by Mill almost half a century earlier are immediately evident. Like Mill, Wells attaches a high degree of significance to individuality and its unhindered cultivation. Indeed, Mill's emphasis on the assertion of individuality as the essential ingredient of human happiness finds ample resonance in Wells's statement that 'To have free play for one's individuality is [...] the subjective triumph of existence'. The high degree of significance Wells attaches to individuality and, relatedly, its unique nature ('with its deepening insistence upon individuality and upon the significance of uniqueness') emerge directly from the perspective he had elucidated in the 'Scepticism of the Instrument'. Wells's insistence in that paper that all individualities are unique is, when applied to human society in *A Modern Utopia*, transformed into an urgent recognition of the need to allow each individual to pursue their development according to their own unique nature, which 'steadily intensifies the value of freedom'.

Mill prefigures Wells in the manner in which the latter relates the uniqueness of each individual to the need of an intensification of personal freedom. This of course refers to the passage of *On Liberty* in which Mill insists that since individuals are more diverse in their characters than they are in their dress requirements, it is imperative that they are provided with ample scope to develop their character. An additional parallel between Wells and Mill evident in the passage cited above concerns Mill's insistence that, rather than constituting a cognate part of civilisation, it is imperative for individuality itself to be recognised as an essential part of human life. His statement that 'until at last we begin to see liberty as the very substance of life, that indeed it is life' reveals that in *A Modern Utopia*, Wells is attempting to adhere to the principle that Mill perceives as yet unfulfilled in his contemporary society and recognise 'that the free development of individuality is one of the leading essentials of well-being'.[48]

While Wells attaches a considerable degree of significance to the assertion of individuality in *A Modern Utopia*, he is careful to point out that 'since man is a social creature, the play of will must fall short of absolute freedom' (31). His statement that 'Perfect human liberty is possible only to a despot who is absolutely and universally obeyed' (31) reveals that – in accordance with Mill – Wells's emphasis on the assertion of individuality does not diminish his sense of the individual's responsibility towards society. Indeed, the two principles which Wells identifies as restricting 'the play of will' for man as a social creature are identical to those conditions that Mill had specified in *On Liberty* as limiting the assertion of individuality. First of all, Mill's refrain that the freedom of each individual is in part limited by the reciprocal freedom of others finds resonance in Wells's comment in *A Modern Utopia* that, apart from that exercised by a despot, 'All other liberty is a compromise between our own freedom of will and the wills of those with whom we come in contact' (31). Secondly, Mill's insistence that each person must bear his share 'of the labours and sacrifices incurred' for defending society is recalled in Wells's statement that, as well as being restricted by the rights of others, individual liberty is limited 'by considerations affecting the welfare of the community as a whole' (31).

In terms of imposing restrictions on the play of individual will, Wells points to how 'a general prohibition in a state may increase the sum of liberty, and a general permission may diminish it' (31). He uses the example of the considerable degree of liberty we gain by the loss of the common liberty to kill, which means that 'one may go to and fro in all the ordered parts of the earth, unencumbered by arms or armour, free of the fear of playful poison, whimsical barbers, or hotel trap doors' (32). As a consequence of the social mayhem that would ensue from the liberty to kill and other threatening freedoms, Wells considers that: 'in a modern Utopia, which finds the final hope of the world in the evolving interplay of unique individualities, [...] the State will have effectually chipped away just all those spendthrift liberties that waste liberty, and not one liberty more, and so have attained the maximum general freedom' (32). This passage of *A Modern Utopia* instantly recalls Mill's statement in *On Liberty*, that: 'The only freedom which deserves the name, is that of pursuing our own good in our own way, so long as we do not attempt to deprive others of theirs, or impede their efforts to obtain it.' Although a comparison of these remarks reiterates that both men attach a high degree of significance to individuality while at the same time emphasising that its expression should not impinge on the freedom of others, it would be inaccurate to assume that Wells merely appropriates the principles first outlined by Mill in *On Liberty*. The crucial development to occur in *A Modern Utopia*, evident from the passage cited above, is that these principles emerge as an integral part of social relations. Whereas Mill had established the urgent necessity of recognising the significance of individuality, for Wells the fulfilment of individuality becomes a primary objective of the utopian state itself. Thus in *A Modern Utopia* it is the State, rather than some one individual, which will endeavour to 'chip away' those liberties which threaten to impinge upon the freedom of others thus attaining 'the maximum general freedom' that is necessary in facilitating 'the final hope of the world [it finds] in the evolving interplay of unique individualities'.

The probable influence of Mill can also be identified in Wells's consideration of 'two distinct and contrasting methods of limiting liberty; the first is Prohibition, "thou shalt not," and the second Command, "thou shalt" ' (32). Wells favours the former as a means of restricting liberty in *A Modern Utopia*, since while 'Prohibition takes one definite thing from the indefinite liberty of a man, [...] it still leaves him an unbounded choice of actions. He remains free, and you have merely taken a bucketful from the sea of his freedom' (33). His subsequent comment that command or 'compulsion destroys freedom altogether' reveals explicitly that Wells concurs with Mill's insistence in *On Liberty* that the individual cannot rightly be compelled in thought or action unless he or she presents a danger to the safety or liberty of others or the well-being of the community as a whole. In a passage which confirms that he conforms to Mill's distinction that children are to be regarded differently concerning liberty, Wells emphasises that in *A Modern Utopia* he is endeavouring to avoid the use of compulsion as a means of restricting liberty: 'I think indeed there should be no positive compulsions at all in Utopia, at any rate for the adult Utopian – unless they fall upon him as penalties incurred' (33). Wells utilises the fictional dimension of the work in order to facilitate his claim that there are no compulsions in *A Modern Utopia*. This is particularly apparent as the two protagonists present themselves for the second time to a public office in order to discover what fate awaits them in Utopia following the completion of their employment in the factory making wooden toys. While he informs these two earthly travellers that the committee of identification has suggested they consult first with a professor of anthropology and then their doubles, the utopian official emphasises that they are *not compelled* to follow this recommendation: ' "There's no positive compulsion" ', he insists (212).

A further aspect of Wells's consideration of personal autonomy that is entirely absent from Mill's account in *On Liberty* is freedom of movement. His consideration of freedom of movement is necessitated by the global scale of the modern Utopia, or as Wells himself recognises 'the very proposition of a World State speaking one common tongue carries with it the idea of a world population travelled and travelling to an extent quite beyond anything our native earth has seen' (41). Wells thus stresses that an essential characteristic of his Utopia is that the entire world will not only be relatively free from the restrictions of enclosure but 'will [also] be open and accessible and as safe for the wayfarer as France or England is to-day' (41–2).

The fact that its population is migratory beyond any earthly precedent means that Wells must devise an accurate means of verifying personal identification for his Utopia: 'If the modern Utopia is indeed to be a world of responsible citizens, it must have devised some scheme by which every person in the world can be promptly and certainly recognised' (146).[49] He conceives a system of indexing which records not only the individual's movements but also material facts including those relating to marital status, parentage and criminal convictions. Wells envisages that an index extending to include the entire utopian population 'could be housed quite comfortably on one side of Northumberland Avenue' (146–7). His remark that this 'index would be classified primarily by some unchanging physical characteristic, such as we are told the thumbmark and fingermark afford' (147) reveals the influence of Galton's research into fingerprints on the creation of a means of personal verification in *A Modern Utopia*.[50] In his work on *Fingerprints*, first published in 1892, Galton demonstrates that the composition of the pattern of a fingerprint provides an accurate means of verifying personal identity: 'the numerous bifurcations, origins, islands, and enclosures in the ridges that compose the pattern, are proved to be *almost beyond change* [emphasis in original]'.[51] Galton's influence can also be detected in Wells's use of index cards as a means of recording the characteristics of each individual. In his book on *Fingerprints*, Galton had advocated the accumulation of finger and thumb prints from members of the population which could be indexed on cards stored in boxes.[52] Wells develops this idea by making his index cards transparent so a photographic copy can be relayed wherever it is necessary to establish a person's identity. The presence of thumb marking apparatus in various utopian institutions including inns and post offices means that in its efficiency in establishing the location of its citizens the utopian state is compared to an eye, and one which will slowly apprehend the existence of the terrestrial protagonists 'as two queer and inexplicable particles disturbing the fine order of its field of vision' (149).

In order to demonstrate his point that the modern Utopia allows plentiful scope for individual cultivation, Wells ensures that the first character his protagonists encounter on this alternative world is one who opposes the founding principles of the utopian state. His stated opposition to the technological advance which characterises Utopia demonstrates that the blond haired heretic has been allowed to develop an uncustomary character in accordance with those principles established by Mill. Indeed, the presence of the blond haired heretic reveals that Wells's emphasis on the uniqueness of all individualities assumes the same practical application as Mill's insistence upon individuality. For the first utopian inhabitant encountered by the protagonists constitutes exactly the type of 'different experiment of living' advocated by Mill. The fact that – having paid for his keep and thus discharging his obligation to the community – the blond haired man 'spent all the leisure time he could gain in going to and fro lecturing on "The Need of a Return to Nature," and on "Simple Foods and Simple Ways"' (106), reveals that Wells agrees wholeheartedly with Mill's assessment that the worth of different modes of living ought to be proved practically where people see fit to try them.

In addition to substantiating the parallels between him and Mill, the presence of the blond haired heretic also signifies a significant development in Wells's thought. For in foregrounding a figure who possesses an uncustomary character, Wells is endeavouring to demonstrate that in his Utopia he successfully avoids the compression of individuality that had occurred in the lunar society of *The First Men in the Moon*. However, the outlook possessed by the blond haired man also hints that this Utopia may not be so sympathetic as the narrator claims. The man's relentless scorn towards technological advance serves only to emphasise his radically intolerant attitude towards the vast majority of utopian society.

The attitude of the blond haired heretic towards the two protagonists reveals an instance which demonstrates how the fictional aspect of the work overturns the narrator's intentions for *A Modern Utopia*. For this man's stubborn refusal to even consider as a possibility the narrator's story that he and the botanist come from another world – ' "You and your friend, with his love for the lady who's so mysteriously tied – you're romancing!" ' (119) – undercuts the narrator's stated intention that he and the botanist would derive additional comfort from the idea of the welcome they will receive in the universally tolerant society of Utopia: 'To us, clad as we are in mountain-soiled tweeds and with no money but British bank notes negotiable only at a practically infinite distance, this must needs be a reassuring induction' (38).

It should be noted that the intolerance of the blond haired heretic towards technological advancement and his sometimes irrational insistence on a return to simple means – emphasised by his argument with the botanist – emerges from Wells's desire to satirise those Utopias, such as William Morris's *News From Nowhere*, which resist the progress of the modern world and instead advocate a return to nature as the ideal condition for mankind. Considering its subversion of the pre-existing tradition of utopian literature, *A Modern Utopia* should be regarded as a continuation of Wells's first scientific romance, *The Time Machine*. Rather than being presented with a guide whose purpose is to explain how their contemporary society transformed into a more ordered world, as is the case with Dr Leete in Edward Bellamy's *Looking Backward*, in each of these Wells works the protagonist is forced to actively interpret the utopian landscape for himself. Whereas in *The Time Machine* the Traveller is presented with a series of clues which gradually allow him to solve the puzzle posed by the fate of humanity, the narrator of *A Modern Utopia* is frustrated in his attempts to locate those individuals who provide the guiding will of Utopia. Like the Time Traveller, the narrator complains regarding the absence of a cicerone when confronted with the back to nature enthusiast whom he is sure constitutes the very 'antithesis' of those who order this world: 'When one comes to Utopia one expects a Cicerone, one expects a person as precise and insistent and instructive as an American advertisement – the advertisements of one of those land agents, for example, who print their own engaging photographs to instil confidence and begin, "You want to buy real estate" ' (110). The narrator's comment regarding his discussion with the first utopian inhabitant he meets indicates a further dimension of Wells's satire of contemporary utopian literature: 'One expects to find all Utopians absolutely convinced of the perfection of their Utopia, and incapable of receiving a hint against its order' (110–11). For in placing the heretic – or as the narrator terms him 'this purveyor of absurdities!' (111) – at the forefront of his modern Utopia, Wells undercuts the ortho-dox utopian narrative in which a cicerone such as Dr Leete not only explains the conception of a more organised world to his visitor but is also invariably able to answer any objections that the protagonist may invoke against the purpose of the society that he now finds himself in. Although he obstructs the narrator's attempts to locate the organising 'will' on this alternative earth, Wells stresses that the presence of the blond haired man is perfectly in accordance with the conception of a society that allows for a generous recognition of individual differences, since 'Irrelevance is not irrelevant to such a scheme, and our blond-haired friend is exactly just where he ought to be here' (111).

It is exactly the same insistence on the assertion of individuality which marks out a world that is no longer unanimous in its ideals as the distinctive characteristic of the modern Utopia, that accounts in part for Wells's rejection of Galton's implication that young persons of the elite should be encouraged to intermarry. For Wells, the compul-sory pairing of human beings is an absurdity not only in that it consti-tutes a misunderstanding of what the term individuality implies, but also because it deprives persons of 'the supreme and significant expres-sion of individuality, [which] should lie in the selection of a partner for procreation' (164).

There is a further aspect to his critique of Galton that is essential to understanding the development of Wells's thought leading up to the publication of *A Modern Utopia*. This concerns the absence in Galton's work of any consideration of environmental factors in the success of human beings. Thus in 'The Problem of the Birth Supply' Wells laments the fact that a gifted man from the poorer strata of society must pur-chase his attainment at the cost of his posterity, since 'he must either die childless and successful for the children of the stupid to reap what he has sown, or sacrifice his gift'.[53] Similarly, at the Sociological Society meeting of 1904 Wells points out that Galton's research ignores 'the consideration of social advantage, of what Americans call the "pull" that follows any striking success'.[54] For Wells, the fact that the sons of great scientific men are often great scientific men themselves 'may after all be far more due to a special knowledge of the channels of profes-sional advancement than to any distinctive family gift'.[55]

While in his autobiography Wells considers that 'The Problem of the Birth Supply' is the only part of *Mankind in the Making* that is of longstanding worth, the chapter entitled 'Certain Wholesale Aspects of Man-Making' is in fact massively significant since it constitutes the first attempt on the part of the author to apply his concept of the artificial factor in mankind to the question of mass humanity.[56] To reiterate, for Wells in 'Human Evolution, An Artificial Process' the artificial factor of mankind constitutes the traditions, education and morals that have evolved with the development of organised humanity and that are essential to the continued progress of civilisation. Following on from this in the third part of *Mankind in the Making*, at the same time as he reinstates the view that it is not possible to consciously raise the average human heredity, Wells emphasises that to develop the artificial element of humanity is within the grasp of social reformers in contemporary society: 'We are going to consider how it is built up and how it may be built up, we are going to attempt a rough analysis of the whole complex process by which the civilised citizen is evolved from that raw and wailing little creature.'[57]

For Wells, the child must receive certain minimum standards of comfort and stimulation that include a warmly lit room and the support of a readily available doctor.[58] However, he acknowledges that such conditions are the privilege of a wealthy few in contemporary England, and that the vast majority start handicapped: 'they are born into insanitary and ugly or inconvenient homes, their mothers or nurses are ignorant and incapable, there is insufficient food or incompetent advice [...] and there is not enough sunlight for them'.[59] The consequence of these conditions is that the development of the artificial factor that is essential to the progress of civilisation is retarded in each individual: 'the far graver and sadder loss, [is] the invisible and immeasurable loss through mental and moral loss undeveloped', writes Wells.[60] Wells is also disconcerted by the fact that the vast majority of infant mortality involves 'children of untainted blood and good mental and moral possibilities'.[61]

The key word in terms of proposing a solution to the unacceptable conditions endured by a substantial number of the population is wholesale. For Wells believes it is possible to alter these conditions immediately with the establishment of minimum standards that are applicable throughout society. One such expedient concerns the condition of houses. He insists that with slight modifications to existing legislation, a national standard of dwelling could be established. Any house that did not meet this standard would be pulled down. Wells also stresses that there should be legislation against overcrowding. In a comment that anticipates his distinction in *A Modern Utopia* between the liberty of adults and the dependency of children, Wells states that while six mature individuals may choose to sleep together in a crowded dwelling, 'directly children come in we touch the future'.[62] Consequently, it is imperative that: 'The minimum permissible tenement for a maximum of two adults and a very young child is one properly ventilated room capable of being heated, with close and easy access to sanitary conveniences, a constant supply of water and easy means of getting warm water.'[63]

Wells acknowledges that a universal insistence on such expedients will bear heavily on the resources of poorer parents, but considers that the establishment of a minimum wage can counter this. A reference to Beatrice and Sidney Webb in 'Certain Wholesale Aspects of Man-Making' suggests that Wells is indebted to their recently published *Industrial Democracy* (1902) for this conception.[64] The Webbs present the minimum wage as a necessary counter to the debilitating effects of physical deterioration upon the national stock, which 'would be determined by practical inquiry as to the cost of food, clothing, and shelter physiologically necessary, according to national habit and custom, to prevent bodily deterioration'.[65] In order to impress the need of a minimum wage on the capitalist class, the Webbs point out that such a minimum would be low. It is immediately evident that Wells's minimum wage is more generous that that of *Industrial Democracy*, since it not only provides for 'the maintenance of himself and his wife and children above the minimum standard of comfort' but also covers 'his insurance against accidental death or temporary economic or physical disablement' as well as a 'provision for old age and a certain margin for the exercise of his individual freedom'.[66] Of course, this last emphasis on the exercise of freedom anticipates the degree of significance attached by Wells in *A Modern Utopia* to the assertion of individuality.

While the mechanism of the minimum wage ensures that the corresponding minimum conditions for nurturing offspring are universally affordable, there remains the difficulty of parents who neglect their children. While he acknowledges that there is an apparent dilemma between taking the children away from their parents and removing an obstacle to the breeding of the unfit on the one hand, and leaving the children to face cruelty on the other, Wells stresses that 'There is a quite excellent middle way'.[67] This consists of making the parent a 'debtor to society on account of the child for adequate food, clothing and care for at least the first twelve or thirteen years of life, and in the event of parental default to invest the local authority with exceptional powers of recovery in this matter'.[68] Wells states that having established minimum standards of education, nutrition and health for childrearing, any parents whose offspring fell below these standards would have their child removed from them and forced to pay for the cost of a suitable maintenance for that child. Similarly, parents who were either neglecting or abusing their offspring would be forced to pay maintenance for a child no longer in their care. In either scenario, Wells envisages the strictest of penalties for parents failing to make these payments. For example, they might be compelled to work off their debts: 'If the parents failed in the payments they could be put into celibate labour establishments to work off as much debt as they could, and they would not be released until their debt was fully discharged.'[69]

A final aspect of 'Certain Wholesale Aspects of Man-Making' that is relevant to developing our understanding of *A Modern Utopia* concerns Wells's consideration of the remaining problem of the unemployed. He points out, however, that the establishment of the minimum wage, supported by a widespread network of employment bureaux, would suggest that these people are unsuitable for employment, and that improved housing conditions will have swept away the hiding place of individuals unsuitable to succeed in life: 'They would exist, but they would not multiply – and that is our supreme end.'[70] Wells foresees that, being unable to earn a wage for themselves, such individuals would be the necessary recipients of a future public charity which would constitute a more organised version of those in the contemporary world.

This last statement reveals that repressing the reproduction of the least desirable sections of the community is a far more significant endeavour for Wells than it is for Galton. This difference of emphasis emerges from the contrasting interpretations of the theory of natural selection held by Wells and Galton respectively. Indeed, Wells is adamant that Galton has misunderstood the manner in which competition functions amongst the members of species in the natural world, since his conception of 'positive' eugenics reveals: 'something of that same lack of a fine appreciation of facts that enabled Herbert Spencer to coin those two most unfortunate terms, *Evolution* and the *Survival of the Fittest* [emphasis in original]'.[71] While he acknowledges that the implication of these two terms is that the *best* reproduces and survives, Wells points out that 'really it is the *better* that survives, and not the *best* [emphasis in original]'.[72] For him, the reality of the case is that the inferior usually perish and that the average of the species usually rises 'but not that [as is implied by Galton] any exceptionally favourable variations get together and reproduce'.[73] Since the 'way of Nature has always been to slay the hindermost', Wells insists the primary application of the theory of natural selection within human society resides in the possibility of 'prevent[ing] those who would become the hindermost being born'.[74] Consequently, he concludes his response to Galton's address to the Sociological Society with the controversial statement: 'It is in the sterilisation of failures, and not in the selection of successes for breeding, that the possibility of an improvement of the human stock lies.'[75]

Despite his attempt to differentiate himself from the work of Spencer, Wells's reading of nature in fact aligns him with a Spencerian position. Indeed, an unsigned review in *Academy and Literature* explicitly relates to the work of Spencer, Wells's insistence in *Mankind in the Making* that the permanent way to end the ills of the world is to repress the reproduction of people below a certain standard while at the same time encouraging the multiplication of superior types: 'But why not have gone to the fountain head and refer to the Spencerian dictum that the most detrimental result of any social action is "to encourage the production of the unworthy at the expense of the worthy." '[76]

In *A Modern Utopia*, competition among individualities to reproduce is an essential characteristic of Wells's conception of a kinetic Utopia which cannot ignore the fact of evolution. Even though he had chosen to use the term better rather than best to describe the mechanism by which the average of a species rises, Wells in *A Modern Utopia* concurs exactly with Spencer's imperative that hindering the reproduction of the inferior while encouraging the multiplication of the superior is essential to the progress of *homo sapiens*: 'These people [the inferior] will have to be in the descendant phase, the species must be engaged in eliminating them; there is no escape from that, and conversely people of exceptional quality must be ascendant' (123). However, there is a hugely significant difference between the conceptions of Wells and Spencer concerning the responsibility of society in ordering this biological imperative. For Spencer, society in its corporate function should do nothing to protect those individuals unable to succeed in the competition that is life. Precisely the 'Sin' of Legislators is their endeavour to redistribute wealth which, warns Spencer, threatens to endow the inferior with the means to reproduce their number while at the same time diminishing the capacity of the superior to multiply. Wells, conversely, considers that it is possible to humanise the conflict that must inevitably ensue from the competition to reproduce: 'And if it can so be contrived that every human being shall live in a state of reasonable physical and mental comfort, without the reproduction of inferior types, there is no reason whatever why that [the material needs of all persons being met] should not be secured' (124).

Wells's acknowledgement of the necessity of reproductive competition in *A Modern Utopia* is accompanied by the same insistence upon minimum standards that had characterised the third section of *Mankind in the Making*. In his attempt to reconcile the imperative of reproductive competition with the acknowledgement of the necessity for collective minimum standards, Wells endeavours to resolve the debate between individualism and collectivism generated by the type of opposing interpretations of evolutionary theory advanced by Spencer and Huxley respectively. In attempting to resolve the individualism-collectivism debate, Wells draws substantially upon contemporary discussion. One contribution to this debate is Charles Richmond Henderson's article, 'Definition of a Social Policy Relating to the Dependent Group', which was published in *The American Journal of Sociology* in 1905.[77] A reference to *The American Journal of Sociology* in *A Modern Utopia* reveals that Wells was familiar with the periodical, and it is possible that he may have read Henderson's article. There are striking parallels in the manner in which each writer reconciles a Spencerian biological imperative with his own insistence on minimum standards of human welfare.

Henderson's article is intended to facilitate the construction of a social policy dealing with dependent groups such as children, the unemployed and criminals. Since a social policy seeks to fulfil a recognisable good, it must be concerned to establish a minimum standard of life for all citizens. A fundamental consideration of establishing a minimum standard of life demands that: 'As a nature-object every person must have a certain minimum of food and shelter, and, normally, the race-interest asks for provision for propagation, maintenance, and protection of healthy offspring.'[78] Henderson regretfully informs us that 'People by the tens of thousands are trying to exist and bring up children in homes which are unfit for human habitation, and on food which is insufficient to meet the minimum requirements of growth'.[79] A correlated minimum, particularly in relation to the maintenance of healthy offspring, is that of establishing universal standards of education. In this respect, Henderson observes that 'all countries which have compulsory school attendance, at least up to a certain age, declare thereby that they have adopted a minimum standard of education'.[80]

In *A Modern Utopia*, Wells identifies precisely the same fundamental conditions as crucial to the establishment of minimum standards. Like Henderson, Wells observes that in the contemporary world there is for the multitude 'only miserable houses, uncomfortable clothes, and bad and insufficient food' (124). Wells of course envisages that his modern Utopia 'will certainly have put an end to that', since: 'It will insist upon every citizen being properly housed, well nourished, and in good health' (124–5). This insistence on the part of Wells of course emerges from his consideration in *Mankind in the Making* of those factors, such as poor houses and insufficient food, which retard the development of the artificial factor that is so essential to progress in society. Wells's artificial factor is the equivalent to Henderson's idea of the 'race interest'. The emphasis on the artificial factor throughout *A Modern Utopia* creates an inevitable tension in the work between social improvement and biological evolution. Both perspectives are in fact essential to Wells's conception of social progress and indeed to his idea that *A Modern Utopia* should constitute a kinetic, or continually progressing, world. The ethos towards continual striving in Utopia is emphasised by the fact that its minimal standards are continually rising, a fact revealed by the Voice's comment on housing: 'Any house, unless it be a public monument, that does not come up to its *rising standard* of healthiness and convenience, the Utopian State will incontinently pull down [emphasis added]' (125). One factor which facilitates artificial evolution is universal education, and like many of the countries Henderson mentions it is compulsory in Wells's Utopia.

A further parallel between Wells and Henderson concerns the expedient of the minimum wage. Henderson is adamant that the 'only rational starting-point is a minimum standard below which public morality – expressed in sentiment, custom, trade-union regulations, moral maxims, and law – will not permit workers to be employed for wages'.[81] Henderson is assured that the establishment of a minimum wage will lead to the demise of the 'parasitic' industries as well as the sweated worker. He is equally adamant, however, that 'being a community interest [the establishment of a minimum wage], should not be left to trade unions, but should be, as far as possible, a matter of law and governmental action'.[82] Henderson also uses the capacity of the individual to work as a measure of social dependency, with those being unable to secure employment at the minimum wage being transferred to the category of the unemployed. These unemployed could then be referred to charity, with Henderson calling for a better understanding between public and private agencies of relief.

As in *Mankind in the Making*, the minimum wage of *A Modern Utopia* is determined as necessary not only for the maintenance of physical and mental welfare but also for the exercise of personal freedom. His use of the phrase 'Standard of Life' reveals that Wells broadly concurs with Henderson's insistence that the establishment of a minimum wage would eradicate the sweated worker. He also concurs with Henderson's point that the State should be responsible for establishing the level of the minimum wage. Where Wells differs from Henderson concerns his provision of universal welfare for the temporarily unemployed: 'It will find him work if he can and will work, it will take him to it, it will register him and lend him the money wherewith to lead a comely life until work can be found or made for him, and it will give him credit and shelter and strengthen him if he is ill' (125). Such welfare provisions signify a shift in Wells's thought, since at the time of writing *Mankind in the Making* he had concurred with Henderson's view that the unemployed should be referred to charity. In *A Modern Utopia*, however, the State acts as the reserve employer of labour. The unemployed can choose to work in one of a number of toilsome, but not incapacitating, jobs which contribute to the common good. Far from being received 'with any insult of charity' (127), such employment would be regarded as a public service.

As indicated, an additional parallel between Wells and Henderson concerns the manner in which each of these men attempts to reconcile the biological imperative that the inferior should not breed, with his own insistence on minimum standards. Discussing the necessity of positive social selection, Henderson points out that it is imperative that the inferior do not multiply: 'It is more than formerly assumed that persons who cannot improve, or at least will not degrade, the physical and psychical average of the race, should be prevented, so far as possible, from propagating their kind.'[83] However, it is for him equally imperative that the process of positive social selection should not be left to those same destructive forces at work in nature, since this 'would mean, first of all, that hundreds of thousands of our fellow-men who fail in competition would starve or freeze before our eyes in the street'.[84] The same instinct for sympathy which leads to the moral obligation to establish minimum standards dictates that those same minimum standards are extended to those who are regarded as too inferior to breed, or as Henderson puts it elsewhere: 'In spite of the powerful and influential protest of Mr. Herbert Spencer, the civilized nations have gone on their way of extending the positive agencies of benevolence.'[85]

As inferred, Wells concurs entirely with the imperative that inferior members of the human species should not breed, or as he puts it in *A Modern Utopia*: 'the ideal of a scientific civilisation is to prevent those weaklings [who would perish in nature] being born' (163). Yet he also states elsewhere that while we must compete to give birth 'we may heap every sort of consolation prize upon the losers in that competition' (163). A passage from the chapter entitled 'Failure in a Modern Utopia' neatly summarises Wells's insistence on the difference which must necessarily exist between artificial selection as an essential characteristic of social progress and natural selection:

> The way of Nature in this process is to kill the weaker and the sillier, to crush them, to starve them, to overwhelm them, using the stronger and more cunning as her weapon. But man is the unnatural animal, the rebel child of Nature, and more and more does he turn himself against the harsh and fitful hand that reared him. He sees with a growing resentment the multitude of suffering ineffectual lives over which his species tramples in its ascent. In the Modern Utopia he will have set himself to change the ancient law. No longer will it be that failures must suffer and perish lest their breed increase, but the breed of failure must not increase, lest they suffer and perish, and the race with them. (123)

This passage reveals that, like Henderson, Wells believes that the process of selection should not be left to those same destructive processes – the crushing, starving, and overwhelming of the weak – which operate in the animal and plant kingdoms. Nor should it be left to the brutal struggle for survival among savages, since civilised man increasingly 'turns[s] himself against the harsh and fitful hand that reared him'. The instinct for sympathy in the modern world mentioned by Henderson is recalled by Wells's comment that: 'He sees with a growing resentment the multitude of suffering ineffectual lives over which his species tramples in its ascent.' His statement that failures need no longer 'suffer and perish lest their breed increase' emphasises that Wells concurs entirely with the widely articulated notion expressed by Henderson that minimum standards should be extended to all citizens, regardless of reproductive value.

In order to become a parent, the inhabitants of *A Modern Utopia* must be 'established in work at a rate above the minimum' (127). Wells thus broadly agrees with Spencer's insistence that there is a close correlation between economic success and the right to breed offspring. A statement in *A Modern Utopia* equating insolvency with unworthiness would appear to align Wells with a particularly severe interpretation of Spencer. However, this would be to misunderstand the context in which this comment appears. His insistence on minimum standards and welfare provisions not only ensures that the inferior no longer suffer, it is also essential to Wells's endeavour to construct an equal basis for competition between unique individuals, or as he puts it in the work: 'in Utopia everyone will have had an education and a certain minimum of nutrition and training; everyone will be insured against ill-health and accidents; there will be the most efficient organisation for balancing the pressure of employment and the presence of disengaged labour, and so to be moneyless will be clear evidence of unworthiness' (134). Such a basis is of course entirely absent from the work of Spencer. Furthermore, whereas Spencer is adamant that benevolence on the part of policy makers has disastrous implications for the future of *homo sapiens*, Wells insists that his minimum standards will facilitate social progress. Taken together, the aim of his welfare expedients 'is not to rob life of incentives but to change their nature, to make life not less energetic, but less panic-stricken and violent and base, [and] to shift the incidence of the struggle for existence from our lower to our higher emotions' (139–40). This will 'neutralise the motives of the cowardly and bestial' thus enabling 'the ambitious and energetic imagination which is man's finest quality' to 'become the incentive and determining factor in [human] survival' (140).

The narrator of *A Modern Utopia* enthuses over the efficient welfare system of the world state in which he has appeared, and makes a somewhat unpatriotic comparison with the terrestrial globe: 'Compared with our world, it is like a well-oiled engine beside a scrap heap' (153). However, the claim that welfare provisions are efficiently managed in Utopia provides an additional example of how the fictional dimension of the text undercuts the narrator's claim of what Utopia would be 'like'. The narrator reflects that in the case of a man who finds himself without money or employment in a district of Utopia unknown to him: 'One imagines him resorting to a neat and business-like post-office, and stating his case to a civil and intelligent official' (135). The important word here is *imagines* because it implies that the narrator's observation in this respect forms part of his speculations about Utopia rather than an actual attribute of the world he and the botanist visit. When the two terrestrial protagonists recognise the urgency of their financially stricken plight and consequently seek employment at the public office, the reality of Utopia reveals itself. Rather than being dealt with by the civil and intelligent individuals envisaged by the narrator, they in fact generate a considerable amount of confusion among the petty bureaucrats with whom they are confronted. It should further be noted that the utopian officials to whom they attempt to explain their case are no more tolerant of the protagonists' story that they have appeared from another world than the heretic had been. Initially, the narrator had stated that the thought of universal tolerance should provide a reassuring introduction to Utopia for two men dressed in tweed.

Yet the surprise reaction of the male official, the first of the Samurai encountered in the work, to the clothing of the protagonists hints that the dress code of Utopia might not be so permissive after all: 'He looks from her to us gravely, *and his eye lights to curiosity at our dress* [emphasis added]' (142). The narrator had also compared the efficiency of the utopian state to an eye which would apprehend instantly the existence of the dual protagonists. However, when this eye locates the two earthmen, it does not know what to do with them. Additionally, the identification of the two travellers with their utopian doubles intensifies the confusion of the public office episode.

Despite the confusion they generate, the protagonists do of course eventually secure employment. That they work in a utopian factory enables Wells to uphold the earlier contention that the industrial infrastructure of *A Modern Utopia* will be free of the sweated worker, since as the narrator states: 'that brooding stress that pursues the weekly worker on earth, that aching anxiety that drives him so often to stupid betting, stupid drinking, and violent and mean offences will have vanished out of mortal experience' (199).[86] It is highly appropriate that the narrator and botanist work in a factory making wooden toys, since such playthings provide precisely the level of stimulation that Wells had specified in *Mankind in the Making* as crucial to the development of the artificial factor in childhood. However, with the minimum standards which safeguard the mental and physical development of children already in place – and continually fostered by the role of women, discussed below – the primary focus of accumulating the artificial factor of mankind shifts elsewhere in *A Modern Utopia*.

In 'Human Evolution, An Artificial Process', Wells states that the 'artificial factor of mankind – and that is the one reality of civilisation – grows, therefore, through the agency of eccentric and innovating people, playwrights, novelists, preachers, poets, journalists, and political reasoners and speakers'.[87] In accordance with this dictum a crucial qualification to join the Samurai, the ruling elite of *A Modern Utopia*, is to have made a significant contribution to the continuing accumulation of this 'one reality of civilisation', or as the narrator's utopian double terms it: 'he had to hold the qualification for a doctor, for a lawyer, for a military officer, or an engineer, or teacher, or have painted acceptable pictures, or written a book, or something of the sort' (250). Even a cursory glance at what is considered to constitute a contribution to the artificial factor in each of these sources reveals an unmistakeably biographical bias on the part of Wells, since he himself fulfilled two of these roles.

Biography aside, his emphasis on the significance of innovation in accumulating the artificial factor reiterates Wells's alignment with Mill's notion that originality is an important element in human affairs. Mill's emphatic insistence on the importance of genius finds resonance in Wells's poietic type, one of four temperaments he distinguishes in *A Modern Utopia*. Similar to Mill's definition of genius, this creative class of mind is characterised by 'the desire to bring the discoveries made in such excursions, into knowledge and recognition' (236). Wells concurs with Mill's assessment that the unhindered cultivation of genius, or the poietic type of mind, is essential to continued social advancement: 'the forms of the human future must come also through men of this same type, and it is a primary essential to our modern idea of an abundant secular progress that these activities should be unhampered and stimulated' (237).[88]

As inferred, the position Wells ascribes to women in *A Modern Utopia* is in many senses defined by his insistence that the accumulation of the artificial factor is imperative to the progress of humanity. In his discussion of women, the narrator of the work 'suppose[s] the Modern Utopia equalises things between the sexes in the only possible way, by insisting that motherhood is a service to the State and a legitimate claim to a living' (168). In this regard the State will not only pay the mother a gratuity upon the birth of a child, it will also reward her with regular sums sufficient to keep her and her child in independent freedom, 'so long as the child keeps up to the minimum standard of health and physical and mental development' (169). In other words, these payments are contingent upon the satisfactory development of the child's capacity to accumulate the artificial factor.

Once efficient childrearing is recognised as a service to the State, Wells anticipates that a mother 'is as much entitled to wages above the minimum wage, to support, to freedom, and to respect and dignity, as a policeman, a solicitor-general, a king [...] or anyone else the State sustains' (168).[89] The advantages Wells associates with the endowment of motherhood include economic independence from her husband. In proposing that motherhood becomes the primary or even sole profession of women – or as he puts it in *A Modern Utopia*, a career of wholesome motherhood would be 'the normal and remunerative calling for a woman' (169) – Wells appears unable to separate the social status of women from their reproductive role as mothers. Indeed, Wells stresses that his Utopia will do 'its best to make thoroughly efficient motherhood a profession worth following' (169). Since Wells himself stresses the importance of education to human development, it may be argued that the wider agencies of socialisation – including the compulsory education up to the age of 14 that is a feature of *A Modern Utopia*, or the employment of nannies which Wells on the whole rejects in the work – might contribute to the nurturing of the child, leaving the mother free to compete with men in the remaining professions. The reactionary nature of Wells's endowment of motherhood is further emphasised by the fact that, although women are allowed to join the governing classes in *A Modern Utopia*, female Samurai must bear children.

Wells's emphasis on motherhood as the 'proper' profession for women emerges from his insistence in *A Modern Utopia* that women are inferior to men in their capacity to compete in other careers. His comment that the inferiority of women concerning their 'inability to produce as much value as a man for the same amount of work' (167) is beyond question would undoubtedly have infuriated contemporary campaigners for women's rights, not to mention modern feminists. While the entire notion of endowing motherhood now appears a conservative one, it highlights the subsequent difficulties that Wells creates for himself in his attempt to reconcile personal freedom and social efficiency, which centres on the issue of reproduction.

Despite the narrator's claim that there will be much less interference in sexual relations in Utopia than there is any terrestrial state, reproduction is in fact the most highly regulated sphere of this world order. It is also the issue which most explicitly reveals how Wells's preoccupation with social efficiency impinges on his notion of individual freedom.

Wells delineates a number of preconditions which must be fulfilled before parentage is attained: 'the contracting parties must be in health and condition, free from specific transmissible taints, above a certain minimum age, and sufficiently intelligent and energetic to have acquired a minimum education' (171). It should immediately be noted that being forced to supply the above information prior to the attainment of parentage would be considered as a huge infringement of civil liberties in modern society. In his attempt to reconcile social efficiency and individual liberty in his endowment of motherhood, Wells, in imposing so many preconditions to parentage, in fact limits the expression of choice rather than creates it. The economic independence which would result from the endowment of motherhood in *A Modern Utopia* would restrict a woman's choice to those reproductive partners who fulfil the criteria constructed by Wells, since she would presumably be unable to choose a partner who did not conform to these preconditions. Moreover, his adherence to specified conditions that must be fulfilled before attaining parentage undercuts the entire thrust of Wells's assertion that the cardinal expression of individuality is the choice of a mate for procreation, since this choice can only be made within the perimeters of those potential partners who fulfil these pre-existing criteria.

Wells's attitude towards those couples that produce offspring without fulfilling these criteria reveals that, despite his claims elsewhere in the novel, there are in fact compulsions in Utopia. Similar to those parents in *Mankind in the Making* who would be forced to work in labour establishments in order to pay off debts related to their offspring, people who have children but fail to meet these qualifications would be compelled to pay for the nurture of an infant that had been taken into the care of the State: 'we shall insist that you are under a debt to the State of a peculiarly urgent sort, and one you will certainly pay, even if it is necessary to use restraint to get the payment out of you: it is a debt that has in the last resort your liberty as security' (165).[90]

The complex structure of *A Modern Utopia* creates an element of ambiguity as to whether the narrator's reflections concerning reproduction actually form part of Utopia or whether they constitute an additional aspect of the narrator's speculations concerning Utopia. There is a hint that his entire discussion of marriage and reproduction in Utopia form part of a daydream which the narrator initiates as a means of temporarily evading the botanist's preoccupation with his 'lost' love. Reflecting upon the tendency of his companion to brood, the narrator complains that: 'The old Utopists never had to encumber themselves with this sort of man' (161). Yet precisely the reason why the narrator is encumbered 'with this sort of man' is that, unlike the older Utopists, Wells does not pretend that he can change the essential nature of humankind. Rather he limits himself to contemporary humanity and is therefore burdened with its restrictions. Whereas the classical nowheres present an altered humanity in a perfect world, the modern utopian explorer is destined to find that his vision of a rational world is constantly disturbed by the emotions, preoccupations and intolerance that characterise the human race as it exists in 1905. While the narrator's speculations concerning reproduction in Utopia might well form part of a daydream contrived to spite the botanist, this should not be used to detract from the fact that the views expressed in this section of the text are identifiable with those of Wells, as is revealed by the obvious line of continuity with *Mankind in the Making*. Rather, it should be considered as a further aspect of the difference between what the narrator imagines Utopia will be 'like' and the actual constitution of the world in which he and the botanist find themselves.

Remaining with the idea that Utopia might use the liberty of the individual as security in cases where persons fail to fulfil their obligations, there is a further compulsion in *A Modern Utopia* that is of comparable magnitude. This concerns the enforced exclusion of specified categories of dependent from mainstream society. Returning to Henderson's notion of 'positive social selection', he stresses that while humanity cannot risk facing the consequences that would ensue from the rapid multiplication of inferiors, an economically viable solution is apparent: 'The method of segregation, as a device of negative social selection, is already at work and its results are before us.'[91] For Henderson, it would be quite practicable, for example, to maintain a woman of childbearing age in a farm colony where she does not breed. In *A Modern Utopia*, Wells employs the identical method of segregation that was widely debated in his contemporary moment. Like Henderson, Wells believes that: 'You must resort to a kind of social surgery' (128). This 'social surgery' comprises segregating classes of dependents, including lunatics, criminals, alcoholics and drug takers on celibate islands where they will not be able to interfere with the freedoms of others.

Whereas Henderson is willing to accept that safeguarding the liberty of the majority necessitates restricting the freedom of the few, Wells insists that the concept of segregation can be reconciled with the notion of individual liberty for those placed on his island colonies. That there are no prisons in *A Modern Utopia* appears to have been influenced by Beatrice Webb having forwarded to Wells a draft of a tract she had written on penal reform. In a response to this draft, Wells reminds Webb of the cruel treatment meted out to prisoners by their jailors, stating that: 'the *practical administration of the details of the business* [of running prisons] *have to be entrusted to rather low common men* [emphasis in original]'.[92] This comment finds resonance in the narrator of the work's statement that there are to be no jails in Utopia since: 'No men are quite wise enough, good enough and cheap enough to staff jails as a jail ought to be staffed' (130). Wells argues that the increased freedom granted to criminals can be extended to all the inhabitants of his islands, since the State will endeavour to 'give these segregated failures just as full a liberty as they can have' (130). However, Wells's comment that 'there will be no freedoms of boat building' undercuts his attempt to reconcile liberty with segregation, since his island occupants are thereby denied the freedom of movement that is one of the chief principles of Utopia. Despite Wells's claim to the contrary, they are in fact prisoners. The vision of these island colonies portrayed in *A Modern Utopia* is not, however, without novelistic irony. Wells indeed appears at points to raise questions deliberately concerning his own sincerity in proposing segregation as a solution to social problems, as indicated by his comment that: 'there is no reason why the islands of the hopeless drunkard, for example, should not each have a virtual autonomy' (130).

In a review of *Mankind in the Making*, Havelock Ellis commented on how this novelistic irony clouded Wells's view of criminology: 'he proceeds to cast contempt on the study of criminology'.[93] While Wells is contemptuous of criminology at points in his work, his attitude to the criminal in his work up to and including *A Modern Utopia* is an ambivalent one. In 'The Problem of the Birth Supply', he points out: 'A criminal is no doubt of less personal value to the community than a law-abiding citizen of the same general calibre, but *it does not follow that for one moment that he is of less value as a parent* [emphasis in original].'[94] In his contribution to the Sociological Society debate, Wells emphasises the importance of environmental constraints, stating that: 'I am inclined to believe that a large proportion of our present-day criminals are the brightest and boldest members of families living under impossible conditions, and that in many desirable qualities the average criminal is above the average of the law-abiding poor, and probably of the average respectable person.'[95]

Yet for all his earlier stress on the importance of environment, Wells in *A Modern Utopia* nonetheless concurs entirely with Galton's imperative that criminals should not breed. A startling omission from *A Modern Utopia*, especially in terms of the above statement from 'The Problem of the Birth Supply', is any measure of contingency provision for the children of criminals. There again, Wells endeavours to ensure that extreme caution is exercised prior to excluding criminals from mainstream society, or as he puts it in the work: 'You must not too hastily imagine these things being done – as they would be done on earth at present – by a number of zealous half-educated people in a state of panic at a quite imaginary "Rapid Multiplication of the Unfit"' (128).

There is a moment in *A Modern Utopia* that reveals Wells's rejection of a mechanism for sterilising the unfit which had been articulated by one of his contemporaries, and concerns a reference to W. A. Chapple's book, *The Fertility of the Unfit* (1903). Chapple's book constitutes an example of the kind of imaginary panic at a rapid multiplication of the unfit cited by Wells. As its title suggests, it is preoccupied with the apparent rapidity at which the 'unfit' are breeding at the same time as those displaying more desirable qualities are showing more restraint towards producing offspring. In order to redress the balance, Chapple advocates the implementation of tubo-ligature as a means of artificially inducing sterilisation in the wives or partners of criminals or others considered 'unfit'. Chapple is at pains to point out that tubo-ligature is an operation that can be performed with simplicity: 'A simple ligature of each Fallopian tube would effectually and permanently sterilise, without in any way whatever altering or changing the organs concerned, or the emotions, habits, disposition, or life of the person operated on.'[96] For Chapple, this remains the most 'humane' way of repressing the fertility of the unfit, since it avoids the side effects that must inevitably result from operations to sterilise men or from the cruder procedures that might be performed upon women, which include altered emotions and hormone levels. Chapple envisages that, faced with the burden of more children than they can provide for, the sexual partners of the unfit would willingly submit to this operation.

Wells's curt statement in *A Modern Utopia* that works such as *The Fertility of the Unfit* merely constitute 'a not very well criticised literature' (130) suggests only mild opposition on the part of Wells concerning Chapple's idea of tubo-ligature. However, in a subsequent debate in the pages of *The New Age* – discussed below – Wells is much more scathing in his criticism of 'These schemes for ligaturing the ducts of unlucky criminals', which he describes as 'silly and ineffectual'.[97] Wells's statement in *A Modern Utopia* that it may 'not [be] necessary to enforce' any separation between male and female criminals is open to two distinct interpretations. The first of these is that, having induced the 'artificial' sterilisation of the females, it would not be necessary to further interfere in the sexual relations of the unfit. The second of these is that Wells is responding sardonically to Chapple's claim that the lovers of criminals would happily submit to the operation of tubo-ligature.

While his views on eugenics continue to generate passionate debates in the present-day, Wells in fact stirred up considerable controversy in his contemporary moment. There was a particularly interesting debate in the pages of *The New Age* in 1910, which was conducted between Wells and C. W. Saleeby.[98] Saleeby had written an article in which he suggested that Wells was now more favourable to Galtonian eugenics than he once had been. Wells responded with a furious rebuttal of this claim, rejecting as 'absolutely untrue' Saleeby's assertion that 'I have since heartily assented' to the propositions of eugenics, and emphasising that: 'I am quite at one with Mr. Chesterton and Mr. Shaw in regarding such "Eugenics" as Dr. Saleeby propounds in your last issue as childish nonsense with cruel possibilities.'[99] This in turn drew a counter response from Saleeby, who pointed to what he considered to be the glaring inconsistencies of his opponent's views, and stressed the ' "cruel possibilities" ' implicit in Wells's apparent willingness – expressed at the Sociological Society – to sterilise failures.[100]

While Saleeby's counterargument is not without merit, a second letter from Wells which constitutes the final instalment of this miniature debate and is entitled 'The Sham Science of Eugenics', possesses far greater value for the purpose of foregrounding the complexities and inconsistencies of his own views on eugenics as expressed between the serialisation of *Mankind in the Making* in 1902–1903 and the appearance of *The New Age* material in 1910. First of all, Wells attempts to clarify his earlier opinion which apparently advocated the sterilisation of failures by making the rather curious statement that: 'To treat my statement that it is only by the sterilization of failures, i.e., the lack of offspring, that a species progresses, into an admission that types can now be distinguished for deliberate sterilization, shows a real ingenuity in misconception.'[101] Wells's use of the term sterilisation to denote non-production of offspring in this instance is highly peculiar. There would have been little doubt among his contemporaries, however, that the term sterilisation refers exactly to methods of ensuring that certain individuals do not produce offspring.

Wells next reiterates his opposition to the notion of 'positive' eugenics by stating that: 'no sane sociologist is for mating So-and-So perforce to a second So-and-So or for sterilizing Such-a-person on the strength of a chance'.[102] However, aside from the distinct conceptions of positive and negative eugenics, he does consider it a separate issue 'to discuss such a modification of social institutions as will increase the reproductive possibilities of the So-and-Sos, and make it less likely that the Such-a-persons will leave offspring'.[103] For Wells, precisely the reason why eugenics in its present form constitutes a 'sham science' is its continuing insistence on monogamy: 'At present we western Europeans have matrimonial institutions that limit the possible legal children of the most wonderful creatures alive to the number one single partner can give them, and the possible variations upon their heredity to what that partner can introduce, and any science of Eugenics that does not begin upon that and concentrate upon that as its essential question is, I hold, just arrant bosh.'[104] The hint of polygamy contained in this passage of course recalls the more radical aspects of *A Modern Utopia*, which includes a discussion of group marriages. However, prior to examining the work in the light of the above passage, it is first appropriate to identify a perceptible shift in Wells's views on eugenics.

It will be recalled that in 'The Problem of the Birth Supply', Wells had carefully maintained a distinction between personal and reproductive value. Hence, while possessing beauty is a desirable personal trait, it cannot be relied on as part of any reproductive equation. It must be stressed, however, that such a distinction is entirely absent in the above statement from *The New Age*. For Wells's emphasis on stimulating the fertility of 'the most wonderful creatures alive' by increasing their number of sexual partners, and consequently the amount of variation upon their heredity, suggests that personal and reproductive values have now fused. His identification of certain individuals possessing enhanced reproductive values now in fact aligns Wells with Galton. Indeed, it would appear that his rejection of Galton is motivated more by Wells's insistence upon the emphasis on the individual's right to choose a pro-creative partner as he articulates in *A Modern Utopia*, and less by any rejection of the possibility of identifying particular individuals who should be particularly encouraged to reproduce.

It is possible to review *A Modern Utopia* with this closer alignment between Wells and Galton in mind. In his discussion of parentage in the novel, Wells states that 'it must be open to every man to approve himself worthy of ascendency [sic]' (123). This comment suggests that, like Galton, Wells advocates stimulating the fertility of certain sections of the community. However, there is a crucial difference between the manner in which each of these men approaches the difficulty of pre-cisely whose fertility should be stimulated. Whereas Galton advocates endowing marriages among the privileged classes, Wells's insistence on minimum standards means that all members of the community have an equal opportunity of proving themselves worthy of parentage.

Considering the views articulated in *A Modern Utopia*, it is also possible to enquire whether Wells's advocacy of polygamy in his letter to *The New Age* contains a gender bias. The narrator of the earlier work consid-ers that the chastity of the wife is imperative to the utopian marriage. For the husband, on the other hand, such restraint is only desirable and ought to be encouraged only to avoid: 'a variable amount of emotional offence to the wife [which] [...] may wound her pride and cause her vio-lent perturbations of jealousy' (174). Such opinions of course stand in a highly ironic relation to Wells's own loose sexual morals. With this in mind, it is likely that his identification of the necessity to increase the number of variations – and hence partners – of the 'most wonder-ful creatures alive' not only refers solely to men but also has a definite biographical bias, which may indeed be construed as a blatant piece of self-justification on behalf of Wells.

Having discussed the treatment of failures and the role of women, the narrator of the work remains frustrated in his attempts to identify the controlling 'will' of Utopia. As indicated previously, in *A Modern Utopia* Wells subverts the existing tradition of utopian literature which provides the protagonist with a guide to the new social arrangements. This theme continues as the narrator fears Utopia is 'swallowing me up' (199) as he and the botanist await their fate in the toy factory. Finding himself contrasting the fragmentary glimpse of Utopia he has attained with his preconception that he would be presented with a series of generalisations, the narrator comments that: 'I had always imagined myself as standing outside the general machinery of the State – in the distinguished visitors' gallery, as it were – and getting the new world in a series of comprehensive perspective views' (199). It is around the point in the novel at which he encounters his utopian 'double', who as a Samurai represents the organising 'will' of Utopia, that the opposition between the narrator's speculations concerning Utopia and the material reality of the world state becomes most readily apparent.

The narrator is keen to emphasise the absence in Utopia of the class distinctions that characterise the contemporary earth. Thus he points out concerning the dress of the women: 'There is little difference in deportment between one class and another' (202). Furthermore, he is careful to foreground that the utopian scheme of classifying individuals avoids recourse to such categories as capitalist and labourer, and is based instead upon a provisional division of individuals into one of four temperaments: the Kinetic, the Poietic, the Dull and the Base. Yet despite this articulation of his ideal that Utopia does not contain class divisions, the narrator's own interaction with the population of this alternative earth in fact exposes rigid class divisions that reflect those on his own world. Hence, precisely the reason why he cannot engage his fellow factory workers in his desire to discuss government is because they share the same limited interest in politics as the 'lower' classes on earth: 'These people about me are everyday people, people not so very far from the minimum wage, accustomed much as the everyday people of earth are accustomed to take their world as they find it' (200). The manner in which the narrator regards 'the better social success of the botanist' is also significant in revealing how the class distinctions of Utopia mirror those on earth (201). Thus the narrator complains that the two unintelligent looking women with whom his companion converses are fine for a lower emotional type such as the botanist, but are not of the class of individual to whom he longs to speak. In this respect, his meeting with his utopian 'double' is significant not only for stirring up within the narrator the same emotional turmoil that characterises the botanist, but also for its fulfilment of his desire to meet someone from his own class.

The Samurai class to which his utopian 'double' belongs further highlights the stark opposition between the narrator's imagined ideal and the actual characteristics of utopian society. As the narrator of the work acknowledges, Plato's Guardians provided the inspiration for the Samurai. In his characterisation of the Samurai, Wells also attempts to resolve the difficulty in his own thought concerning the relation between those in possession of esoteric knowledge and the general population. Whereas in *The Invisible Man* he had warned of the dangers of potential leaders of men becoming severed from society, in *A Modern Utopia* Wells introduces the idea of an annual journey designed to cleanse the Samurai of any egotistical ambitions.

However, the Samurai actually highlight the difficulties involved in creating a class possessing superior knowledge to the rest of society. For despite the narrator's continual insistence upon the tolerant nature of utopian society, the Samurai do not allow for dissent. Rather, they maintain a quasi-religious doctrine which must be followed in order to gain access to the Samurai order. The Samurai have no interest in a multiplicity of truths, only their own truth. From the perspective of the exclusive manner in which the Samurai organise knowledge, such voices as that of the blond haired heretic are made to look ridiculous rather than essential to human progress.

In order to conclude this discussion, it is appropriate to examine the opposition between the narrator's speculations and the material reality of Utopia in the context of Wells's overall strategy in *A Modern Utopia*. There can be little doubt that Wells actively desires the utopian ideals expressed by the narrator of his work. After all, the opinions articulated in *A Modern Utopia* are consistent with those expressed in *Mankind in the Making*, and should be regarded as the fruition of the process of intellectual development Wells underwent between the publication of *Anticipations* in 1901 and the work's appearance in 1905. This being the case, it is perfectly legitimate to examine the ambiguities of *A Modern Utopia* as reflecting the complexities of Wells's thought at the moment he wrote the work.

Hence, for all the insistence on individuality in *A Modern Utopia*, Wells's continued emphasis on efficiency often impinges on individual liberty. The various preconditions for parentage Wells establishes undercut his earlier insistence that the selection of a mate constitutes the supreme expression of individuality, since that choice is restricted to those individuals who fulfil these criteria. Wells's entire attitude to eugenics is revealing in highlighting the glaring inconsistencies of his own position. Although he had initially criticised Galton's schemes to endow specified sections of the community, Wells himself eventually concurs with the notion that particular individuals should be encouraged to reproduce because they are more likely to produce high quality offspring.

This type of inconsistent attitude towards the leading scientific figures of his contemporary moment also defines Wells's attitude towards the writings of Spencer. Although he had argued vigorously against Spencer in his early journalism and indeed in *The War of the Worlds*, Wells in fact appropriates the Spencerian imperative that the weaker members of the species *homo sapiens* should not breed in his conception of the kinetic Utopia. Curiously, the fact that his kinetic Utopia merges this imperative with his own version of 'ethical' evolution indicates that – as his conception of the scientific romance develops into the twentieth century – Wells attempts to reconcile the opposing interpretations of the significance of natural selection produced by Spencer and Huxley respectively.

However, further discussion of *A Modern Utopia* must also bear in mind that his attempt at philosophical discussion is inextricably bound with Wells's novelistic endeavour. He knew that any immediate realisation of his sought after world state must inevitably be restricted to the persons living in the year 1905. It is precisely because of this realisation that Wells utilises a complex narrative structure in *A Modern Utopia*, whereby the fictional texture continually undercuts the desire of the narrator for a better future. This is why the narrator – who can perhaps also be understood as a blatant piece of self-irony on the part of H. G. Wells himself – is continually haunted by the intolerance, pettiness and emotions of contemporary humanity. Nowhere is the manner in which the restrictions of contemporary humanity impinge on the utopian ideal more apparent than in the ending of the work, in which an intense emotional outburst from the botanist upon encountering the double of his 'lost' love finally bursts the utopian 'bubble'. Although this outburst results in both the dissipation of his utopian rationality and a return to the comparative drabness of earthly London for him and the botanist, the narrator concedes that: 'It is good discipline for the Utopist to visit this world occasionally' (324). This statement has a particular resonance for the overall conception of *A Modern Utopia*. For although Wells adheres to the pre-existing endeavour of the genre by imagining improved conditions for mankind, he is emphatic that the modern Utopia cannot divorce itself from the restrictions of present-day humanity. This for Wells constitutes the limits of any *Sociological Holiday*, which exists to propose alternative horizons for the human race.

8
Conclusion

At the outset of this book, I suggested that the conception of Wells as something of a 'founding father' of science fiction has worked to obscure the extent to which his early work is grounded in the discourses of contemporary science. By focusing on the relationship between science *and* fiction – rather than on science fiction – this study has shown that Wells's scientific romances were immersed in the discourses of science in the 1890s and early years of the twentieth century. Indeed, Wells's early fiction exemplifies how the literature of this period provided a means of intervention in a range of topical scientific debates – and in the social, psychological and ethical disputes stimulated by science. The study of Wells's scientific romances is significant for the history of science, since it confirms the importance of literature in contributing to debates that have, until recently, been lost to view. This is true, for example, of the way in which *The Island of Doctor Moreau* responds to new theories of the relations between humans, animals and language.

By investigating Wells's evolving response to 'leading men of science' as part of the scientific engagement of his early fiction, this book has shown that it is necessary to reassess his relationship to the work of T. H. Huxley and Herbert Spencer. Wells does not endorse absolutely Huxley's conception of 'ethical' evolution. As I have argued, from *The Time Machine* onwards he places an emphasis on competition that is largely absent from the writings of Huxley. This is not to understate the influence of Huxley on Wells. On the contrary, Huxley's insistence on the importance of ethical evolution is the obvious inspiration for Wells's identification of morals, culture and education – or, the 'acquired factor' – as the basis for the meaningful progression of *homo sapiens* in 'Human Evolution, An Artificial Process'. Wells's adherence to the co-operative principles of Huxley's ethical evolution as an author of scientific romances is, as I have demonstrated, revealed most explicitly in *The War of the Worlds*.

Yet Huxley was not the only principal scientific figure to influence the development of Wells's scientific romances. For all the scornful remarks he made concerning Spencer in the 1890s, Wells in fact appropriated significant elements of Spencer's work as his scientific romances became increasingly sociological after 1900. In particular, he appropriated the Spencerian imperative that the weaker members of the human species should not breed. As indicated, the kinetic Utopia of *A Modern Utopia* attempts to reconcile the radically opposing worldviews encapsulated by the work of Huxley and Spencer respectively. From a modern perspective, it is interesting to note that Wells's kinetic Utopia synthesises ideas that would now be distinctly opposed on the left and right political wings.

The type of inconsistency he displays towards Spencer is, to a lesser extent, evident in Wells's attitude towards the work of Francis Galton. While he is relatively consistent in his rejection of the entire notion of 'positive' eugenics throughout much of his career as an author of scientific romances, Wells in fact aligns some of his arguments with particular facets of Galton's work in *A Modern Utopia*. Particularly, Wells appears to agree that certain individuals are more worthy of attaining parentage than others – although, it should be emphasised, from a more equitable basis than Galton.

Wells's often disparaging attitude towards principal scientific figures persists even after he has completed the bulk of his scientific romances. Returning to 'The So-Called Science Of Sociology', he described the effect on the reader of Spencer's development hypothesis in the following terms:

> He [Spencer] believed that everything was finally measurable; he believed that individuality (heterogeneity) was and is an evolutionary product from an original homogeneity; and the thought that it might be inextricably in the nature of things probably never entered his head. He thought that identically similar units build up and built up, atoms, molecules, inorganic compounds, organic compounds, protoplasm, conscious protoplasm, and so on, until at last the brain reeled at the aggregation.[1]

Given that at the moment the essay appeared in May 1905 Wells had already modified Spencer's development hypothesis in *Anticipations* and appropriated his imperative that the weak of the species should not breed from *Mankind in the Making* onwards, there is a marked irony about this passage. Perhaps his desire to critique figures like Spencer whilst having already appropriated significant aspects of their work is indicative of Wells's desire to displace them and establish himself as the leading individual in scientific modernity. Thus in the above statement he is attempting to elevate his own insistence that each inorganic and organic being is unique above Spencer's model that all evolution is characterised by the movement from homogeneity to heterogeneity.

In concluding this study, it is appropriate to briefly examine the role of Wells's scientific romances in prefiguring the future direction of his work. The humorous element of a text like *The Invisible Man*, for instance, anticipates the comedy of Wells's social novels. By far the most enduring aspect of the scientific romances in the context of Wells's life work (aside from his lifelong preoccupation with science) is his commitment to the formation of a world state.[2] In *Men Like Gods* (1923), for example, he presents a more advanced version of the global order of *A Modern Utopia*.

As he sought means to campaign for the formation of a world state, Wells utilised the tropes he had first employed in the scientific romances. In historical writings such as *The Outline of History* (1920), and in its shorter companion *A Short History of the World* (1922), he begins with pre-human history in order to emphasise the comparative insignificance of *homo sapiens* and to point to the need for humanity to unite in a world state in order to meet the challenges of history.[3] This of course recalls the manner in which he invokes a cosmic perspective in such novels as *The War of the Worlds* so as to emphasise the importance of co-operation as a means through which humanity can overcome its relative insignificance in the natural order.

Not all of the themes introduced in the scientific romances persist in Wells's subsequent writings, however. I have shown how the development of his scientific romances was characterised by Wells's increasing insistence on the need to allow for the unhindered development of unique individualities in the organisation of society. Yet as Wells's literary and political career developed, he increasingly emphasised the importance of the species over the individual. Indeed, even the characterisation of the distinct individual 'types' who populate his social novels remains inextricably bound with Wells's analysis of the challenges facing *homo sapiens*, or as Roslynn Haynes puts it: 'If the human species as a whole was a cumbersome topic for literature, the nearest manageable approximation was a panoramic view of society as a whole [...] so that the study of a "typical" member within his natural milieu might serve as a reasonable statement of the species as a whole.'[4]

While Wells himself might have increasingly emphasised the importance of collectivism, the tension between social efficiency and individual development found in works like *The First Men in the Moon* and *A Modern Utopia* is symptomatic of the continued relevance of his scientific romances in the twenty first century. As much as ever, governments, social reformers, and political parties continue to contest the appropriate degree of state intervention in individual activities, thus continuing the individualism-collectivism debate that Wells attempts to resolve in works like *A Modern Utopia*. Wells's idea in that work of using biometric data kept on index cards as a means of verifying personal identity has a definite contemporary resonance. Recent plans by the British government to compel all citizens to carry personal identity cards containing biometric data, for example, have caused considerable controversy. While the idea of the world state first tentatively alluded to at the end of *The War of the Worlds* has not – or at least has not yet – materialised, the concept remains a deeply fascinating one in an increasingly interdependent world. Indeed, Wells's recognition in works like *Anticipations* that the increasing interdependence of the world community was an inevitable outcome of improvements in communication and transport means that he foresaw the emergence of globalisation long before the concept was generally acknowledged.

The enduring appeal of Wells's scientific romances can, perhaps, be attributed to his capacity to popularise scientific concepts for a broader audience and to dramatise the implications of scientific developments in an extraordinary narrative form. At the beginning of the twenty first century, in which technological advancements will undoubtedly assert an even greater influence on society, the skill of effectively communicating science and the implications of scientific discovery which Wells possessed is more necessary than ever.

Notes

1 Introduction

1. H. G. Wells, Interview with the *Weekly Sun Literary Supplement*, 1 December 1895; reprinted in 'A Chat with the Author of *The Time Machine*, Mr H. G. Wells', edited with comment by David C. Smith, *The Wellsian*, n.s. 20 (1997), 3–9 (p. 8).
2. Wells himself labelled his early scientific fantasies as 'scientific romances' when he published a collection with Victor Gollancz entitled *The Scientific Romances of H. G. Wells* in 1933, thus ensuring the adoption of the term in subsequent critical discussions of his work. The term appears to have originated with the publication of Charles Howard Hinton's *Scientific Romances* (1886), a collection of speculative scientific essays and short stories.
3. It should be noted, however, that Wells's controversial second scientific romance, *The Island of Doctor Moreau* (1896), did not appear in a serialised form. However, *The Invisible Man* was published in *Pearson's Weekly* in June and July 1897, *When the Sleeper Wakes* was published in *The Graphic* between January and May 1899, *The First Men in the Moon* was published in the *Strand Magazine* between December 1900 and August 1901 and *A Modern Utopia* was serialised in the *Fortnightly Review* between October 1904 and April 1905.
4. A number of Wells's most significant scientific essays have been available for some time in an anthology, *H. G. Wells: Early Writings in Science and Science Fiction*, ed. by Robert M. Philmus and David Y. Hughes (London: University of California Press, 1975).
5. 'A Chat with the Author of *The Time Machine*', p. 6.
6. In an appreciative review of T. H. Huxley – who had lectured him as a student at the Normal School of Science (now part of Imperial College, London) – Wells himself indicates that he had begun reading the periodicals during his days as a student: 'we borrowed the books he [Huxley] wrote, we clubbed out of our weekly guineas to buy the *Nineteenth Century* whenever he rattled Gladstone or pounded the Duke of Argyle'. H. G. Wells, 'Huxley', *Royal College of Science Magazine*, 13 (1901), 209–11 (p. 211).
7. For a partly dissenting view, see Leon Stover, 'Applied Natural History: Wells vs. Huxley', in *H. G. Wells Under Revision*, ed. by Patrick Parrinder and Christopher Rolfe (London and Toronto: Associated University Presses, 1986), pp. 125–33.
8. Brian Stableford, *Scientific Romance in Britain, 1890–1950* (London: Fourth Estate, 1985), pp. 11–17.
9. In his *Experiment in Autobiography*, 2 vols (London: Gollancz, 1934), Wells himself acknowledged the role of earlier Education Acts in his success as a writer: 'The Education Act of 1871 had not only enlarged the reading public very greatly but it had stimulated the middle class by a sense of possible competition from below', II, 507.

10. For a more detailed discussion of the precursors of the scientific romance, see Stableford's *Scientific Romance in Britain*, especially chapter 2, 'Scientific Romance and Its Literary Ancestors', pp. 18–43.
11. Roslynn D. Haynes, *H. G. Wells: Discoverer of the Future, The Influence of Science on His Thought* (London: New York University Press, 1980).
12. William Greenslade, *Degeneration, Culture and the Novel, 1880–1940* (Cambridge: Cambridge University Press, 1994).

2 Heart of Darkness: *The Time Machine* and Retrogression

1. V. S. Pritchett, *The Living Novel* (1946) (London: Arrow: 1960), p. 127.
2. Unsigned Notice, *Daily Chronicle*, 27 July 1895, p. 3; reprinted in *H. G. Wells: The Critical Heritage*, ed. by Patrick Parrinder (London: Routledge & Kegan Paul, 1972), pp. 38–9 (p. 38).
3. What distinguished Wells was his use of a technological device which allowed its user to control their journey through time. Previous time travel narratives had used more simplistic means of transporting the protagonist in time. Edward Bellamy, for example, used a hypnotic sleep in his *Looking Backward* (1888) in order to transfer his protagonist forward to the year 2000. Mark Twain, in contrast, used a bang on the head as a means of moving his central character back in time in *A Connecticut Yankee in King Arthur's Court* (1889). Of course, Wells himself would use a hypnotic sleep in *When the Sleeper Wakes* (1899), in which the protagonist, Graham, awakens in the year 2100 to discover a nightmarish version of the industrialised socialist Utopia envisaged by Bellamy. On time travel narratives before and after *The Time Machine*, see W. M. S. Russell, 'Time Before and After *The Time Machine*', *Foundation*, 65 (1995), 24–40.
4. *Daily Chronicle*, p. 38.
5. Unsigned Notice, *Review of Reviews*, 11 (1895), 263.
6. It should be noted that, while those notices that did appear were favourable, *The Time Machine* was not widely reviewed. Indeed, an anonymous reviewer in the *Review of Reviews* remarked: 'I cannot understand why so little attention has been paid in the Press and elsewhere to the remarkable story which Mr. Wells is contributing to the pages of the New Review.' Unsigned, 'Will the Future be to the Cannibals? A Nightmare of Civilisation' [review of *The Time Machine*], *Review of Reviews*, 11 (1895), 346.
7. Letter to Elizabeth Healey, December 1894, *The Correspondence of H. G. Wells*, ed. by David C. Smith, 4 vols (London: Pickering and Chatto, 1998), I, 226.
8. Geoffrey West, *H. G. Wells: A Sketch for a Portrait* (London: Howe, 1930), pp. 291–2. In one of these versions as reported by West the upper and lower world inhabitants are not yet distinct species and the disruptive presence of the time travellers results in the working population of the underworld rising up to massacre the idle surface dwellers. This of course prefigures *When the Sleeper Wakes*. Interestingly, in his *H. G. Wells: Traversing Time* (Middletown, Connecticut: Wesleyan University Press, 2004), W. Warren Wagar argues that *When the Sleeper Wakes* should be envisioned as a 'prequel' to *The Time Machine*:

> Instead of A.D. 802,701, the year is A.D. 2100, a little more than two centuries from the publication date of the novel. The fission of humanity

into two separate and degenerate species has not yet occurred, but the warfare between capital and labor that will ultimately lead to it has become acute. (p. 67)

9. The *National Oberver* version of *The Time Machine* is reprinted in *Early Writings in Science and Science Fiction*. Both the *National Observer* version and 'The Chronic Argonauts' are reprinted in *The Definitive Time Machine: A Critical Edition of H. G. Wells's Scientific Romance*, ed. by Harry M. Geduld (Bloomington and Indianapolis: Indiana University Press, 1987). 'The Chronic Argounauts' is also reprinted in Bernard Bergonzi's *The Early H. G. Wells: A Study of the Scientific Romances* (Manchester: Manchester University Press, 1961).

10. Henry Holt published a slightly earlier version of the novel, with the erroneous name 'H. S. Wells' printed on the title page, on 7 May in New York. However, the Heinemann text published in Britain on 29 May is generally acknowledged as the 'final' version. For a more detailed account of the development of *The Time Machine*, see Bernard Loing, 'H. G. Wells at Work 1894–1900: A Writer's Beginnings', *The Wellsian*, n.s. 8 (1985), 30–7. Loing investigates the construction of *The Time Machine* more fully in his *H. G. Wells À L'oeuvre: Les débuts d'un écrivain* (1894–1900) (Paris: Didier, 1984). See also, Robert M. Philmus, 'H. G. Wells's Revisi(tati)ons of *The Time Machine*', *English Literature in Transition, 1880–1920*, 41 (1998), 427–52.

11. As Wells's biographers Norman and Jeanne MacKenzie point out: 'The new geology, the new astronomy, the new mathematics and the new physics were all sciences vitally concerned with time.' *The Time Traveller: The Life of H. G. Wells* (London: Weidenfeld and Nicolson, 1973), pp. 121–2.

12. Patrick Parrinder, *Shadows of the Future: H. G. Wells, Science Fiction and Prophecy* (Liverpool: Liverpool University Press, 1995), pp. 41–2.

13. Parrinder, *Shadows of the Future*, p. 42.

14. It should be noted, however, that the 1960 George Pal film version of *The Time Machine* projects the contemporary setting of the novel forward to the beginning of the new century.

15. *The Works of H. G. Wells: Atlantic Edition*, 28 vols (London: Unwin, 1924–1927), I, *The Time Machine, The Wonderful Visit and Other Stories*, p. 5. Subsequent references to this edition will be cited in parenthesis in the text. Wells was probably familiar with 'Modern Mathematical Thought', a transcription of Newcomb's address published in *Nature*, 49 (1894), 325–9. On developments in theories of the fourth-dimension since *The Time Machine* was published, see Alan Mayne, 'The Virtual Time Machine: Part II – Some Physicists' Views of Time Travel', *The Wellsian*, n.s. 20 (1997), 20–31.

16. In his *H. G. Wells's The Time Machine: A Reference Guide* (London and Westport, Connecticut: Greenwood, 2004), John Hammond acknowledges the reference to Newcomb, but overlooks the Medical Man's recollections, leading him to conclude: 'We may infer therefore that the after-dinner conversation at Richmond takes place in the early months of 1894' (p. 21).

17. Kathryn Hume, for example, remarks on the way in which the Time Traveller utilises primitive energy in her article, 'Eat or be Eaten: H. G. Wells's *Time Machine*', *Philological Quarterly*, 69 (1990), 233–51.

18. See Stephen Derry, 'The Time Traveller's Utopian Books and his Reading of the Future', *Foundation*, 65 (1995), 16–24; also see Fernando Porta, 'One

Text, Many Utopias: Some Examples of Intertextuality in *The Time Machine*', *The Wellsian*, n.s. 20 (1997), 10–20.

19. Edward Bellamy, *Looking Backward* (1888) (New York: Signet, 1960), p. 37.

20. The absence of a companion is no doubt an additional factor in stimulating the Traveller's fearful behaviour. In Edward Bulwer-Lytton's *The Coming Race* (1871) (Stroud: Alan Sutton, 1995), the protagonist's companion comments: '"A trusty companion halves the journey and doubles the courage"' (p. 3). Wells himself would later employ this convention in *A Modern Utopia*, in which the narrator explicitly acknowledges that the presence of his botanist travelling companion substantially reduces his fears as he is transported to an alternative earth.

21. Bulwer-Lytton, *The Coming Race*, p. 5.

22. The manner in which the Time Traveller's imagination generates his fears prefigures Prendick's actions in *The Island of Doctor Moreau*. During the Leopard Man's pursuit of him, Prendick acknowledges that his own imagination contributes to his complete unnerving. Of course, in the Martians in *The War of the Worlds*, Wells introduces characters that appear to confirm the Traveller's fear that humanity might develop into something inhuman and overwhelmingly powerful.

23. Bulwer-Lytton, *The Coming Race*, p. 8.

24. 'In the Golden Age' was the title given to one of 16 chapter titles used in the original Heinemann edition of the novel. These titles were: I Introduction; II The Machine; III The Time Traveller Returns; IV Time Travelling; V In the Golden Age; VI The Sunset of Mankind; VII A Sudden Shock; VIII Explanation; IX The Morlocks; X When the Night Came; XI The Palace of Green Porcelain; XII In the Darkness; XIII The Trap of the White Sphinx; XIV The Further Vision; XV The Time Traveller Returns; XVI After the Story (this final chapter includes the epilogue). Wells later rearranged these 16 original titles into 12 when he published the *Atlantic Edition* of his complete works. For a discussion of the inadequacies of many reprints of *The Time Machine*, and indeed other of the scientific romances, see David J. Lake, 'The Current Texts of Wells's Early SF Novels: Situation Unsatisfactory (Part 1)', *The Wellsian*, n.s. 11 (1988), 3–12; 'The Current Texts of Wells's Early SF Novels: Situation Unsatisfactory (Part 2)', *The Wellsian*, n.s. 12 (1989), 21–36.

25. John Barlow, *On Man's Power over Himself to Prevent or Control Insanity* (1843); extracts reprinted in *Embodied Selves: An Anthology of Psychological Texts 1830–1890*, ed. by Jenny Bourne Taylor and Sally Shuttleworth (Oxford: Oxford University Press, 1998), pp. 243–6.

26. Henry Maudsley, *Responsibility in Mental Disease* (London: Henry S. King, 1874), p. 269. Significantly, Maudsley would later participate in the same roundtable discussion of eugenics as Wells at a meeting of the Sociological Society in May 1905.

27. Parrinder, *Shadows of the Future*, pp. 49–64.

28. It is as this point in *The Time Machine* that the Time Traveller's actions correspond to those of the narrator of *The Coming Race* as he encounters the first Vril-ya, thus substantiating Derry's contention that: 'The awe and terror and fear of inimical powers that the sight of living Vril-ya strikes in the narrator of *The Coming Race* has its equivalent in the Time Traveller's reactions to the White Sphinx'. 'The Time Traveller's Utopian Books', p. 19.

This moment also reveals another significant difference between the Time Traveller's introduction to the future and that of Julian West. In contrast to the Traveller's falling asleep after the exhaustion of his emotion, Julian West at least has a comfortable bed in which to recover his strength following his shock concerning the length of time he has slept: 'Feeling partially dazed, I drank a cup of some sort of broth at my companion's suggestion, and, immediately afterward becoming very drowsy, went off into a deep sleep.' Bellamy, *Looking Backward*, p. 39.

29. Maudsley, *Responsibility in Mental Disease*, p. 295.
30. Maudsley, *Responsibility in Mental Disease*, p. 296.
31. Maudsley, *Responsibility in Mental Disease*, p. 296.
32. For a more detailed account of the significance ascribed to nervous energy in Victorian medical science, see Janet Oppenheim, *'Shattered Nerves': Doctors, Patients and Depression in Victorian England, 1850–1914* (Oxford: Oxford University Press, 1991).
33. The disease and decay suggested by the Sphinx have often been linked to Wells's critique of British Imperialism. In the course of the novel, Wells makes a number of classical references which seem contrived to emphasise the futility of the imperial project. For example, the Time Traveller remarks: ' "I fancied I saw suggestions of old Phoenician decorations" ' (33). With this reference to Phoenician culture, Wells may have intended to critique the British Empire by contrasting its relative historical insignificance with the enduring influence of classical culture. On the significance of the Sphinx in the novel, see David J. Lake, 'The White Sphinx and the Whitened Lemur: Images of Death in *The Time Machine*', *Science-Fiction Studies*, 6 (1979), 77–84; Frank Scafella, 'The White Sphinx and *The Time Machine*', *Science-Fiction Studies*, 8 (1981), 255–65.
34. H. G. Wells, 'The Refinement of Humanity', *National Observer*, n.s. 11 (April 1894), 581–2 (p. 581).
35. On the fusion of realism and utopianism in *The Time Machine*, see Patrick Parrinder, *'News from Nowhere, the Time Machine* and the Break-up of Classical Realism', *Science-Fiction Studies*, 3 (1976), 265–74.
36. Porta, 'One Text, Many Utopias', p. 18. Porta uses *Looking Backward* as an example of how the protagonist of the utopian story often finds love in the future, since Julian West marries the great-granddaughter of his lover.
37. Porta, 'One Text, Many Utopias', p. 18.
38. Porta, 'One Text, Many Utopias', p. 18.
39. Porta, 'One Text, Many Utopias', p. 18.
40. Parrinder, *Shadows of the Future*, p. 59.
41. Wells's continuing awareness of such discourses in revealed in 'A Slum Novel' [his review of Arthur Morrison's *A Child of the Jago*], *Saturday Review*, 82 (1896), 573.
42. Andrew Mearns, *The Bitter Cry of Outcast London* (1883); extracts from Mearns's text are reprinted along with a selection of other discourses on the poor in *Into Unknown England, 1866–1913*, ed. by Peter Keating (Manchester: Fontana, 1976), pp. 91–111.
43. Mearns, 'Bitter Cry', p. 95.
44. The implications of this apparent inversion of the class system are discussed below. The relationship between Wells's early romances and Conrad's novel

is examined by Patrick A. McCarthy, *'Heart of Darkness* and the Early novels of H. G. Wells: Evolution, Anarchy, Entropy', *Journal of Modern Literature*, 13 (1986), 37–60.

45. T. H. Huxley, 'The Struggle for Existence in Human Society' (1888), in *Collected Essays By T. H. Huxley*, 9 vols (London: Macmillan, 1903), IX, *Evolution and Ethics and Other Essays*, 195–236 (p. 217).

46. Huxley, 'Struggle', pp. 217–18.

47. In *Mankind in the Making* (London: Chapman & Hall, 1903), Wells produces his own account of the necessary responsibilities of the State.

48. Wells, *Experiment in Autobiography*, I, 201.

49. T. H. Huxley, 'Evolution and Ethics' [The Romanes Lecture] (1893), in *Collected Essays by T. H. Huxley*, IX, *Evolution and Ethics and Other Essays*, 46–86 (p. 81).

50. Huxley, 'Evolution and Ethics', p. 83.

51. Huxley, 'Struggle', p. 199.

52. Letter to T. H. Huxley (May 1895), *The Correspondence of H. G. Wells*, I, 238.

53. Edwin Ray Lankester, *Degeneration: A Chapter in Darwinism* (London: Macmillan, 1880).

54. Indeed, Lankester later wrote a long and praising review of Wells's *Anticipations* (1901) entitled 'The Present Judged by the Future', Supplement to *Nature*, 65 (1902), pp. iii–v. Lankester then authored an appreciative notice of 'H. G. Wells' in the *English Illustrated Magazine*, 31 (September 1904), 614–17. The two men first became acquainted in the 1880s and became very good friends in 1904. They remained friends and correspondents until Lankester's death in the 1920s.

55. Lankester, *Degeneration*, p. 29.

56. Lankester, *Degeneration*, p. 32.

57. Lankester, *Degeneration*, p. 33.

58. Lankester, *Degeneration*, p. 33.

59. Lankester, *Degeneration*, pp. 59, 60.

60. In *Degeneration*, Lankester states that: 'Elaboration of some one organ *may* be a necessary accompaniment of Degeneration in all the others; in fact, this is very generally the case' (p. 32). See also William Greenslade, 'Fitness and the Fin de Siècle' in *Fin de Siècle/Fin du Globe*, ed. by John Stokes (Basingstoke: Macmillan, 1992), pp. 37–51 (p. 40).

61. Francis Galton, *Inquiries into Human Faculty and its Development* (1883) (London: J. M. Dent, 1928), p. 14.

62. Galton, *Inquiries*, p. 14.

63. Greenslade, 'Fitness', p. 43.

64. Galton, *Inquiries*, p. 16.

65. See also John S. Partington, *'The Time Machine* and *A Modern Utopia*: The Static and Kinetic Utopias of the Early H. G. Wells', *Utopian Studies*, 13 (2002), 57–68 (pp. 60–1).

66. Galton, *Inquiries*, p. 220.

67. Galton, *Inquiries*, p. 214.

68. Galton, *Inquiries*, p. 17.

69. Galton, *Inquiries*, p. 14.

70. Wells, 'The Refinement of Humanity', p. 581.

71. In 'Ancient Experiments in Co-Operation', *Gentleman's Magazine*, 273 (1892), 418–22, Wells had already emulated Huxley's opposition to the economic individualism of Spencer by emphasising the pivotal role that co-operation plays in the evolution of the organism.

72. Hume, 'Eat or be Eaten', p. 242. In a review published just a few months after *The Time Machine*, Wells himself reiterated something of the dilemma articulated in his first novel: 'In brief, a static species is mechanical, an evolving species suffering – no line of escape from that *impasse* has as yet presented itself [emphasis in original]'. H. G. Wells, 'Bio-Optimism' [review of *The Evergreen: A Northern Seasonal* by Patrick Geddes et al.], *Nature*, 52 (20 August 1895), 410–11 (p. 411).

73. In his *Liberalism and Sociology: L. T. Hobhouse and Political Argument in England, 1880–1914* (Cambridge: Cambridge University Press, 1979), Stefan Collini notes that the terms individualism and collectivism came into being in the 1880s to denote opposing reactions to the issue of state intervention.

74. Collini, *Liberalism and Sociology*, p. 29.

75. Collini, *Liberalism and Sociology*, p. 31.

76. The embarrassment which the Time Traveller feels regarding his actions recalls the shame of the narrator of *The Coming Race* following his flight from the hideous reptile, leaving the body of his companion to be devoured by the monster.

77. John Huntington, *The Logic of Fantasy: H. G. Wells and Science Fiction* (New York: Columbia University Press, 1982), p. 44.

78. Indeed, the Traveller himself seems to acknowledge the comparative physical weakness of the Morlocks: '"I could not imagine the Morlocks were strong enough to move it [the Time Machine] far away"' (82).

79. Bernard Bergonzi, '*The Time Machine*: An Ironic Myth' in *H. G. Wells: A Collection of Critical Essays*, ed. by Bernard Bergonzi (London: Prentice-Hall, 1976), pp. 39–54 (p. 51).

80. John Huntington, '*The Time Machine* and Wells's Social Trajectory', *Foundation*, 65 (1995), 6–15.

81. Huntington, 'Social Trajectory', pp. 6–7.

82. Huntington, 'Social Trajectory', p. 13.

83. H. G. Wells, 'Zoological Retrogression', *Gentleman's Magazine*, 271 (1891), 246–53.

84. Patrick Parrinder, *H. G. Wells* (Edinburgh: Oliver and Boyd, 1970), p. 21.

85. Parrinder, *H. G. Wells*, pp. 21–2.

86. H. G. Wells, 'On Extinction', *Chambers Journal*, 10 (1893) 623–4; reprinted in *Early Writings in Science and Science Fiction*, pp. 169–72.

87. Wells, 'On Extinction', p. 170.

88. Wells, 'On Extinction', p. 171.

89. Wells, 'On Extinction', p. 172.

90. Mary Shelley's novel, *The Last Man* (1826), might well have been Wells's source here. In *The War of the Worlds*, the narrator fears that he is 'the last man alive' following the Martian invasion of the earth.

91. Ernst Haeckel, *The Evolution of Man* (1879); extracts from Haeckel's text are reprinted in *Embodied Selves: An Anthology of Psychological Texts 1830–1890*, pp. 308–11 (pp. 309, 310).

92. Wells, 'Zoological Retrogression', p. 246.
93. Wells, 'Zoological Retrogression', p. 247.
94. Lankester, *Degeneration*, p. 75.
95. In this respect, Wells might have provided the inspiration for George Orwell's later novel, *Nineteen Eighty-Four* (1949). In this dystopian fiction, party members purposefully endeavour to eliminate abstract concepts from the English language, or 'Newspeak' as it is now called. This is intended to deprive the individual of the conceptual skills which might allow him or her to resist party doctrine.
96. Kathryn Hume notes: 'Indeed the Morlocks provide him with a welcome excuse to exercise powers not wanted in London.' 'Eat or be Eaten', p. 239.
97. Huxley, 'Evolution and Ethics', pp. 51–2.
98. Huxley, 'Evolution and Ethics', p. 52.
99. Huntington, *The Logic of Fantasy*, p. 51.
100. H. G. Wells, 'The Biological Problem of To-day', *Saturday Review*, 78 (December 29, 1894), 703–4 (p. 704).
101. H. G. Wells, 'The Rediscovery of the Unique', *Fortnightly Review*, n.s. 50 (July 1891), 106–11 (p. 111).

3 'An Infernally Rum Place': *The Island of Doctor Moreau* and Degeneration

1. Friedrich Nietzsche, *Beyond Good and Evil* (1886) (Harmondsworth: Penguin, 1990), p. 102.
2. Basil Williams, *Athenauem*, 9 May 1896, pp. 615–16; reprinted in *H. G. Wells: The Critical Heritage*, p. 51.
3. Unsigned Review, *Review of Reviews*, 13 (1896), 374–6 (p. 374).
4. *The Works of H. G. Wells: Atlantic Edition*, II, *The Island of Doctor Moreau, The Sleeper Awakes*, ix. Subsequent references to this work will be cited in the text.
5. Parrinder, *Shadows of the Future*, p. 56.
6. For a more detailed account of vivisection in the nineteenth century, see Richard Deland French, *Antivivisection and Medical Science in Victorian Society* (London: Princeton University Press, 1975).
7. Wells, 'Zoological Retrogression', p. 247.
8. Wells, 'Zoological Retrogression', p. 246.
9. Wells, 'Zoological Retrogression', p. 253.
10. Wells, 'Zoological Retrogression', p. 253.
11. Reed, John R., 'The Vanity of Law in *The Island of Doctor Moreau*' in *H. G. Wells Under Revision*, ed. by Patrick Parrinder and Christopher Rolfe (London: Associated University Presses, 1986), pp. 134–44.
12. For an account of the relations between homosexuality and degeneration, see Ed Cohen's *Talk on the Wilde Side* (London: Routledge, 1993).
13. Max Nordau, for example, in his *Degeneration* (1892) (London: University of Nebraska Press, 1993), regarded Wilde as an English representative of the aesthete: 'It is asserted that he walked down Pall Mall in the afternoon dressed in doublet and breeches, with a picturesque biretta on his head, and a sunflower in his hand, the quasi-heraldic symbol of the Aesthetes' (p. 317).

14. Wells's inspiration for this near cannibal act was probably provided by a well-publicised recent court case that would have been fresh in the minds of many of his readers. In the case of *Regina v. Dudley and Stephens* (1884), a court ruled that the actions of two British sailors who had resorted to cannibalism in order to survive at sea were not justified.
15. Unsigned, *Review of Reviews*, 374.
16. H. W. Wilson, 'The Human Animal in Battle', *Fortnightly Review*, n.s. 60 (1896), 272–84.
17. H. G. Wells, 'Human Evolution, an Artificial Process', *Fortnightly Review*, n.s. 60 (1896), 590–5.
18. Wilson, 'The Human Animal', p. 273.
19. Wilson, 'The Human Animal', p. 274.
20. Wilson, 'The Human Animal', p. 274.
21. Wilson, 'The Human Animal', p. 274.
22. Wilson, 'The Human Animal', p. 273.
23. The importance of the culinary theme in Wells's fiction is discussed in Peter Kemp's *H. G. Wells and the Culminating Ape* (London: Macmillan, 1996), pp. 7–72.
24. Letter to the Editor, 7 November 1896, *Saturday Review*, 82 (1896), 497. Mitchell's review of *The Island of Doctor Moreau* was published in the *Saturday Review* on 11 April 1896.
25. Mitchell responded to these comments in a letter that appeared immediately after Wells's in the 7 November issue of the *Saturday Review*. Mitchell argued that the most recent research did not in fact support Wells's claims. He also pointed out that his criticism appeared to have generated valuable publicity for Wells's novel.
26. H. G. Wells, 'The Limits of Individual Plasticity', *Saturday Review*, 79 (19 January 1895), 89–90.
27. Wells, 'The Limits of Individual Plasticity', p. 90.
28. The novel's engagement in contemporary debates concerning animals and language has been almost entirely overlooked by previous criticism. The lone exception to this trend, other than my own research, is Christine Ferguson's *Language, Science and Popular Fiction at the Victorian Fin-de-Siècle: The Brutal Tongue* (Aldershot: Ashgate, 2006). Chapter 4 of Ferguson's study, 'The Law and the Larynx: R. L. Garner, H. G. Wells, and the Dehumanization of Language' (pp. 105–30), examines the way in which both Garner's research and *The Island of Doctor Moreau* subvert linguistic humanism. For Ferguson, the novel undercuts the assumptions of the very anti-vivisection rhetoric with which it has so often been aligned: 'If [...] [in the discourse of animal rights activists] the existence of animal language made brutes equivalent to primitive humans, the same faculty in *Moreau* suggests that human language is an instinctual, debased, and largely irrational function of a random biology' (p. 106).
29. See Gregory Radick's 'Morgan's Canon, Garner's Phonograph, and the Evolutionary Origins of Language and Reason', *British Journal for the History of Science*, 33 (2000), 3–23.
30. R. L. Garner, 'The Simian Tongue [I]', *New Review*, 4 (1891), 555–62; reprinted in *The Origin of Language*, ed. by Roy Harris (Bristol: Thoemmes, 1996), pp. 314–21 (p. 314).

31. Garner, 'The Simian Tongue [I]', p. 320.
32. R. L. Garner, 'The Simian Tongue [II]', *New Review*, 5 (1892), 424–30; reprinted in *The Origin of Language*, pp. 321–7 (p. 325).
33. Radick, 'Morgan's Canon', p. 14.
34. H. G. Wells, 'The Mind in Animals', *Saturday Review*, 78 (1894), 683–4. This review appeared in the same edition (22 December) as one of Wells's articles, 'Another Basis For Life'.
35. Wells, 'The Mind in Animals', p. 683.
36. Wells, 'The Mind in Animals', p. 683.
37. Morgan's distinction between intelligence and reasoned action comes in his 'The Limits of Animal Intelligence', *Fortnighly Review*, n.s. 54 (1893), 223–39. Due to the faculty of intelligence, which 'is ever on the watch for fortunate variations of activity and happy hits of motor response' an animal may appear to be reasoning abstractly, but truly reasoned action is always accompanied by powers of introspection concerning a particular action, which is not displayed by animals (p. 239).
38. On Wells's satirical intentions in the novel, see John Hammond, '*The Island of Doctor Moreau*: A Swiftian Parable', *The Wellsian*, n.s. 16 (1993), 30–41.
39. Unsigned Review, *The Guardian*, 3 June 1896; reprinted in *H. G. Wells: The Critical Heritage*, p. 53.
40. In his preface to the *Atlantic Edition* of *The Island of Doctor Moreau*, Wells himself termed the novel 'a theological grotesque' (ix). For a discussion of the relationship between the novel's theological subtext and the hostile reviews this generated, see Gorman Beauchamp, '*The Island of Doctor Moreau* as Theological Grotesque', *Papers on Language and Literature*, 15 (1979), 408–17.
41. Frank McConnell, *The Science Fiction of H. G. Wells* (New York: Oxford University Press, 1981), p. 105.
42. Wells, 'Human Evolution', p. 593.
43. Wells, cited in Reed, 'The Vanity of Law', p. 142.
44. Extracts from Spencer's text *The Principles of Sociology* (1876) are reprinted in *The Fin de Siècle: A Reader in Cultural History c. 1880–1900*, ed. by Roger Luckhurst and Sally Ledger (Oxford: Oxford University Press, 2000), pp. 321–6.
45. Spencer, *Principles*, p. 322.
46. Spencer, *Principles*, p. 322.
47. Spencer, *Principles*, p. 322.
48. This preface does not appear in all editions of the novel and is not included in the *Atlantic* text. However, the preface is included in the recently published Penguin Classics *The Island of Doctor Moreau*, ed. by Patrick Parrinder (London: Penguin, 2005), pp. 5–6.
49. William Greenslade, *Degeneration, Culture and the Novel*, p. 74.
50. Mary Jeune, 'The Homes of the Poor', *Fortnightly Review*, n.s. 47 (1890), 67–80.
51. Jeune, 'The Homes of the Poor', p. 68.
52. See Roslynn Haynes, *H.G. Wells: Discoverer of the Future*, p. 27.
53. Fernando Porta, 'Narrative Strategies in H. G. Wells' Romances and Short Stories (1887–1910)' (doctoral thesis, University of Reading, 1996), p. 172. A book version of Porta's study is available in Italian, *La scienza come favola: Saggio sui scientific romances di H. G. Wells* (Salerno: Edisud, 1995).

54. I owe this observation to Professor Owen Dudley Edwards of the University of Edinburgh.
55. In his 'H. G. Wells at Work 1894–1900: A Writer's Beginnings', Bernard Loing notes the influence of *Frankenstein* on the first draft of *Moreau*, most revealingly signified by the initial presence of a wife and son for Moreau: 'in a hypothetical further development, their function might have been to serve as ritual victims for some terrifying monster of Moreau's' (p. 36).
56. In her article, 'Vivisected Language in H. G. Wells's *The Island of Doctor Moreau*', *The Wellsian*, n.s. 29 (2006), 20–35, Kimberley Jackson establishes an important context in which to understand Moreau's self-indulgent activities. She points out that the Cruelty to Animals Act of 1876 sought to keep the physical suffering of vertebrate animals to a minimum, justifying it only 'if it serves a purpose in the pursuit of "physiological knowledge" or the "alleviation of suffering"' (p. 21). Examined in the context of Jackson's remark that, in the context of the scientific consensus established by this act, 'the bodily violence must be able to be reconciled, not only with the moral code, but also with the corresponding "body" of knowledge and lead ultimately to its fulfilment' (p. 21), Moreau's experiments cannot be justified. Indeed, in a revealing statement, Prendick indicates that what disturbs him most about Moreau's work is that the Beast Folk's suffering does not lead to scientific fulfilment: 'Had Moreau had any intelligible object I could have sympathised at least a little with him. I am not so squeamish about pain as that. I could have forgiven him a little even had his motive been hate. But he was so irresponsible, so utterly careless' (123).
57. I am again indebted Professor Owen Dudley Edwards in this instance.
58. Nordau, *Degeneration*, p. v.
59. Nordau, *Degeneration*, p. 43.
60. Thus John R. Reed writes that: 'Like Moreau, Wilde believed he could shape the world to his own taste. Both were destroyed by the schemes they begot' ('The Law of Vanity', p. 143).
61. Unsigned, *Review of Reviews*, p. 374.
62. W. S. Lilly, 'The New Naturalism', *Fortnightly Review*, n.s. 38 (1885), 240–56 (p. 252).
63. In *Degeneration*, Nordau considers zoophilia, 'or excessive love of animals', as an integral trait of the degenerate (p. 315).
64. The intertextual relations of the novel are further investigated in Porta's thesis. See especially his discussion, 'Textual Islands: Open Influences and Closed Intertextualities in *The Island of Doctor Moreau*', pp. 155–79.
65. In her 'Vivisected Language in H. G. Wells's *The Island of Doctor Moreau*', Jackson persuasively argues that the violence of Moreau's vivisection pervades the text as a whole: '*The Island of Doctor Moreau* is thus a story of the interrelation of literary and scientific vivisection, the two "operations" violently intertwined' (p. 22). For Jackson, not only are Moreau's hybrid animals the victims of his brutal experiments, 'it becomes clear that every element of the text is susceptible to vivisection, and is indeed victimised by its violence' (p. 22). The literary vivisection of the text is, Jackson states, performed by the way in which inanimate objects and the organic forms of the island act like the tools of vivisection, 'cutting' like the scalpel, or responding by 'bleeding' like the victims of Moreau's experiments: 'The adjective "sharp" is used in the

novella no less than 16 times, with regard to speaking, looking, turning [...] in addition to the numerous references to things which cut and stab' (p. 24).

66. This of course parallels the manner in which the Time Traveller acquires the characteristics of the Morlocks.

67. Porta, 'Narrative Strategies', p. 167.

68. Wells, 'Human Evolution', p. 590.

69. Wells, 'Human Evolution', p. 595.

70. Indeed, in 'Bio-Optimism', Wells effectively argues the opposite of the conclusion he later arrives at in 'Human Evolution': 'As a matter of fact Natural Selection grips us more grimly than ever did, because the doubts thrown upon the inheritance of acquired characteristics have deprived us of our trust in education as a means of redemption for decadant families' (p. 411). Of course, these doubts are not apparent in the way in which Prendick acquires the characteristics of the Beast People.

71. In his book, *Faces of Degeneration: A European Disorder c. 1848–1914* (Cambridge: Cambridge University Press, 1989), Daniel Pick points out that 'the threat of levelling or homogenisation' (p. 86) is an important characteristic of degeneration.

72. This corresponds to Ferguson's observation concerning this aspect of *The Island of Doctor Moreau*: 'Rather than becoming human through its speech, the articulate animal testifies to the fact that language is an artefact of a bestial past rather than an evolutionary attainment'. *Language, Science and Popular Fiction*, p. 7.

4   Science behind the Blinds: Scientist and Society in *The Invisible Man*

1. H. G. Wells, 'The Chronic Argonauts' (1888), reprinted in Bernard Bergonzi, *The Early H. G. Wells*, pp. 187–214 (p. 209).

2. Unsigned Review, *Literature*, 1 (30 October 1897), 50–1 (p. 50).

3. Unsigned, *Literature*, p. 50. In a now famous passage, Joseph Conrad afterwards termed Wells 'Realist of the Fantastic' in response to his achievement in combining fantasy and realism in *The Invisible Man*. Letter to H. G. Wells, dated 4 December 1898, *J. Conrad: Life and Letters*, ed. by Georges Jean-Aubry (New York: Doubleday, 1927), pp. 249–50.

4. *Arnold Bennett and H. G. Wells*, ed. by Harris Wilson (London: Hart Davies, 1960), pp. 34–5 (p. 34).

5. Clement Shorter, Review in *Bookman*, 8 (October 1897), viii; reprinted in *H. G. Wells: The Critical Heritage*, pp. 58–9 (p. 59).

6. Bergonzi, *The Early H. G. Wells*, p. 116. *A Grotesque Romance* was of course the subtitle of *The Invisible Man* upon publication.

7. Kirpal Singh, 'Science and Society: A Brief Look at *The Invisible Man*', *The Wellsian*, n.s. 7 (1984), 19–23 (pp. 21–2).

8. Robert Sirabian, 'The Conception of Science in Wells's *The Invisible Man*', *Papers on Language and Literature*, 37 (2001), 382–403 (p. 383). While he recognises Wells's achievement in emphasising the necessity of both observation and the imagination to scientific enquiry, Sirabian does not place the villagers' speculations about Griffin in the context of Wells's educational journalism.

9. Bergonzi, *The Early H. G. Wells*, p. 115.
10. H. G. Wells, Letter to the *Educational Times, The Correspondence of H. G. Wells*, I, 169–73 (p. 172).
11. H. G. Wells, Letter to the *Educational Times*, p. 172.
12. H. G. Wells, 'Science, in School and After School', *Nature*, 50 (27 September 1894), 525–6. Wells's article provoked intense interest in the pages of *Nature*, with the issue of 15 November 1894 publishing responses from W. B. Crump and Grace Heath, *Nature*, 51 (1894), 56–7.
13. Wells, 'Science, in School', p. 525.
14. Wells, 'Science, in School', p. 525.
15. Wells, 'Science, in School', p. 526.
16. Wells, 'Science, in School', p. 526.
17. H. G. Wells, 'Science Teaching – An Ideal and Some Realities', *Educational Times*, 48 (1 January 1895), pp. 23–9; this article was originally given as a lecture before the College of Preceptors on 12 December 1894. Wells explores the themes developed in 'Science Teaching' in 'The Sins of the Secondary Schoolmaster', *Pall Mall Gazette*, 59 (15 December 1894), 1–2.
18. 'The Sequence of Studies' is the title used by Wells in his review of three books, all of which neglect to show 'a particle of that progressive reasoning process which is the very essence of genuine scientific study', *Nature*, 51 (1894), 195–6 (p. 196). That is, they fail to establish evidence as to why something is so.
19. Wells, 'Science Teaching', p. 24.
20. Wells, 'Science Teaching', p. 24.
21. Wells, 'Science Teaching', p. 25.
22. Wells, 'Science Teaching', p. 25.
23. T. H. Huxley, 'Science and Culture' (1880), in *Science and Culture and Other Essays* (London: Macmillan, 1881), pp. 1–23.
24. Huxley, 'Science and Culture', p. 6.
25. Huxley, 'Science and Culture', p. 7.
26. Huxley, 'Science and Culture', p. 5.
27. Wells, 'Science Teaching', p. 25.
28. Wells, 'Science Teaching', p. 25.
29. Wells, 'Science Teaching', p. 25.
30. H. G. Wells, 'Popularising Science', *Nature*, 50 (26 July 1894), 300–1 (p. 301).
31. *Atlantic Edition*, Vol. III, *The Invisible Man, The War of the Worlds, A Dream of Armageddon*, p. 7. Subsequent references to this work will be cited in the text.
32. Anne B. Simpson, 'The "Tangible Antagonist": H. G. Wells and the Discourses of Otherness', *Extrapolation*, 31 (1990), 134–47 (p. 145).
33. Sirabian, 'The Conception of Science', p. 389.
34. Karl Pearson, *The Grammar of Science* (London: Walter Scott, 1892), pp. 7–9.
35. Pearson, *Grammar*, p. 7.
36. Pearson, *Grammar*, p. 8.
37. Pearson, *Grammar*, p. 8.
38. Pearson, *Grammar*, p. 8.
39. For an intelligent account of the changing status of induction in the nineteenth century, see Jonathan Smith, *Fact and Feeling: Baconian Science and the Nineteenth-Century Literary Imagination* (London: University of Wisconsin Press, 1994), especially pp. 11–44.

40. Sirabian, 'The Conception of Science', p. 390.
41. Sirabian, 'The Conception of Science', p. 391.
42. Sirabian, 'The Conception of Science', p. 391.
43. John Tyndall, 'Scientific Use of the Imagination' (1870), in *Fragments of Science: A Series of Detached Essays, Addresses and Reviews* (London: Longmans, Green and Co., 1876), pp. 423–57.
44. Tyndall, 'Scientific Use', p. 425.
45. Tyndall, 'Scientific Use', pp. 425–6.
46. Tyndall, 'Scientific Use', p. 425.
47. Tyndall, 'Scientific Use', p. 428.
48. Tyndall, 'Scientific Use', p. 449.
49. Tyndall, 'Scientific Use', pp. 446–7.
50. A similar point is made by Sirabian, 'The Conception of Science', p. 389.
51. See also Sirabian, 'The Conception of Science', p. 402.
52. See also Jeanne Murray Walker, 'Exchange Short-Circuited: The Isolated Scientist in H. G. Wells's *The Invisible Man*', *Journal of Narrative Technique*, 15 (1985), 156–68. While Murray Walker does not relate the novel explicitly to Wells's educational journalism or contemporary debates over scientific method, she does comment on how Griffin's alienation from the Iping community in part emerges from the villagers' inability to either employ or comprehend scientific forms of thinking.
53. Bergonzi, *The Early H. G. Wells*, p. 114.
54. Bergonzi, *The Early H. G. Wells*, p. 114.
55. Wells, 'The Chronic Argonauts', p. 189.
56. Wells, 'Popularising Science', p. 300. Wells's insistence on the need for researchers to facilitate intelligent communication with the rest of society continues the emphasis of earlier 'public scientists' who, according to Frank M. Turner in his book *Contesting Cultural Authority* (Cambridge: Cambridge University Press, 1993), 'recognized that they must nurture a friendly constituency within the political nation' (p. 206). Turner applies the term 'public science' to those who argued for the wider social utility of scientific advances (p. 203). His account of the three stages of public science in nineteenth-century Britain indicates that most public scientists had become disillusioned with the lack of state support by the end of the 1800s. *Contesting Cultural Authority*, pp. 203–28. The evidence offered by Turner's analysis, therefore, suggests that Wells's anticipation of an ever proliferating State funding was unusually optimistic for the time. As Turner himself acknowledges, just a few years later in *Anticipations* (1901), Wells himself would be objecting to the manner in which the emerging class of experts were being denied a political voice (p. 220). (See Chapter 6 of the present study.)
57. Wells, 'Popularising Science', p. 300.
58. Wells, 'Popularising Science', p. 300.
59. Wells, 'Popularising Science', p. 300.
60. Wells, 'Popularising Science', p. 300.
61. Wells, 'Popularising Science', p. 300.
62. Wells, 'Popularising Science', p. 300.
63. Wells, 'Popularising Science', p. 301.
64. Wells, 'Popularising Science', p. 301.
65. Of course, the comedy of this incident exposes how little education these supposedly leading members of the community have received. For all

his apparent scientific training as a general practitioner, Cuss wrongly assumes that the stranger's diary contains Russian. Bunting, who had 'no Greek left in his mind worth talking about' (69), fears that this fact will be momentarily exposed. This humorous moment accentuates the manner in which Griffin's use of technical language further confuses those whose scientific education has been neglected. While he is clearly using the vicar and the doctor to satirise the rudimentary education even of those in positions of social authority, the emphasis of 'Popularising Science' suggests that Wells would share Bunting's frustration at there being ' "no diagrams" ' and ' "No illustrations throwing light" ' (69) on the nature of Griffin's research.

66. Walker sees Griffin's refusal to publish his scientific data as symptomatic of the unwillingness to enter into social exchange which finally leads to his alienation from society. 'Exchange Short Circuited', p. 156.

67. Following *The Island of Doctor Moreau*, Wells is again drawing upon the topical controversy surrounding vivisection. Like Moreau, Griffin is breaking the 1876 Cruelty to Animals Act since his experiment on the cat serves no medical or scientific utility.

68. Christopher Marlowe, *Dr Faustus* (1604) (London: A & C Black, 1986), III, pp. 2, 56.

69. It should be noted, however, that Griffin is much less playful in his use of physical intimidation to 'stimulate' the will of Mr. Thomas Marvel.

70. The element of social comedy in the novel relates to the humour employed in Wells's non-scientific romances, especially *The Wonderful Visit* (1895) and *The Wheels of Chance* (1896). It also prefigures the comical realism of Wells's social novels, particularly *Kipps* (1905) and *The History of Mr Polly* (1910).

71. H. G. Wells, 'Morals and Civilisation', *Fortnightly Review*, n.s. 61 (February 1897), 263–8 (p. 268).

72. The manner in which Griffin becomes severed from social reality explicitly recalls Victor Frankenstein: 'I wished, as it were, to procrastinate all that related to my feelings of affectation until the great object, which swallowed up every habit of my nature, should be completed.' Mary Shelley, *Frankenstein: or The Modern Prometheus* (1818) (Oxford: Oxford University Press, 1980), p. 55.

73. The way in which Griffin equates his attainment of invisibility with personal gain recalls Pearson's refrain that scientific training in itself does not necessarily guarantee good citizenship: 'It is the scientific habit of mind as an essential for good citizenship, and not the scientist as sound politician that I wish to emphasise.' *A Grammar of Science*, pp. 9–10.

74. H. G. Wells, 'The Origin of the Senses', *Saturday Review*, 81 (9 May 1896), 471–2 (p. 471).

75. Wells, 'Senses', p. 472.

76. Simpson, 'The Tangible Antagonist', p. 135.

77. Singh, 'Science and Society', p. 21.

78. Sirabian, 'The Conception of Science', p. 394.

79. Sirabian, 'The Conception of Science', p. 395.

80. A similar point is made by Sirabian, 'The Conception of Science', p. 387.

81. Kemp, of course, had apparently earlier ' "demonstrated conclusively" ' (107) the impossibility of corporeal invisibility.

82. Wells, 'Morals and Civilisation', p. 267.

83. See, for example, Patrick Bridgwater, *Nietzsche in Anglosaxony* (Leicester: Leicester University Press, 1972), pp. 58–60.
84. Robert Louis Stevenson, *The Strange Case of Dr Jekyll and Mr Hyde* (1886) (Oxford: Oxford University Press, 1998), p. 9.
85. Stevenson, *Dr Jekyll and Mr Hyde*, p. 25
86. Stevenson, *Dr Jekyll and Mr Hyde*, p. 25.
87. Of Wells's fictional responses to anarchism, 'The Stolen Bacillus' (1894) remains the most relevant to modern day fears of terrorism. In this earliest Wells short story, an anarchist consumes a potion he has stolen from a bacteriologist's laboratory with the intention of polluting the entire water supply of London. Although – in an ironic twist to the plot – this 'deadly cholera germ' turns out to have little effect other than turning the skin blue, the story possesses a chilling resonance at a moment when Western governments are investing considerable resources in order to counter the potentially devastating consequences of biological or chemical warfare. For an examination of 'The Stolen Bacillus' in the context of contemporary tales of anarchism, see Yorimitsu Hashimoto, 'Victorian Biological Terror: A Study of "The Stolen Bacillus"', *The Undying Fire*, 2 (2003), 3–27.
88. H. G. Wells, 'The Country of the Blind' (1904), reprinted in *The Complete Short Stories of H. G. Wells*, ed. by John Hammond (London: Dent, 1998), pp. 629–48 (p. 640). Nunez's ambitions are soon deflated as he realises that the inhabitants of the valley of the blind have adapted their other senses to compensate for not possessing sight. Nunez's experience is prefigured in *The Invisible Man* as Griffin, feeling at first ' "as a seeing man might do [...] in a city of the blind" ' (139), finds himself fleeing from a blind man: ' "I saw in time a blind man approaching me, and fled limping, for I feared his subtle intuitions" ' (p. 144).
89. Wells, 'Ancient Experiments', p. 418.
90. Wells, 'Ancient Experiments', p. 418.
91. Gustave Le Bon, *The Crowd: A Study of the Popular Mind* (1896) (London: T. Fisher Unwin, 1913).
92. Le Bon, *The Crowd*, p. 32.
93. Le Bon, *The Crowd*, p. 36.

5　The Descent of Mars: Evolution and Ethics in *The War of the Worlds*

1. H. G. Wells, 'The Man of the Year Million', *Pall Mall Gazette*, 57 (6 November 1893), 3–6; reprinted in *H. G. Wells: Journalism and Prophecy, 1893–1946*, ed. by W. Warren Wagar (London: Bodley Head, 1965), pp. 3–8 (p. 4). Wells later published a slightly revised version of this essay as 'Of a Book Unwritten' in *Certain Personal Matters* (London: Lawrence & Bullen, 1898), pp. 161–84.
2. Wells had referred to the possibility of life on Mars as early as his address to the Debating Society at the Normal School of Science on 19 October 1888. This address appeared in the College magazine as 'Are the Planets Habitable?', *Science Schools Journal*, 15 (1 November 1888), 57–8.
3. *The Works of H. G. Wells: Atlantic Edition*, III, *The Invisible Man, The War of the Worlds, A Dream of Armageddon*, p. 220. Subsequent references to this work will be cited in the text.

4. Bergonzi, *The Early H. G. Wells*, p. 134. See also Stephen Arata, *Fictions of Loss in the Victorian Fin de Siècle* (Cambridge: Cambridge University Press, 1996), p. 110.

5. *The War of the Worlds* has also been examined as one of a number of nineteenth-century fictions in which the fall of the Thames Valley leads to the invasion of London (and, by extension) the country as a whole. See Patrick Parrinder, 'From Mary Shelley to *The War of the Worlds*: The Thames Valley Catastrophe', in *Anticipations: Essays on Science Fiction and its Precursors*, ed. by David Seed (Liverpool: Liverpool University Press, 1995), pp. 58–74.

6. Unsigned Review, *Saturday Review*, 85 (29 January 1898), 146–7 (p. 146).

7. See Robert Crossley, 'H. G. Wells, Visionary Telescopes and the "Matter of Mars"', *Philological Quarterly*, 83 (2004), 83–115.

8. H. G. Wells, 'The Things that Live on Mars', *Cosmopolitan Magazine*, 44 (1908), 335–42.

9. Percival Lowell, *Mars* (1895) (London: Longman's, 1896), p. 122.

10. Lowell, *Mars*, p. 208.

11. Lowell, *Mars*, p. 209.

12. Robert S. Ball, 'Mars', *Fortnightly Review*, n.s. 52 (1892), 288–303.

13. H. G. Wells, 'Another Basis For Life', *Saturday Review*, 78 (1894), 676–7; the article by Ball which Wells was referring to was 'The Possibility of Life in Other Worlds', *Fortnightly Review*, n.s. 56 (1894), 718–29. There is a later relationship between the context in which Wells's and Ball's work was published. Ball's article on 'Comets' was published in the same volume of the *Strand Magazine* as *The First Men in the Moon*, 21 (1901), 393–9.

14. Letter to the Editor of *Academy*, c.10 November 1897, *The Correspondence of H. G. Wells*, I, 292.

15. Ball, 'Mars', p. 294.

16. Ball, 'Mars', p. 289.

17. Ball, 'Mars', p. 302.

18. Ball, 'Mars', p. 291.

19. The implications of the Martians' treatment of humans for humans' treatment of animals are discussed below.

20. H. G. Wells, 'Intelligence on Mars', *Saturday Review*, 81 (4 April 1896), 345–6.

21. H. G. Wells, 'Through a Microscope' (1894); reprinted slightly modified in *Certain Personal Matters*, pp. 238–45. References are to this later version.

22. Wells, 'Through a Microscope', p. 244.

23. Wells, 'Through a Microscope', p. 245.

24. Ball, 'Mars', p. 288.

25. Unsigned, 'A Strange Light on Mars', *Nature*, 50 (1894), 319.

26. 'A Strange Light', p. 319.

27. 'A Strange Light', p. 319.

28. H. G. Wells, 'The Extinction of Man', *Pall Mall Gazette*, 59 (25 September 1894), 3; reprinted in a slightly extended form in *Certain Personal Matters*, pp. 172–9 (pp. 178–9). The relevance of this essay to *The War of the Worlds* is also discussed by Bergonzi, *The Early H. G. Wells*, p. 132.

29. Of course, the narrator later encounters the dead body of the landlord, whose neck has been broken.

30. H. G. Wells, *The Correspondence of H. G. Wells*, I, 213–4.

31. Wells was probably familiar with the article Allen wrote on 'Spencer and Darwin', which appeared in the *Fortnighly Review*, n.s. 61 (1897), 251–62.

Appearing in the same volume as Wells's 'Morals and Civilisation', Allen's article argues vigorously for the need to recognise the full significance of Spencer's thought.

32. This series of articles formed the basis of Spencer's *Man Versus the State* (1884).
33. Herbert Spencer, 'The Sins of Legislators', *Contemporary Review*, 45 (1884), 761–75.
34. Spencer, 'The Sins of Legislators', p. 765.
35. Spencer, 'The Sins of Legislators', p. 765.
36. Spencer, 'The Sins of Legislators', pp. 765–6; 766.
37. Spencer, 'The Sins of Legislators', p. 766.
38. Spencer, 'The Sins of Legislators', p. 763.
39. See also Simpson, 'The "Tangible Antagonist": H. G. Wells and the Discourse of Otherness'. While she recognises how 'people reveal their actual isolation from one another just as their need for solidarity becomes imperative', Simpson concludes that the various narrative perspectives of the text 'confirm a single view of the solitariness of existence without offering sustained hope for a cure' (p. 145). Understood as a critique of individualism, however, the splintering of humanity in the face of the alien invasion points to the importance of co-operation as a means to reduce the solitariness of existence.
40. T. H. Huxley, 'Evolution and Ethics', p. 82.
41. 'What We Saw from the Ruined House', *Pearson's Magazine*; reprinted in *The Collector's Book of Science Fiction by H. G. Wells*, Selected by Alan K. Russell (Secaucus, New Jersey: Castle, 1979), pp. 83–7 (p. 85).
42. Roslynn Haynes, *H. G. Wells: Discoverer of the Future*, p. 74.
43. Huxley, 'Evolution and Ethics', p. 83.
44. Parrinder, *H. G. Wells*, p. 37.
45. Extracts from 'The Man of the Year Million' are reprinted in the *Broadview Press* edition of *The War of the Worlds*, ed. Martin A. Danahay (Peterborough, Ont.; Orchard Park, New York: Broadview, 2003), pp. 203–6.
46. Wells, 'The Man of the Year Million', p. 4.
47. Wells, 'The Man of the Year Million', p. 4.
48. Wells, 'The Man of the Year Million', p. 5.
49. Wells, 'The Man of the Year Million', p. 6.
50. Wells, 'The Man of the Year Million', p. 5.
51. Wells, 'The Man of the Year Million', p. 5
52. Wells, 'The Man of the Year Million', p. 7.
53. Jonathan Swift, *Gulliver's Travels and Other Writings* (1726) (Oxford: Oxford University Press, 1976), p. 182.
54. Several critics have remarked on how the Martians' characterisation warns against separating the intellect from the capacity for human sympathy. In his *H. G. Wells*, Geoffrey West paraphrases Wells on his intentions in the characterisation of the Martians: '*The Invisible Man* and *The War of the Worlds* illustrated the dangers of power without moral control, the development of the intelligence at the expense of human sympathy' (pp. 108–9).
55. Wagar, *Traversing Time*, p. 56.
56. Patrick Parrinder, 'How Far Can We Trust the Narrator of *The War of the Worlds*?', *Foundation*, 77 (1999), 15–24 (p. 18).

57. Parrinder, 'How Far', p. 18.
58. Wells, 'Ancient Experiments', p. 421.
59. Wagar, *Traversing Time*, p. 57.
60. Kathryn Hume, 'The Hidden Dynamics of *The War of the Worlds*', *Philological Quarterly*, 62 (1983), 279–92 (p. 282).
61. Herbert Sussman, *Victorians and the Machine: The Literary Response to Technology* (Cambridge: Harvard University Press, 1968), p. 179.
62. Bergonzi, *The Early H. G. Wells*, p. 134.
63. Bergonzi, *The Early H. G. Wells*, p. 135.
64. Bergonzi, *The Early H. G. Wells*, p. 135.
65. H. M. Havelock-Allan, 'A General Voluntary Training to Arms *Versus* Conscription', *Fortnightly Review*, n.s. 61 (1897), 85–99; 'England's Military Position: Its Present Weakness, Its Vast Undeveloped Strength', *Fortnightly Review*, n.s. 62 (1897), 19–41; the first of these articles appeared in the same volume of the *Fortnightly Review* as Wells's 'Morals and Civilisation', 263–8.
66. Havelock-Allan, 'A General Voluntary Training', p. 89.
67. Havelock-Allan, 'A General Voluntary Training', p. 89.
68. Havelock-Allan, 'A General Voluntary Training', p. 91.
69. Havelock-Allan, 'A General Voluntary Training', p. 92.
70. Havelock-Allan, 'England's Military Position', p. 26.
71. Havelock-Allan, 'England's Military Position', p. 27.
72. Havelock-Allan, 'England's Military Position', p. 29.
73. Havelock-Allan, 'England's Military Position', p. 30.
74. For a discussion of how *The War of the Worlds* prefigures developments of twentieth-century warfare, see Charles E. Gannon, ' "One Swift, Conclusive Smashing and an End": Wells, War, and the Collapse of Civilisation', *Foundation*, 77 (1999), 35–46. See also R. T. Stearn, 'Wells and War: H. G. Wells's Writings on Military Subjects, before the Great War', *Wellsian*, n.s. 6 (1983), 1–15.
75. Archibald Forbes, 'The Warfare of the Future', *Nineteenth Century*, 29 (1891), 782–95.
76. Forbes, 'The Warfare of the Future', p. 793.
77. Forbes, 'The Warfare of the Future', p. 793.
78. Forbes, 'The Warfare of the Future', p. 794.
79. Unsigned, *Saturday Review*, pp. 146–7.
80. Huxley, 'Evolution and Ethics', pp. 80–1.
81. This inference that the Martians will use humanity as a food source recalls Jonathan Harker's fear in *Dracula* (1897) that Count Dracula plans to create an army of slaves out of the British population (Bram Stoker, *Dracula* (1897) (Oxford: Oxford University Press, 1998)). For a more sustained account of the parallels between *The War of the Worlds* and *Dracula*, see R. J. Dingley, 'Count Dracula and the Martians', in *The Victorian Fantasists*, ed. by Kath Filmer (London: Macmillan, 1991), pp. 13–24.
82. John Huntington, *The Logic of Fantasy*, p. 84.
83. See also Simpson, 'The Tangible Antagonist', p. 142.
84. *The Works of H. G. Wells: Atlantic Edition*, IV, *Anticipations and Other Stories*.
85. Wells, *Anticipations*, pp. 256–7.
86. Wells, *Anticipations*, p. 257.
87. Wells, *Anticipations*, p. 258.

88. Wells, *Anticipations*, pp. 245–6.

89. Wells, 'Human Evolution', p. 592.

90. Wells, 'Human Evolution', p. 594.

91. Wells, 'Human Evolution', p. 594.

92. The narrator's vision prefigures a passage from Wells's 'The Discovery of the Future', *Nature*, 65 (1902), 326–31. Wells supposes that a day will come when 'beings who are now latent in our thoughts and hidden in our loins, shall stand upon this earth as one stands upon a footstool, and shall laugh and reach out their hands amidst the stars' (p. 331).

93. Wells, 'Through a Microscope', p. 162.

6   'Science is a Match that Man Has Just Got Alight': Science and Social Organisation in *The First Men in the Moon*

1. Wells, 'The Rediscovery of the Unique', p. 111.

2. *The Works of H. G. Wells: Atlantic Edition*, VI, *The First Men in the Moon and Some More Human Stories*, ix. Subsequent references to this work will be cited in the text.

3. Wells's statement here can be immediately contrasted with Jules Verne's response to the novel. Verne argued vigorously that Wells's novels – *The First Men in the Moon* included – do not make the same rigorous use of science as his own work: ' "No, there is no *rapport* between his work and mine. I make use of physics. He invents. I go to the moon in a cannonball, discharged from a canon. Here there is no invention. He goes to Mars in an airship, which he constructs of a metal which does away with the laws of gravitation" '. Jules Verne, cited in Ingvald Raknem, *H. G. Wells and his Critics* (London: George Allen & Unwin, 1962), p. 406. However, an appreciative review of *The First Men in the Moon*, entitled 'A Lunar Romance' and appearing in the science periodical *Nature*, does not concur with Verne's assessment of the scientific basis of his own work. Instead, the anonymous reviewer quickly points to the 'scientific blunders and improbabilities of the most glaring character' which litter Verne's account of an attempted journey to the moon, before considering the more thoroughly scientific basis of Wells's new novel: 'Mr. Wells has produced a book of a very different character; he has made himself master of the little we know about the moon, and thought out the possibilities with the greatest care, and the result is a narrative which we will venture to say is not only as exciting to the average reader as Jules Verne's, but is full of interest to the scientific man.' *Nature*, 65 (1902), 218–19 (p. 218).

4. Norman and Jeanne MacKenzie, *The Time Traveller*, p. 151.

5. Prof. John H. Poynting, 'Recent Studies in Gravitation', *Nature*, 62 (23 August 1900), 403–8 (p. 405).

6. Poynting, 'Studies in Gravitation', p. 405.

7. Poynting, 'Studies in Gravitation', p. 406.

8. Poynting, 'Studies in Gravitation', p. 408.

9. This of course discounts *When the Sleeper Wakes*, which does portray a global community. However, this earlier novel cannot really be construed as a world state, because Graham's awakening reveals the conflict and

oppression on which this community is predicated. There is, of course, conflict in *The First Men in the Moon*, but the hostility between different classes of Selenites strengthens rather than weakens the lunar world state, since each class expresses pride in its particular activity. Crucially, no outside force or awakening can disrupt the global order of the Selenites.

10. The sections detailing lunar society originally formed a late addition to the version of the text serialised in the *Strand Magazine* and other periodicals. David Lake traces the development of the novel in his introduction to the Oxford World Classics edition of *The First Men in the Moon*, ed. by David Lake (New York: Oxford University Press, 1995), pp. xiii–xxvii. According to Lake, Bedford's landing at Littlestone was intended as the end of the story. Having submitted the 'finished' novel for serial publication, however, Wells had the inspiration to write 'Cavor's radio messages, [and] sent this extra part to the monthly magazines' (xxii). These changes were then incorporated into the first British and American book editions of the novel, with some revisions, thus resulting in 'the novel that is familiar to Wells's [subsequent] readers' (xxii). Included in Wells's correspondence is a letter to *New Magazine* in which he informs the Editor of his intention to alter the concluding chapter of the story and requesting that every effort be made to incorporate this. Letter to the Editor, *New Magazine*, 21 July 1900, *The Correspondence of H. G. Wells*, I, 361.

11. Huntington, *The Logic of Fantasy*, pp. 87–97.

12. Wells, *Anticipations and Other Papers*, p. 3.

13. Letter to Winston Churchill, *The Correspondence of H. G. Wells*, I, 457.

14. Huntington, *The Logic of Fantasy*, p. 88.

15. Cavor's near asphyxiation of the terrestrial globe recalls, 'The Man Who Could Work Miracles' (1898). In that short story, the protagonist – George McWhirter Fotheringay – discovers that he has suddenly acquired miraculous powers. After performing a number of minor miracles under the watchful encouragement of the local clergyman Mr Maydig, Fotheringay causes a catastrophe when he stops the earth's rotation: 'everybody and everything had been jerked violently forward at about nine miles per second – that is to say, much more violently than if they had been fired out of a cannon. And every human being, every living creature, every house, and every tree – all the world as we know it – had been so jerked and smashed and utterly destroyed'. 'The Man Who Could Work Miracles' (1898), reprinted in *The Complete Short Stories of H. G. Wells*, pp. 399–412 (p. 410).

16. Wells, *Anticipations*, pp. 61–2.

17. Wells, *Anticipations*, p. 63.

18. Wells, *Anticipations*, p. 64.

19. Wells, *Anticipations*, pp. 69–70.

20. Wells, *Anticipations*, p. 87.

21. Wells, *Anticipations*, p. 74.

22. Wells, *Anticipations*, p. 81.

23. Wells, *Anticipations*, p. 77.

24. Wells, *Anticipations*, p. 76.

25. Wells foresees that the impact of science will, for example, have a revolutionary impact on the military. He writes that: 'a new sort of soldier will emerge, a sober, considerate, engineering man'. *Anticipations*, p. 85.

26. Wells, *Anticipations*, p. 124.
27. Wells, *Anticipations*, p. 125.
28. Herbert Spencer, 'The Social Organism' (1860), reprinted in *Essays: Scientific, Political, Speculative*, 3 vols (London: Williams and Norgate, 1868), I, 384–428.
29. Wells, *Anticipations*, p. 136.
30. Wells, *Anticipations*, pp. 136–7.
31. Wells, *Anticipations*, p. 132.
32. Wells, *Anticipations*, p. 147–8.
33. Wells, *Anticipations*, p. 154.
34. Wells, *Anticipations*, p. 155.
35. Robert Wallace, 'The Psychology of Capitalist and Labourer', *Fortnightly Review*, n.s. 54 (1893), 676–85.
36. Wallace, 'Capitalist and Labourer', p. 677.
37. Wallace, 'Capitalist and Labourer', p. 677.
38. Wallace, 'Capitalist and Labourer', p. 677.
39. The desire of Bedford to own all the wealth in the world recalls the plot of *When the Sleeper Wakes*. In that novel, the protagonist, Graham, awakens after 200 years to discover that he does indeed possess half the wealth in the world.
40. Huntington, *The Logic of Fantasy*, p. 91.
41. Huntington, *The Logic of Fantasy*, p. 91.
42. This is surely a joking reference to A. T. Simmons, a friend of Wells's from the Normal School of Science. The joke is seemingly completed by the fact that Bedford signs his manuscript with the 'respectable' name Wells.
43. T. S. Eliot, 'Wells as Journalist' (1940), in *H. G. Wells: The Critical Heritage*, p. 320.
44. Parrinder, *H. G. Wells*, p. 36.
45. Richard Gregory, Letter to H. G. Wells, 22 June 1899, *The Correspondence of H. G. Wells*, I, 342–3 (p. 342).
46. Arnold White, 'The Unemployed', *Fortnightly Review*, n.s. 54 (1893), 454–63.
47. White, 'The Unemployed', p. 461.
48. White, 'The Unemployed', p. 461.
49. Wells of course creates potential difficulties for himself here. Any attempt on the part of the English-speaking communities to lead the formation of the world state could simply be construed as an alternative form of the imperialism Wells satirises in *The First Men in the Moon*.
50. Wells is employing a degree of anachronism, since Galton (b. 1822) lived until 1911.
51. Francis Galton, 'Intelligible Signals between Neighbouring Stars', *Fortnightly Review*, n.s. 60 (1896), 657–64.
52. Galton, 'Neighbouring Stars', p. 657.
53. Galton, 'Neigbouring Stars', p. 658.
54. Galton, 'Neighbouring Stars', p. 663.
55. Charlotte Sleigh, 'Empire of the Ants: H. G. Wells and Tropical Entomology', *Science as Culture*, 10 (2001), 33–71.
56. John Lubbock, *Ants, Bees, and Wasps: A Record of Observations On the Habits of the Social Hymenoptera* (London: Kegan Paul, Trench, & Co, 1885).
57. H. G. Wells, 'The Duration of Life', *Saturday Review*, 79 (1895), 248.

58. Wells, 'Duration', p. 248.
59. Lubbock, *Ants, Bees, and Wasps*, p. 1.
60. Lubbock, *Ants, Bees, and Wasps*, p. 181.
61. Lubbock, *Ants, Bees, and Wasps*, p. viii
62. Wells would later explore favourable conditions for the development of insects in 'The Empire of the Ants' (1905).
63. Percival Lowell, *Mars*, p. 2.
64. This is of course what Wells had argued in 'Another Basis for Life', in which he posits silicon-aluminium life forms as a possible alternative to carbon based organisms.
65. Lubbock, *Ants, Bees, and* Wasps, p. 67.
66. Lubbock, *Ants, Bees, and Wasps*, p. 182.
67. It should be noted here that Lubbock's work indicates a broader context for some of the speculations in Wells's scientific journalism. In 'Intelligence on Mars' (1896), Wells himself had pointed out that there was no necessary reason for extraterrestrials to possess the same senses as *homo sapiens*, let alone the same sensory range.
68. Lubbock, *Ants, Bees, and Wasps*, p. 294.
69. Lubbock, *Ants, Bees, and Wasps*, p. 10.
70. Lubbock, *Ants, Bees, and Wasps*, p. 20.
71. The high degree of specialisation of function among the Selenites is, of course, highly Spencerian. The influence of Spencer's development hypothesis on Wells's construction of lunar society will be explored later.
72. *Authorial Preface* to *The Scientific Romances of H. G Wells* (London: Gollancz, 1933), pp. vii–x; reprinted as an appendix to the Everyman edition of *The Invisible Man* (London: Everyman, 1995), pp. 139–43 (p. 141).
73. Unsigned, 'A Lunar Romance', p. 218.
74. Wells, *Anticipations*, p. 120.
75. Wells, *Anticipations*, p. 120.
76. Wells, *Anticipations*, p. 121.
77. Wells, *Anticipations*, p. 122.
78. Wells, *Anticipations*, p. 122.
79. Wells, *Anticipations*, p. 124.
80. Wells, *Anticipations*, p. 124.
81. Wells, *Anticipations*, p. 125.
82. As the reviewer in *Nature* also noted, this passage also points to the intolerance of contemporary earthly society.
83. Wells's use of colour to signify allegiance to a particular social group is prefigured in *When the Sleeper Wakes*.
84. Wells, *Anticipations*, p. 242.
85. Wells, *Anticipations*, p. 242.
86. Sleigh, 'Empire of the Ants', p. 44.
87. Wells, *Anticipations*, p. 242.
88. Sleigh, 'Empire of the Ants', p. 44.
89. Wells, *Anticipations*, p. 183.
90. Wells, *Anticipations*, p. 89.
91. Wells, *Anticipations*, pp. 212–13.
92. The regularity of journeys of vast distances that will inevitably form part of the landscape of the future is recalled in a statement from the first message Cavor radios back from the moon: ' "We arrived," he says, with no

more account of our passage through space than if we had made a journey in a railway train' (216). Wells would later address the Fabian Society on the impact of 'Locomotion and Administration' in March 1903. This paper was recollected in *Mankind in the Making* and in the same volume of Wells's collected works as *Anticipations*, pp. 283–304.

93. Wells, *Anticipations*, pp. 88–9.
94. Unsigned Review, *The Daily Telegraph* (14 November 1901), p. 11.
95. H. G. Wells, Letter to the Editor, *Clarion*, 22 April 1904, 3.
96. Jonathan Swift, 'A Modest Proposal' (1729), reprinted in *Gulliver's Travels and Other Writings*, pp. 439–46.
97. Swift, 'A Modest Proposal', p. 441.
98. Swift, 'A Modest Proposal', p. 442.
99. Wells, *Anticipations*, p. 184.
100. Wells, *Anticipations*, p. 184.
101. Jonathan Swift, *Gulliver's Travels*, p. 128.
102. Swift, *Gulliver's Travels*, p. 128.
103. Wells, *Anticipations*, p. 201.
104. Wells, *Anticipations*, p. 201.
105. Wells, *Anticipations*, p. 204.
106. Spencer, 'The Social Organism', p. 399.
107. Spencer, 'The Social Organism', p. 399.
108. Spencer, 'The Social Organism', p. 403.
109. Spencer, 'The Social Organism', p. 403.
110. Spencer, 'The Social Organism', p. 408.
111. Spencer, 'The Social Organism', p. 395.
112. H. G. Wells, 'The So-Called Science of Sociology', *Independent Review*, 6 (May 1905), 21–37.
113. Wells, 'So-Called', p. 27.
114. Bedford's actions prefigure not only the emphasis on competition in the 'kinetic' Utopia of *A Modern Utopia* but also much later Wells writings. The emphasis on the need for competition in the evolutionary process is very much apparent in *The Science of Life* (1931). In this work, Wells – along with his son G. P. (Gip) and Julian Huxley – wrote: 'Without constant struggle and competition, Evolution could not have occurred; without the failure and death of innumerable individuals, there could have been no gradual perfection of the type; without the extinction of great groups, there could have been no advance of life as a whole.' H. G. Wells, Julian Huxley and G. P. Wells, *The Science of Life* (Garden City, New York: Doubleday, Doran, 1931), p. 639.
115. Wells, *Anticipations*, p. 81.
116. Wells not only endorses his conception in 'Human Evolution' but notably also in a review of Lloyd Morgan's *Habit and Instinct* appropriately titled 'The Acquired Factor'. Wells congratulates the author for diminishing the significance of the inherited factor in mankind. He writes that what Morgan has shown is that man is the most static of all living things, and 'that human evolution is a quite different process from that which has differentiated animal species, is instead the evolution of a mental environment'. In a passage which explicitly recalls the argument of 'Human Evolution', Wells indicates what he considers Morgan to have successfully

shown: 'The development of the modern man by example, precept, subtle suggestion, the advantage of an ancient and growing tradition of living, is his real, perhaps his only difference, from his ancestor of the Age of Stone.' 'The Acquired Factor', *Academy*, 51 (January 1897), 37.

117. Wells would of course attempt exactly this in *Mankind in the Making*.
118. Wells, 'Rediscovery', p. 107.
119. Wells, 'Rediscovery', pp. 106–7.
120. 'A Slip under the Microscope' (1895); reprinted in *Atlantic Edition*, VI, *The First Men in the Moon and Some More Human Stories*, pp. 393–419 (p. 399). Subsequent references will be cited in the text.

7   The Limits of a Sociological Holiday: Social Progress in *A Modern Utopia*

1. *The Works of H. G. Wells: Atlantic Edition*, IX, *A Modern Utopia and Other Discussions*, p. 7. Subsequent references to this work will be cited in the text.
2. Wells, 'The So-Called Science of Sociology', p. 34.
3. H. G. Wells, *A Modern Utopia* (London: T. Fisher Unwin, 1905), p. viii.
4. See, for example, John S. Partington, 'The Death of the Static: H. G. Wells and the Kinetic Utopia', *Utopian Studies*, 11 (2000), 96–111.
5. Krishan Kumar, *Utopianism* (Milton Keynes: Open University Press, 1991), p. 96.
6. Kumar, *Utopianism*, p. 96.
7. Kumar, *Utopianism*, pp. 96–7.
8. Wells published two further scientific romances in the Edwardian era, *In the Days of the Comet* (1906) and *The War in the Air* (1908). It is in *A Modern Utopia*, however, that the strands of debate initiated in his earlier scientific romances converge. After *The War in the Air*, Wells returned only once to the genre of the scientific romance, with the publication of *Star Begotten* (1937).
9. This professorship, at University College, London, was first held by Galton's student Karl Pearson (1911).
10. Francis Galton, 'The Possible Improvement of the Human Breed under the Existing Conditions of Law and Sentiment', *Nature*, 64 (1901), 659–65.
11. Galton, 'Possible Improvement', p. 659.
12. Galton, 'Possible Improvement', pp. 662–3.
13. Galton, 'Possible Improvement', p. 663.
14. Galton, 'Possible Improvement', p. 663.
15. Galton, 'Possible Improvement', p. 663.
16. Galton, 'Possible Improvement', p. 664.
17. H. G. Wells, 'The Problem of the Birth Supply', *Fortnightly Review*, n.s. 72 (1902), 704–22.
18. Wells, 'Birth Supply', p. 708.
19. Wells, 'Birth Supply', p. 711.
20. Wells, 'Birth Supply', p. 709.
21. Wells, 'Birth Supply', p. 708.
22. Wells, 'Birth Supply', p. 709.

23. Wells, 'Birth Supply', p. 709.
24. H. G. Wells, [discussion] 'Eugenics: Its Definition, Scope and Aims' in *Sociological Papers*, ed. By Francis Galton (London: Macmillan, 1904), pp. 58–60 (p. 60). Wells was responding to Galton's ideas as part of a debate organised by the Sociological Society. Galton's address on eugenics, and the roundtable debate which Wells participated in, also appeared in the *American Journal of Sociology*, 10 (1904), 1–25.
25. H. G. Wells, 'Scepticism of the Instrument', reprinted as an appendix to *A Modern Utopia, Atlantic Edition*, IX, *A Modern Utopia and Other Discussions*, 335–54.
26. Wells, 'Scepticism', p. 339.
27. Wells, 'Scepticism', p. 339.
28. Wells, 'Scepticism', p. 341.
29. Wells, 'Scepticism', p. 339–40.
30. Wells, 'Scepticism', p. 340.
31. Indeed, in 'Discoveries in Variation', *Saturday Review*, 79 (9 March 1895), 312, Wells had already acknowledged the pre-eminence of Darwin among those interested in the significance of minuscule differences between individuals of the same species: 'It has long been known that the individuals of any species differ from each other in innumerable minute respects. These differences occur in every organ, in every part of the body, and, naturally, it has occurred to many, from Darwin and Wallace onwards, that the differences between species may have been compounded of such minute differences between individuals'.
32. Charles Darwin, *On the Origin of Species* (1859) (Ware: Wordsworth, 1998), p. 42.
33. *Anticipations and Other Papers*, p. 251.
34. Edmund Gosse, cited in Norman and Jeanne MacKenzie, *The Time Traveller*, pp. 167–8.
35. The until recently neglected liberal dimension to Wells's political thought is also explored by Richard Toye, 'H. G. Wells and the New Liberalism', *Twentieth Century History*, 19 (2008), 156–85.
36. John Stuart Mill, *On Liberty* (1859) (London: Penguin, 1985), p. 68.
37. Mill, *On Liberty*, p. 69.
38. Mill, *On Liberty*, p. 141.
39. Mill, *On Liberty*, p. 72.
40. Mill, *On Liberty*, p. 69.
41. Mill, *On Liberty*, p. 133.
42. Mill, *On Liberty*, p. 120.
43. Mill, *On Liberty*, p. 130.
44. Mill, *On Liberty*, pp. 129–30.
45. H. G. Wells, 'The Organisation of the Higher Education', *Fortnightly Review*, n.s. 74 (1903), 353–72 (p. 370).
46. H. G. Wells, 'Political and Social Influences', *Fortnightly Review*, n.s. 74 (1903), 928–49 (p. 941).
47. Frederic Harrison, 'John Stuart Mill', *Nineteenth Century*, 40 (1896), 487–508.
48. Mill, *On Liberty*, p. 120.

49. It should be noted that Mill would not necessarily agree with Wells's emphasis in the novel that the State should necessarily be able to verify the identity of each individual.
50. Wells had already explored the implications of such a means of verification of personal identity for the crime fiction genre in 'The Thumbmark' (1894). In this short story, the presence of apparatus for taking thumbprints leads to the exposure of a mysterious anarchist.
51. Francis Galton, *Fingerprints* (London: Macmillan, 1892), p. 9.
52. Galton, *Fingerprints*, pp. 145–6.
53. Wells, 'Birth Supply', pp. 720–1.
54. Wells, 'Eugenics', p. 59.
55. Wells, 'Eugenics', p. 59.
56. H. G. Wells, 'Certain Wholesale Aspects of Man-Making', *Fortnightly Review*, n.s. 72 (1902), 1078–96.
57. Wells, 'Man-Making', p. 1078.
58. On the issue of minimum standards and the social policy Wells advances, see also Partington, 'The Death of the Static', pp. 106–8.
59. Wells, 'Man-Making', p. 1082.
60. Wells, 'Man-Making', p. 1084.
61. Wells, 'Man-Making', p. 1085.
62. Wells, 'Man-Making', p. 1092.
63. Wells, 'Man-Making', pp. 1092–3.
64. Sidney and Beatrice Webb, *Industrial Democracy* (London: Longman, 1902).
65. Webb and Webb, *Industrial Democracy*, pp. 774–5.
66. Wells, 'Man-Making', p. 1094.
67. Wells, 'Man-Making', p. 1091.
68. Wells, 'Man-Making', p. 1091.
69. Wells, 'Man-Making', p. 1091.
70. Wells, 'Man-Making', p. 1095.
71. Wells, 'Eugenics', pp. 59–60.
72. Wells, 'Eugenics', p. 60.
73. Wells, 'Eugenics', p. 60.
74. Wells, 'Eugenics', p. 60.
75. Wells, 'Eugenics', p. 60.
76. Unsigned Review of *Mankind in the Making*, *Academy and Literature*, 65 (26 September 1903), 285–6; reprinted in *H. G. Wells: The Critical Heritage*, pp. 90–3 (p. 93).
77. Charles Richmond Henderson, 'Definition of a Social Policy Relating to the Dependent Group', *The American Journal of Sociology*, 10 (1905), 315–34.
78. Henderson, 'Definition of a Social Policy', p. 318.
79. Henderson, 'Definition of a Social Policy', p. 320.
80. Henderson, 'Definition of a Social Policy', p. 321.
81. Henderson, 'Definition of a Social Policy', p. 319.
82. Henderson, 'Definition of a Social Policy', p. 322.
83. Henderson, 'Definition of a Social Policy', p. 328.
84. Henderson, 'Definition of a Social Policy', p. 329.
85. Henderson, 'Definition of a Social Policy', p. 330.

86. This interest in the plight of the sweated worker is a further aspect of *A Modern Utopia*'s engagement in debates conducted in a transatlantic context. See, for example, Annie Marion MacLean, 'The Sweat Shop in Summer', *The American Journal of Sociology*, 9 (November 1903), 289–309.

87. Wells, 'Human Evolution, an Artificial Process', p. 594.

88. Two further parallels between Mill's definition of genius and Wells's concept of the poietic type of mind are apparent. First of all, Mill's notion that geniuses are *more individual* than other people is recalled by Wells's recognition that utopian philosophers would value the heightened individuality of the poietic type. Second, Mill's insistence that genius cannot conform to rigid social categories without hurtful compression to both the individual and his or her contribution to progress resonates in Wells's comment that utopian social policy: 'would not only regard the poietic element as the most important in human society, but would perceive quite clearly the impossibility of its organisation' (243).

89. Wells's endowment of motherhood scheme reveals how immersed he is in contemporary ideas. In 'The Marriage Contract in its Relation to Social Progress', *Fortnightly Review*, n.s. 77 (1905), 479–85, Vere Collins argues that maternity 'should be made a charge on the State' and that: 'Every woman might draw an allowance in respect of her children, subject to their being brought up properly, and might herself be entitled to a pension on attaining a certain age' (483).

90. It should be emphasised, however, that Wells's use of compulsion in this instance is not entirely incompatible with a liberal perspective. Indeed in *On Liberty*, Mill considers that it is perfectly reasonable to employ the mechanism of compulsion in cases where a man fails to uphold his obligations to others, and makes use of an example that prefigures the work of Wells: 'as for instance to support his children, it is no tyranny to force him to fulfil that obligation by compulsory labour if no other means are available' (167–8).

91. Henderson, 'Definition of a Social Policy', p. 330.

92. Letter to Beatrice Webb, 29 April 1904, *The Correspondence of H. G. Wells*, II, 25.

93. Havelock Ellis, *Weekly Critical Review*, 19 February 1904; reprinted in *H. G. Wells: The Critical Heritage*, pp. 94–8 (p. 96).

94. Wells, 'Birth Supply', p. 713.

95. Wells, 'Eugenics', p. 59.

96. W. A. Chapple, *The Fertility of the Unfit* (Melbourne: Whitcombe and Tombs, 1903), p. 112.

97. H. G. Wells, 'The Sham Science of Eugenics', *The New Age*, 7 (19 May 1910), 71.

98. I am indebted to Professor Patrick Parrinder, of the University of Reading, for bringing this debate to my attention.

99. H. G. Wells, 'Eugenics: To the Editor of "The New Age"', *The New Age*, 7 (12 May 1910), 44.

100. C. W. Saleeby, 'Dr. Saleeby Replies: To The Editor of the New Age', *The New Age*, 7 (12 May 1910), 44.

101. Wells, 'Sham Science', p. 71.

102. Wells, 'Sham Science', p. 71.

103. Wells, 'Sham Science', p. 71.
104. Wells, 'Sham Science', p. 71.

8 Conclusion

1. H. G. Wells, 'The So-Called Science of Sociology', p. 29.
2. Warren W. Wagar's *H. G. Wells and the World State* (New Haven: Yale University Press, 1961) remains the classic account of Wells's commitment to the formation of a world state.
3. For an account of the central significance of *The Outline of History* to Wells's work, see Wagar's *Traversing Time*, pp. 162–81.
4. Roslynn D. Haynes, *H. G. Wells: Discoverer of the Future*, p. 167.

Bibliography

Wells's writings

Fiction

'The Chronic Argonauts' (1888), in *The Early H. G. Wells: A Study of the Scientific Romances*, ed. by Bernard Bergonzi (Manchester: Manchester University Press, 1961), pp. 187–214.

The Collector's Book of Science Fiction by H. G. Wells, selected by Alan K. Russell (Secaucus, New Jersey: Castle 1979).

The Complete Short Stories of H. G. Wells, ed. by John Hammond (London: Dent, 1998).

'The Country of the Blind' (1904), in *The Complete Short Stories of H. G. Wells*, ed. by John Hammond (London: Dent, 1998), pp. 629–48.

The Definitive Time Machine: A Critical Edition of H. G. Wells's Scientific Romance, with an introduction and notes by Harry M. Geduld (Bloomington and Indianapolis: Indiana University Press, 1987).

The First Men in the Moon (1901), ed. by David Lake (New York: Oxford University Press, 1995).

The First Men in the Moon (1901), ed. by Patrick Parrinder (London: Penguin, 2005).

The Island of Doctor Moreau (1896), ed. by Patrick Parrinder (London: Penguin, 2005).

'The Man Who Could Work Miracles' (1898), in *The Complete Short Stories of H. G. Wells* ed. by John Hammond (London: Dent, 1998), pp. 399–412.

A Modern Utopia (London: T. Fisher Unwin, 1905).

'Prospecting Begins' [serialised instalment of *The First Men in the Moon*], *Strand Magazine*, January 1901, 37–41.

'The Refinement of Humanity', *National Observer*, n.s. 11 (1894), 581–2.

Select Conversations with an Uncle (Now Extinct) with Two Hitherto Unreprinted Conversations, ed. by David C. Smith and Patrick Parrinder (London: H. G. Wells Society, 1991).

'A Slip under the Microscope' (1895), in *The Works of H. G. Wells: Atlantic Edition*, 28 vols (London: Fisher Unwin, 1924–1927), VI, *The First Men in the Moon and Some More Human Stories*, 393–419.

The Time Machine (1895), ed. by Patrick Parrinder (London: Penguin, 2005).

Tono-Bungay (1909), ed. by Patrick Parrinder (London: Penguin, 2005).

The War of the Worlds (1898), ed. by Martin A. Danahay (Peterborough, Ontario; Orchard Park, New York: Broadview, 2003).

'What We Saw from the Ruined House', [serialised instalment of *The War of the Worlds*], in *The Collector's Book of Science Fiction by H. G. Wells*, selected by Alan K. Russell (Secaucus, New Jersey: Castle, 1979), pp. 83–7.

When the Sleeper Wakes (1899) (London: Dent, 1994).

The Works of H. G. Wells: Atlantic Edition, 28 vols (London: T. Fisher Unwin, 1924–1927), VI, *The First Men in the Moon and Some More Human Stories* [1925].

The Works of H. G. Wells: Atlantic Edition, 28 vols (London: T. Fisher Unwin, 1924–1927), III, *The Invisible Man, The War of the Worlds, A Dream of Armageddon* [1924].

The Works of H. G. Wells: Atlantic Edition, 28 vols (London: T. Fisher Unwin, 1924–1927), II, *The Island of Doctor Moreau, The Sleeper Awakes* [1924].

The Works of H. G. Wells: Atlantic Edition, 28 vols (London: T. Fisher Unwin, 1924–1927), IX, *A Modern Utopia and Other Discussions* [1925].

The Works of H. G. Wells: Atlantic Edition, 28 vols (London: Unwin, 1924–1927), I, *The Time Machine, The Wonderful Visit and Other Stories* [1924].

Scientific, educational and literary writings

'The Acquired Factor' [review of C. Lloyd Morgan's *Habit and Instinct*], *Academy*, 51 (1897), 37.

'Ancient Experiments in Co-Operation', *Gentleman's Magazine*, 273 (1892), 418–22.

'Another Basis for Life', *Saturday Review*, 78 (1894), 676–7.

'Are the Planets Habitable?', *Science Schools Journal*, 15 (1888), 57–8.

'The Biological Problem of To-day', *Saturday Review*, 78 (1894), 703–4.

'Bio-Optimism' [review of *The Evergreen: A Northern Seasonal* by Patrick Geddes et al.], *Nature*, 52 (1895), 410–11.

'Discoveries in Variation', *Saturday Review*, 79 (1895), 312.

'The Duration of Life', *Saturday Review*, 79 (1895), 248.

'The Extinction of Man' (1894), in *Certain Personal Matters* (London: Lawrence & Bullen, 1898), pp. 172–9.

With R. A. Gregory, *Honours Physiography* (London: Joseph Hughes, 1893).

'Human Evolution, an Artificial Process', *Fortnightly Review*, n.s. 60 (1896), 590–5.

'Huxley', *Royal College of Science Magazine*, 13 (1901), 209–11.

'The Influence of Islands on Variation', *Saturday Review*, 80 (1895), 204–5.

'Intelligence on Mars', *Saturday Review*, 81 (1896), 345–6.

Interview with the *Weekly Sun Literary Supplement*, 1 December 1895; reprinted in 'A Chat with the Author of *The Time Machine*, Mr H. G. Wells', edited with comment by David C. Smith, *The Wellsian*, n.s. 20 (1997), 3–9.

Letter to the Editor, *Clarion*, 22 April 1904, 3.

Letter to the Editor, 7 November 1896, *Saturday Review*, 82 (1896), 497.

'The Limits of Individual Plasticity', *Saturday Review*, 79 (1895), 89–90.

'The Man of the Year Million' (1893), in *H. G. Wells: Journalism and Prophecy, 1893–1946*, ed. by W. Warren Wagar (London: Bodley Head, 1965), pp. 3–8.

'The Mind in Animals', *Saturday Review*, 78 (1894), 683–4.

'Morals and Civilisation', *Fortnightly Review*, n.s. 61 (1897), 263–8.

'Of a Book Unwritten', *Certain Personal Matters* (London: Lawrence & Bullen, 1898), pp. 161–84.

'On Extinction' (1893), in *Early Writings in Science and Science Fiction*, ed. by Robert M. Philmus and David Y. Hughes (London: University of California Press, 1975), pp. 169–72.

'The Origin of the Senses', *Saturday Review*, 81 (1896), 471–2.

'Popularising Science', *Nature*, 50 (1894), 300–1.

'Preface', *The Scientific Romances of H. G. Wells* (1933), in *The Invisible Man* (1897) (London: Everyman, 1995), pp. 139–43.

'The Rediscovery of the Unique', *Fortnightly Review*, n.s. 50 (1891), 106–11.

'Scepticism of the Instrument' (1903), reprinted as an appendix to *The Works of H. G. Wells: Atlantic Edition*, 28 vols (London: Fisher Unwin, 1924–1927), IX, *A Modern Utopia and Other Discussions*, 335–54.

'Science, in School and after School', *Nature*, 50 (1894), 525–6.

'Science Teaching – an Ideal and Some Realities', *Educational Times*, 48 (1895), 23–9.

'The Sequence of Studies', *Nature*, 51 (1894), 195–6.

'The Sins of the Secondary Schoolmaster', *Pall Mall Gazette*, 59 (1894), 1–2.

'A Slum Novel' [review of Arthur Morrison's *A Child of the Jago*], *Saturday Review*, 82 (1896), 573.

Textbook of Biology (London: University Tutorial Press, 1893).

'The Things that Live on Mars', *Cosmopolitan Magazine*, 44 (1908), 335–42.

'Through a Microscope' (1894), in *Certain Personal Matters* (London: Lawrence & Bullen, 1898), pp. 238–45.

'Zoological Retrogression', *Gentleman's Magazine*, 271 (1891), 246–53.

Sociological, historical and prophetical writings

'Certain Wholesale Aspects of Man-Making', *Fortnightly Review*, n.s. 72 (1902), 1078–96.

'The Cyclist Soldier', *Fortnightly Review*, n.s. 68 (1900), 914–28.

'The Discovery of the Future', *Nature*, 65 (1902), 326–31.

[Discussion] 'Eugenics: Its Definition, Scope and Aims', in *Sociological Papers*, ed. by Francis Galton (London: Macmillan, 1904), pp. 58–60.

'Eugenics: To the Editor of "The New Age"', *The New Age*, 7 (1910), 44.

Mankind in the Making (London: Chapman & Hall, 1903).

New Worlds for Old (London: Archibald Constable, 1908).

'The Organisation of the Higher Education', *Fortnightly Review*, n.s. 74 (1903), 353–72.

The Outline of History (1920) (London: Cassell, 1961).

'Political and Social Influences', *Fortnightly Review*, n.s. 74 (1903), 928–49.

'The Problem of the Birth Supply', *Fortnightly Review*, n.s. 72 (1902), 704–22.

With Julian Huxley and G. P. Wells, *The Science of Life* (Garden City, New York: Doubleday, Doran, 1931).

'The Sham Science of Eugenics' [Letter to the Editor], *The New Age*, 7 (1910), 71.

A Short History of the World (1922) (London: Watt, 1929).

'The So-Called Science of Sociology', *Independent Review*, 6 (1905), 21–37.

The Works of H. G. Wells: Atlantic Edition, 28 vols (London: Unwin, 1924–1927), IV, *Anticipations and Other Papers* [1924].

Collected writings

Certain Personal Matters (London: Lawrence & Bullen, 1898).

H. G. Wells: Early Writings in Science and Science Fiction, edited, with critical commentary and notes by Robert M. Philmus and David Y. Hughes (London: University of California Press, 1975).

H. G. Wells's Literary Criticism, ed. by Patrick Parrinder and Robert M. Philmus (Sussex: Harvester Press, 1980).

Autobiographical writings and letters

The Correspondence of H. G. Wells, 4 vols, ed. by David C. Smith (London: Pickering and Chatto, 1998).
Experiment in Autobiography, 2 vols (London: Gollancz, 1934).

Primary texts

Allen, Grant, 'Spencer and Darwin', *Fortnightly Review*, n.s. 61 (1897), 251–62.
Ball, Robert S., 'Comets', *Strand Magazine*, 21 (1901), 393–9.
—— 'Mars', *Fortnightly Review*, n.s. 52 (1892), 288–303.
—— 'The Possibility of Life in Other Worlds', *Fortnightly Review*, n.s. 56 (1894), 718–29.
Barlow, John, *On Man's Power over Himself to Prevent or Control Insanity* (1843); extracts reprinted in *Embodied Selves: An Anthology of Psychological Texts 1830–1890*, ed. by Jenny Bourne Taylor and Sally Shuttleworth (Oxford: Oxford University Press, 1998), pp. 243–6.
Bellamy, Edward, *Looking Backward* (1888) (New York: Signet, 1960).
Bourne Taylor, Jenny and Sally Shuttleworth, eds, *Embodied Selves: An Anthology of Psychological Texts 1830–1890* (Oxford: Oxford University Press, 1998).
Bulwer-Lytton, Edward, *The Coming Race* (1871) (Stroud: Alan Sutton, 1995).
Chapple, W. A., *The Fertility of the Unfit* (Melbourne: Whitcombe and Tombs, 1903).
Collins, Vere, 'The Marriage Contract in its Relation to Social Progress', *Fortnightly Review*, n.s. 77 (1905), 479–85.
Conrad, Joseph, *Heart of Darkness* (1899) (Harmondsworth: Penguin, 1995).
Crozier, J. B., 'H. G. Wells as a Sociologist', *Fortnightly Review*, n.s. 78 (1905), 417–26.
Crump, W. B., 'Science Teaching in Schools', Letter to the Editor, *Nature*, 51 (1894), 56.
Darwin, Charles, *On the Origin of Species* (1859) (Ware: Wordsworth, 1998).
Defoe, Daniel, *The Life and Adventures of Robinson Crusoe* (1719) (Harmondsworth: Penguin, 1965).
Forbes, Archibald, 'The Warfare of the Future', *Nineteenth Century*, 29 (1891), 782–95.
Galton, Francis, *Essays in Eugenics* (London: The Eugenics Education Society, 1909).
—— *Fingerprints* (London: Macmillan, 1892).
—— *Inquiries into Human Faculty and its Development* (1883) (London: J. M. Dent, 1928).
—— 'Intelligible Signals between Neighbouring Stars', *Fortnightly Review*, n.s. 60 (1896), 657–64.
—— 'The Possible Improvement of the Human Breed under the Existing Conditions of Law and Sentiment', *Nature*, 64 (1901), 659–65.
—— ed., *Sociological Papers* (London: Macmillan, 1904).
Garner, R. L., 'The Simian Tongue [I]', reprinted in *The Origin of Language*, ed. by Roy Harris (Bristol: Thoemmes, 1996), pp. 314–21.
—— 'The Simian Tongue [II]', reprinted in *The Origin of Language* (Bristol: Thoemmes, 1996), pp. 321–27.

Haeckel, Ernst, *The Evolution of Man* (1879); reprinted in *Embodied Selves: An Anthology of Psychological Texts 1830–1890*, ed. by Jenny Bourne Taylor and Sally Shuttleworth (Oxford: Oxford University Press, 1998), pp. 308–11.

Harrison, Frederic, 'John Stuart Mill', *Nineteenth Century*, 40 (1896), 487–508.

Havelock-Allan, H. M., 'A General Voluntary Training to Arms *Versus* Conscription', *Fortnightly Review*, n.s. 61 (1897), 85–99.

—— 'England's Military Position: Its Present Weakness, Its Vast Undeveloped Strength', *Fortnightly Review*, n.s. 62 (1897), 19–41.

Heath, Grace, 'Science Teaching in Schools', Letter to the Editor, *Nature*, 51 (1894), 56–7.

Henderson, Charles Richmond, 'Definition of a Social Policy Relating to the Dependent Group', *The American Journal of Sociology*, 10 (1905), 315–34.

Hurd, Percy A., 'The New Imperialism', *Contemporary Review*, 72 (1897), 171–83.

Huxley, T. H., 'Evolution and Ethics' [the Romanes Lecture] (1893), in *Collected Essays By T. H. Huxley*, 9 vols (London: Macmillan, 1903), IX, *Evolution and Ethics and Other Essays*, 46–86.

—— 'Science and Culture' (1880), in *Science and Culture and Other Essays* (London: Macmillan, 1881), pp. 1–23.

—— 'The Struggle for Existence in Human Society' (1888), in *Collected Essays By T. H. Huxley*, 9 vols (London: Macmillan, 1903), IX, *Evolution and Ethics and Other Essays*, 195–236.

Jean-Aubry, Georges, ed., *J. Conrad: Life and Letters* (New York: Doubleday, 1927).

Jeune, Mary, 'The Homes of the Poor', *Fortnightly Review*, n.s. 47 (1890), 67–80.

Keating, Peter, ed., *Into Unknown England, 1866–1913* (Manchester: Fontana, 1976).

Lankester, Edwin Ray, *Degeneration: A Chapter in Darwinism* (London: Macmillan, 1880).

—— 'H. G. Wells', *English Illustrated Magazine*, 31 (1904), 614–17.

—— 'The Present Judged by the Future' [review of *Anticipations*], Supplement to *Nature*, 65 (1902), iii–v.

Le Bon, Gustave, *The Crowd: A Study of the Popular Mind* (1896) (London: T. Fisher Unwin, 1913).

Lilly, W. S., 'The New Naturalism', *Fortnightly Review*, n.s. 38 (1885), 240–56.

Lowell, Percival, *Mars* (1895) (London: Longman's, 1896).

Lubbock, John, *Ants, Bees, and Wasps: A Record of Observations on the Habits of the Social Hymenoptera* (London: Kegan Paul, Trench, & Co, 1885).

Luckhurst, Roger, and Sally Ledger eds, *The Fin de Siècle: A Reader in Cultural History c. 1880–1900* (Oxford: Oxford University Press, 2000).

Maclean, Annie Marion, 'The Sweat-Shop in Summer', *The American Journal of Sociology*, 9 (1903), 289–309.

MacQuery, T. H., 'Schools for Dependent, Delinquent, and Truant Children in Illinois', *The American Journal of Sociology*, 9 (1903–1904), 1–23.

—— 'The Reformation of Juvenile Offenders in Illinois', *The American Journal of Sociology*, 8 (1902–1903), 644–54.

Maeterlinck, Maurice, 'In the Hive', *Fortnightly Review*, n.s. 69 (1901), 465–75.

Marlowe, Christopher, *Dr Faustus* (1604) (London: A & C Black, 1986).

Maudsley, Henry, *Responsibility in Mental Disease* (London: Henry S. King, 1874).

Mearns, Andrew, *The Bitter Cry of Outcast London* (1883); extracts reprinted in *Into Unknown England, 1866–1913*, ed. by Peter Keating (Manchester: Fontana, 1976), pp. 91–111.

Mill, John Stuart, *On Liberty* (1859) (London: Penguin, 1985).

Mitchell, P. Chalmers, 'Letter to the Editor', *Saturday Review*, 82 (1896), 498.

—— 'Mr Wells's "Dr. Moreau"', *Saturday Review*, 81 (1896), 368–9.

Morgan, C. L., 'The Limits of Animal Intelligence', *Fortnightly Review*, n.s. 54 (1893), 223–39.

Morris, William, *News from Nowhere* (1890) (Harmondsworth: Penguin, 1998).

Newcomb, Simon, 'Modern Mathematical Thought', *Nature*, 49 (1894), 325–9.

Nietzsche, Friedrich, *Beyond Good and Evil: Prelude to a Philosophy of the Future* (1886) (Harmondsworth: Penguin, 1990).

Nordau, Max, *Degeneration* (1892) (London: University of Nebraska Press, 1993).

Orwell, George, *Nineteen Eighty-Four* (1949) (Harmondsworth: Penguin, 1989).

Parrinder, Patrick, ed., *H. G. Wells: The Critical Heritage* (London: Routledge & Kegan Paul, 1972).

Pearson, Karl, *The Grammar of Science* (London: Walter Scott, 1892).

Plato, *The Republic*, Translated by Desmond Lee (Harmondsworth: Penguin, 1987).

Poynting, John H., 'Recent Studies in Gravitation', *Nature*, 62 (1900), 403–8.

Saleeby, C. W., 'Dr. Saleeby Replies: To the Editor of the New Age', *The New Age*, 7 (1910), 44.

Shelley, Mary, *Frankenstein: or The Modern Prometheus* (1818) (Oxford: Oxford University Press, 1980).

—— *The Last Man* (1826) (Oxford: Oxford University Press, 1994).

Spencer, Herbert, *The Data of Ethics* (London: Williams and Norgate, 1897; repr. 1907).

—— *The Principles of Sociology* (1876); extracts reprinted in *The Fin de Siècle: A Reader in Cultural History c. 1880 – 1900*, ed. by Roger Luckhurst and Sally Ledger (Oxford: Oxford University Press, 2000), pp. 321–6.

—— 'The Sins of Legislators', *Contemporary Review*, 45 (1884), 761–75.

—— 'The Social Organism' (1860), in *Essays: Scientific, Political, Speculative*, 3 vols (London: Williams and Norgate, 1868), I, 384–428.

Stead, W. T. [Unsigned], 'The Latest Apocalypse of the End of the World' [review of *The War of the Worlds*], *Review of Reviews*, 17 (1898), 389–96.

Stevenson, Robert Louis, *The Strange Case of Dr Jekyll and Mr Hyde* (1886) (Oxford: Oxford University Press, 1998).

Stoker, Bram, *Dracula* (1897) (Oxford: Oxford University Press, 1998).

Swift, Jonathan, *Gulliver's Travels and Other Writings* (Oxford: Oxford University Press, 1976).

—— 'A Modest Proposal' (1729), in *Gulliver's Travels and Other Writings* (Oxford: Oxford University Press, 1976), pp. 439–46.

Thomas, W. I., 'The Psychology of Race-Prejudice', *The American Journal of Sociology*, 9 (1903–4), 593–611.

Tyndall, John, 'Scientific Use of the Imagination' (1870), in *Fragments of Science: A Series of Detached Essays, Addresses and Reviews* (London: Longmans, Green and Co., 1876), pp. 423–57.

Unsigned, 'A Lunar Romance' [review of *The First Men in the Moon*], *Nature*, 65 (1902), 218–19.

Unsigned, 'A Strange Light on Mars', *Nature*, 50 (1894), 319.

Unsigned, 'Will the Future be to the Cannibals? A Nightmare of Civilisation' [review of *the Time Machine*], *Review of Reviews*, 11 (1895), 346.

Unsigned Review [of *Anticipations*], *The Daily Telegraph* (14 November 1901), 11.

Unsigned Review of *The Invisible Man*, *Literature*, 1 (1897), 50–1.

Unsigned Notice of *The Invisible Man*, *Saturday Review*, 84 (1897), 321–2.

Unsigned Review of *The Island of Doctor Moreau*, *Review of Reviews*, 13 (1896), 374–6.

Unsigned Notice of *The Time Machine*, *Review of Reviews*, 11 (1895), 263.

Unsigned Review of *The War of the Worlds*, *Saturday Review*, 85 (1898), 146–7.

Wallace, Robert, 'The Psychology of Capitalist and Labourer', *Fortnightly Review*, n.s. 54 (1893), 676–85.

Webb, Sidney, and Beatrice Webb, *Industrial Democracy* (London: Longman, 1902).

White, Arnold, 'The Unemployed', *Fortnightly Review*, n.s. 54 (1893), 454–63.

Wilson, Harris, ed., *Arnold Bennett and H. G. Wells* (London: Hart Davies, 1960).

Wilson, H. W., 'The Human Animal in Battle', *Fortnightly Review*, n.s. 60 (1896), 272–84.

Secondary texts

Arata, Stephen, *Fictions of Loss in the Victorian Fin de Siècle* (Cambridge: Cambridge University Press, 1996).

Batchelor, John, *H. G. Wells* (Cambridge: Cambridge University Press, 1985).

Beauchamp, Gorman, 'The Island of Doctor Moreau as Theological Grotesque', *Papers on Language and Literature*, 15 (1979), 408–17.

Bergonzi, Bernard, *The Early H. G. Wells: A Study of the Scientific Romances* (Manchester: Manchester University Press, 1961).

—— 'The Time Machine: an Ironic Myth' in *H. G. Wells: A Collection of Critical Essays*, ed. by Bernard Bergonzi (London: Prentice-Hall, 1976), pp. 39–54.

Brantlinger, Patrick, *Rule of Darkness: British Literature and Imperialism, 1830–1914* (Ithaca, New York: Cornell University Press, 1988).

Bridgwater, Patrick, *Nietzsche in Anglosaxony: A Study of Nietzsche's Impact on English and American Literature* (Leicester: Leicester University Press, 1972).

Bristow, Joseph, *Empire Boys: Adventures in a Man's World* (London: Harper Collins, 1991).

Brome, Vincent, *H. G. Wells* (1951) (London: Stratus, 2001).

Chamberlain, Edward and Sander Gilman, eds, *Degeneration: The Dark Side of Progress* (New York: Columbia University Press, 1986).

Cohen, Ed, *Talk on the Wilde Side* (London: Routledge, 1993).

Collini, Stefan, *Liberalism and Sociology: L. T. Hobhouse and Political Argument in England, 1880–1914* (Cambridge: Cambridge University Press, 1979).

Costa, Richard Hauer, *H. G. Wells* (Boston, Massachusetts: Twayne, 1985).

Crossley, Robert, 'H. G. Wells, Visionary Telescopes and the "Matter of Mars"', *Philological Quarterly*, 83 (2004), 83–115.

Derry, Stephen, 'The Time Traveller's Utopian Books and his Reading of the Future', *Foundation*, 65 (1995), 16–24.

Dickson, Lovat, *H. G. Wells: His Turbulent Life and Times* (London: Macmillan, 1969).

Dingley, R. J., 'Count Dracula and the Martians', in *The Victorian Fantasists*, ed. by Kath Filmer (London: Macmillan, 1991), pp. 13–24.

Doughty, F. H., *H. G. Wells: Educationalist* (London: J. Cape, 1926).

Ferguson, Christine, *Language, Science and Popular Fiction at the Victorian Fin-de-Siècle: The Brutal Tongue* (Aldershot: Ashgate, 2006).

Foot, Michael, *H. G: The History of Mr. Wells* (Washington, DC: Counterpoint, 1995).

Forrest, D. W., *Francis Galton: The Life and Work of a Victorian Genius* (London: Elek, 1974).

French, Richard Deland, *Antivivesection and Medical Science in Victorian Society* (London: Princeton University Press, 1975).

Gannon, Charles E. ' "One Swift, Conclusive Smashing and an End": Wells, War, and the Collapse of Civilisation', *Foundation*, 77 (1999), 35–46.

Greenslade, William, *Degeneration, Culture and the Novel, 1880–1940* (Cambridge: Cambridge University Press, 1994).

—— 'Fitness and the Fin de Siècle' in *Fin de Siècle/Fin du Globe*, ed. by John Stokes (Basingstoke: Macmillan, 1992), pp. 37–51.

Haight, Gordon S., 'H. G. Wells's "The Man of the Year Million" ', *Nineteenth-Century Fiction*, 12 (1958), 323–6.

Hammond, John, *An H. G. Wells Companion* (London and Basingstoke: Macmillan, 1979).

—— *H. G. Wells and the Modern Novel* (New York: St. Martin's Press, 1988).

—— ed., *H. G. Wells: Interviews and Recollections* (London: Macmillan, 1980).

—— *H. G. Wells's The Time Machine: A Reference Guide* (London and Westport, Connecticut: Greenwood, 2004).

—— '*The Island of Doctor Moreau*: A Swiftian Parable', *The Wellsian*, n.s. 16 (1993), 30–41.

Hashimoto, Yorimitsu, 'Victorian Biological Terror: A Study of "The Stolen Bacillus" ', *The Undying Fire*, 2 (2003), 3–27.

Haynes, Roslynn, *H. G. Wells: Discoverer of the Future, The Influence of Science on His Thought* (London: New York University Press, 1980).

Hillegas, Mark, *The Future as Nightmare: H. G. Wells and the Anti-Utopians* (New York: Oxford University Press, 1967).

Hume, Kathryn, 'Eat or be Eaten: H. G. Wells's *Time Machine*', *Philological Quarterly*, 69 (1990), 233–51.

—— 'The Hidden Dynamics of *The War of the Worlds*', *Philological Quarterly*, 62 (1983), 279–92.

Huntington, John, *The Logic of Fantasy: H. G. Wells and Science Fiction* (New York: Columbia University Press, 1982).

—— '*The Time Machine* and Wells's Social Trajectory', *Foundation*, 65 (1995), 6–15.

Jackson, Holbrook, *The Eighteen Nineties: A Review of Art and Ideas at the Close of the Nineteenth Century* (London: Grant Richards, 1913).

Jackson, Kimberley, 'Vivisected Language in H. G. Wells's *The Island of Doctor Moreau*', *The Wellsian*, n.s. 29 (2006), 20–35.

Jones, Greta, *Social Darwinism and English Thought: the Interaction between Biological and Social Theory* (Brighton: Harvester, 1980).

Kemp, Peter, *H. G. Wells and the Culminating Ape* (London: Macmillan, 1996).

Kern, Stephen, *The Culture of Time and Space 1880–1918* (Cambridge, Massachusetts: Harvard University Press, 1983).

Kumar, Krishan, *Utopianism* (Milton Keynes: Open University Press, 1991).

Lake, David, 'The Current Texts of Wells's Early SF Novels: Situation Unsatisfactory (Part 1)', *The Wellsian*, n.s. 11 (1988), 3–12.

—— 'The Current Texts of Wells's Early SF Novels: Situation Unsatisfactory (Part 2)', *The Wellsian*, n.s. 12 (1989), 21–36.

—— 'The White Sphinx and the Whitened Lemur: Images of Death in *The Time Machine*', *Science-Fiction Studies*, 6 (1979), 77–84.

Ledger, Sally, and Scott MacCracken, eds, *Cultural Politics at the Fin de Siècle* (Cambridge: Cambridge University Press, 1995).

Loing, Bernard, *H. G. Wells À L'oeuvre: Les débuts d'un écrivain (1894–1900)* (Paris: Didier, 1984).

—— 'H. G. Wells at Work 1894–1900: A Writer's Beginnings', *The Wellsian*, n.s. 8 (1985), 30–7.

McCarthy, Patrick A., '*Heart of Darkness* and the Early novels of H. G. Wells: Evolution, Anarchy, Entropy', *Journal of Modern Literature*, 13 (1986), 37–60.

McConnell, Frank, *The Science Fiction of H. G. Wells* (New York: Oxford University Press, 1981).

MacKenzie, Norman and Jeanne MacKenzie, *The Time Traveller: The Life of H. G. Wells* (London: Weidenfeld and Nicolson, 1973).

Mayne, Alan, 'The Virtual Time Machine: Part II – Some Physicists' Views of Time Travel', *The Wellsian*, n.s. 20 (1997), 20–31.

Morton, Peter, *The Vital Science: Biology and the Literary Imagination, 1860–1900* (London: Allen & Unwin, 1984).

Murray Walker, Jeanne, 'Exchange Short-Circuited: The Isolated Scientist in H. G. Wells's *The Invisible Man*', *Journal of Narrative Technique*, 15 (1985), 156–68.

Oppenheim, Janet, '*Shattered Nerves': Doctors, Patients, and Depression in Victorian England, 1850–1914* (Oxford: Oxford University Press, 1991).

Parrinder, Patrick, 'From Mary Shelley to *The War of the Worlds*: The Thames Valley Catastrophe', in *Anticipations: Essays on Science Fiction and its Precursors*, ed. by David Seed (Liverpool: Liverpool University Press, 1995), pp. 58–74.

—— *H. G. Wells* (Edinburgh: Oliver and Boyd, 1970).

—— 'How Far Can We Trust the Narrator of *The War of the Worlds*?', *Foundation*, 77 (1999), 15–24.

—— '*News from Nowhere, The Time Machine* and the Break-Up of Classical Realism', *Science-Fiction Studies*, 3 (1976), 265–74.

—— ed., *Science Fiction: A Critical Guide* (London and New York: Longman, 1979).

—— *Science Fiction: Its Criticism and Teaching* (London and New York: Methuen, 1980).

—— *Shadows of the Future: H. G. Wells, Science Fiction and Prophecy* (Liverpool: Liverpool University Press, 1995).

—— With Christopher Rolfe, eds, *H. G. Wells under Revision* (London and Toronto: Associated University Presses, 1986).

Partington, John S., 'The Death of the Static: H. G. Wells and the Kinetic Utopia', *Utopian Studies*, 11 (2000), 96–111.

—— 'The Time Machine and A Modern Utopia: The Static and Kinetic Utopias of the Early H. G. Wells', *Utopian Studies*, 13 (2002), 57–68.

Philmus, Robert M., 'H. G. Wells's Revisi(tati)ons of *The Time Machine*', *English Literature in Transition, 1880–1920*, 41 (1998), 427–52.

Pick, Daniel, *Faces of Degeneration: a European Disorder, c. 1848–c. 1918* (Cambridge: Cambridge University Press, 1989).

Porta, Fernando, *La Scienza come favola: Saggio sui scientific romances di H. G. Wells* (Salerno: Edisud, 1995).

—— 'Narrative Strategies in H. G. Wells' Romances and Short Stories (1887–1910)' (doctoral thesis, University of Reading, 1996).

—— 'One Text, Many Utopias: Some Examples of Intertextuality in *The Time Machine*', *The Wellsian*, n.s. 20 (1997), 10–20.

Pritchett, V. S., *The Living Novel* (1946) (London: Arrow, 1960).

Pykett, Lyn, ed., *Reading Fin de Siècle Fictions* (London: Longman, 1996).

Radick, Gregory, 'Morgan's Canon, Garner's Phonograph, and the Evolutionary Origins of Language and Reason', *British Journal for the History of Science*, 33 (2000), 3–23.

Raknem, Ingvald, *H. G. Wells and His Critics* (London: George Allen & Unwin, 1962).

Reed, John R., 'The Vanity of Law in *The Island of Doctor Moreau*' in *H. G. Wells Under Revision*, ed. by Patrick Parrinder and Christopher Rolfe (London: Associated University Presses, 1986), pp. 134–44.

Russell, W. M. S., 'Time before and after *The Time Machine*', *Foundation*, 65 (1995), 24–40.

Scafella, Frank, 'The White Sphinx and *The Time Machine*', *Science-Fiction Studies*, 8 (1981), 255–65.

Seed, David, ed., *Anticipations: Essays on Early Science Fiction and its Predecessors* (Liverpool: Liverpool University Press, 1995).

Showalter, Elaine, *Sexual Anarchy: Gender and Culture at the Fin de Siècle* (London: Bloomsbury, 1991).

Simpson, Anne B., ' "The Tangible Antagonist": H. G. Wells and the Discourse of Otherness', *Extrapolation*, 31 (1990), 134–47.

Singh, Kirpal, 'Science and Society: A Brief Look at *The Invisible Man*', *The Wellsian*, n.s. 7 (1984), 19–23.

Sirabian, Robert, 'The Conception of Science in Wells's *The Invisible Man*', *Papers on Language and Literature*, 37 (2001), 382–403.

Sleigh, Charlotte, 'Empire of the Ants: H. G. Wells and Tropical Entomology', *Science as Culture*, 10 (2001), 33–71.

Smith, Jonathan, *Fact and Feeling: Baconian Science and the Nineteenth-Century Literary Imagination* (London: University of Wisconsin Press, 1994).

Stableford, Brian, *Scientific Romance in Britain, 1890–1950* (London: Fourth Estate, 1985).

Stearn, R. T. 'Wells and War: H. G. Wells's Writings on Military Subjects, before the Great War', *Wellsian*, n.s. 6 (1983), 1–15.

Stokes, John, ed., *Fin de siècle/Fin du Globe* (Basingstoke: Macmillan, 1992).

—— *In the Nineties* (Hemel Hempstead: Harvester Wheatsheaf, 1989).

Stover, Leon, 'Applied Natural History: Wells vs. Huxley', in *H. G. Wells Under Revision*, ed. by Patrick Parrinder and Christopher Rolfe (London and Toronto: Associated University Presses, 1986), pp. 125–33.

Sussman, Herbert, *Victorians and the Machine: The Literary Response to Technology* (Cambridge: Harvard University Press, 1968).

Toye, Richard, 'H. G. Wells and the New Liberalism', *Twentieth Century History*, 19 (2008), 156–85.

Turner, Frank M., *Contesting Cultural Authority* (Cambridge: Cambridge University Press, 1993).

Turner, Jonathan H., *Herbert Spencer: A Renewed Appreciation* (London: Sage, 1985).

Wagar, W. Warren, *H. G. Wells and the World State* (New Haven, Connecticut: Yale University Press, 1961).

—— *H. G. Wells: Traversing Time* (Middletown, Connecticut: Wesleyan University Press, 2004).

West, Geoffrey, *H. G. Wells: A Sketch for a Portrait* (London: Howe, 1930).

Index

Unless otherwise stated, all books, articles and short stories indexed below are by H. G. Wells

CPSIA information can be obtained
at www.ICGtesting.com
Printed in the USA
LVHW030447261119
638462LV00011B/823/P